Advance Praise

"*Gone by Sundown* is an extremely timely novel that traces the origins of a racist atrocity and its effects on residents from bottom-dwelling working class blacks and whites, to the 'French colored' and merchants higher up the social ladder, to union agitators and mine owners at the top of local society. Peter Leach has the story-teller's heart of Harper Lee and the sociologist's eye of Frank Norris."

    —Tim W. Brown, author of *Second Acts*

"Almost no other novel treats the creation of sundown towns. *Gone by Sundown* thus amounts to a one-volume antidote to American amnesia. On top of that, it's a good read."

    —James W. Loewen, author of *Lies My Teacher Told Me* and *Sundown Towns*

"*Gone by Sundown* takes us into a world and sensibility that is fresh, resonant and provocative. Peter Leach writes of a great wrong done by ordinary people, and does so with quiet fervor, displaying sadness and pity for all."

    —Daniel Woodrell

Gone by Sundown

a novel

by Peter Leach

Winner of the Gival Press Novel Award

Arlington, Virginia

Published by Gival Press, an imprint of Gival Press, LLC.

For information please write:
Gival Press, LLC
P. O. Box 3812,
Arlington, VA 22203
www.givalpress.com

First edition
ISBN: 978-1-92-8589-61-7
eISBN: 978-1-92-8589-67-9
Library of Congress Control Number: 2011925419

Cover: Arthur Witman Photograph Collection, Western Historical Manuscript Collection, University of Missouri-St. Louis.

Design by Ken Schellenberg.

Acknowledgements

Bernie Schram, Anne Woodhouse, Mark McBride of Mississippi Lime, Bonita and Robert Rehm of Rehm's Place; Jerry Holliday, Martha Roth, and Madeline Jett of the Anvil Saloon, Carl Ekberg, Jim Baker of the Felix Valle State Historic Site, Margaret Brown, Beth Scott, Don Heldman, Donna Charron, Barbara Hankins, Bill and Patti Naeger, Mark L. Evans; Dwayne Lause of Quarry Workers Local 829; John Jones, Barbara Steiger, Jerri Bequette, Becky Kist, Mercedes Rodriquez, Bernice Noble, Sharon Tucker, and Linda Schaper of the Ste. Genevieve branch of Ozark Regional Library.

Historical Note

GANGS OF ARMED WHITE MEN ACTUALLY DID GO AROUND TO THE BLACK people of Ste. Genevieve, Missouri on the night of October 12, 1930 and order them to leave by 5 o'clock the next day. What set them off was the murder of two white quarry workers by three of the so-called transient Negroes brought in from down South by the lime companies to work in the quarries and kilns at half the going rate of pay. That is the main event of the tale that follows.

I also have used other actual occurrences in Ste. Genevieve in the 1930s—the long and bitter strike in the lime works from May to November 1939, the Mississippi River flood of 1937, the murder of Ethel Fahnstock by Holt Hardy on September 27, 1935, and the public hanging of Hardy on March 6, 1937. I have changed the order of the public events.

—PL

1.

WHEN LON CAME BACK FROM THE DAIRY SHOW, ZENO TOLD HIM ABOUT the shooting of the white men. Two black men and a black woman were arrested and said to have confessed. As the crowd gathering in the streets threatened to mob the jail, the sheriff put blankets over the heads of the suspects, ran them out through the courthouse basement to his own automobile, and drove them to St. Louis.

Lon asked, "Where Cap?"

"Out making speeches. Inebriated."

"We need to get him home."

"Unh-hunh."

Their youngest brother Cap fought in the World War. With his veterans' preference he had secured employment as a rural mail carrier. He studied the works of W. E. B. Dubois and Marcus Garvey, and was known for speaking his mind in the presence of white people.

"Where Cletus at?"

"Gone looking for him."

Cletus was the sharecropper boy who stayed in the cabin out back.

ON CLEARING OUT THE FILES FROM HIS PRIVATE PRACTICE AS HE WENT ON senior status, The Honorable Sidney Redmond came upon several boxes of court documents, clippings, and interview notes in the matter of Lee Guy Taylor, Columbus Jennings and Vera Fox Rogers. They were accused of shooting two white men at the ferry landing a mile north of Ste. Genevieve and dumping them in the river. One was still alive, paralyzed from the waist down with a bullet lodged in his spine. He said when the three Negroes saw him trying to paddle to shore, they threw rocks at him.

The night after the arrests and alleged confessions of the three suspects, gangs of armed white men went around to all the colored people they could find and ordered them to leave town by five o'clock the next day.

Although what they were accused of occurred fifty miles down the river, they were incarcerated in the St. Louis City Jail. You still would visit clients in their cells then and the first thing you notice about the place is the pervasive body odor of unwashed men, the smell of urine and vomit and fecal matter from overflowing toilets, some days with a fresh redolence of Lysol and industrial-strength ammonia. The second thing you notice is the noise, just, pandemonium. You cannot hear yourself think in that madhouse. It is like a symphony orchestra of a thousand instruments all tuning up and a chorus of prima donnas all practicing different scales, angry shouts, diatribes, gossip, scheming, hustling this and that, blaring radios, flushing toilets, the clanging of steel doors, sometimes a man screaming, guards threatening, cajoling, all echoing and reechoing in that cavernous space with stone and concrete walls, and the inmates running around loose and left to their own devices. The penitentiary is bad enough but there at least they must go to sweat-shop jobs in the prison industries for most of the day. In the St. Louis City jail for the most part they are waiting for trial or sentencing and too poor to make bail and have nothing to do from when they are let out of their cages in the morning until lock-down at night except eat and shit and menace and abuse and slander and generally torment and harass and make life miserable for each other. It is not a happy place. So he visited them one after the other, Taylor and Jennings on different tiers in the main jail, and Mrs. Vera Rogers in the Annex for Women & Children and Insane Prisoners. Le Guy Taylor was a sly, dapper man, sepia colored, who migrated north when the chicken plant in West Memphis, Arkansas shut down. Columbus Jennings, a country boy from Jericho Junction who drifted along with Taylor, was a sickly green brown like the pods on a locust tree. The high yellow Vera Fox Rogers, no doubt once a lovely woman but wasted and worn down, said she was married to a man in Crystal City who beat her.

They were three scared Negroes. The account each one gave was designed to put as little of the blame as possible on him or herself, and as much as possible on the other two. But they agreed in material ways which were strikingly different from the accounts in the newspapers, and, from their signed confessions.

The most important difference was that the white man who survived for 36 hours, Rauscher, would have you believe the shootings took place in a premeditated robbery. Taylor, Jennings, and Mrs. Rogers all insisted that they just needed a ride up to the landing, while the white men wanted to see the Negro craps game and agreed to drive them there for a dollar and fifty cents. But as soon as they got in the car the white men were talking trash to Mrs. Rogers and seemed to think she was a prostitute and her companions were her pimps. They all declared Rauscher insulted Mrs. Rogers.

Talking to Redmond then and in testimony at his trial Taylor stated that he told the white man to stop acting that way and said *You would get sore if a Negro were talking like that to a white woman.* Rauscher stopped the machine and reached back and hit Taylor in the stomach saying *So you are sore, are you?*

Taylor denied throwing the white men into the river and also denied stoning the one who was still alive as he tried to swim to the bootleggers' barge. Both Jennings and Mrs. Rogers asserted that Taylor fired the shots and claimed he helped drag the men to the river bank and push them in. They also said he participated in throwing rocks at them.

Redmond counseled his three clients to beware of jailhouse snitches, and to say nothing to custodial personnel about their cases. They should refuse to be interviewed further by police or anyone else representing the State unless he was present. This is a provision of the law that is more honored in the breach than in the observance. He told them their first order of business was to get a change of venue out of Ste. Genevieve County, indeed out of the entire 27th Judicial Circuit of five counties, where there was obvious and flagrant prejudice against them.

2.

HE HAD ONLY THE NAME OF A MRS. BROOKS WHO WAS SAID TO BE IN SERvice to the household of the owner of the largest of the quarry and lime companies and to have a daughter attending Lincoln, the state college for Negroes. As you know places of public accommodation then were permitted to refuse service to people of color, and what you did when you traveled was to find a Negro boarding house or a home in the community that would let you a room. The possibilities in Ste. Genevieve were extremely limited due to the exodus of black people after threats from gangs of armed white men.

His directions were to a gray frame house with white trim on the St. Mary road just past the bridge over the South Fork. After asking again at a gas station and again at a dry goods store, he found what seemed to be the house and with Espy one step behind he went up on the gallery and rang the bell.

At the corner of his eye he saw the flutter of a curtain as if someone had looked out to see who it was. Then they waited. And waited. He rang the bell again. The door opened at most two inches to the length of a brass-plated latch chain. The voice of someone he could not see asked, "Who is it?"

He identified himself and young Mr. Espy and their business, that they were the attorneys appointed by the court to represent the people accused of killing the two white men. Once you are an established attorney, public defender work will cost you money. But in the Depths of the Depression, the chump change the court paid for it could be your income.

Assuming this was Mrs. Brooks, Redmond said they had been given her name as someone they might prevail upon to offer them lodging. They would pay, of course.

"Oh, not here," the voice said. "We already was run off by American Legions, and be walking on eggs ever since we were permitted to return."

"Permitted to return?" he asked.

"We are on the Good Negroes list, law-abiding colored people that were born here and own property."

"You know that is in flagrant violation of the Fourteenth Amendment to the United States Constitution, besides the U.S. Criminal Code number--"

"Because we returned?"

"That you were driven out under threats and intimidation in the first place, and in the second place that these hoosiers have the arrogance to suppose it is up to them whether you may come or go or move sideways. ... It just infuriates me!"

"Mr....Redmont...is that you name?"

"Redmond."

"Mr. Redmond, you don't live here."

With that she abruptly shut the crack in the door so you could feel the breath of air like from a six-foot fan and hear three lock-bolts slamming home.

On the gallery of the house next door was a large middle-aged white woman with a pleasant face. She sat in a rocking chair with a book on her lap and a toddy glass on the bench beside her. He bade her good evening.

"Bon soir," she said. "Can I help your gentlemen?"

He introduced himself and Espy and told her their business and that they were looking for a place to stay the night.

She introduced herself as Leola Amoreaux, and when she insisted they sit down Redmond took a ladder-back chair by the wall and Espy perched on the top step. "Ordinarily I would say go to the Ribeau brothers next door on the other side," she told them. "But we had some unpleasantness there...You may know about it."

"Ribeau?...The mail man?"

"A gang of drunken fools called him out. Said they wouldn't hurt him, he just had to leave town."

Redmond took out his memo book and made a notation.

"He got away from them and Father T. hid him in the church basement. But he was a nervous wreck and they put him on the train to St. Louis, and he checked himself into a sanitarium there...They say he's not coming back."

Redmond said they knew about it in a general way but what she was telling them was helpful.

"*Helpful?*" she asked. "In what way?"

"To establish prejudice...that our clients could not get a fair trial in Ste. Genevieve."

"Of course not."

"Would you be willing to sign our motion for a change of venue...as a local witness?"

"I'd have to think about that."

He told her they planned to be there most of the next day and possibly the day after, and he changed the subject back to where they might stay for the night.

The white woman seemed relieved that they did not press her to agree to sign as a witness. She said she brought up the trouble at Ribeaus' because she had a feeling that the men who had it in for Cap—he gathered this was the mail man—that they were keeping an eye on the house. He said he thought those men had been arrested, but she said more than fifty were out there in the road and only five or six arrested, and all of them were turned loose with a slap on the wrist as soon as the National Guard left town.

She said she saw what happened to them with her neighbor, and the only other Colored she could think of to direct them to were Irene and Otis Bouchard on Gabouri Street but Otis had a drinking problem. "Charley and Sarah Garesche' the last I heard are still staying in the basement of the Catholic church...They are scared, Mr. Redmond. I would be too. Geraldine Brooks is scared to death. You mustn't blame her too much for shutting the door in your face."

He said he understood.

"You go on to the Bouchards, and if that doesn't work out...well...you come on back here. Lord knows, I have room... since Vital died and the girls left the nest. I just knock around in this old place."

He was touched. Not many white women would offer to put up two strange black men, especially in a backwater Missouri town spoiling to lynch them some niggers.

"I just don't think it would be advisable for you to stay at the Ribeaus. Their house is *watched*. A sharecropper boy staying in the cabin out back simply *disappeared...*he *vanished. ...*So, if Irene and Otis hesitate--and she might with Otis' drinking ... you had better just stay here."

"You are a good-hearted woman, Mrs. Amoreaux," he said. "But from the impression I am getting of this town, you might well be putting yourself in harm's way."

"Thank you, ma'am," said Espy. "We can't let you do that. You would be ostracized at the very least."

"*Ostracized...*Now that's a good word."

"Did I use it correctly?"

"You certainly did. That is just the right word, and it has already happened. I am being ostracized in place. Everyone knows I was the one who called the Sheriff when the crowd gathered at the Ribeaus.' They don't have a telephone."

Redmond said, "All the more reason why we can't impose on you."

"Look...I could pretend to be offended. I could...cry. I could say please let me do this because it will make me feel good---which is true...as far as it goes...I will be honest with you... There are hateful, mean people in this town, but we are not all of us like that. Some of us are from old French families that go way back to when this place was on the map. They married their Indian women in the church and sometimes their Negro women. They left property to them, and the priests baptized their children. They were all buried in the same graveyard. Nearly half of them were Negro, and the Spaniards down in New Orleans did not like it that they were allowed to carry firearms. A number of them were free. This was a cosmopolitan place back then. We were *on maps of the world.* Now we are mostly Catholic Germans and ignorant hillbillies, with a few of the old families who ought to know better...I'm not going to defend what the town did after those two white men were killed. That was... *unconscionable...*one of those words we should not use lightly...It was an *enormity...*committed against innocent, law-abiding....But, I suppose you know too....the labor situation had something to do with it."

Redmond said he needed to know more about that.

"Well, one of the lime companies advertised in newspapers down south for quarry workers at half the pay of the union workers. Most of the people who came were sharecroppers, turned off because the farmers were buying tractors. Enough moved here to frighten us, enough to be resented. Unfortunately your clients were among them."

"Yes, ma'am." Although the woman Mrs. Rogers grew up in Crystal City, their other two clients were from West Memphis and all three were perceived as what she said...*transient niggers.*

"Mr. Redmond....and Mr. Espy....if I may use the word in a quotation, to the laid-off white quarry workers, they are *nigger scabs*....Which is no excuse. It's just a fact. And more than half of the crowd that went around in cars armed to the teeth and most of them drunk ordering Negro people to leave town....were lime workers...and what a beautiful excuse the killing of those two white men was....and let me tell you, Chomeau and Rauscher were not good men, but that doesn't matter. They were a *cause.*"

"Yes, Mrs. Amoreaux...that is very like my own understanding of what happened." He would have to say that at that point he was struggling not to show how delighted he was that this obviously decent and intelligent white woman saw clearly to the heart of the matter. And if she were to testify, it was a foregone conclusion that their change of venue would be granted.

"But of course all that is no excuse, just....how it came to pass."

"Yes, ma'am," he said, "and surely the court will grant us a change of venue."

Mrs. Amoreaux shook her head as if you had thrown cold water in her face and said, "Don't count on it."

"Ma'am?"

"The court that decides that sits right here in Ste. Genevieve, Missouri."

"If the court decides against us and my clients are tried here, it will be a lynching."

"....I wish you well, Mr. Redmond."

He shifted in his chair and looked at Espy.

"And Mr. Espy," she said.

"We thank you, Mrs. Amoreaux," Redmond said and stood up. "We need to get moving."

"Where?" she asked.

"Well, I thought perhaps the Ribeau brothers."

She shook her head. "It's too late....after ten o'clock. You'll just have to stay here."

They went back and forth with her politely declining but she insisted, and he supposed she honestly did want them to stay there and would be if not necessarily hurt or offended, *disappointed* if they refused.

She showed them in and down a plain hall to what she called "the girls' room" with narrow beds on each side of the window on the back gallery and her vegetable garden that sloped up to a bluff face in the moonlight. She told them us to bring in their grips and get settled, showed them the bathroom across the hall, and invited them to join her for a nightcap.

When they had followed her instructions, they went out again to the front gallery. She poured real bottled-in-bond bourbon for them not moonshine in two thick bottom glasses and left it to them to mix or not with Vess soda or creek water, and they settled down again—she in her rocking chair by the bench, Redmond on the chair by the wall, and Espy again at the top of the steps leaning back against a post.

They were done talking with her on the business that brought them there, and he was relieved when she said, "Now you gentlemen tell me about yourselves."

Redmond said he lived in the Ville neighborhood of St. Louis where he grew up, that his papa was a dentist and his mama a school teacher. He attended Oberlin College in Ohio, received his law degree from Howard University in Washington, D.C., and returned to St. Louis to practice. He told her, "We have a house on Cote Brilliant Avenue. My wife Evelyn is a beautician and we have one child, Jack who is seven years old and already has turn. We thank his grandmother for that. She lives downstairs."

"He *has turn?*" their hostess asked.

"Good manners," he said. "Respect. It is a common expression in the Negro community."

"Sometimes one of my pupils would use an expression I hadn't heard before."

"It was funky expressions they *had heard before* got you attention from my teachers," he said, "with a ruler across your knuckles."

"You teach school?" Espy asked.

"I went back to it after the girls were grown."

"I imagine you are a good teacher."

"Thank you....Are you from St. Louis, Mr. Espy?"

"No, ma'am. I was born in Jefferson City where my father is a custodial officer at the state penitentiary. My mother works in domestic service. I have a younger brother and three sisters. I attended Lincoln Institute there, from which I received my law degree under a special arrangement with the University of Missouri."

"....There was something about that in the newspapers."

Redmond tried to catch Espy's eye but he continued and Redmond shrugged. It was his business.

"Yes, Ma'am," he said. "Lloyd Gaines sued for admission to the University of Missouri Law School on the grounds that no separate but equal facility was available for Negroes.... He lost in the Boone County court, but the Eastern District of Missouri Appellate Court reversed them and ordered his admission. Before the University could decide whether to appeal to the state supreme court, Lloyd disappeared. Some in the Negro community believe he was murdered."

"You knew him?"

"Yes, ma'am. I admired him. He took up for little kids in the school yard."

Redmond said, "We do not know that he is a victim of foul play. He might have found his situation too stressful....suffered some kind of nervous breakdown....and just chose to disappear."

"He dead, Sidney. You don't have to shuck and jive for Mrs. Amoreaux."

"I stand corrected. I take that in good spirit, John."

"I knew that you would."

Mrs. Amoreaux said, "I wouldn't be at all surprised if he was murdered."

They sat there a while. She hauled herself up and refilled their glasses. They had wrung their hands enough over the sins of white people. Redmond asked about her late husband and her daughters.

"Vital was a pharmacist....Gabrielle's married to a mining engineer and lives in New Mexico. Vivienne is a nurse in St. Louis."

She showed them pictures, told stories about them. Her husband supplied liniment and animal medicine to one of the Ribeau brothers who had a thriving practice as an unlicensed veterinarian. "When Vivienne was little she was always pestering me to let her go next door and watch Lon doctor the animals. He would explain what he was doing, let her think she was helping him."

"And she went into nursing?" Espy said.

"Oh, Lon Ribeau is the reason. White farmers come to him. He cures their kye and kine."

Redmond said you hear stories like that from slavery times, how white people believe Colored have a way with animals. "There was a famous Negro jockey in Kentucky who belonged to a Mr. Belknap."

"Of course they pay Lon only half as much as the young DVM in Weingarten."

"Like the croppers that come here to work in the lime kilns," said Espy.

He took a particular interest in the sharecroppers. His mother knew the house mother of the sorority at Lincoln Institute that canceled their spring prom, and took the money to buy canned milk and cooking oil to take to the croppers the previous winter when they were camping out along the highway.

"What is worse to you," Mrs. Amoreaux asked, "the man who believes a Negro should get half the pay for the same work, or the man who makes money when he takes it?"

Redmond could not think when he had such an honest conversation with a white person, and that was many years ago.

3.

IN THE MORNING WHEN REDMOND WENT OUT TO HIS CAR, SOMEONE HAD written with soap on the windshield:

Nigger you have til sundown

The tires had been slashed.

A chestnut brown man in a white shirt was watching him and Espy from the gallery steps of what their hostess had given them to understand was the brothers Ribeau house. The man looked this way and that and over his shoulder, and with an air of self-consciousness walked toward them but stopped a few feet away. He said, "Can I be of assistance to you gentlemen?"

They agreed that the one spare tire in the boot in front of the passenger-side running board was not going to solve the problem. They discussed various possibilities. Ordinarily a punctured tire could be repaired with a patch on the inner-tube. Long deep slashes all the way through the side walls were another matter. "Be from a stout knife," said the man. "Or a sling blade."

They also agreed that the legend on the windshield was part of the problem. "Somebody want you gone, but he fix it so you can't." They contemplated this conundrum.

They returned to the question of what was to be done about the four flat tires. If they set blocks under the axles they could remove the wheels and take them to a service station. Or they could purchase four new tires, or just four new inner-tubes and take their chances on them blistering out through the slashes.

The man looked over his shoulder and to the right and to the left, and said, "Beg you pardon. I be Alonzo Levi Ribeau...*dit* Lon."

Espy and Redmond introduced themselves and they all shook hands.

"I know you gentlemens not from here, cause you can count the Negro peoples that remain in this town on the fingers of you hands, and my brothers and me be three of them."

They told him their business.

This information made him even more skittish. He looked to his right and to his left and behind his back all over again. "Well, I have to get up to Mr. Rozier's or I be late for work." He walked on past them to the corner of a street that went up the bluff on a steep incline, then came back part way. "Be five gas stations," he said. "Three don't want you business if you Negro." He told them where the other two were and walked off, then came back again. He said his job was to chauffeur Mr. Rozier and he was not allowed to joyride on personal business. But maybe he could come back in Mr. Rozier's automobile and give them a lift.

He proved unable or unwilling to do this.

They used up two hours attending to the problem—at the second gas station they visited they found a black man willing to drive them back to Redmond's car in the tow truck with four new tires and tubes, in turn jacking up the front and back end and removing the wheels, going through the laborious process of removing the flats from the rims and putting the new tires on, and filling the first three from the compressed air tank on the tow truck, and when it ran out, pumping up the last tire with a hand pump. He acted as if he were doing them a tremendous personal favor, as if they were an annoying interruption of his more important work. Or it might have been that he was scared of being observed helping them and ashamed, and this was his way of showing it. After paying the 16 dollars and 45 cents for this, Redmond had 3 dollars until the end of next week.

They finally set out with sandwiches that Mrs. Amoreaux had prepared for them. They parked across from the courthouse and walked up and down the streets of the Ste. Genevieve business district going in one establishment after another. The people in most of them were at least civil, several were friendly enough, some were rude, and some just outright hostile.

The proprietor of Odile's Lace and Notions on 3rd Street was friendly and talkative and seemed to see matters much the same way as Mrs. Amoreaux. "Oh, they won't get a fair trial here," she said. "I'm afraid not." But when Redmond asked her to sign their motion, she hesitated. "It will be a matter of public record?"

Redmond had to allow that it would.

"I'm sorry, Mr. Redmond, but I just can't. I would lose half my trade."

He thanked her for her time and they moved on.

They tried at Ziegler's Tobacco & Art Supplies, with a Coca-Cola sign by the door. A man he supposed was Ziegler asked, "May I help you gentlemen?"

Espy stated their business and asked if he would care to sign their petition for a change of venue.

He looked them over and shook his head.

Espy was offended and halfway out the door when the man came gimping out from behind the counter. One leg was shorter than the other and he wore an elevator shoe. "Wait," he said. "If you don't have enough by the end of the day..."

Redmond kept a list of the places they went.

The girl at Bouvarie's General Merchandise and the desk clerk at Vorst's Hotel and the man at Koettig's Jewelers all were friendly, but like the woman at Odile's Lace and Notions—on Redmond's list Odile Bernays—they were afraid of losing trade if they signed. The woman at Kuch's bakery on Merchant street said oh no the Negro people can't get a fair trial here but she would be put out of business if she signed. She said she was sorry and gave them a bag of day-old jelly donuts.

As soon as they walked in the Silver Café on Main Street the waitress said, "We don't serve Colored."

"We are not here to get served," Redmond said.

"Then get out."

They did.

The woman at Tlapek Real Estate also was quite rude. Before he could introduce himself she said, "We don't sell to Negroes. We don't rent to Negroes, and we are not listing any more properties to sell for Negroes."

"That's not why we are here," Redmond said.

"Why, then?"

He told her their business.

"You should be grateful those people are even having a trial, and you get some work out of it."

They went to Firmin's Dry Goods, Rozier's Bank, Elder Manufacturing, the Palace Bar, the Main Street Saloon, Nauman's Butcher Shop, Basler's Mortuary, the Detchmendy Hotel, the Elpers & Inman law office, Cap Donze's Cut-Rate & Bus Stop, Oberle's Sausage, Stewart's Sinclair gas station, the *Herald* newspaper office, Okenfuss Hardware, the Creole Dairy, the Stanton Ford Dealership, Standard Oil, Vic Sexauer's Tavern, and other places that he did not write down as they were running out of time. No one would sign their motion for a change of venue.

They went back to Ziegler's Tobacco & Art Supplies. The door was locked and the sign hanging inside the glass said CLOSED.

Early on they had noticed two men who seemed to be following them, and as the day wore on they saw others. By four o'clock there were at least six and no longer furtive but openly dogging them.

The clerk's office would close at five.

Espy and Redmond discussed it back and forth as they went along. Not knowing anyone in town before they came, the merchants and businesses were the ones they approached. They were reluctant to go knocking on the doors of white people in white neighborhoods with dogs and young hoodlums to follow and taunt them. They were ever mindful of the threat written in soap on the windshield of Redmond's car, and the tire-slashing. They were scared.

Redmond supposed that the names of the handful of Negro residents who remained in Ste. Genevieve would carry less weight than white people, and the response of Mrs. Brooks was not encouraging. Mrs. Amoreaux they had kept back as their ace in the hole, thinking when they set out that morning that surely they would be able to get enough signatures to do without hers, which would only expose her to more aversion. Now they calculated that with her and one other they would have at least the statutory minimum of two affidavits, and the other could be one of the Ribeau brothers or Mrs. Bouchard.

No one answered the door at Bouchard's, although he suspected someone was there. He guessed it was Mrs. Bouchard.

At the Ribeaus he got the feeling they really were not home, but probably still at work.

At Mrs. Amoreaux's house, a colored boy was raking leaves. They went up on the gallery and knocked on the door although no light was showing in the early dark and the old car that had been in the driveway was gone. "She ain't there," the boy said.

He asked if he had an idea when she might be back.

"She gone to visit her daughter at St. Louis."

Two cars had followed them and were parked nose-to-tail behind Redmond's car like a funeral procession waiting for the mourners to finish up at the graveside. As they came down to the road, men got out of the cars and gathered around them. The boy with a rake made himself scarce.

Redmond said, "Good evening, gentlemen."

A red-nosed little peckerwood with his thumb stuck in his belt asked them, "You know when sundown is?"

Redmond said, "So you are the one who vandalized my car?"

The white men looked at each other. They were not used to a Negro talking up to them in this way. Redmond was trying to keep the involuntary twitching behind his knees from reducing him to the overall shakes. One of them advised him to talk civil. He was a big fellow with a lot of chin who looked like the picture of Mussolini after he conquered Ethiopia and made the cover of *Life* Magazine.

Redmond asked the first one, "What is your name?"

"A. J. Crowley. *Mister* Crowley to you."

"That name sounds familiar."

The effect of this was remarkable. One of the other men said, "You had better go home, A.J."

The little red-nose man whirled around and cursed the man who had said that, and three of the others got back in the second car and it made a quick U-turn.

Redmond said to the local Mussolini, "As attorneys, we are officers of the Court."

He seemed to be intelligent enough to have some idea of the implications of that. He sidled back a few steps saying, "Well, you have been warned."

Redmond stood his ground, and Mussolini-in-an-American-Legion-cap got in the other car and it made a U-turn and peeled off.

Redmond was honest-to-goodness just plain shaking all over. His teeth chattered until he clamped his mouth shut. Espy said, "Sidney, whatever got into you?"

He shook his head and said, "Something going on."

They found out later that the little peck Crowley and at least two of the men with him were among the six who had actually been arrested in the incident at the Ribeau house and were on probation.

They got back to the courthouse just as the clerk was about to lock the door to his office, and turned in their motion for a change of venue without any affidavits from local citizens.

Once they were beyond the city limits and the stretch of graded gravel and onto the paved highway, he stepped on the gas. By ten o'clock that night, they were crossing the South Broadway bridge over the River Des Peres into St. Louis.

WHEN LON RIBEAU WENT ACROSS THE CREEK INTO TOWN FOR THE FIRST time after the vigilantes had come to his door, he saw people looking out over their curtains like he was the plague. They were keeping themselves away from it.

Except for Will Bouvarie. He came out of his dry goods and said, "Don't you let them scare you, Lon. Stand your ground. If they make trouble, I have a Springfield rifle you can borrow any time. Just give me a holler." He visited with Lon right out there on Merchant street, shook his hand, and went on to the hotel bar for his noontime bitters.

Ken Oberle the butcher came along. He said, "Lon, if they cause you any more trouble, there's always a place for you at our house. Your brothers too." Gary Schram told him the same thing, the Aubuchons too.

Most of the people though were just looking through their curtains. Neighbors talked about him and his brothers behind their backs, how they let the house run down, Lon's animal doctoring. They said Zeno would not step off the sidewalk to let a white man pass. Cap would get a snoot full and run his mouth.

Just a few stood by them. You remember who.

Lon went on to the bank to see Frank Rozier Jr. who was running it since old Mr. Rozier semi-retired. He had some documents he wanted him to keep safe for him. Young Frank said, "You people keep quiet and out of sight, and all this will blow over." He said it might be a good idea if they went away for a while and came back when things calmed down.

Lon drew himself up and said, "I was not afraid of the Kaiser and I am not afraid now. I not going to leave here till I be a corpse."

Young Frank said it was just a suggestion.

"Same for Zeno and Cap, sir."

All three Ribeau brothers had served in the World War.

Their grandfather Jean Ribeau was a white man who came there over a hundred years ago from France, and he bought their grandmother Felicite from Janis the tavern keeper and married her in the church. Lon was in service to old Mr. Rozier, whose father owned their grandmother's sister Odile. He could recall them speaking together in French. *"Grandpère e' Grandmère parlez vous together,"* he would say. *"Noi son le frère Ribeau."* Their mother was caramel brown. Lon was the same color; Zeno black as tar, and Cap was *cafe' au lait*. People said he could pass. Zeno labored at Jenkins-Gillis lime company. Cap with his veterans' preference worked for the U.S. Postal Service.

The vigilantes came to their door because Cap had a white man's job.

The Negro lawyer from St. Louis whose tires were slashed made him extremely nervous. Those men were watching the house.

Lon wondered about the boy Cletus who stayed in the old slave crib out back. He disappeared that night.

4.

AS IT BECAME GENERALLY KNOWN IN THE ST. LOUIS NEGRO COMMUNITY
that he was representing the suspects in the killing of the two white men, refugees from the
mass eviction came to Redmond for advice and assistance. Some came alone, others in couples or family groups, mothers with young children and babes in arms, great-grandparents.
They climbed the six flights of stairs to his office overlooking an air shaft in the old Wain-
wright Building on Chestnut Street. A few were respectably dressed and grammatical with a
manner that bespoke Negro middle class. Most were poor and threadbare and gave account
of themselves in rural dialect from the Missouri Boot Heel and the cotton south.

Among them was the sharecropper boy Cletus Johnson who was staying with the Ribeau brothers and had been a work mate of Taylor and Jennings. Seeking further to establish
that they could not get a fair trial in Ste. Genevieve, Redmond wanted to hear why he had
fled. He also asked about the circumstances of his employment there, and about the long
strike at the white quarries.

CLETUS SAID THE MAN AT THE GATE SENT HIM TO SEE MR. JENKINS IN THE
caboose. The white man asked if he had ever done quarry work. He told him he had done
agricultural work since he was eight years old.

"Shucking corn...chopping cotton?"

"I done that."

"You one of those sharecroppers who camped out on the highway?"

"Papa was."

"You a agitator?"

"No, sir."

A little man with bandy legs by a stand-up desk with blueprints, Jenkins had kinky
white hair like old colored men. He said, "It's twenty-five cents."

That was what Cletus had read in the newspaper. He had it in his pocket in case they
tried to gyp him down. He said, "Yes, sir."

"I need a boy on the pulverizer...What did you say your name was?"

"Cletus. Cletus Johnson."

"Day shift is seven to four. Go with Mr. Walker there."

A white Negro with squinty pink eyes pushed back from another high desk where he was messing with an adding machine and put on dark glasses, and Cletus followed him on out. He asked, "Where you from, Cletus?"

"Samos."

"Where's that?"

"Pemiscot County...down the Boot Heel."

All around on three sides were white cliffs and on the ground lime dust. They came to a building like a cotton gin but what they ginned was cooked limestone, grinder shafts going round and round so loud that you raised you voice like to a deaf person. Walker took him to a coal black middle-aged man he called Zeno, said here is the new boy and Cletus' name.

Zeno told him he needed a tin hat and horse-leather gloves and that would come out of his first pay and there was a one week hold-back so the first money he saw would be a week from Saturday. He took him over to a booth by the door, and on the wall were four hooks with numbers, and on two of them were tin hats. He handed him one and said you can adjust the headband.

It was all greasy and nasty against his forehead from the man who wore it before.

"Cost you two dollars," Zeno said. "A new one is five." He handed him a pair of new gloves. "That's a dollar."

"They pay me to work here?" Cletus asked. "Or I has to pay them?"

"How much they give you chopping cotton?"

"*Picking*, you paid by the sack." Hump and don't mind if your fingers bleed, you could take down some money.

"How come you not doing it then?"

Cletus just shook his head and looked down.

"Jenkins lay off a white man to hire you on."

"What for he do that?"

"Cause he has to pay the white man fifty cents."

THE MAN UP ON THE PLATFORM BY THE TRACK TIPPED THE HOPPER CARS into the kiln that cooked the water out. Taylor the man who did that was out sick. Two men were supposed to work down by the conveyor raking off any impurities and rocks bigger than a fist. CJ was doing that by himself.

Zeno put Cletus up on the platform. It was a hard job. You pulled the pin so the hopper swung free, then pushed up on the rod handle to tip it. Little bits of rock spilled down, and CJ would holler at him.

Zeno shared out some of his dinner with Cletus. When the other man was off relieving himself he said, "CJ bad in the head this morning. Don't mess with him."

Cletus believed he was suffering from the excess consumption of alcohol and maybe that was also what Taylor was out sick from. CJ stood for Columbus Jennings. Taylor they called Lee Guy. Zeno was the boss over the three of them and ran the pulverizer.

AT THE END OF THE SHIFT OLD ZENO KEPT HIM BACK, THEN WENT OUT THE gate beside him. He said Walker told him he was a church nigger.

Cletus hunched up, shook his head.

"Say you one of them camped on the highway, Reverend Whitfield's people."

"You know about that?"

"Everybody know...Mrs. Roosevelt, *Jet* Magazine ."

"Lots of good it done us."

"Made niggers proud!"

"Sic the state police on us, dump us in the spillway."

"You comprehend that?"

He comprehended that. Reverend Whitfield said, *We going to starve anyway, might as well do it out on the highway for all the world to see.* Cletus used to think Reverend Whitfield walked on water and was the bravest man he knew after his papa. But his papa could not read or write. When they were out on the highway, white boys took his sister up the ditch and gave her a trick baby. Cletus was an *eye-for-a-eye* nigger since. He said, "...I was raised a church nigger."

"All I be saying is, you different from these low, shiftless, transient colored come here from the advertisement down south."

Cletus was not about to tell him he had one of those advertisements in his pocket.

ZENO TOOK CLETUS HOME WITH HIM. A BACHELOR, HE LIVED WITH HIS TWO bachelor brothers Alonzo and Cap Louis Ribeau in an old French house on the south bottom road. Lon cooked the dinner that he called a haricot because it had beans, white beans and cut up rabbit meat. Lon was in service to Mr. Rozier the banker, Zeno the boss of the pulverizer and south kiln at Jenkins-Gillis Lime Company, and Cap had a good government job as a mail man.

Zeno was black as tar, Lon a medium brown like a cigar, and Cap a high yellow with blue eyes and he could pass. Cletus hoped he did not give offense when he asked them, "You whole brothers?"

They said that's right.

"How come you all such a different color?"

They looked at each other, shook their heads and laughed.

"Folks wonder," Zeno said.

"Only they too bashful to ask," said Lon.

"It's Mendel's Law," Cap said.

"What's that?" Cletus asked him.

"How far you gone in school?"

"Tenth grade."

"You never study Mendel's Law in biology?"

"No, sir. We just have general science."

"Our grandaddy was a white man," Lon said.

"Louis Ribeau, same as Cap," said Zeno. "He marry Odalie that belong to Mr. Janis."

"Mendel a Austrian monk like to tend his garden, and he experiment. Fertilize a red sweet pea from a white sweet pea and write down the colors of the flowers that grow from they seeds. One be red, two pink, one white."

"Why don't they all be pink?"

"That is Mendel's Law."

"You funning me."

"It's in the *World Book* encyclopedia."

"Don't make sense."

Zeno and Lon looked at each other and laughed.

Cap went to the book shelf by the window with a row of heavy green books just alike except each was a different letter of the alphabet. He took one out and came back to the table and read from it. "Mendel's Law..."

All three of them and Cletus too drank red wine from jelly glasses, and Cap refilled his from the cut glass pitcher in front of him on the table. Lon made the wine from grapes they grew up the hill in the back yard. He said they owned to the top of the bluff that was just a steep hill along there, one arpent wide and used to run all the way to the Mississippi River. An arpent was a French acre. In his wine Cap got disputatious about Mrs. Roosevelt and Senator Bilbo and the rights of colored people.

Zeno said, "That trash in Merchant Street bottom don't deserve no rights. Give us a bad name." Most of the transient Negroes lived in cribs in the bottoms at the end of Merchant Street around the depot, some out at Modoc landing where the ferry came.

Lon said, "Cap read in the *World Book*. He read in it every night, one letter of the alphabet after another. What letter you on now, Cap?"

"I gone through them all twice, be at G the third time. Be reading on Gandhi. Read on him in the *Fair Play* newspaper too."

Zeno asked, "What for he go around in that big diaper and sandals?"

"He dress like the poor people. They follow him too. *Five hundred thousand* follow him on his Salt March to the sea...Be how he going kick the English out of India."

"He do it too," said Lonzo. "All them English lords and ladies."

"American colored be a colonized people," said Cap.

"You talk like that to you honky postal patrons, they string you up on the pecan tree," said Zeno.

"Cracker trash, sic they dogs on me."

"Reverend Whitfield preach on Gandhi," said Cletus.

"See, this boy here know about Gandhi."

"Get death threats in the night, has to hide up at St. Louis."

"Hear that, Cap?" Zeno say. "Even this boy know better."

THEY SAID CLETUS WAS WELCOME TO STAY BY THEM AND PAY SOME FOR board, but Mrs. Brooks next door with her daughter Clementine attending Lincoln College in Jefferson City had a spare room. They went over to the Brooks' house. Zeno told Cletus she was in service to Mrs. Mathews the wife of the boss of the biggest lime company Bluff City, and George Brooks was the custodian at Valle Catholic High School. They had dinner guests, Charles and Sarah Garesche'. Charles was the sexton for the Catholic church, Sarah the housekeeper for the priests Father Van and Father Horn.

Mrs. Brooks was bragging on the rich white woman she worked for Mrs. Harry B. Griswold Junior. "She is so concerned about the old French houses. She and some of her friends in the Colonial Dames are taking up a collection amongst their wealthy friends to buy the old rundown Bolduc house, and fix it up to show for the better class of tourists."

"Won't that be lovely," said Auntie Garesché.

"Suppose that include us, Charlie?" Zeno asked.

"We the better class of colored people."

"In Ste. Genevieve we the creme de la creme."

"Only way we get in the door is to wash the windows or serve whores' ovaries on a tray."

"Or fetch the mail to them." Cap said.

Then Mrs. Brooks was going on about what a wonderful man Mr. Harry B. Griswold Junior was, how he treated the men who worked for him right. "Pay them decent pay, not like that horrible Old Man Jenkins that bring up trash from down South."

"This boy here trash?" Zeno asked.

"Why of course not, Zeno," said Mrs. Brooks.

"He just hired on. Come from...where at?"

"Samos."

"Samos...down the Boot Heel. His daddy a sharecropper... turned off."

"I did not mean--"

"Camped on the highway...one of Reverend Whitfield's people."

"Oh, my heart goes out to them. Everyone's does...My Clemmie and her sorority sisters drove down from Lincoln with old clothes. Called off they spring dance and took the money they was going to spend on a new frock to buy can milk for the little babies, rice and beans. Those poor people, out there by the highway in the snow."

"That the ideal," Cletus said. "Make the peoples feel sorry."

"Geraldine," Zeno asked, "what you doing with Clementine's room now she off at the college?"

"Why, that is her room. She need it for her holidays, for the summer vacation. That always be my precious Clemmie's room till the day I die."

"Just asking."

"...Oh."

"We was wondering," Lonzo said, "this boy here with three old bachelors."

"Oh. Of course...What was your name again?"

"Cletus."

"Cletus...why you daddy be evicted?"

"All the croppers round Samos be put off...Most the croppers at Wilson City, Wyatt put off last year. Farmers steal our parity payment and buy tractors, go to day labor."

"I find that hard to believe."

"Reverend Whitfield say they breaking up the whole sharecropper system. Buy tractors, sell the mules for dog food."

"Well, Cletus, I surely am impressed with how you speak...with how well-spoken you are. You have a fine little mind. But the farmers steal you payments? I just can't believe that."

Standing off to the side by Cap, Cletus said to her lady-like brown face, "Mrs. Brooks, you a fool."

WHEN THEY WERE BACK AT THEIR HOUSE, LONZO, ZENO AND CAP TRIED TO act all serious and embarrassed. Cletus said his Papa and Mama raised him to respect his elders and he did, and he was over next door as their guest and he appologized, "I sincerely do."

Lonzo said, "Well, Cletus--"

"Yes, son..." say Zeno.

Then Cap, Zeno, and finally Lonzo--all three of them were just laughing like they would never quit. They laughed and laughed, looked at each other, and laughed some more.

"She say--"

"Well!"

"We tried."

Lon said, "You all remember when she got me to waiter for Tertius' wedding?" He explained to Cletus, "That be old Griswold' son. The old man already Junior so the son be Harry Griswold the Third, call him Tertius.

"Geraldine say the girl's family just nobodies in South St. Louis so the wedding be in Ste. Genevieve and the groom's family having the reception at the Knights of Columbus. I be there in my waiter coat serving cocktails and glasses of champagne off my waiter tray out on the gallery standing by Tertius and his best friend George, and George be dipping Ritz crackiers one after another into the bowl of little black fish eggs.

"After a while old Mr. Harry Griswold himself come up and say, 'Get you cotton-picking fingers out of there!'

"'Oh, sir, I'm sorry,' George say. He a tall shambling fellow with eyeglasses, back off against the wall.

"'That is Beluga caviar that I flew in from Russia at a cost of sixteen hundred dollars and you are chomping it down like peanut butter.'"

"Poor George," Cap said.

"You remember when Tertius in knee pants, go around town with a big fellow talk British say from Scotland Yard?" Zeno asked.

"Be his bodyguard," Cap said. "They afraid he be kidnapped."

"Ain't nobody going to kidnap me," Cletus said.

That set them off laughing all over again.

So Cletus stayed with old Cap and Lonzo and Zeno. They fixed up the old summer kitchen out back so he could have some privacy. He helped out tending the vegetable garden and paid a dollar a week. Lonzo was in charge the cooking and Zeno and Cap and Cletus took turns helping him out and cleaning up after.

Their diet was different from what Cletus was used to, with more greens and squash and tomatoes, turnips and beets and beans. They did not do any deep fat frying like his mama with chicken and hush puppies. They *sautéed* in the skillet on just a little butter and cooked the meat with vegetables. He took a liking to it and had more regular bowel movements.

He also took a liking to the wine they made. At supper they always a tall jar of the red wine on the table. Down home booze was the Devil's brew, why men beat on their women, went to rob and cut each other, and women commit fornication, leaving children by themselves to go hungry, set the house on fire. Old church people criticized Reverend Whitfield because he did not preach on it. Cletus' papa said he took a drink himself now and then, and so did Jesus. Maybe sometime the old Ribeau boys got into a second jar, or Cap did, but they just played cribbage, sat on the gallery watching the evening birds catch June bugs and said *How you doing?* to people passing by.

Cletus pestered Lonzo to show him how to make it.

FOR A WHILE LEE GUY AND CJ DID NOT PAY THE SHARECROPPER BOY CLEtus Johnson much mind. They each did their tasks and had little business with each other except when something went wrong. Then they seemed to be noticing how Zeno treated Cletus differently, as if he was his little brother or his nephew—not just a hand. At dinner break Lee Guy asked Cletus, "You stay by Ribeaus?"

"That's right."

"What they do for women?"

"They not married."

"They not interested in womens?" CJ asked. He was a sickly brown with a big round face, always looking to Lee Guy when he talked.

"How I know?" Cletus asked. "I stay in the crib out back, pay a dollar."

"Has good jobs," Lee Guy said. "Old Zeno classified a fireman, be paid sixty cents same as a white man."

"They old enough."

"One have a position with the U.S. Postal Service."

"Be a mail man," Cletus said.

"I say it wrong?"

"Say it any way you want."

"No. You corrected me, like I a silly nigger talking fancy."

Cletus just shook his head.

"How come they not married?" CJ asked.

"They old-family Colored from the time of the Frenchmens. Not many that kind of womens here to pick from. Mrs. Geraldine Brooks married to George, Sarah Garesche' to Charley."

"They a higher class Negro?" Lee Guy asked.

"You can say it that way."

"There he go. Criticize how I talk."

Cletus shut his mouth.

The next day at dinner time Lee Guy started in again. "What those old boys *do?* Fuck you up the rectum? Suck dick?"

Cletus stared at him. Lee Guy was a foxy dapper negro, sepia colored.

"What for he stare at me like that. Suppose he want to suck *my* dick?" Lee Guy pretended to unbutton his pants.

CJ looked at him as if to say that was enough.

"After me, do CJ."

CJ told him, "I not playing."

Cletus thought to himself *the knife in my pocket has blood on it.* If Lee Guy laid a hand on him, he would cut him.

"What that boy done to you?" CJ asked.

"He criticize how I talk."

Cletus knew his Bible, before the Jesus part. *An eye for an eye, a tooth for a tooth.*

"Why you so hateful this morning? Vera on the rag?"

Cletus was not scared of Lee Guy Taylor. He would slash him criss cross. He had conked hair, supposed to be a ladies' man.

"What he doing there, hand in his pocket?"

Cletus stared at him, and kept his mouth shut.

"You playing with it?"

Cletus was not playing. He had a four-inch lock blade knife that would cut paper endways.

"Go to fight on the job," CJ told him, "old Jenkins fire you ass quicker than a union man....*Me* too, cause I suppose to be you friend."

"You right," Lee Guy said. "I tend to this boy later."

IN THE AFTERNOON LITTLE PIECES OF ROCK FELL AROUND CLETUS FROM UP on the platform where Lee Guy was working. One the size of a brick hit his wrist and raised a welt. After a while a substantial rock hit him on top of his shoulder where at the arm joint so he lost hold of the rake, and it was moving down the belt among the cooked rock.

CJ grabbed it out and hollered at him, "That rake go in the mix, old Man Jenkins grind you down with it!"

Cletus took back the rake, and hurried to catch up with what he was supposed to be doing.

Zeno came around from where he was tending the fire and asked, "What you hollering about?"

CJ told him, "This ignorant boy lost hold, rake jam up the pulverizer."

"You need to be more careful, son," Zeno said. "We cooking chemical lime here, not cement."

"Yes, sir."

"That rake do jam up the shaft, we has to clock out till it fixed."

"I be more careful." As he said it he saw CJ with a smirk on his green-black face looking up over his head. He turned around, and Lee Guy up on the platform was bent over with both hands across his mouth to keep from laughing out loud.

Zeno was walking away.

Cletus called, "Mr. Ribeau...!"

He came back.

Cletus snitched. "I lost hold of the rake because a rock hit me here." He twisted to show where it tore his shirt, passed his hand over the place, showed him the smear of blood.

Zeno looked at him, then up at Lee Guy. "Taylor, come down here!"

Lee Guy stared hard at Cletus. He came down the iron ladder as if he weighed a thousand pounds, and he dared Zeno to tell him to hurry.

When he finally was down and had come over to them, Zeno said, "Taylor, that happen again, I know it be on purpose."

"Come on, Zeno," Lee Guy said, "all that rock bouncing down. You know a piece going to fall now and then."

"You understand what I be saying?"

"Put that boy up on the platform. See what—"

"You on probation…! I be going down now, write it up."

The next day just little bits of rock fell now and then. Zeno came up, checked on them. Then another *big* rock fell, this one on Cletus' head and knocked his tin hat off.

He reached out quick to grab it, lost his balance, and squatted back down just in time or he would have sprawled out on the cooked rock moving to the pulverizer.

Zeno had just come up again and was standing behind CJ.

Cletus did not see him. He went straight for the ladder up to the platform, and was halfway up when a hand grabbed his ankle.

Cletus came down, backed off. This was between Lee Guy and Zeno.

"Taylor…! *Come down here!*"

This time the way Lee Guy came down the iron ladder was more normal but he did not hurry. He came over to Zeno and said, "What you want now?"

Zeno did not raise his voice. He just told him, "You suspended rest of this week without pay…Come back Monday on time. One more piece of rock fall or any other monkey business, you terminated for cause and a bad reference."

This time LeGuy was not talking back. He stood staring at Cletus trying to intimidate him and make him look down. Cletus stared his own hard stare with his hand on the knife in his pocket.

"And you menace this boy in any way, I whip you sorry ass till you wish you was dead."

Lee Guy spat by Cletus' shoe.

5.

COME MONDAY LEE GUY TAYLOR WAS SWEET AS PIE, SAID LAST WEEK HE WAS
out of sorts. "Cletus...that you name, Cletus?"

Cletus nodded.

"I apologize." He held out his brown hand.

CJ caught his eye as if to say Lee Guy was sincere, and Cletus shook his hand.

"We all has to get along."

"I need this job," Cletus said.

"We all needs this job," CJ said.

"Don't be nothing in West Memphis," said Lee Guy.

"That where you all from?" Cletus asked.

"West Memphis, Arkansas. Be working in the chicken plant. Chicken plant close
down."

"I be from the country near there, Jericho Junction," CJ said.

Lee Guy shared out some cold biscuits that he said Vera made for them.

They asked and Cletus told them he came to Ste. Genevieve from an advertisement in
the newspaper, and they saw one of them too. He did not say too much about camping on the
highway after they were all evicted. They heard of it, the Croppers on the highway.

"Don't brag on it to Old Man Jenkins," CJ said. "He think you a Union agitator."

AT SUPPER CLETUS TOLD ZENO AND HIS BROTHERS THAT LEE GUY TAYLOR
made up to him, and said come down to Merchant Street bottoms to the juke joint.

"Oh, that be a place to stay away from," Lonzo said. "Niggers get drunk, cut and beat
on each other...Most every Tuesday the *Fair Play* newspaper tell about police called in over
the weekend .... Domestic disputes, drunk and disorderly, and just all-around trouble and
crime."

Zeno shook his head like he heard all this before.

"Be the den of iniquity," Lonzo said. "Jezebel, Bathsheba, and the Whore of Babylon just
lying in wait. Come out of there with you shirt on backwards and you pants on inside out."

Zeno was trying to look serious.

Cap didn't say anything. He went there himself when he tired of his *World Book*.

Cletus said well he could take it or leave it. Through the week he was too tired even to think on it. But with just a half day Saturday and his first whole pay since he paid off on the tin hat and horse-leather gloves, he sifted on down there.

The joint was around behind the depot in a place with a checkerboard sign for the feed company, a dirty line around the walls from the last flood. Men stood out on the gallery and the gravel street, women and men together crowded inside talking, laughing, standing around and sitting on benches at long tables. The bar was the old feed store counter. Lon said they called it the Creamery because it was next to the ice house that used to have a big walk-in icebox to keep cream, and it was the first place in town you could get ice cream. Smoke and funk from all the peoples hung in the air with perfume, barbecue, sewage and a dead animal smell from the slough out back.

Where the ceiling was two stories high people were dancing to the juke box, a man singing...

> Woman, don't talk me to death
> Cause I not ready to die.

By the pool table was a picture on the wall, a white woman in a swim suit drinking a Lemp Red Lager.

Cletus stood by the front, nobody paying him any mind.

Outside were more trestle tables under the cottonwood trees, and bits of lint hung in the air. Cletus was gawking around when a thump high on his back made him jump as if he were snake-bit, and it was Lee Guy.

He said come on over by him and Vera, and CJ was there too. Cletus followed him to the last table under the trees, with bottles in paper bags, and Vess soda and an ice bucket, and some tin cups. People made room for him.

He took a cup of white whiskey from the moonshine barge with Vess red pop. It tasted like chemicals but he drank some, then mostly pretended to drink.

Vera was a fine brown woman but drunk and worn-out looking. She just nodded toward him, looking off somewhere.

Lee Guy asked him about the Ribeau brothers, what they all did. "Lonzo in service to Mr. Rozier?"

"That's right," Cletus said.

"What all he do for him?"

"Tend the garden. Prepare his lunch. Answer the telephone ...Drive him places, run errands."

"Drive a Lincoln Zephyr."

"I believe that the kind of car."

"When he run errands, Rozier always with him or by himself sometime?"

"Sometime by himself." Cletus was wondering what Lee Guy had in mind.

"He ever run a errand for himself?"

"He not suppose to."

"Or for you...if you ask him real nice."

"He not suppose to do that."

"Ribeau always do what he suppose to do?"

"Far as I know."

"What about you, Cletus?"

"What for you asking all this?"

"Nothing. Just...we need a car."

CLETUS TRIED TO TELL LONZO WITHOUT ZENO KNOWING, SO HE WOULD not be snitching again. But they were brothers. Cletus said, "He have a revolver. When he drunk, we go down by the river, shoot tin cans."

SUNDAY CLEMMIE BROOKS PAID A CALL ON THE RIBEAUS. SHE SAID SHE WAS not supposed to talk to Cletus because he was disrespectful to her mama. He apologized all over again, said his papa would whip him. Cap and Zeno grinned and shook their heads.

She was having a philosophical conversation on Marcus Garvey, whether black people had to secede from white people before they could have dignity.

They were talking back and forth using big words from Cap's *World Book* and her Professor Green. Cletus tried to place her among the college girls who had come to their camp. After a while he said, "Miss Brooks, excuse me, but I do not recall you amongst the young ladies from the Alpha Gamma Pi Sorority that come to our camp."

"Did my mother say I was?"

"I believe so. That is my recollection."

Miss Clemmie Brooks rolled her eyes and asked the Ribeaus if they recalled her saying that.

Lonzo nodded and said he believed she did.

"Cletus...that you name? Cletus, the kindest way to say it is Mama exaggerates."

She said she was in Professor Green's American Social History class and a member of the sorority but she was doing her practicum teaching and going through a difficult time with her fiancé and decided not to go. She did donate the money she was going to spend on her dress for the spring promenade.

Cletus nodded and shrunk up inside. She was a lovely red-brown young woman the color of polished walnut, with freckles across her nose and cheeks. He already was having thoughts of asking her to walk with him by the river, and go to the picture show. But he did not believe she would have the time for a funky little country nigger like him.

He was mistaken.

She might not want to be his jo, but she did have an idea to use him to practice-teacher on. She asked, "Cletus, how much education you have?"

He told her he satisfactorily completed tenth grade in the Charleston, Missouri colored high school.

"You are not attending school at the present time?"

"No, ma'am. Be going on eighteen years old. I has to work."

"Did you know you can get your high school diploma by independent study?"

"I hear something about that...for the mens in the penitentiary."

"It's not just for men in the penitentiary. You get materials from the Harris Normal School in St. Louis. I can help you with it."

After that most Sunday afternoons Cletus went next door to the Brooks' house, and had his lesson with Miss Clemmie in the parlor where she had piano and voice pupils too. She told him what they were doing was like slave Sunday School.

He told her, "I don't be a slave."

"Cletus, we could have us a philosophical discussion about that as well. What I be talking about is the Africans Sunday School movement of the ante bellum days that we study about in Professor Green's course along with Reconstruction, the rise of the Ku Klux Klan, the invention of Jim Crow, and Marcus Garvey and the Back-to-Africa Negro Nationalism movement."

"Yes, ma'am."

"In the South and Border states be against the law to teach slaves to read. Missouri have a state law, you go to prison if they catch you teaching slaves to read."

"Yes, ma'am."

"But you know what the Reverend Mr. Elijah Lovejoy did?"

"No, ma'am."

"He had his Sunday School on a old house boat on the Mississippi River!"

"Yes, ma'am."

"What you think of that?"

"I know how to read."

"I know that, child. I don't be disrespecting you...I just think it's interesting."

"I had plane geometry, declamation and rhetoric, general science..."

"That's *fine*, Cletus. You don't have far to go. We'll get you that diploma in no time."

"Then what?" he asked.

"After you have achieved your high school equivalency?"

"Still the Depression. Don't be no jobs."

"Education set you free, Cletus."

"I *be* free. My papa and mama free. Grandma be *set* free by Abraham Lincoln."

"Free from ignorance, Cletus. Free from inequality to white people."

"More white mens than colored out of work."

"That's cause there *are* more white people. Far more."

"*Percentage* be the same."

"Good for you, you know about percentage."

"I not ignorant!"

"I not saying you ignorant...Remember when your papa wanted to send a letter to the sorority girls to thank them for bringing food and clothes to you when you were camped on the highway...and he had to ask you to write it for him?"

"How you know about that?"

"Professor Green read it to our class."

"Just cause he can't read and write my papa not ignorant. He wise...he a *brave* man."

"That is my impression."

"Don't you ever call my papa ignorant!"

"I don't. Old Francois Valle was the richest man in Ste. Genevieve. The Spanish made him commandant, and he was illiterate."

"See? You refute you own argument."

"But Francois Valle was a white man. He owned forty slaves."

"Reverend Whitfield make my papa Captain of the Sweet Home church group on the highway. He a good farmer too."

"I respect that, Cletus. But you have a big advantage that he doesn't. You can read and write."

"I works at hard labor, Lee Guy drop rocks on my head. Breathe in the lime dust...I rather chop cotton."

"You won't always work at hard labor, not if you have your high school equivalency... But it's not just that. We have to *make ourselves* equal to white people...I know, we already are. But mostly they don't see that...We have to make ourselves so they don't have any excuse...be educated...have good personal hygiene...don't do stupid crime...so they don't have any excuse to disrespect us. You understand what I be saying?"

"Yes, ma'am."

Clemmie had a voice pupil waiting when she finished with Cletus.

While her mother was showing him out she said, "Cletus, I need to have a word with you." She stopped by the door and showed where he tracked mud on the hallway carpet and asked him please to remember to wipe his feet. Then out on the gallery she said she was sorry to have to bring this up but she needed to speak of his personal hygiene. "How often do you bathe?"

"Twice a week."

"I'm sorry to have to ask you this, but will you please also be sure to bathe on Sunday morning before you come here. When you been here, you unwashed country nigger funk *suffuse* the parlor. When Clemmie's next pupil come, she be embarrassed."

"Yes, ma'am."

"One of her pupils is white!"

"Cleanliness next to godliness."

"Are you mocking me?"

"Yes, ma'am."

THE NEXT SUNDAY HE SUPPOSED HE WOULD NOT BE WELCOME AT THE Brooks' for his lesson, and Lonzo pestered him to go along with him to the Catholic church. Colored were allowed up in the slave gallery in back. Old Father wore a high black hat that Lonzo said was his Monseignor hat. He preached on the Loaves and the Fishes.

Father Van stood by the church house door shaking everybody's hand as they came out. Lonzo waited to go at the end so no white people had to wait behind them. The Priest shook his brown hand as if they were best friends.

He asked if Cletus was a good Catholic boy like Alonzo and his brothers. He said no sir and sifted on by.

WHEN THEY GOT BACK, CAP SAID HIS FRIENDS TAYLOR AND CJ CAME LOOKing for him. "In a automobile they say they borrowed," Cap said. "With a fine brown fox name Vera....say they want to take you for a Sunday drive."

THE NEXT EVENING WHEN CLETUS CAME ALONG AFTER WORK, CAP WAS sitting up on the gallery with his jelly glass of wine and he called to him, "We need to talk to you."

He stopped.

"Go on wash up."

In his crib he changed out of his work clothes all caked with sweat and lime dust. Then in the yard at the pump he splashed water on his face and arms, washed his hands with a piece of brown soap in the coffee can, and wiped them on his pants.

Cap was already sitting at his end of the table, a wine jug by. Zeno and Lonzo brought out plates. Cap poured them wine, and for Cletus too. He waited for them to start in on him but they just ate. Lonzo talked about how Mr. Rozier said Mrs. Griswold came to him about the bank going in with her Colonial Dames on the old Bolduc house. Everybody finished eating, and Cletus cleared off the plates and sat down again.

"Now, Cletus," Zeno said, "there is something we need to talk to you about."

"What did I do now?" They had been on him for little things.

Cap took a paper out of his shirt pocket, unfolded it, and handed it to him. It was a WANTED poster. "That you?"

Cletus eyes blurred looking at it. It said Cletus Johnson, Negro, age 18 was wanted for the attempted murder of James Thomas "J. T." Griswold near Samos, Pemiscot County, Missouri. He thought at least it did not have his picture. Then he thought of that Professor taking his pictures of all of them to make the world see their plight. He asked, "You going to have me arrested?"

Cap took a long breath, and sighed. He shook his head.

"What you want me to do?" He thought on Lee Guy and C. J. talking dirty about the bachelor Ribeau brothers.

"Don't jump to no conclusion."

He wiped the back of his hand across his eyes.

"I copped this off the wall two days ago. I could not believe it was you."

They all were looking at him to see what he would say. If he bare-face denied it or said mind your business, they would send him on his way or call the sheriff. He could think of nothing but to tell the truth. "....He rape my sister."

"You care to tell us about it?" Zeno asked.

"Be at Sweet Home church. That the fourth place they move us to. We all evicted from where we cropping, camp on the Sikeston highway. The Governor he send State Police, load us in trucks, dump us off behind the levee at Dorena out of sight. Then they take us to a old dance hall at New Madrid, and last be this little one-room country church. We make tents from old quilts, sleep on the floor between the pews. We more than a hundred camp there, outhouse overflowed so you can't use it no more. Peoples go up the ditch in the woods to do they business, come down with flux and—"

Lonzo interrupted. "We know you all suffer out on the highway and in the camps, but what for you try and kill a white boy?"

"I be *telling* you."

"James Thomas Griswold."

If he was going to chastise him, Cletus would shut his mouth.

"He any relation to the Peerless Lime Griswold?"

"Let Cletus tell his story," Zeno said.

"White boys one of them Mr. Griswold son J.T. come---"

"*Our* Mr. Griswold?" Lonzo asked.

"He a farmer....own farms, a cotton gin....I got no ideal who he related to."

Zeno gave Lon a hard look.

"White boys shoot tin cans off the fence post, J.T. and he friends lurk around, spy on the womens doing they business. Catch Josephine by herself all cramped up from the flux, take her off a ways, three, four white boys *bone* her....all of them. None of the womens tell me cause they afraid what I do...."

"This J.T.," Cap asked, "You acquain'ted with him?"

"Use-to I thought we was friends. J.T. and he older brother William we run together." William was interested in the Indian mounds, collected arrow heads and pieces of old broken pots that he said Indians made. Their hideout was on an Indian mound with trees and brush growing up out of it. They dug down to make their fort to some big flag stones. They lifted them off and when they dug some more, they found a skeleton.

"Sweet Home church not a mile from where Mr. R.C. Griswold evict us from....J.T. and he friends come around our raggedy camp, come to dog us, talk trash. J. T. say, 'You trespassing.' I say we use to be friends. 'Got us a Ford tractor,' he say. Act like he forgot my name.

"I have a ideal what he done to my sister, be sure when I see her puke. Say I go back hide in the woods, tend to business with J.T. Griswold. ... Josephine cry. Mama be crying, Auntie Rue, all the womens has to pray on me. Old time country niggers they pray you down, turn the other cheek. Josephine stay by me, watch when I try to run off. I go down in the weeds and willows by the clear creek under the bridge, she waiting on the other side. She take my hand, say, 'Cletus, be my business.' I ask her *You my sister?* 'They put you away.' *Think I lay around wait for police?* 'Hurt a white boy you be lynched.' *Has to catch me first.* 'Crackers have they excuse. Set they dogs on us, burn us all out.' She trying to shame me."

"You *cut* him?" Lon asked.

Cletus was looking down.

"He die?"

He shook his head.

They looked at him a long time then at each other as if to wait for who was going to talk first. Lon said, "That boy is a fugitive from justice."

"What kind of justice he get down the Bootheel....in Samos?" Cap said.

Zeno looked at one of them, then the other. "Cletus," he said, "We need to talk it over amongst ourselves."

He got up from the table. Lon said, "You run off now, boy, we *will* go to the Sheriff."

He looked down at the floor. He did not study any such thing until Lon gave him give him the idea.

Cap told his brother to quit ragging on the boy.

Cletus went out and sat on the back gallery. He thought how Lonzo kissed up to the white man. Cap talked back. Zeno the oldest had the good sense. If they sent him on his way, he wondered where he would go.

St. Louis was big enough that not everybody knew your business. Reverend Whitfield went to St. Louis, hiding out.

Clemmie Brooks was a student at Lincoln Institute in Jeff City and he believed she was his friend even if he was disrespectful to her mother again, but that professor with his picture and the sorority girls knew him. One of them Miss Adele James, she was a fox. She went walking up the fence row with him among the trees, taught him to French kiss. Cletus had saved up a few dollars what with the Ribeaus not charging him hardly anything to stay by them and feed him too.

He looked out past the pump and the old slave cabin where he cribbed up the grass slope to the trees at the top. It was hardly what you would call a bluff except that just a little ways further were limestone cliffs again. They were in the shadow from the sun going down but you could see it shine on the other side of the trees up there and on the birds that fly high catching bugs. The big one with a white stripe on the wing was a nighthawk.

A dog barked, a woman hollered for her children to come home.

They were taking their sweet time. The shutters were open. He heard the sound of voices but could not make out what they were saying. He moved to just under the window and scrunched down. He heard Lon's voice, then Zeno trying to be patient. The talking stopped. He slid back to over by the door, and Cap came out.

He followed him in, and Zeno nodded for him to sit down. He looked to Cap and Lon as if to be sure they agreed, and that he was going to tell the verdict. "You can stay, Cletus," he said, "but *on conditions.*"

Cletus looked from one to the other of them. Lon did not meet his eye.

"You lay low. Stay out of trouble....Don't tell you business to everybody."

"....All right."

"And don't you go hanging with Lee Guy and C.J....One of them find out, have that over you head..." Zeno caught his eye.

"I understand."

Lon said, "Stay out of Mabel's place, and--"

"Wait a minute," Cap said.

"....That low nigger juke joint."

"No, now, we not giving you a penny ante list of *do* and *don't*," said Cap, who liked to go there sometimes himself. "Just use common sense."

"That Mabel she signify, tell you one thing, tell me something else.....*ingratiate* herself."

Cap and Zeno looked at Lon like they were waiting until he could keep his mouth shut. Then Zeno said, "We agree on this.... Stop paying the dollar a week....Save you money.... cause if they do come looking, you need to scoot....Go someplace not a small town everybody know you business....Maybe we give you a name of someone can help you out."

Cletus' eyes blurred over again. He tried to thank them. Words refused to come out right.

ONE EVENING THEY WERE OUT ON THE GALLERY WHEN A WHITE BOY CAME along looking for Otis Bouchard who lived around on Gabouri Street.

Cap asked, "He owe you money?"

Zeno said, "He not in a good humor."

The white boy named Lester just had to see Otis Bouchard. The men he worked with took up a collection and he must give it to Otis.

Cap said he would just stay drunk longer. Zeno said give it to his wife, and the white boy said where at? Zeno said, "Cletus here will show you."

So Lester and Cletus were walking by the creek to Bouchards. Cap and Zeno had been talking about more troubles at the white quarries and how one way or another it would come down on them. Cletus tried to study this out, "How come Otis be fired?"

Lester did the who-shot-john this way and that before the stone truth came out: *AFL did not allow colored.* When the white men got their union last year, they let colored already working by them stay on, like Otis. They took their dues money and wrote their names down without saying they were colored. As Cletus understood it, some peckerwood snitched. The union boss came down from St. Louis and said the companies had to fire all the colored by the closed shop contract.

6.

THE SHOOTING OF RAUSCHER AND CHOMEAU WAS IN THE EARLY MORNING hours of Sunday October 12. Five o'clock Monday afternoon was the deadline for all black people to leave town, and the incident at the Ribeaus' was Tuesday night. Espy and Redmond were there Thursday and that night, and returned home Friday night.

By long distance telephone which he could ill afford and from other sources, and finally a second trip to Ste. Genevieve which he undertook with some trepidation, Redmond discovered what he could about the two dead white men. His purpose was to investigate the claim of his clients that killing them was in self-defense, and to examine the coroner's report.

He took the train.

Just across the tracks was a joint called the Creamery that his clients had told him was where they met the white men. The one customer was face down on the bar, the woman behind it studying her dream book. She would identify herself only as Mabel and she contradicted Redmond's clients. She said they were at a private party at the home of a Negro named Fisher and the two white men crashed it.

"People always laying the beef on me," she said. "Anybody cut, beat on by her man, it started at Mabel's."

He asked if she knew the victims.

"They be in here other times. A lot of white mens. Old Mr. Griswold' jackass son. He talk like a jackass. 'HEE-haw...HEE-haw.'"

"What about Chomeau and Rauscher?"

"They trash. Just...low down trash...Rauscher a big man. Try to intimidate you. Drive a truck for one of the lime companies. He set here, cry in his beer...Disrespect his wife. Say he could win a prize on her at the fair. He big. She real big. I seen her in the grocery, a boy tormenting her for treats. He say she fat on purpose to spite him. Too fat to fuck, too big to beat on. Only they must get down sometime. Has nine, ten childrens."

Redmond asked where they lived.

"Otis...?" She poked the inebriated customer. "Otis, you worked at that white quarry. Where Rauscher stay at?"

Otis required time to re-orient himself.

"That big peckerwood, drive a truck."

"What for you asking me that?"

"One time he say something about old lime kilns."

"The old Peerless kiln...? That be up the hollow."

"Where at?"

"Mosher Hollow."

Redmond asked how far, and he said three or four miles.

The woman told him Chomeau had a nickel and dime insurance business on the side, the kind where you put in a quarter every week but if you miss a payment the policy is canceled and they keep your money.

The inebriated man Otis was the only other patron, although they were interrupted by two rough-looking white men who came in with beer kegs and rolled empties out the open back door. The woman had imbibed some herself. He studied to encourage her volubility without seeming to interrogate.

"Mr. Fisher ask Chomeau and Rauscher to leave, say he don't want white and black peoples together at a party in his home...They gone to the party trolling for womens...Out in the yard Lee Guy, C.J. and Vera they trying to get this Negro man Smithton has a old truck to drive them to Modoc landing where they a dance and a craps game. He refuse....Chomeau and Rauscher still hanging about by the gate, they overhear. Say they drive them to the craps game for a dollar and fifty cents.

"Come to the railroad trestle, they arguing. Rauscher he make immoral and insulting propositions to Mrs. Rogers. C.J. and Lee Guy they call him down...He reach back and strike C.J. Stop the car and they all fall out fighting, Rauscher and C.J. on one side the car, Lee Guy on the other. C.J. beat Rauscher on the head with his gun, he hear a shot on the other side of the car. Say Rauscher bigger and stronger, he afraid he get hold of his gun, shoot him with his own gun, so he fire off all his bullets to empty it. He not in mind to kill that white man...Taylor come around the car and he say to Rauscher, 'You a tough son of a bitch.' Then shoot him. Just shoot him...He already shot Chomeau. That Chomeau stone dead.

"CJ come in here one scared nigger. They interrogate him the first time and turn him loose. I tell him get his black ass to St. Louis. Man go up to the City looking, be like three specks in a pot of pepper."

"What about the people at the party they were going to?"

"Peoples that stay up at Modoc, they hear the shots....Crazy girl Talulah, her mama the midwife, she run up to look, say, 'Be Chomeau the *in*surance man!' They crowd up to *see*. Taylor and CJ they dragging the fat man Rauscher to the river bank. Crazy Talulah down on Chomeau like a dog on a bone. Go to open his pants, *cut* him. Womens pull her off."

"Did she....*cut* him?"

"She fixing to. Grab holt of his johnson."

His clients did not mention any of this. It behooved them for him to know whatever the Law might also know in order to adequately prepare for their defense. He had encountered this before. They hold back on you. The result could be an unpleasant surprise in court.

REDMOND NEEDED TO VISIT THE SCENE, TO BE ABLE TO VISUALIZE IT. "HOW far is the trestle from the river?" he asked.

"You can see to where the trees stop....Be a ways to drag a dead man."

He looked out the back door at empty tables under the Catalpa trees. He asked if there was anybody else he could talk to.

She said, "They gone...All my trade."

"Anybody who was there....lives out that way?"

"They gone in the wind like smoke from a fire, like ashes. They scattered. Vigilants come around, say, 'You be gone out of here by five o'clock Monday.' They gone....They mostly come to this town cause they has no place else to go. Now they gone to they next no-place-else-to-go. I don't even know where they all come from, let alone where they go....A number of them was sharecroppers. *Tractored off.*"

"*Anybody* I can talk to....Anybody at all?"

She told him maybe the white woman at the Anvil Tavern, Mrs. Janis. "It right by. Her hired girl and some patrons come out to see."

Anybody else?"

"That crazy girl's mama Beaulah Misplait, she talk to you. Only hers one of the houses burnt. She gone."

HE FOLLOWED MABEL'S DIRECTIONS TO LA HAYE STREET WHERE IT RAN along the north fork of Gabouri Creek. Five houses in a row whose back yards abutted on the creek were reduced to burnt hulks, an iron bed frame, twisted stove pipe, heaps of ashes and blackened debris. The eight houses across the way were deserted, some locked up, the doors of others gaping open. All the furniture had been looted from one little house, the straw from the bed ticks strewn on the floor. On the wall in a room with a smashed door was a photograph of a baby in a christening dress, and on the narrow porch a rag doll.

REDMOND WENT SEEKING THE PRIEST THEY CALLED FATHER VAN. THE spire of the Catholic church was visible all over town. He went to the plain brick house next door to it, and a suspicious black woman in a maid's uniform answered the bell. "What you doing at the front door?"

He identified himself and his business.

"Father ain't here."

He was not sure he believed her. "From what I have heard of the good father, I believe he would want to see me...."

"I *told* you--"

"Where is he?"

She started to say none of his business but thought better of it. "At the retreat."

He nodded.

"All the priests be down at the retreat at Perryville...at that old school for priests."

"You must be Mrs. Sarah Garesche'. I understand you and your husband had to take refuge here when the—"

"I ain't going to talk about none of that with no strange nigger from nowhere."

Redmond shook his head. One of his own people treating him badly on behalf of white people made him sad.

THE LAST TRAIN HE COULD CATCH TO RETURN TO ST. LOUIS WAS AT FOUR o'clock. He did not wish to miss it and be in this town after sundown. The white woman at the Anvil tavern might or might not consent to speak with a strange Negro man, and what she might tell him might or might not be helpful in the defense of his clients. Also he wanted to visit the scene, but he was not sure how long it would take to walk out there and back to the train station. One thing that he knew it was necessary for him to do was to see the Coroner's reports.

He followed the sign to an office in the courthouse basement. He waited while the woman annoyed at his interrupting her crocheting made a telephone call. She reported that Dr. Deichman was busy seeing patients, and for all they knew he was a reporter for that Negro newspaper in St. Louis. He assured her he was a licensed attorney and that his clients were charged with murder in the first degree and he was entitled to see the Coroner's reports. In fact he would be derelict if he did not. She resumed her crocheting and dismissed him, "That's what Doctor says."

He went across to a door with a legend in the frosted glass: Clerk of the Circuit Court, LEO J. KARL. He went in and asked if any of the judges were *in camera*. The man who came to the doorway of an inner office said Magistrate Judge Siebert was, and Redmond identified himself and his business and asked to see him. Mr. Karl recalled from when he filed the petition for a change of venue and with a civility that was lacking in the Coroner's office, he directed him to the second floor.

Judge Siebert's chambers consisted of a musty little office with crumbling plaster and a window that looked across the square to the side of the Catholic church. The Judge made a point of not standing, of not inviting him to sit, of not shaking his Negro hand. He wore a brown vest with a heavy gold watch chain drooping across his belly.

"Redmond...?" he asked.

"Yes, your honor."

"I assume you are a licensed attorney--"

"I passed the Missouri Bar seven years ago."

"Doctor Deichman's question was legitimate."

"I am in the Blue Book, the Official Manual of the State of--"

"I understand. You might have asked to see me before you went to the Coroner's office."

"A white attorney would not have to do that."

"He would if he was unknown to us."

"I am retained on behalf of my clients by the Public Defenders' Office for the Eastern District of Missouri!"

"Mr. Redmond....calm down."

"Yes, your honor."

"This is a sensitive matter...Sensational and exaggerated stories about us have appeared in the newspapers of St. Louis...and elsewhere...most of it barefaced lies."

Redmond held his peace.

"One of them is particularly galling. I suppose you are familiar with a Negro newspaper in St. Louis that calls itself the *Argus?*"

The editor-and-publisher Donald Suggs was a neighbor and friend of his, but he only shrugged.

"I take that to mean you are."

He barely nodded.

Siebert picked up a folded newspaper, Redmond supposed one of the two local weeklies the *Herald* or the *Fair Play*, and read, "'*In what purports to be an expose` of the unchristian, brutal treatment inflicted upon the murderers of Paul Rauscher and Jerry Chomeau and on the transient riffraff as well as the native colored of this city, a St. Louis Negro newspaper calls the citizens of Ste. Genevieve bloodthirsty and vicious.*'

"I call your attention to this: '*After members of the Knights of Columbus had taken communion, they went out onto the steps of the Catholic Church and began to circulate a petition ordering all Negroes to leave town. Father Van of the church attempted to interfere but was warned to keep out...Dr. Deichman, prominent white physician, was the chief instigator of the petition.*'

"That is a damned lie... a *slander* on this whole town. We will not stand for it, Mr. Redmond!"

He felt himself not for the first time treated by a white individual as the personification of all people of color, not merely as a representative but as the *protagonist*, to blame for all the sins and crimes black people have or may have committed. In this case what offended the white man was the story of what he had done as told by a Negro. Redmond was weary of his own indignation, sometimes outrage from the countless times this had occurred, an indignation he could rarely afford to express. In this instance he wanted to pity the white man, to think he was playing into his hands.

He stood silent before him.

"...I will inform Mrs. Schwendt that you are authorized to see the reports."

When he returned to the Coroner's office, the woman was sullen but compliant. At a counter along a side wall for the purpose, he made a note of the number of Chomeau's file and copied excerpts from what was filled in the blanks on the printed form. Three lines had been rubbed out and written over. He returned the file.

He asked for the report on Rauscher. Here too lines had been rubbed out and written over, *'At the autopsy a rock was found to have penetrated his skull and stuck in his brain.'* According to the news reports, he died from the operation to remove the bullet from his spine.

AT THE END OF THE BASEMENT HALLWAY WAS THE SHERIFF'S DEPARTMENT, the frosted glass door standing open. He went in and identified himself to the deputy at the high front desk and asked if he might see Sheriff Picou. The deputy had gimlet eyes and a military haircut but was perfectly respectful. He went over to another open doorway and said a few words, then turned and motioned with his head for him to come along. He went through the swinging gate in the low barrier, and the deputy withdrew.

"Come in, Mr. Redmond," said the Sheriff. He leaned across his desk to shake hands, which was a matter of some sensitivity to people of color then, and still was. Redmond felt that many white people supposed because their skin was brown that they were unclean.

Redmond told him he appreciated how he acted quickly to move his clients out of harm's way.

Picou shrugged and said that was his job.

Ordinarily Redmond would go to the coroner to ask about the condition of the bodies. But gauging by the reception he got in his Deichman's office, he was reluctant to do that. He asked the Sheriff, "Did you see the bodies?"

"...Yes."

"What about their condition?"

"They were dead, from gunshot wounds and having rocks thrown at them."

"Anything else you noticed?"

"Mr. Chomeau's clothing was disheveled...His trousers were unbuttoned and his a... male organ was hanging out."

"Intact...?"

He gives Redmond an odd look.

He did not explain.

"...That is correct."

HE BARELY HAD TIME TO CATCH HIS TRAIN. IN THE BACK OF THE COACH AS it rattled along he could see across the river to the bluffs on the Illinois side, golden in the setting sun. He thought of his forebears a hundred years ago who looked across from a Slave State and saw *Freedom* there. More often than not, the ones who crossed the river for it were hunted down and returned to be chastised. He thought of that word. *Chastised.* It was how you made a woman chaste, a slave obedient. He wondered how he would have borne it.

7.

ON HIS RETURN ONE OF SEVERAL REFUGEES WHO CAME TO HIS OFFICE CON-cerned about property they had been forced to abandon was the midwife Beaulah Misplait. He took statements from all of them and drafted a class action suit against the town of Ste. Genevieve and certain white individuals they recognized in the squads of armed men who came to them delivering the ultimatum to leave town. Most of them offered to pay him what they could but were destitute. He said he was taking up their action on a contingency basis, and he would accept a fee only if they were awarded monetary damages.

A mocha brown woman with sagging bosom and ample hips, the midwife apologized for bringing along the child of her crazy daughter who ran off to Crystal City. Where she was staying there was nobody she trusted to leave her with. Redmond assured her his clients often brought children or other family members with them. He asked the lovely dark amber little girl, "And what is your name?"

His secretary Mrs. Simmons took off the ear piece to the Dictaphone she was transcribing from and smiled at her.

"Felicite," the child said. She was wearing a gray cardigan sweater several sizes too large for her over a thin summer dress.

"I have a boy named Jack who I imagine is about your age."

"He in school?"

"Why, yes. His auntie teaches school."

"Felicite misses her school," her grandmother said. "The children in the school by where we staying torment her, say she *country*."

"Well, if it's the same school my boy goes to and he's one of them, I'll give him a good licking when he comes home."

Young Felicite brightened up. This seemed to be a satisfying prospect.

Redmond turned to his secretary and asked, "Mrs. Simmons, is there something Felicite could help you with?"

"Why, yes," she said. "If she would be so kind. I have all these letters to deadbeats to go in the mail—you did sign them all, sir; or, I did for you—and it would be a big help if she could fold them and put them in envelopes and put the stamps on."

Young Felicite seemed agreeable.

After taking her grandmother to the open door of the other private office and introducing her to his associate John Espy, he ushered her into his own office and closed the door. He watched her take it all in—the framed diploma on the wall, the pictures of his wife and Jack on the credenza, the view of the air shaft, some of the windows across the way broken and boarded up. She sat warily on the edge of the court-house chair in front of his desk.

After she had made her statement for the class-action suit about the armed white men coming to her door and causing her to flee for her life to St. Louis, Redmond said as he imagined she knew he was representing Mr. Jennings, Mr. Taylor, and Mrs. Rogers who were accused of killing the white men. He said he understood one of the white men, Chomeau, was not well-liked. "Can you tell me anything about him?"

"No more than anybody. He collect for the two-bit life insurance."

"Did your daughter have some of Mr. Chomeau's insurance?"

"What for you asking me that?"

"To help me defend my clients."

"You want to know about my daughter, talk to her youself."

"Mabel Detchmendy said she went to mutilate Chomeau's body."

"That old whore Mabel can kiss my booty!"

"She indicated that a white doctor who lost his license had a particular animus against you."

"His license be suspended for a while. Maybe he got it back. Anyways, he practicing same as ever."

"What is his name?"

"*Deichman.*"

"*Deichman?* The Coroner?"

"That be him."

Redmond said he heard that while the Sheriff was interrogating his clients, a local doctor was on the church steps after mass trying to get people to sign a petition to force all Negroes to leave town.

"Dr. Emil Deichman. He the nastiest most hateful man you will ever see, just go out of his way malicious toward Colored....I will give you a for instance. This woman Tillie Beauvais be in service to a white family. They wealthy prominent peoples in this town, street they live on name for them. Tillie a mature intelligent colored woman and the missus and children all just love her. She like a member of the family.

"Well, Deichman told them she have the syphilis and they better get rid of her before she give it to the whole family. So they go and fire her and seal off her room and fumigate it, and the childrens has to keep washing they hands whenever they touch anything the Negro woman has touched. It was a big emotional upset for them cause they all was crazy about her....Later on he laugh and say he have no ideal if she has the syph or not but she going around with a nigger man that does, so she probably get it."

"I heard the priest drove him off."

"Old Father Van, he drive him off like Jesus drive the moneychangers from the Temple.... Deichman my *bête noir.* You comprehend French?"

"I had a year of it in college."

"He stone hate niggers. Have a special hate on me."

"Why is that?"

"I birth babies....for white womens too. *Poor* womens. He say I 'practicing medicine without a license'...when he have his license suspended his own self."

"Why was that?"

"Well, you hear different stories...He prescribe morphine for himself. He prescribe it for rich peoples down from St. Louis...He perform Dilation-and-Curettage in the back room...I been accused of that myself....I be the *cut rate*...And a woman. Womens trust me.

"He come home fresh from osteopath doctor school, only trade he can get be Colored. And he get none of the birthing at all. Colored come to me.

"His big chance was the explosion at Jenkins-Gillis after the World War when a whole wagon load of the dynamite went off. Lots of mens killed, injured. The two older white doctors call him in, and he have white patients after that."

Redmond was particularly interested in this Dr. Deichman. He asked, "What else can you tell me about him?"

"My mamma be the laundress to his mamma," Beaulah Misplaits said. "She go to a different white woman different days, take me with her when I out of school. Let me turn the wringer. I help her hang the clothes on the line, hand her clothes pins, fold clothes."

Ludwig Emil Deichman was in high school then. They called him just Emil. The last summer before he went off to the osteopath college Beaulah's titties had begun to show, and he hung around. Her mamma spoke up to him. She said "Emil, you let that girl work!"

"He say some stupid shit like *She's too pretty to work.*"

Beaulah never did study him. She told her mamma she did not like how that Emil looked at her. Her mamma did not like it either but you could not tell *his* mamma anything. Her boy could do no wrong. She was a docent for the Colonial Dames. She showed rich white women from St. Louis around that old French house, only she was not a Dame herself. You had to be from the old First Families for that. Mr. Deichman owned the biggest barber shop, with four chairs. Sometimes he pulled teeth.

Emil hung around on wash days as if he were a dog and young Beaulah a bitch in heat. He drove her mamma to distraction always in the way and underfoot. Her mamma told him, "You get on away from here, boy, or you going to get all wet."

He laughed and looked at Beaulah.

"I has to throw out this dirty water," she said, "and it splash all on you."

He tried to be sneaky and follow her and her mamma home to see where they lived, but they saw him skulking along.

Next laundry day at Deichmans' Beaulah's mamma left her at home. She went berry-picking with her little cousins Celeste and Sharlene out along the creek. The backs of the yards along there ended in shrubs and trees and a broken-down fence. There was a swatch of creek bottom out behind, fallow in weeds and berry briers around the edges and a big patch at one end. Children played there, made their hideouts. The creek bank was bluff on the other side up to Ziegler street.

So they were picking blackberries. Celeste was eight years old, Sharlene a year and a half older. Beulah had recently turned thirteen. Somebody was watching them. She did not see who it was, just knew someone was there.

She supposed it was her oldest brother Tyrone. He was on parole, just laying around the house. It was mainly because of him that her mamma was taking her with her to her laundry work. Not that he would mess with young Beaulah himself, but he was a bad influence. His friends came around. He was supposed to stay in the Jeff City prison seven years for manslaughter only he was paroled in four because he found Jesus.

She saw a rustle in a sumac bush, somebody trying to sneak going away. So she would think they were gone.

Before long he came walking along by the creek pushing through branches not trying to sneak, like a different person. It was Emil. He had an old dirty lard bucket she would bet he picked up in the creek. Acting like he was surprised he said, "Why, hello, Beaulah. What are you doing here?"

She was of a mind not to answer him but she said, "…Picking berries."

"I was out to pick berries myself. Is this a good place?"

"Belong to peoples that have they houses along South Gabouri Street."

"But they don't *own* the property."

"Mamma own our place. Louis and Vivienne Dufour, Mayottes, Lalumondiers all up and down here own they place."

"But just here is weeds along the creek. The creek right of way."

"You *trespassing.*"

"You talking smart to me?"

Celeste and Sharlene were backing off. They knew something was not right.

"I can pick berries here if I want."

Beaulah went on to picking. She would ignore him.

"Why can't you be nice?….I'm nice to you."

She did not say anything.

"Being colored doesn't matter to me, you know."

She kept herself from answering back.

"A pretty girl is a pretty girl."

He had sidled up to her, picking on the same bush.

"This here is my bush."

"Sorry. Didn't know you owned it."

"We *own* this patch from the end of our back yard to the creek and on across the creek to the back yards up on the next."

"Niggers don't *own*. They rent."

"You just *said....*"

"What?"

He had come up behind her trying to rub himself on her hind end. She jinked away, and he wrapped his arms around her, felt up her little titties. "You turn loose!"

Celeste and Sharlene ran off.

WHEN THEY CAME BACK WITH TYRONE, EMIL HAD THROWN HER DOWN. HE lay on her, reaching up her skirt. She twisted this way and that, bit and scratched. He held her wrists.

She saw Tyrone loom up. He was a big boy. Emil was just turning to look when Tyrone fetched him a hard kick and he was wearing his steel toes from when he used to work in the quarry. Emil scrambled on all fours like a dog, then was just standing up when Tyrone slapped him with the flat of his hand up side the head with all his might.

Emil fell down hard. He held his jaw. He was crying.

HER MAMA TOOK THEM ALL TO FATHER VAN. SARAH GARESCHE' HIS HOUSE-keeper told them to go around to the back. Father rebuked her, led them himself up the hall from the kitchen into the priest's house study. Sometimes biggity Colored would do you the worst.

Father took them in the study and said sit down, please sit down. They sat in the leather chairs. All around on the walls were books in glass-front book cases, a Jesus nailed to his cross high on the wall.

Her mama did the talking, how Emil hung around while she was trying to work, made eyes at Beaulah. She told how she left her at home because he was a pest, and about him coming on her in the berry patch and threw her down. She told about Celeste and Sharlene going to fetch Tyrone.

Father asked Beaulah to tell it. She felt shy but he was patient. It came out nearly the same because what her mamma had told was what Beaulah told *her*, and she told it back to the priest.

"And he lay on top of you and put his hand up your skirt?"

She said *yessir.*

"Did you entice him, my child?"

She sat looking at his feet in purple slippers, and shook her head.

Then he sweated her brother like in catechism. He asked him when he kicked and slapped the white boy, what was in his heart? Tyrone looked down like he was ashamed.

Reported for parole violation, he would be back in the prison.

Mama asked Father Van, "Suppose the white boy charge assault on Tyrone."

TYRONE FOUND EMPLOYMENT RUNNING HOOCH FOR THE BOOTLEGGERS. He stayed on their barge cooking it. If the Law inquired of him, they would say he had gone up to East St. Louis.

Her mamma quit Deichmans, and went Tuesdays to Miss Lucy Donze instead. She was a midwife. Mostly she went to the woman's house, but sometimes a young girl all swollen up came to her door. Her mamma washed the sheets from the birthing, and Beaulah hung them out.

One day with a girl in labor, Miss Lucy asked her to help out. She watched how she did, learned birthing herself. The summer after, she had her assist her on a regular basis. If she was paid a dollar, she gave Beaulah a quarter. If she was paid four dozen eggs, Beaulah took home a dozen to her mamma.

Most women Lucy tended were white but she did not refuse Colored. Old Bonita Scruggs who birthed for colored was getting on. She died. Colored women came to Beaulah for birthing ever since.

8.

REDMOND WENT AGAIN ON THE TRAIN TO STE. GENEVIEVE TO FILE THE class action suit on behalf of the refugees who had been forced to abandon property, and to continue his investigations on behalf of his clients accused of killing the white men. He wanted to go out and get the lay of the land at the scene of the crime and talk to Mrs. Janis and the hired girl at the Anvil Tavern. Also he recalled Cletus Johnson saying the white boy Lester who came seeking Otis Bouchard boarded there.

He delivered the papers for the class action suit to the office of Clerk Leo Kerl, insisted on a signed acknowledgement of their receipt, and got out before some fresh affront caused him to seethe and clench his teeth with anger that he dare not express.

It was more than two miles out North Main Street and Modoc Road to the ferry landing, and he was glad he had comfortable old boots from when he worked summers during college at Vulcan Foundry and his second-best but warm overcoat in the chilly sunshine of late October. Once he passed the north fork of Gabouri Creek and the rail yards, there were long straggling rows of rundown houses and shacks between the road and the bluff. Almost all the yards were littered household goods—mattresses, chairs, chests of drawers, clothing hastily abandoned. Approaching the Poor Farm there were also rows of shacks and shanties on the other side of the road. Except for an isolated plume of smoke or here and there a barking dog, they were deserted.

After the Poor Farm the gravel road curved gradually down hill toward the tracks and as he passed the trees along the base of an outcropping of the bluff, he saw the Frisco trestle.

He studied to visualize the night of the killings as Rauscher had described it to the police captain at the hospital in St. Louis before he died and printed in the *Fair Play*, the story that almost all the white people in Ste. Genevieve believed without question. According to Rauscher he was driving and as they approached the trestle, Taylor said, "Stop the car." He got out with a gun in his hand and told him and Chomeau to get out, and Jennings got out and he also had a gun. They backed the white men up against the trestle abutment and robbed them. Disgusted with how little he got from Chomeau, Taylor shot him dead.

The big man Rauscher had begun to fight Jennings and the woman Vera said, "Shoot that man dead before he get up on you!" Jennings claimed he could not get his automatic pistol to work and it was Taylor who shot Rauscher, who fell and played dead. From there they dragged him to the river.

Redmond continued on under the trestle and down the steep incline beside the ferry landing to the rip rap along the bank counting his steps—210. Two steps to a pace was 105 paces, and a pace was 5 feet. 525 feet to where the water line was that day, October 23rd. The river was well within its banks. So far as he knew there had been no dramatic rise or fall in the eleven days since October 12th.

He counted steps on the way back but this time noticing what would be the Anvil, a solid limestone edifice with first and second floor galleries and three dormer windows to the attic with chimneys at either end, and as he could see as he drew closer a two-story ell off the back. Railroad tracks curved off into a hollow past the front of it. As he retraced his steps under the trestle to where Rauscher said he and Chomeau were backed up against the abutment, you would not have been able to see what happened from the Anvil, but you certainly could hear the shots—some time between one and two in the morning.

Redmond unbuttoned his overcoat and took a memo pad from the inside jacket pocket of his suit and made a rough sketch and some notes. He examined the concrete of the abutment to either side of the road, although he recalled that both bullets had been recovered from the bodies of the white men. At least one heavy rain had fallen since the 12th and he could see no telltale footprints or pattern of knocked-down weeds or crushed grass. He put the memo book away, buttoned his overcoat, and strode toward the Anvil across the spur of tracks in the hollow, again glad that he was not wearing his frequently polished and re-soled lawyer shoes for days in court.

Here he faced an old conundrum. He supposed if he walked in the front door like a patron he would not necessarily be shot dead, but he would have the undivided attention of everyone in the room. They would be thinking *Who is that Negro? What does he want here?* It might well cross their minds that he intended to rob them or to commit mayhem or even slaughter—perhaps in revenge for what he might regard as the enormity of the insult that had been committed against people of his color by the righteous white people of this town.

He might be able to exchange a few civil words with the good host or Mrs. Janis who he supposed was his wife or the hired girl and state his business, and one or another of them might have taken him off out of sight of their patrons and talked a while to him. But it would be unpleasant and fraught with disagreeable and even dangerous possibilities, including that he would lose his temper and give them a piece of his mind.

As he picked his way across the tracks in the hollow he concluded not to stand on his dignity as an attorney and officer of the court and instead to go where Colored were expected to go, around back. An attached barn and a chicken coop together with the ell formed a courtyard between the back of the tavern and the bluff, and by what would be the back door to the kitchen was a young white man sitting on the end of a keg cleaning fish. Redmond addressed him with deference as if he were just another country Negro who knew his place, "Good afternoon, sir."

The young man frankly stared at him, waiting Redmond supposed for him to explain himself.

"I am Sidney Redmond, an attorney...from St. Louis."

The young white man simply nodded. He had set down the filleting knife and the catfish he was gutting in the pail by his feet.

"I am from the Public Defenders' Office of the Eastern District of Missouri. I have been assigned to represent Columbus Jennings, Lee Guy Taylor, and Mrs. Vera Fox Rogers who are accused of killing two...white men here on the night of October 12th."

"Good luck."

"Yes, well...May I ask your name?"

"Dodge....Lester Dodge."

"...I have heard of you from a young Negro man named Cletus Johnson."

Young Mister Dodge seemed perplexed.

"He said you came looking for Otis Bouchard."

"Oh...*Cletus.*"

"He told me you wanted to give him some money that you and your work mates collected when he was terminated."

"That was unjust."

"Not many white men would do that." Or colored either Redmond would have to admit if the white man were treated unjustly.

"Otis saved my life."

"How is that?"

"It's a long story."

"I might be interested to hear it."

"If you don't mind me talking while I gut fish."

"No, sir....You catch all those fish?"

He nodded. "It's how I pay my keep...in the strike."

"I know about that only in a general way."

"We been out since May 17th."

"That is a long strike."

"Five months, and the lime company bosses have still got their heads up their ass."

"I have been told that the labor situation was a factor in the reaction of white people in Ste. Genevieve to the killings. It is my contention that my clients could not get a fair trial here."

"They *almost* was lynched ."

"I have heard that the lime companies brought in displaced Negroes from down south to work at half the union rate of pay."

"Mister...what did you say your name was?"

"Redmond."

"I can tell you more than you want to know about that."

9.

IN THE FEED SACK TIED TO HIS BELT LESTER DODGE HAD THREE BOILED PO-tatoes in the waxed paper from store bread, his caliper, and a clean pair of socks. He pondered what account he would give of himself at the lime works. The truth was he had been discharged from Crystal City for posting a CIO handbill on company property.

Nobody was in the gate house, so he walked on by.

He went in a side door to the tall barn-like building where the machinery noise was coming from, and the first man he encountered he had to holler in his ear, *"The superintenent... the boss...Where's he at?"*

"You mean Bondurant...has a cripple arm?"

"The one that hires you on."

"Not likely."

"Where's he at?"

"There was a accident."

"I need to see him."

The man jerked his head to the left.

Lester started up the hollow.

He calls after him, "Say! You need you a tin hat."

Lester nodded like he understood and his fairy godmother would make a shiny tin hat appear on his head. She was working on it and the fellow did not need to worry himself. He and the others in the building had tin hats on their heads like doughboys and perhaps they were left over from the World War and painted white. He pulled his leather slouch cap down so the little bill was across his eyes and he was looking out of his private cave and the falling rocks could not get him. His mama gave him that cap when they took him on to apprentice in the machine shop at Crystal City Glass.

He walked on up the floor of the hollow that was packed dirt and chat and bare lime rock to where you start to see a whole cliff face with a row of squared-off tunnels cut into it. Then you walk up a ways from the floor of the hollow to another wide flat. You don't see until you get closer how it is bigger than a ball field cut in there with lines of big square posts going off different ways. Narrow tracks came out of it, and off to one side was a line of beat-up tipple carts on little wheels.

Nobody was around but as he drew nigh he could see lights back in there and then other lights moving around and some kind of commotion. He would walk in toward it but the narrow tracks ran every which way, and maybe he would be run over by a train of carts or get lost or they would arrest him. He went out to the front and sat on a crate by one of the columns that held the roof up and waited.

He said over to himself the story he had concluded to tell this Bondurant. *I had a difference with my supervisor.* He would ask what about. *He was disrespectful to a woman at a dance,* he might say. *Not on company time?* he would ask. Or he might say, *Not on company property?* And Lester would say, *No, sir,* and he would be satisfied and hire him on. Or so he might hope.

After a while he heard somebody coming but stayed where he was sitting out of the way. It was two fellows with a crumpled man on a stretcher, the purple blood congealed in his mashed-in chest like a sink hole. Walking beside the stretcher was a little white-haired man in a short sleeve khaki shirt that he believed was Bondurant. They did not pay any mind to Lester and he sat tight until they had passed on.

He was not sure he studied this line of work.

When they came back without the dead man he had stood up and was leaning against the column by the tunnel mouth, and the one that had to be Bondurant came on ahead and said, "Who the hell are you?"

Lester told him his name and that he was looking for work.

"What kind?"

"...Labor."

"You ever done quarry work?"

"I dug tiff some around home."

"Where is that?"

"Mineral Point."

"What's your name again?"

"Lester Dodge."

He wrote in his pocket book and said, "Fifty cents."

"If that is what the work is worth." Lester took down sixty cents an hour in the machine shop.

The man cocked his head like he might ask another question or change his mind.

Lester looked off to the side.

"Go on with Henry. He will show you what to do."

Lester went to shake hands with Bondurant but it was his right arm that was shriveled from the elbow down.

Of the two other men he supposed the older one who was short and stout was Henry. He followed them into the wide front part of the mine that was ten degrees cooler than outside then down the tunnel they had emerged from. The younger one had greasy black hair down over his collar and a slouching way about him and he picked up that his name was Walter. When they came to where they had been working there was another fellow and a colored man sitting there slack and glassy-eyed like they had given up all hope and the end was near. Henry introduced one as his boy Little John. The colored man was Otis.

Before them was rock face with spikes driven in to mark it off in rows and a scaffold to where they were drilling. On the ground was a slab three feet thick and big as a barn door that had been pried up at one corner and rocks and timbers wedged under it. Henry gave Lester the tin hat of the dead man and set him and Otis and Walter to break up the fallen slab with picks and ten-pound hammers into head-size pieces and load them into the tipple cart.

When the siren went off they got their dinner buckets and settled down and Lester squatted off to the side and treated himself to another boiled potato. They spoke of the man who was killed. His name was Sam Ehler and he was fifty years old and left behind his wife and four sisters and two brothers and a number of step children and nephews and nieces.

"That big rock?" Lester asked.

"He was drilling," said Little John.

"It smashed down on him so the drill was stuck in his chest," said Walter. "He was trying to scream but he couldn't get no air to do it."

"He lived five minutes," said Little John.

"He was a quiet, hard-working man," said Henry.

Otis looked as if he had something to say but thought better of it.

"What about Sam's hat?" Walter asked.

"You will need to get you a tin hat of your own," said Henry. "They take it out of your first pay."

Lester asked him, "When is that?"

"Week from Friday."

He swallowed, thinking he could get hungry by then.

By the four o'clock siren he was bone tired and the blisters on his hands had blisters with blisters on them. As they walked out toward the gate-house Henry asked him, "You got you a place to stay?"

Lester said not actually.

Henry said he could not promise anything but he had an idea. Halfway to town at the ferry landing was the Anvil tavern with garret rooms for two or three lodgers and perhaps Janis would give him credit.

The bluff was right by the river and the river had risen over the road, so they walked along the tracks. They passed two caves and another working quarry with a row of the old square tower kilns, then a stretch where the bluff was nearly straight up two hundred feet high, then a barge dock where they loaded up from the lime plants, and the ferry landing. Back in from the landing was a tight little hollow with houses on both sides and one old mansion, and between the tracks and the river where the terrace widened out an old stone warehouse.

The tavern was at the mouth of the hollow so that from the gallery you could see what came off the ferry and down the bottom road where it ran on into town. He followed Henry— he had told him his last name was Maheu—in the front door and they sat at the shiny wood bar. The busty girl with her hair in yellow pigtails rolled tight on each side of her head drew a pint for Henry. Lester had 37 cents to his name and shook his head when she looked at him. Henry was not buying but it was hard times and he was trying to help him out and he knew that was more important than treating him to a beer, but it would have been nice.

Henry asked the girl, "The boss around?"

"Which one?" she asked.

"The one that wears pants."

She said he would be back any time now and went to serve two more fellows who had sat at the bar.

When she had done with them she came back and said to Henry they were all sorry to hear about Sam. Henry choked up, said they were schoolboys together, and he must pay a call on Dora.

"A boy lost his right hand just last week," said the girl. "Seems like every other day is some kind of accident."

"Ain't it the truth," said one of the other two men who Henry said worked at Western Lime. Where Lester had signed on was Bluff City Cement.

"And poor Ray Fahnstock. They ordered him to stay on for a double shift when he wasn't feeling right, and he dropped dead of a heart attack. Fifty-two years old."

"How is Ethel making out?" Henry asked.

"Runs a machine all day at Elder Shirtwaist."

Henry introduced Lester as a new hire, and they went on at such a rate speaking of men who were maimed and killed or died young that he wondered if they were making sport of him. One told how a big rock fell off a tipple car that was too full and it broke through Don Basler's tin hat and he needed 23 stitches to stop the bleeding from his scalp. They strove to outdo each other in reciting these tales. Another recalled how Fred Dunlap had a compound fracture of his leg and contusions on his head at Peerless Quarry. Not long before that a man named Spraul was killed.

"That was at Bluff City," Henry said.

"He got *cremated*," said one of the Western Lime fellows.

"How did that happen, Henry?" the other Western fellow asked.

"It was over at the other pit," Henry said, "but I went and saw him, what was left. He was driving one of them big Mack trucks when the chassis just bent and broke under a twelve-ton load. That's what they said, twelve ton. Where it busted was right under the cab so's the steering wheel and dash buckled in and crushed him and you hope it killed him right then because it busted the gas line under his seat and the gas caught fire and Andy Huck that was riding with him jumped out just in time and *Whoosh!* just like that the cab is a ball of fire and he was...well, he was cremated."

"I heard the smoke was so bad they had to go to town and get the gas masks out of the museum so's they could go down in and get his remains out."

"They done that but by the time they come back the smoke was cleared enough we could go down in and get him. Just burnt bones and ashes with clinker in it. Had to scrape the last of him up with a little shovel and a whisk broom."

"It gives you pause."

It gave Lester pause too, for fifty cents an hour.

After a while Janis came in and Henry said, "This is the fellow I took on this morning, after...well, you know about that..."

Janis said they were all sorry about Sam Ehler, and for a while they had to talk about that some more and how were Dora and the children and will the lime company do anything for them?

Then Henry asked Janis, who went by Frank, would he consider putting up Lester on credit till a week from Friday in one of his rooms in his attic.

The friendly look went out of Janis's face and he said, "Oh, no. All my rooms is let."

Lester expected this and was thinking maybe he would head on down the road to see if he could find a safer line of work. If he got hungry enough and did not mind working with mostly colored he could chop cotton. The crews for that you moved from place to place and he heard they put you up in bunk houses or croppers' cabins.

Janis looked around the room and in another kind of voice he said, "So nothing's happened?"

Henry looked out the side of his eyes like he was not sure this was something to discuss in front of Lester but he said, "They are talking open shop and a ten per cent pay cut."

Janis's eyebrows went up in a *look*.

"Bondurant says we listened to them outside agitators and look where it got us."

"Jack O'Hare says they tried the same thing at Crystal."

Lester pricked up his ears.

A little red-haired woman came in that just crackled and sparked and not a hundred pounds wringing wet. Lester concluded this was Janis's Missus, Emma. "O'Hare?" she asked. "He's our man. What we need is a sit-down strike."

"I know Jack," Lester said.

They all turned and looked at him.

"He is a steward at Crystal City Glass...where I was working at in the shop." It was Jack who gave him the CIO handbill he was discharged for *disseminating*. That was what they called it. '*You are discharged for disseminating CIO propaganda.*' Stuck it on the door to a toilet stall. A rat saw him.

Janis looked him over again but with a different kind of expression on his face. He seemed to think about it before he said, "Henry brought us this young fellow he just took on, in case there's a room upstairs and we could give him credit to pay day."

The Missus said she would show him up to the room soon as she checked on the kitchen girl.

So the deal was done and he had a room and board.

PAYDAY HE WENT WITH LITTLE JOHN AND WALTER AND THEIR FRIEND
Clyde to a dance. When he got into the car Clyde had a shotgun in his hand. Walter asked
him why. He said, "I might see a rabbit on the way."

As they rode along Walter asked him again, "Why must you bring your shotgun,
Clyde?"

"The Falkners might be there."

When they came out of the woods to where you could see the Weingarten house lit up
across the hollow and hear the concertina, he asked them to stop and let him out.

They went on to the dance and Lester just had a fine time. It was a big old German farm
house and the entire third floor was the ballroom like a barn loft where you looked up at the
roof beams and a high-up balcony at one end with a five-piece band. Weingarten took a dollar
from you for the music and set-ups and you brought your own hooch or he would sell you his
moonshine or bottle beer. His wife had laid out sandwiches and deviled eggs and neighbor
women and girls brought covered dishes and pies and cakes. Walter and Little John said you
can sleep over for ten cents, men on the ballroom floor and women down in the bedrooms, and
hot breakfast is another ten cents.

They did not stay on until the morning.

Kith and kin and marrieds and steady couples sat at tables around the sides but plenty
of girls had come stag and they mostly sat together or stood chatting and primping along the
wall. He screwed up his courage and no girl he asked outright turned him down, though one
or two were stuck-up and one kind of sullen. A number of the dances were polkas and fast
waltzes and what they call a *shottish* and another the name as best he could make it out was
a *lendler,* and those he begged off.

One girl he fancied and contrived to dance with most with was named Ethel, who said
she worked at Elder shirtwaist factory and when he was with her and a polka started up she
would not allow him to sit out but declared she would teach him to do it. With her light brown
hair in a pigtail wound on top of her head and rhinestone bangles from her stick-out ears she
looked quite the high-toned lady, and if she made her own frock from a pattern book she had
a knack. Her dress-up shoes were old and cracked though and she did not put on airs. He
persuaded her to come with him downstairs to the kitchen for a bite to eat and had it in the
back of his mind to ask her if she might like to go outside for a breath of fresh air.

They were in the kitchen and he had just put some sauerkraut on his cold pork sandwich
on dark rye bread when it was like the shot went off inside his own head. It was *that close* and
people jumped out of their skins and hollered and bumped into each another ducking this

way and that. Ethel grabbed on to him and he stood by the cook-stove with his arm around her saying whoever done it run off. He had a pretty good idea who that was, and felt ashamed of himself that neither he nor Little John or Walter said a word to Falkner or old Weingarten. The shot was fired through the open window over the cellar door and the charge struck Falkner in the throat so his life's blood poured out onto the pie safe.

Lester saw Walter in the doorway jerking his head to give him to understand he had better come pretty damn quick if he wanted a ride, and it just tore him up to have to cut out sudden on Ethel. He said the fellows he rode with were leaving, but might he see her again? She looked at him like she was making up her mind. "I sing in the choir," she said.

He asked her where at?

"Evangelical Lutheran...in town."

10.

THE SUN WAS RED COMING UP OVER THE BLUFFS ON THE ILLINOIS SIDE AND by the time Lester had shaved and eaten his grits and bacon and the fog had burnt off, it was already a steam bath walking into town. The gravel road was on the bluff side of the tracks, and the bottom got wider as he went along and you could see where the river bank was by the tops of the trees across the mud and high water that had crept up in the night.

On a stone bridge he crossed a creek that was backed up from the river and one side was the railroad fill that made do for a levee and on the other side was the town. He asked the way and on South Gabouri Street by another branch of the creek that was backed up with river water, he found the Lutheran church. Cut in the stone over the door was: *Ev. Luth. Kreuz Kirche 1869.*

He sat off to one side in the back pew while the Preacher preached away thumping his Bible and pointing his finger this way and that. The choir sat behind him sideways in dark blue robes and he saw Ethel the second-one-in on the third row, and caught her eye. The Preacher was talking about how they must be on their guard against atheism and the Reds who got their orders from Moscow and had taken over the CIO and mostly were Jews and were hard-hearted and to blame for how the Roman soldiers scourged and crucified Jesus, and they must not lay it all on Chancellor Hitler who made the trains run on time.

He finally ran out of gas and said, "It is more blessed to give than to receive," and sat down, and two men in boiled collars passed little baskets for you to put your money in, and the choir stood up and sang. It was in a foreign language that he supposed from what was cut in the stone over the door was German, but the tune was like one of the hymns that stuck in his mind from when he was obliged to go to church.

Glorious things of thee are spoken

Zion, city of our God.

When they were done the preacher prayed some more prayers, and announced the last hymn number, and people opened the hymn books and sang along ragged and half-hearted with the choir as they walked out down the aisle two-by-two. The Preacher came last and stood on the steps, and you had to wait for everybody ahead of you to gab with him and shake his hand.

Among the people standing around outside to visit, he caught up to Ethel. She was with a half-pint boy and a woman of whom she said, "This is my mother...and my brother Delbert."

Her mother reached out to shake hands and said, "Lucy Fahnstock," and the boy shook hands and said how-to-do like he was taught.

Ethel went to change out of her choir robe, and in a nice way her mama inquired about Lester's people and how he came to Ste. Genevieve. He said his papa was Israel Dodge and he worked for the railroad at DeSoto. His uncle got him hired to apprentice in the machine shop at Crystal City Glass, but they were having trouble with the CIO—which was the truth— and he concluded to remove to Ste. Genevieve and see what he could find in the lime works.

She said her late husband was the swing-shift foreman at Bluff City Lime.

He told her he was working at Bluff City himself on the day shift with Henry Maheu. She says oh yes they knew Henry and wasn't it a shame about Sam Ehler and she had taken a casserole to Dora and she was just prostrated with grief. Lester said as he imagined she knew, he was hired on in his place.

She said, "Oh, they don't miss a beat."

"They gave me his tin hat...for the rest of the shift."

"I received a letter of condolence and they referred our name to Catholic Charities and we aren't even Catholic...after seventeen years."

"Did your husband die in an accident?"

"They ordered him to stay on for a double shift when he wasn't feeling right, and he dropped dead of a heart attack."

"That is not right."

"They killed him."

"How long ago?"

"Two years. My daughter wished to attend the Normal School at Kirksville. Now that is out of the question."

When Ethel came back she was wearing the same stylish frock to just below her knees that she wore to the dance, and her mama said they had better get on home or Holt Hardy would be on the doorstep waiting for his Sunday dinner.

"Oh, Mama!"

"When her father was alive this young man got in the habit and——"

"He...*presumes.*"

"Listen," Lester said, "if you have got you a steady fellow——"

"I do *not!*" Ethel says.

"Mr. Dodge is welcome to join us."

"...That would not be pleasant."

"You did say the young man you danced with might come to church. I could tell Mr. Hardy you had other plans."

Ethel kissed her mama's cheek, and they took their leave.

She said she thought about it ahead of time and if he was agreeable, she was going to show him the town. They walked along the street by the backed-up water in the creek branch and when they came to a rundown little house with a wide gallery across the front, she said it was two hundred years old. He was skeptical, so she took him by the hand and led him up to the front door and called, "You who!...Mrs. Bouchard!?"

She concluded Mrs. Bouchard was at church and took him around to the side by the chimney where two of the wall boards had come loose. "See?" she said. "Under the clapboard it is straight-up-and-down logs. That is how the Frenchmen did it."

The street they were on ended at another bridge across the creek and they went up a block to a business street and over to the cemetery, and she took him to see some of the graves. They stopped by a whole row of square stones and the writing on them he knew was French, and she made him squat down low to read one.

Moss and lichen had grown over it and the numbers worn down and he had to puzzle it out with his finger, but he had to allow the date the man was born was seventeen-something, 1716 or 1715, and when he died was seventeen-something too, he believed 1783, or 88. Then he tried the name. "It is F-R-A...not Frank? Or Franklin?"

"Francois," she says. "Francois Valle."

"It's not fake?"

"I can't imagine why it would be."

"You go to St. Joseph to see the house where Jesse James was shot, only it ain't."

"You are a suspicious-hillbilly type."

"I can be."

They walked around the graveyard that was pretty run down and altogether about two acres with a wide sink-hole to one side as if a giant had pressed his whole hand down flat, and a number of the stones were on the high parts between the fingers. He did not see any stones on the bottom of the sink hole but lots of dents and pocks that she said were Colored and Indians. Most of the names were French and German, not many just plain American, and the very old ones were all French.

"You believe me now?" she asked.

"I believe old Francois died a long time ago."

"You are hopeless, Mr. Dodge."

He asked if he might treat her to dinner and where was a nice place?

She said he only got his first wages and had to pay back for his room and board that he got on credit, and she would not allow him to treat.

He said, "I never told you that."

"Your boss was a friend of my papa and looks in on us from time to time."

"Henry has been good to me."

"He says you are a steady worker and you catch on quick."

Naturally Lester was pleased but the idea of her talking to his boss like that somehow made him skittish.

They walked back toward the river and she said this is Merchant Street, and you could tell a number of houses and store buildings were old but mostly they were kept up. She went in a little brick bakery and got four Kaiser rolls. Around the corner they went in Oberle's Market and she bought corn beef and liverwurst and cheese and two tomatoes and some pickles and a cellophane sleeve of Dixie cups. All she would allow him to pay for was a quart Vess lemon-lime soda pop and a bag of Saratoga chips. The store clerk gave them an extra brown paper bag and they went out and she said if he could walk a little ways further they could sit and have their picnic dinner on the river bank where the first old town was. He wondered if she had thought this out beforehand too.

So they walked on a gravel road by the bigger creek from the two forks joined together, and the river was backed up to the lower branches of the willows. Off to the other side in the wide bottom that she called the *grand champs*, the low parts had water on them and the young corn was sticking up like rice.

When they came to the river there was a barge tied off by the rip-rap and a fast-looking motor boat alongside and Ethel asked him, "Want some hooch?"

It was the moonshine barge he had heard about where they cooked the stuff out on the water of the Mississippi River so the police and Sheriff and even the Missouri State Patrol could say *Oh, that is not our jurisdiction.* Lester said, "Sure...why not?"

"I will allow you to go dutch on it. A pint is a dollar."

He wanted to say let me do it but his next payday was two weeks off. He shrugged and fished out a fifty-cent piece.

She went to the highest place on the bank and waved her arm and hollered, "You hoo!"

One of the fellows on the barge saw her and climbed down a ladder into the boat and started the motor. The boat came up and on past them and stopped, and with just a couple of burps and purrs of the motor drifted backwards up the creek mouth to a rickety little dock and the fellow looped a line around the piling. He was a stumpy white man in a fedora hat with stubble on his chin and a big old automatic pistol in a holster under his arm.

Ethel gave Lester two quarters and he went down and said they would like a pint. The man asked, "Gin or Canadian?"

Lester called up to Ethel, and she said gin. Kind of bored and surly as if he thought their piddling business was hardly worth his trouble, the man took their money and handed him an unlabeled pint bottle of a clear liquid that for all he knew was water or kerosene. The bootlegger flicked off the loop of line, gunned his motor, and scooted back to the barge, and then Lester saw one of the other fellows watching them through binoculars.

Ethel saw that too. Without saying anything they moved back to where they could still see out the mouth of the creek to the river and across to the trees on the Illinois side, but a swatch of willows screened them from the men on the moonshine barge.

They sat on packed dirt and gravel where it looked mostly dry and their backs to a drift-wood sycamore log. She got out the Dixie cups, and they mixed the rot-gut and Vess soda pop and had themselves cocktails with their picnic dinner. They talked about different things but she knew what was on his mind, and after she had filled their Dixie cups again she said, "I am at my wits' end about Holt Hardy."

"The fellow that come to Sunday dinner?"

"I suppose he is a nice-enough man but..."

"You said he *presumes.*"

"His family had the farm next to ours. He was in Flat River working at the lead mines, but they shut down and he couldn't find work and came home. Papa felt sorry for him and gave him a job."

"He presumes he is your steady fellow?"

"He is twelve years older. He thinks if he is patient I will come to care for him."

"You may lead a horse to water but you can't make her drink."

She made a noise like a horse blowing so its lips flop together, "Pblpblpbbbl..."

He laughed. It was a good imitation. He said he couldn't tell the difference from a real horse.

"You want to *ride* me?"

Lester did not fancy coarse talk in a woman.

"He is after me constantly, asking me to go with him to dances and parties...He *drinks*... not often. But when he does...it is put the Devil back in hell...Mama has tried as nicely as she can to let him know he is not to join us for Sunday dinner as a matter of course...or to come calling in the evening three and four times in the week. Lately when we see him coming I take to my room...I visit with my girlfriends after work. I could let a room in town if I liked but I hate to leave Mama and my least brother alone out at our place. When Papa was alive with his good job at the lime company, the farm was a sideline. Now it is all they have got...besides the piddling five dollars Mama will take for my keep. And don't think the lime company helps out...Mama drives the tractor...plows, harrows, reaps. Delbert does what he can...tending the chickens and such, but I am the one who must milk the cows and muck out the stalls... Naturally Holt Hardy offers to assist...and make us obliged. Mama has refused him time and again, as I refuse when he presses me to go with him to a dance.

"At least for a while I will be out of his way."

"How is that?"

"I have rehearsals for the pageant." She told him of the bicentennial pageant and how she would be a dancer and also one of the Guionee singers. "He tried to tell me I ought not to do it...that after my days at the shirtwaist factory I will fatigue myself. What fatigues me is having to say no to him. He will not understand. When someone else takes an interest in me, he frightens him away."

Lester did not like the sound of this.

"What are you thinking, Mr. Dodge?"

"It is a hard case."

"And you are not sure you care to involve yourself?"

His back was against the sycamore log and she was leaning against his chest with his arm around her waist. She was unbuttoning her dress.

SATURDAY ETHEL CONTRIVED TO MEET HIM AT HER GIRLFRIEND'S HOUSE in town and then they went to the motion picture show. The idea was to keep Holt Hardy from pestering her if she walked alone from the farm into town on Saturday afternoon. Or if Lester were to appear there to escort her, he would be lurking nearby to spy upon them.

At the Orris Theater they saw one of the latest picture shows, *Poor Little Rich Girl* with Shirley Temple where she runs away from home to join the Vaudeville. Ethel said she was so cute with her dimples, you want to pinch her.

After the show they were walking down the street thinking to have a treat in the ice cream parlor when Lester saw a man in the post office parking lot messing around one of the delivery trucks. He said, "That fellow is up to no good."

"Ignore him," Ethel said.

"I believe he is siphoning gasoline."

"Come *on!*"

He was about to holler *Hey! What are you doing there?*

She hurried him along.

As they were passing the photographer's next door she said, "That is Holt Hardy."

"Siphoning gasoline ten o'clock of a Saturday night from a U. S. Mail truck! And what is he going to do with it?"

"He may hurt you."

"I may hurt him!"

She asked him please do not make a scene.

"I am of a mind to go to the Sheriff's department." Ordinarily he would do no such thing but just this week he had been sweated in the death of Falkner, and whatever this Hardy fellow did he might be suspected of it himself.

While they were enjoying their ice cream sodas there was a commotion up the street. It was at the movie theater and people were gawking up at it and milling about, and the crowd not halfway through the late show coming pretty quick out the door. You could smell the nasty smell of the smoke from old paint and seat cushions and linoleum and see licks of flame behind the painted-over windows on the second floor, then window panes here and there popped and flames burst out. With a sudden *WHOOSH!* you could feel the rush of air sucked out of your lungs and the flames had exploded through the roof blazing yellow and orange with streaks of green and you could see the glow of it on the underside of the dark low clouds and the flickering light on the upper floors of buildings to either side and the tall trees in the yards of the houses across the alley.

Fire bells were ringing and some fellows in fireman hats came bustling up with a red wagon that had only buckets of sand and a hand-pump and had no effect that Lester could see on the raging fire. The entire Theater building was ablaze, and the flames had spread to the hardware on the west. The plate glass windows of the dry goods and tailor shop across the street cracked from the heat. Fine ash drifted like cottonwood lint in the air so you breathed it in with the stinking smoke.

The wind whipped up and it looked as if the dry goods would catch fire. Cartridges and shotgun shells were exploding in the hardware store. A man who must have been the tailor and his wife were running in and out of their shop with armloads of suits and pants and rolls of cloth.

More and more people had converged on Merchant Street and the Ste. Genevieve square with City Hall and the court house and jail, and just across the way was the Catholic church, and you could see sparks settling on the steep roof and on the roof of the school and priest's house. People noticed and a special brigade brought ladders and buckets to save the blessed church. He calculated all but the most aged and infirm of the whole town were there and among them were children of all ages, even babies whose mothers held them as if the sight of the raging fire would vaccinate them against such misfortunes in their future life. Several groups were passing buckets and stretching garden hoses to wet down nearby structures.

Others in the crowd like Ethel and Lester merely gawked and milled about, tolled in and held as if the blaze were the climax to a double feature picture show. Regular fire trucks arrived from distant towns and men in slickers and boots with high-pressure hoses took charge, and in time the flames died down. Small fires flickered here and there and embers glowed among the charred timbers and debris of fallen walls and roofs. People drew back and began to drift away. The spell was broken.

When Lester turned and looked about, he saw a man staring at them from the doorway of a pharmacy half way down the block. It was the man he had seen siphoning gas. He nudged Ethel and said *There he is!* She refused to look.

They walked slowly past the hotel and the ice cream parlor to the corner. Under the boughs of a sycamore tree in the narrow swatch of grass in front of the electric company, Lester stepped ahead and blocked her path. He asked her, "Now will you permit me to go to the Sheriff's department?"

"You must not!"

"He was--this fellow Holt Hardy was siphoning gasoline."

"You do not know it was he."

"You told me so yourself!"

"And I would be pressed to bear witness."

Lester considered this. He was charmed with her person and enthralled by the power of her sex, and she was more than two years older than he was and up to a point it was her business. Yet Lester knew Hardy set the fire. It started in the movie theater after they saw him siphoning gas. He did it out of spite.

He said, "I do not wish to quarrel with you over it."

"Anyhow I am not certain the man was Mr. Hardy."

He wondered if she was afraid of Hardy's wrath, or protective out of softness for him in her heart.

As they walked along out Main Street she held his hand and after a time she said, "I did not see Mary Ann at the fire. She must stay with her aunt when the colored woman is off. I told her not to worry."

"If you come in late?"

"If I do not come in at all."

They walked on out Main Street across North Gabouri Creek—which had begun to spread here and there beyond its banks. They passed the rundown house where her friend lived between the butcher shop and the boarded-up brewery. He could not rid himself of a feeling that they were spied upon. When she put her arm about his waist he naturally put his about hers and his senses were aroused. But it made him more uneasy, as if she too felt spied upon and was flaunting her affection.

Lights still burned at the Anvil but only two cars and a wagon were there. He had his own key to the side door near the back, and they climbed the narrow stair holding hands.

They spent the night in sweet delight.

Yet never far from his mind was Holt Hardy staring at them from the doorway.

11.

AFTER WORK ON MONDAY LESTER FOUND HIMSELF ALONE AS HE CAME down the path to the railroad tracks, and there just back in the shadow of the trees was a man staring at him. It was Holt Hardy. He said, "I need to have a word with you."

He was not so tall nor quite so stout as Lester, yet he had to will himself not to quail before him. Without moving his head he looked about for anything he might lay hands upon to defend himself, a stick, a rock, a railroad spike. He tried to act unafraid, even annoyed that the man was keeping him from his draught of beer at the end of a long hot day. "What about?" he asked him.

"Ethel Fahnstock."

"What do you have to say to me?"

"I know she is going with you."

"She give me to understand that she is free to do that."

"You all went to the moving picture."

He did not say *what business is that if yours?* He supposed it would not be wise to speak of the fire or how he concluded Hardy set it. He did not wish to antagonize the man any more than he already was against him, but he would not snivel. He could not think of a reply.

"*Poor Little Rich Girl,*" Hardy said. "I imagine that show was just her dish of tea."

"I have to say I found it enjoyable."

"That is a women's picture."

Lester did not rise to the bait.

"I would have taken her to the Western double feature…Buck Jones in *Riding for Justice* and Ken Menard in *Phantom Patrol.*"

"I like a good Western." Lester tried to think of one to mention. He had not seen more than half a dozen talking pictures in his life. Then he thought how closely Hardy had studied what was showing at the Orris Theater, and surely he followed them after the fire and saw them walking with their arms entwined, and her going in the door of his lodging.

Hardy continued to stare at him. Finally he said, "I am glad we can speak man to man."

Again Lester could think of no prudent reply.

"Now I must ask you civil…man to man…not to see my darling anymore."

He swallowed. He could not pretend to accede to this request. He said in a quiet manner simply as a matter of fact, "She does not seem to regard herself as your darling."

"That is her folly."

"She is a grown woman."

"You are disputing me."

"I do not wish to pick a quarrel."

"I am the one that her father chose."

"I did not know of that," Lester said although from what she had said he could imagine how the man might cherish such a thought.

Hardy went on to tell him pretty nearly the same as she did about growing up on the farm next door, coming home after the Flat River lead mines shut down, and her father getting him on at Bluff City. "I was made welcome in his home. I took dinner there almost every night. He was concerned for his daughter who had high-flown ideals of going to the normal school. His fondest wish was...for her and me to be married."

Lester was tired of humoring this deluded and presumptuous man. He said what he had said to Ethel that seemed to amuse her. *"You can lead a horse to water, but you can't make her drink."*

"I am sorry that you said that."

"And why are you sorry?"

"I hoped I would not have to hurt you."

Lester waited.

Hardy reached behind him and pulled a knife that must have been in a sheath on his belt in back. The blade was as long as his pecker with a hard-on which he supposed was about average, but long enough to do the job.

He did not hesitate to scream and holler. Either the watchman was not there or was asleep in his little watchmen' house. Anyone working the pulverizer or the kiln you had to shout in his face to be heard over the machinery noise, but like a burglar alarm that keeps ringing once it is set off he continued to scream bloody murder.

Behind him was the trestle over the creek that ran out of the hollow where the lime works was. He ducked and grabbed some ballast rocks and flung them at Hardy then scrambled and jumped down into the gray scummy water with all manner of trash in it and strewn along the sides and he still was looking for something to lay his hand on. Then as Hardy came down after him he scooted on under the railroad tracks and up on the side of the creek nearest the gate shack.

Keeping hold of the knife Hardy was not so quick climbing back up to get at him, and he flung some more ballast rocks at him, and dodging them slowed him down and Lester screamed and hollered some more *Help! Murder! It's a madman loose! Trying to kill me! ... Help!* and just plain screaming and hollering, and he did not care if he did sound like the pretty girl when King Kong the gorilla had gotten hold of her. *Help!...It's a madman!*

Hardy was up on the tracks now and coming at him.

Lester did not exactly see, but it was something out the corner of his eye while his gaze was fixed on the knife blade that he was holding out waist high and closing in. Then Hardy looked off to the side.

Somebody was coming down the path from the lime works.

It was the colored man Otis and he had a two-foot iron rod in his hand of the kind that holds the wooden wheels of a cable spool to the spindle and as big around as your little finger. He held it down low and he was stalking Holt Hardy.

Quick as that Hardy stuck his knife behind his back where he pulled it, trying to bullshit Otis.

Lester was so bold as to hope that if he said Hardy pulled a knife on him and Otis saw it too that Hardy would be discharged. But that would give the man yet another grievance. If he made a complaint at law he supposed at most they might put him under a peace bond. Without a mark upon him he could not well sustain a claim of assault. Again he would have even more cause to do him harm. He would bide his time.

Lester dearly wished he might have the rod in Otis' hand. He would let it hang down the end behind his heel and without warning whip it low to strike the side of Hardy's knee joint, and as he fell he would bring it down on top of his shoulder and split his collar bone like dry kindling. He would be helpless and he could leave him so, or he might strike the side of his elbow on the crazy bone and his other knee joint and collar bone so that he would live out his days a cripple. Or with one hard blow to the back of his skull or his temple on either side Lester would rid the earth of him. So he dearly wished and that he might do it without paying with years in the penitentiary or his neck.

"Go on, Hardy," said Otis. "This boy ain't worth you job."

Hardy stared at him like a carbide drill.

The end of that rod just barely twitched like a horse's tail before he flick's it.

"Me and him was just having a talk…about our business."

"Way he holler…you done finished talking."

Hardy stared at him. You might call it even money between his knife and that rod in Otis' hand like the gladiators in *Ben Hur* one with a net and a frog gig, and the other with a little sword and shield---only this was not a picture show. A thick drill rod or a tree branch stout enough to break a bone, he might bet on the knife. But that thin rod of iron was quick as a whip. Besides, Otis had the rod in his hand and Hardy had put up his knife.

If he pulled it again Lester would jump his back and fix him in a choke hold while Otis broke his knees. He would twist his head backwards and wring it around like a chicken. He never in his life so wished to kill a man and thought on ways to do it, he supposed because he never felt so menaced.

Hardy knew they had got the better of him for now and skulked off. "You can both go to hell," he said.

AS FOR OTIS THE COLORED MAN SEEMED DETERMINED TO ESCAPE BEFORE
it occurred to Lester that he had saved his life. He caught up to him to tell him so and shake
his hand and say he must come with him to the Anvil and allow him to treat him to a draught
at the very least. Otis was reluctant. "I don't be welcome there," he said.

"We will see about that," Lester said but maybe he was whistling Dixie.

Otis consented to walk along with him as far as the hollow by the ferry landing and with
coaxing to the tavern door but he would not enter. "I can drink out here," he said.

The busty girl Hildegard with golden pigtails coiled to the sides of her head was tending
bar and at one end was Frank Janis jollying his guests, and at two tables pushed up together
Walter and Little John were sitting with some fellows Lester had drunk with once before but
did not recall their names. He started to order two draughts but concluded to ask instead for
a bucket and two mugs.

His hands were full and he asked for help at the door. "Say," said Little John, "is that
for me?"

"It is for Otis Bouchard," he said. "He is bashful of drinking with white men."

Janis caught his eye but did not speak.

In the yard under a cottonwood tree was a stand-up table of a wide plank across the ends
of two barrels and as he set the mugs on it and poured for himself and Otis from the gallon
bucket, Little John and Walter came out and joined them. "Otis has done me a good turn,"
Lester said.

Otis shook his head and they both drank.

"He should know better than that," said Walter.

Lester closed his eyes and felt them all at once well up with abundant pity for himself
and began to shake.

"Say, Lester," Little John asked, "what is with you?"

He choked and could scarcely say it, "Otis just——" He had to start over. "He...saved
my life."

"I never," said Otis.

"He *did*."

"I done no such thing," said Otis.

"Holt Hardy was fixing to...to slit my throat." He could not help it. He was sobbing
and shaking and so ashamed that he cursed himself. "God *damn!* I am bawling like a girl."

Walter and Little John looked at each other then back at Lester.

He could only whisper it. "...He saved my life."

"I just happen along."

Lester sniffled and sniveled and wiped the snot and tears on the back of his hand and took a long drink.

"You making too much of it."

He shook his head and told them pretty straight as he recalled it how Holt Hardy lay in wait for him, how at first he talked civil but then he tried to warn him off going with Ethel Fahnstock, and when Lester refused he talked ugly, and then was coming at him with his evil knife and almost surely would have stuck him like a hog and hanged him by the heels to drain. "But Otis come with his iron rod in answer to my cries," he said, "and Hardy put up his knife and slunk away."

Walter and Little John considered this.

Lester filled the glasses all around.

"He backed you," said Walter.

"We would do the same for him," said Little John.

They all drank to Otis and he nodded and grinned but his eyes flicked from hither to yon and back again. Although they were his work mates, he might hope it was not remarked upon that he was drinking with white men.

They drank again to Otis.

The hired girl came out to see if they want another bucket, and Mr. Janis wished her to tell them that Mr. Bouchard was welcome to come and drink with them at the bar or a table inside. "None of our guests now objects," she said, "and when the Frau Janis came down she was angry with Frank for not in the first place making your comrade welcome."

Lester asked Otis, "Shall we go inside?"

"No, sir," he said, and Lester felt strange. Otis was twenty years their senior yet he deferred to all three of the young white men, and on the job he generally spoke only when he was spoken to and took his dinner apart.

"I was thinking we may be ready for another bucket."

"I best get home to Irene," he said. "She worry when I be late." He swallowed the rest of what was in his mug in one long draught, wiped the back of his hand across his mouth, and for the first time grinned a wide grin, Lester imagined mostly in relief that his ordeal of the white boys condescending to drink with him was at an end.

They all shook his hand as if he were a long-lost brother and had now returned, as if they had not just spent ten hours toiling beside him among the rocks and had the day before and expected to on the morrow. They shook hands as if in farewell.

"You did not have to do it," Lester said again.

Otis said, "I know that man."

When he had gone they sat thinking their thoughts to the WEE-zoo...WEE-Zoo...WEE-zoo of the locusts and the twitter of the little birds that dart and sweep to catch them. Lester was thinking that he would not always have a Good Samaritan in earshot of his cries. He said, "I am not shut of Holt Hardy."

"He is a case," Little John said. "He will be your friend... treat you to a draught some evening, and the next day he has recalled some slight he thinks you done him and would rip your thrapple."

"Ethel is at her wits' end," Lester said.

"You and her for sure are going together now?"

"That is my understanding."

"He will track you down."

"I suppose that is the nature of his mind."

Walter said, "We have got Clyde's pistol...for safe-keeping until he gets out of jail."

"If he ever does," said Little John.

"It is a Bulldog Special thirty-eight snub-nose no bigger than your hand."

"Is that a good ideal?" Little John asked.

"People know Hardy. If Lester must shoot him, it is self-defense."

"To pack...at work?"

"Must you snitch?"

"No! And Papa ain't no friend to Hardy. But him and Lester both are fired toot-sweet if Bondurant finds out. And me and you as well for passing it to him."

"He can tote it in his lunch pail."

NO SOONER DID LITTLE JOHN GIVE LESTER THE REVOLVER THAN CLYDE WAS arraigned and charged with murder in the first degree for shooting Falkner. Lester's friends allowed they mainly told the truth when the deputies sweated them down. They said how Clyde asked to ride with them to the dance and brought his shotgun saying he might see a rabbit along the way, then that Falkner and his brothers might be at the dance. They also said Clyde made threats against Falkner the week before, but they hated to say anything to him or to the host and have Clyde down on them.

Clyde at first denied the crime. But after two days in jail and meeting with a Flat River lawyer his mother had retained, he signed a confession to the charge. He said his reason for killing Falkner was he betrayed his sister and would not consent to marry her after she gave birth to a child.

12.

AT THE ROCK FACE WHERE THEY WERE DRILLING NEXT DAY BONDURANT came and fetched Otis away to the office saying he must have a word with him, and by dinner time he had not returned. Nor had he as they went back to work. Near quitting time Lester asked Henry. He said he did not know but something was not right.

In the morning Otis did not report for work. Lester asked again. "Where is Otis?"

Henry shook his head.

"I can not recall when he missed a day," said Little John. "Not since I commenced to work."

"I can think of once," Henry said, "when Irene had the grippe…but he sent word."

"He did not seem to be ailing himself," said Little John.

They hesitated to conclude what well they might from how Bondurant came and got him. It had no rhyme or reason.

Henry caught his eye.

"You never can tell about colored," said Walter.

At dinner time Henry went to the office himself. When he came back he said, "Otis is discharged."

They asked him why. They protested that he was a *worker,* and Walter said he knew his place.

"That's all I know."

At the end of the day Lester asked his leave to talk to Bondurant himself.

"You are always free to do that," Henry said.

"I am obliged to Otis."

Henry considered what to say. Lester believed Little John was careful not to tell his papa things that might get any of them in dutch, and Henry did not sweat him. He doubted

Little John's scruple extended to Holt Hardy. However, Lester imagined Henry in his turn as careful not to let on to him or Walter that he knew of something that he could only know from his own boy, that he did not want them to suppose that Little John bore tales. He said, "Bondurant may tell you to mind your business."

"I would be wrong not to make it my business."

Henry did not gainsay that. He took a long breath and let it out through his teeth. He was troubled. "Lester," he said, "watch yourself. We are walking on eggs here."

LESTER PROCEEDED TO THE PULVERIZER BARN WHERE THEY BAGGED THE quick lime and went to the crib in the corner with two desks and a ice-box, and by the window that looked up the hollow to the rock face was a stand-up desk. That was where he found Bondurant with some kind of a blueprint and a slide rule that he worked with his one good hand.

"Mr. Bondurant?" he asked.

Without turning around he said, "What do you want?"

"I am Lester Dodge."

He said he knew that and still did not turn around. The idea was he must tend some important work and Lester was a nuisance.

"You may say it is not my business, but Otis Bouchard done me a good turn, and--"

"He is discharged."

"But *why*. . .sir?"

Bondurant stepped back and turned to look at him as if he could not conceive of how a common hand would have the gall to question him so. He studied him and shook his head, then asked, "Did Henry put you up to this?"

"No, sir. He . . ."

"He what . . .?"

"When you fetched Otis away and by quitting time he still had not come back, I asked Henry why. He said he did not know, but something was not right."

"'Something is not right.' Those were his words?"

"Yes, sir. But here I come to stand up for Otis and the first thing I do is get Henry in dutch. He is a *good boss*, sir. He makes you do things right but he is fair, and--"

"Do not worry about that, Lester. I want to hear what you have to say."

He was thinking oh-oh now he will play me for a snitch, but he had gotten himself into it. "Yes, sir. In the morning when Otis did not show up for work, we was all concerned. At dinner hour, Henry went to see you himself."

"What did he say about that?"

He thought here was where he was called to play the snitch, but he could see no harm to Henry in the simple truth. "He says, 'Otis is discharged. That is all I know.'"

"Those were his words?"

"Yes, sir."

"He did not tell you anything else."

"He did not."

"You have not gotten Henry in dutch. On the contrary."

"So at the end of the day I ask his leave to talk to you myself. Henry says, 'You are always free to do that.'"

"It is the policy and when you first came in I was short with you, and that is against policy. I beg your pardon."

"Yes, sir." He was amazed that Bondurant the Day Superintendent of the whole works and boss of his boss was showing him such respect, but then he wondered *what is he up to with me?* Yet he rattled on as if this were but a friendly older fellow who took an interest, "So I say, 'I am obliged to Otis—'"

Bondurant started to ask him a question but thought better of it, and nodded for him to go on.

"Henry says that you may tell me to mind my business--"

"Well, I did not come out and say it, but you know…it is unheard-of cheek for a man--especially a green young hand like yourself—to come in here and question a personnel decision about another man."

"Yes, sir. I do know that. I come in here supposing I might well be discharged myself."

"So-far-so-good, Lester. Now then. . .Otis Bouchard must have done you a good turn indeed."

He disliked saying it over and again and to make the words commonplace but he must, "*He saved my life.*"

"How is that?"

Here he wished he had more time to puzzle the matter out. On the one hand if he snitched on Holt Hardy and he was discharged, the man had cause that in his estimation would be enough to end his days, to say nothing of Lester's impertinence in the matter of Ethel Fahnstock. On the other hand if Lester refused to elaborate, Bondurant might dismiss him and he would lose what chance he had to do Otis any good, or even to feel he had done what he could for him. If he tried to think over different ways to say it as he stood before him, Bondurant would suppose he was trimming. He was no fool.

Again Lester told the tale about as he had to Walter and Little John in the presence of Otis. He did not name Holt Hardy but spoke of him as "a man who has a grudge against me," and he tried to make clear that what passed between them was outside the gate to the lime works.

Nevertheless, Bondurant made a point of it. "And just where that this occur?"

"On the railroad tracks and trestle over Fallert's Creek."

"Was this man an employee of Bluff City Lime?"

"Mr. Bondurant, I hope you will grant how I would rather not answer that."

Bondurant considered before he said, "You are correct if you suppose he would be discharged at once…unless what you just told me is a bare-faced lie."

"It is the truth. Otis Bouchard is my witness."

THROUGH THE WINDOW BEHIND HIM LESTER SAW A BIG OLD BLACK CAR come booming up the hollow throwing lime dust every which way, only Bondurant did not hear it over the machines. It shoved right up close, and a red-faced bulldog of a fellow in a blue suit and a Tam-o'-shanter got out and looked around like he was chasing bank robbers. Then he opened the back door and bowed his head as a stout man in English riding boots and khaki knickers got out. He was wearing a Sam Browne belt with a strap down slantwise across his chest and a holster on his hip. While he said something to the one who got out first and Lester imagined was his bodyguard, a young fellow in a seersucker suit and straw hat got out the other side in back. The driver in a shiny bill cap stayed put.

By this time Bondurant had seen them and said out the side of his mouth, *"It is Mr. Griswold."*

The stout one in khaki knickers had already walked in and he said, "Now what is this about having to fire the colored men?"

Bondurant looked at Lester then back to the man to tell him this is something he was not supposed to hear but Griswold took no notice and it was too late anyhow. Lester did not know what he was expected to do and was scared to ask, so he sifted back into the corner by the ice box.

"That is what Secour told me," Bondurant says. "He is not happy about it either." He meant Dick Secour who was the local union rep.

"If he is so unhappy about it," Griswold asked, "why did he make the demand?"

"He said a union member complained."

"Do you know who?"

"I have a pretty good idea."

"What is his name?"

Bondurant looks again at Lester.

Griswold took no notice.

"...Holt Hardy."

Finally the big boss deigned to cast his eyes in Lester's direction. "That boy there?"

"No, sir. This is Lester. Lester Dodge."

"'Lester'?" the big boss asks. Lester nodded. The boss held out his hand. "I am Joe Griswold."

Lester shook his hand.

"Lester, how do you feel about working alongside a colored man?"

"That is what I come to speak with Mr. Bondurant about."

"To complain?"

"*No, sir.* I come to Mr. Bondurant about a colored man that did work alongside me, that I thought the world of—and Henry and Little John did too, but he is discharged."

"Lester, so far as I am concerned if he is a good worker and you all get along, I am glad to have him as an employee."

"Yes, sir."

"But your union...your *international* union has a rule against it. Did you know that?"

"I have heard of some such." It was mainly from the CIO that would be their union instead but he kept that to himself.

"You see?" Griswold said to Bondurant. "This can work to our advantage."

The big boss seemed done with talking to Lester and he looked off to the side toward the door.

"Lester," Bondurant said, "maybe you could wait outside. Or do you have any more you want to speak about with me?"

"Not particularly."

He nodded to say he could leave now.

But Griswold stopped him. "Lester," he said, "what is your last name again?"

"Dodge, sir."

"'Lester Dodge'...Lester, you strike me as a bright lad, and I shall want to speak with you again."

"Yes, sir." First he thought that would be a chance to let him know he was an apprentice machinist and he might do him good, but then perhaps he had some use for him that he might not wish to serve.

As he came out into the sunlight he was thinking too on how he was good and ready for a long cool draught of lager beer, when someone said, "Hello!"

It was the young fellow in the seersucker suit.

"You work here?"

"Yes." I do not say sir.

"Is it hard?"

"Sometimes."

"Just what do you do?"

"Mostly break up the big rocks to middle-size rocks and load them in the hopper car."

He nodded. "I am Joseph Griswold. My *pater* is Junior so that makes me The Third. They call me Tertius." He held out his hand.

"Lester. Lester Dodge," he said.

He shook his soft hand.

"You have a girlfriend?"

That was a fresh question from a stranger just out of the blue but he supposed if you were a rich boy you imagine you could be fresh as you like with a mere working fellow like himself. Or he just might not know better. "I suppose you could say I do."

"You suppose?"

"There is a young lady I am going with."

"Does she have a friend?"

Lester stared at him.

"A pretty friend…who is not going with someone herself?"

He got his drift.

"I am separated from my wife. She's a tramp."

He did not feel called upon to offer his condolences. He supposed he was to take this as the reason he expected Lester to pander for him, besides his being the son and heir. He said, "I do not believe a Ste. Genevieve girl would suit you."

"She might…if she's pretty."

He dearly would have loved to smack this jackass in the face.

"I have a Stutz Bearcat…with a rumble seat."

He shook his head. He more pitied than resented him. He excused himself. "Master Griswold, I have had a long hot day in your father's quarry, and am going home to my manger."

As he turned he saw the red-face fellow in a blue suit and a Scotchman's hat lounging behind him in the shadow where the tin roof hung over, and he jinked so hard his dinner pail rattled. "Easy, mate," the fellow said and gave him a little salute.

What rattled in his lunch pail was Clyde's Bulldog Special.

THE ANVIL WAS CROWDED WITH FELLOWS FROM PEERLESS AND WESTERN Lime. As he sat at the common table to take his supper and lingered after with a pint, they spoke of the colored men. Otis and the others at Bluff City were not the only ones to be discharged. It had happened at all the union lime works, and most of these hillbillies were glad of it.

He moved to the end of the table at his host's left hand and asked him what was going on.

Janis said the quarries laid off their colored men, "all save Jenkins-Gillis."

"But why is that?" Lester asked. He already had put together some idea but it made no sense.

"A. F. of L. does not represent colored," Janis said. "Local 829 is A. F. of L."

"But Otis Bouchard was working for Bluff City by my side. He has been there as long as Henry."

"Lester, to say it ugly but straight out, Ste. Genevieve hates niggers, but we just love our old colored people."

"Otis Bouchard is not a nigger."

"I agree. Dick Secour and Oscar Kampf and a number of the union men agree. When they got their Closed Shop last May, they decided to let the colored men stay on. For the most part I believe they enrolled them and collected their dues the same as anyone else, and the International was none the wiser."

"Until Holt Hardy complained!" Lester said.

"Is that who it was?"

"He done it because Otis crossed him on account of me."

"Holt Hardy. ... I am not surprised."

"Why, it is to bust our union!" I say.

Emma his little red-haired missus chimed in, "Do not put anything past those sons-of-bitches."

He repeated what he heard Griswold say to Bondurant, "'This can work to our advantage.'"

"You need to talk to Dick Secour," said Janis.

"You all should have gone with John L. Lewis and the C. I. O.," said Emma.

"It is too late now," Janis said.

He still paid dues as a active member of Local 829 and came to meetings. They said he worked nearly twenty years for Bluff City as a dynamite-setter, and they fired him as a ring-leader in a bitter fight to organize. The story was that his missus and her people inherited the Anvil about that time, and he became the host.

It sat but a stone's throw from the lime works gates. When he took it over they tried to buy him out, then sicced lawyers on him. But he remained here as a thorn in their side and a staunch friend to the working man.

13.

LESTER WENT SEEKING OTIS BOUCHARD. HENRY HAD TOLD HIM HE LIVED on the St. Mary Road across the south fork where a number of the French colored resided. He went under the railroad track and across the creek that was close to running over the bridge. Off left was the way out to the point where he and Ethel had gotten some hooch off the boot-legger barge and had their picnic.

Straight ahead were old houses one after another all on the side away from the Big Field bottom. They sat close to the road with long narrow back yards that ran to the foot of the bluff. One house you could spit from the gallery to the road. He saw two colored men on a bench in front, and a boy no older than he was sat on the edge with his feet hanging over. They watched him coming and he stopped at the front gate. He told them, "I am looking for Otis Bouchard."

The one in a blue shirt with U.S. MAIL on the sleeve asked,

"He owe you money?"

Lester said the men he worked with took up a collection. "It is not much, but I am sup-posed to give it to him."

"He be glad to see you then."

"He at the Negro joint down by the depot," said the boy.

"You don't want to go in there," said the oldest who was darker and had lime dust on his clothes. "He drunk."

The idea was if he gave him the money he would stay drunk longer. They discussed the matter back and forth and concluded he had better give the money to his wife, Irene.

"House be around on South Gabouri."

The boy Cletus would show him the way.

As they walked by the backed-up water in the creek branch Cletus asked, "You the white boy Otis save you ass?"

Lester did not much like how he said it but allowed that he was.

"How come he fired?"

He said the man who pulled a knife on him filed a grievance.

"But how come Otis be fired? ...Why *all* the Colored?"

Lester told him what he was given to understand. A year ago last May when the lime companies were compelled by law to recognize the union, their Local 829 included all the Colored already working among them, like Otis. They took their dues and kept them on the rolls as members in good standing, but did not identify them to the Union headquarters in St. Louis as Colored. Holt Hardy's grievance exposed their deception. Lester spelled it out, "A F of L is not open to Colored."

They walked on without speaking for a ways.

Lester said, "That is why we should have CIO instead."

"You going to shut us down?"

He was thinking that for a Negro boy this Cletus was no fool. The quarry he worked at was non-union. He saw what happened to Otis as the writing on the wall. Lester would not lie to him. "...There has been talk of it."

He followed along after Cletus and where he stopped was the same rundown house by the creek that Ethel had showed to him and said it was two hundred years old. Now he recalled her saying it was Mrs. Bouchard's. They went up on the gallery and Cletus knocked on the wood part of the screen door. He knocked again and called, "Mrs. Bouchard, it's Cletus... Cletus Johnson...the boy staying by Zeno and Lon and Cap."

He stopped and listened, and called some more, "Mrs. Bouchard...? Irene...? I brought a friend of your husband wants to see you." He listened, then said, "She coming."

She appeared in the screen door in a rumpled house dress like she slept in it, a cut with a purple black scab on her cheekbone and one eye swollen almost shut.

"This be Lester," said Cletus. "He Otis' friend from work."

She looked at him like she knew just who he was. "Oh, yes," she said. She was dark brown and plump with a pretty face and she had her way to talk among white people. "I would invite you in, but half the furniture is broken and things thrown all around. I have not been able to arouse myself to put things to rights."

Lester told her how he and Henry and Little John and Walter all thought the world of Otis and what happened to him was not right. He offered her the envelope.

"We are not destitute," she said.

"It is what we had in our pockets."

"We appreciate the thought." She accepted it.

Lester felt he should say more to her, inquire of Otis.

She excused herself.

AS THEY WALKED BACK THE WAY THEY HAD COME CLETUS SAID, "SHE A sweeper at Elder Shirtwaist. Ashame to go to work, white girls see her husband messed her up."

He supposed he had done right in giving his wife what they collected. It was more than pocket change. Little John and Walter gave half a day's pay each, Henry gave a whole day, Lester put in five dollars which was a day's pay for him and a dollar more, and Ethel insisted he take five dollars from her. It came to twenty-five dollars, altogether more than enough to keep you drunk longer than is good for your health.

He was not keen to speak with Otis now but felt perhaps he should. He inquired of Cletus, "Can you direct me to this joint where he is at?"

"I take you there if you want. But Otis find out you give money to his wife, he just go beat it out of her."

Still he felt he must speak with Otis himself. He followed Cletus down the creek on the other side to the trestle and over to the hotel and down Merchant street past the depot to a ramshackle place that used to be a feed store. It was like when you go into a movie theater from daylight and he bumped into people and excused himself before his eyes got used to the almost dark. They found Otis slouched over with his elbows on the bar, his head down. He scarcely knew Lester, and all that was on his mind was to get them to buy him a drink. But Lester did not have one cent. He put it all in the envelope.

"You...boy! Buy me a drink." Cletus refused. *"Buy me a drink!"*

"No, sir. I suppose to tell you Zeno get you on at Jenkins-Gillis…when you sober."

"Old fool Zeno don't know nothing coming down. I ain't fired. I be *on furlough*."

That set Lester to thinking on what passed between Griswold and Bondurant as he stood not six feet away. He asked, "Otis, when Bondurant took you back to the office, did he make you some kind of promise?"

"Mind you business."

"We hear they are fixing to mess with our contract."

Otis gagged, and vomited on his shoe.

IN THE EVENING AFTER WORK LESTER AND WALTER AND LITTLE JOHN HAD come out into the yard of the Anvil and were gathered around a gallon bucket of beer under the cottonwood tree. "Last night when I met Ethel after her choir practice," Lester said, "Hardy was watching from under the South Fork trestle."

"We can thrash him for you any time you like," said Walter.

"It will take more than that," said Little John.

"He will pull his knife," Lester said.

They both looked at him. He carried the Bulldog Special in his dinner pail to work, and other times it was in his pocket or under the pillow as he slept.

"Shoot him," Walter said.

"I would have to be careful to do it when he has his knife in his hand."

"We might help you set the table."

"If we are the only witnesses, they will discount us as your friends," said Little John.

"I do not know how Ethel would regard me after that." Lester struggled to persuade himself that he acted in self-defense, to protect his dear girl from harm, and to chastise this spiteful selfish fellow for the grief he caused to countless others just to warn him off his jo.

"Or lay in wait for him," Walter says. "Smite him like a steer so he falls to his knees. You drop a wire about his neck and choke it tight so he may not cry out, then pack him in a barrel of lime and roll it into the river."

"It would be better," said Little John, "if we could persuade him to go away from here… and not return."

Lester felt safe among his friends as they conspired against his enemy. He almost felt sorry for him. He was the lone wolf of whom it was said he always turned on friends, accusing them of slights and wrongs they had no idea they committed. Some would forgive him and be his friend once more and make allowances and humor him, but soon or late he must lash out again. The only one who endured as his friend was Ethel's father, who pitied him.

She did too, and he was troubled when he thought on that. He was not so much jealous as concerned that clever as she was and perhaps as well-acquainted with his nature as anyone alive, she supposed he would never do her harm.

14.

IT HAD BECOME GENERALLY KNOWN THAT HOLT HARDY CAUSED THE DIScharge of the colored men. Some would thank him. Others granted a wrong had been done but felt relief that they themselves were spared. Here and there were others like Little John and Henry who regreted the injustice to a man who worked beside them, and thought Hardy should be made to suffer. Lester did not know how many extended the ideal of Solidarity to colored and saw in all this the scheming of the lime companies to bust their union.

He truly believed this and took it for a sanction of what he would do on his own account. In driving out Holt Hardy they would act for the good of all.

As Hardy stalked Ethel to spy out her every move, Lester stalked him and when he did he was armed. As a rule Hardy left the quarries after work by the overgrown road out the back. He proceeded to the old cemetery where Ethel showed Lester the gravestone of Francois Valle who was born two hundred years ago, and he loitered there across from the shirtwaist factory until she came off work at six.

He sat there among the hemlocks about the Detchmendy mausoleum to watch her pass on Market Street. She acted as if she did not know that he was there. Lester supposed that she in fact did not know that he was there too.

He spoke again of Hardy with Little John and Walter. They went over the matter several evenings after work, trying out their different ideas of what they might do. Finally they agreed that they would waylay him among the sink-holes and take him down in the hollow to Fallert's cave.

Besides Lester and Walter and Little John they had recruited Clyde's older brother

Ralph and a tow-headed fellow named Bucholz. They blacked their faces with shoe polish like the minstrel show and were hunched down in two sink-holes by the ruts that were all the road amounted to.

As Hardy came up from the lime works and along a wheel rut that had worn deeper as a footpath, he was talking to himself. The timber was post-oak scrub and cedar with sumac by the path. He was having a regular conversation with his idea of Ethel in his mind.

When he had passed the first sink hole Little John and Lester came up out of the second and stopped across his path. As he turned to go back the other way Walter and Ralph and Bucholz came up behind him. He did not attempt to run. "I ain't scared of you cock-suckers," he said and whipped out his knife.

Lester snatched the Bulldog Special from his belt and as he got it pointed at Hardy he cocked the hammer back and said, "Drop the knife!"

Hardy moved on him to call his bluff.

Bucholz smacked him with a drill rod behind his ear and his legs crumpled from under him so he fell to his knees then flopped forward on the side of his face.

They all five were on him trussing him round and round with twine like a generator coil, and Little John wrapped friction tape around the back of his head over his mouth and more around his jaw and the top of his head. As Lester squatted down to make sure he was breathing, his eyes snapped open. He strained and twitched every which way and the cords in his neck swelled out, and his whole face went red and splotched as he made choked-off sounds of rage.

They wrapped him in a tarpaulin still writhing and twitching, and the other four carried him on their shoulders like pallbearers without a coffin. Lester led the way around the edge of the hollow and down to the cave, which was generally known of but not frequented and he had scouted it out ahead.

The mouth was perhaps thirty feet wide and black from smoke along the ceiling that curved in from up to twenty feet high in the middle to where for a ways back if Lester raised his arms over his head he could not quite touch it, and there were little stalactites sticking down. The flow from a spring ran along one side wall with some cress in it, and on the other a long room crooked off to the left and the ceiling scrunched down to stoop height. They went in there and laid Hardy on the dry clay floor and unwrapped the tarpaulin.

Lester was not sure he had the stomach for this.

Bucholz took the lead on the idea that he was the least-well-known to Hardy and perhaps had done such business before. "Hardy," he said, "the orders is that you must leave here and not come back."

"That is what was resolved," said Ralph.

"We are the telegraph boys for you-know-who-they-are."

"We don't want to hurt you."

"Think he understands?" Walter asked.

They look at Lester.

He nodded.

"Can we talk to you like a man?" Bucholz asksed "or you just scream and holler and piss your pants?"

"Try it," Walter said.

Ralph held Hardy's shoulders down while Bucholz unwrapped the tape from around his mouth.

Hardy worked his jaw a time or two before he said, "I ain't going nowhere. Now turn me loose you son-of-a-bitch."

Bucholz had the drill rod. He tapped the side of Hardy's elbow on his crazy bone.

Hardy defied him to do it again.

Ralph pulled a cigar out of his shirt pocket and took his sweet time getting it lit.

No one would say all that happened in that cave. Bucholz's uncle was a high-up in the Legion and some would tell you they are the next thing to the Klan. Or you hear there is no Klan around there anymore. Ralph had worked in the Illinois coal mines as a union goon or a Pinkerton or both at different times or was a soldier for the Shelton gang that controlled the hooch from East Boogie to Cairo and had sent the Chicago boys limping home more than once. Or that may have been someone else.

Regardless of who they did it for or why, Ralph and Bucholz had experience in this line. Lester did not know about Walter but he took to it. He and Little John did not relish it at all.

The idea was that when Hardy agreed to their demand, or as Bucholz and Ralph said it—the *orders* or the *ruling* or *what was resolved*, as if it was the official meeting of the Ameri-can Legion and the Knights of Columbus and if there was such a thing the Klan and the Chamber of Commerce and perhaps Local 829 and the Elks Club and Red Men and Lions too if not the churches—they would stop. This was not just five fellows thrashing him at a dance or out back of the tavern. This was public business, the town meeting, the ruling of the tribe in council that he was cast out.

When he agreed, they would stop.

He was a child who made a mess or sassed his mama and must say he is sorry and will not do it again. *They* were sorry they must punish him. It hurt them more than him. But so long as he defied them and was *bad*, they must humiliate him and cause him pain.

Only if they must, excruciating pain.

The longer he defied them the more binding his assent would be. An easy man would swear or promise anything before the business fairly started. As Hardy showed little regard for the pain of others, he seemed indifferent to his own. You hear of the Indians torturing those they capture as a matter of course, and among them the most-admired is the one who taunts them to strike him harder and sings his death song as he burns.

They wore him down. But every time Bucholz or Ralph said, "You give? You agree to leave here? You had enough?...Don't make us keep doing this," Hardy answered if only in a feeble voice with a curse.

The last torment and perhaps the worst began when they pulled off his trousers and his drawers and staked down his feet with his legs apart, and Ralph burned him with the cigar in his private parts. Bucholz threatened him with his own knife making little nicks and cuts here and there that left just a thin line or a drop of blood. He said he would castrate him like a shoat and give him his balls in a cup.

Hardy was staunch in his defiance.

They turned him over on his belly.

Bucholz went out with Hardy's knife in his hand and Lester followed. He picked up sticks and cast them aside, then found a sapling of slippery elm and broke off a piece as long as your forearm and stripped the bark at the big end and whittled in to cut off the splinters and make it a knob.

Lester asked him, "What are you fixing to do?"

He was businesslike and solemn, not funning around one bit. "We know what we are about, Lester," he said. "It is on your account."

He held his peace.

As Bucholz went back into the cave Lester sat on a fallen sycamore with his head in his hands, his elbows on my knees. The harm was done. If Hardy should *give* and assents to his banishment, it would not be for long. He would return.

Lester should have killed him.

If he died, they could only pray that they were not found out. Or if they were suspected, that none of them played the snitch. Lester was less concerned that he would go to the law on them. He did not know it for a fact but had an idea Hardy had a history with the law. If nothing else, he had too much pride. He would settle such matters as this on his own.

Or so Lester supposed.

And what of Ethel? He might attempt to keep his mouth shut but she would know within a day that Hardy no longer lurked about. She would remark on it and inquire of him. She could read him like a book.

What they did was to shove the wood up his rectum as he writhed and moaned, then pulled it out reeking of his blood and shit, forced his mouth open, and made as if to jam it down his throat. "He give," said Bucholz. "He swore he would leave and never come back."

Lester regarded him turned over supine again in only his blood-flecked work-shirt.

"Say it again for Lester."

Ralph kicked him in the hip.

Walter told him, "Say it!"

Hardy stared at Lester in defiance.

"Or was you lying?" Ralph asked.

"Say it!" Walter kicked him in the ribs.

Bucholz grabbed his jaw and shoved the stinking faggot of wood in his face.

"I will leave here…"

Walter prompts him, "'and not come back.'"

"I *will* come back and serve each of you as you served me and then some until you beg to die, and--"

Ralph kicked him in the jaw and Bucholz grabbed and forced it open and jammed the faggot in his mouth. He choked with revulsion *eating his own shit* and gagged, his face dark red as he seemed to nod. Bucholz pulled it out.

When Hardy could speak he said in a strained voice that was scarcely more than a whisper, "And not come back."

They all turn to Lester.

"Are you satisfied?" Bucholz asks.

He looked around at each of them in turn until he looked him in the eye and he said, "Yes, my friends. I am satisfied."

They let Hardy put his trousers and boots on, wrapped him again in the tarpaulin, and carried him up the path that ran now on one wheel rut and now on the other to where Little John had parked Henry's car in the weeds by White Sands road. They stuffed Hardy in the trunk.

Little John drove on back streets through town and on south between the bluff and the wide bottom of the Big Field on the road to St. Mary. There they crossed the slough that used to be the main channel of the river and onto Kaskaskia Island and proceeded as far as they could on the mud and gravel road to the eastern shore, where the road ran on the levee, and they looked down on the brown water that was just shy of spreading out beyond its banks. As Walter had promised, by a dock platform floating on oil drums they saw two old rowboats on the bank and a john-boat with an outboard motor.

They took Hardy out of the trunk and carried him down the levee slope and then in the mud and gravel shore weeds to one of the boats. They tipped it on its side to let the rainwater and mosquito wrigglers in it run out, then launched it on the slough. It floated although already you could see it leaked.

When Hardy was in the boat they pulled it by the bow line in the slack water by the jetty way out to the end where driftwood and trash and a dead possum washed past in the current.

They unwrapped the tarpaulin. They had long since cut loose the twine. He lay between the stern and middle seat, too weak to struggle and his voice too strained and choked to cry out. They gave the boat a shove, and soon it was far out and booming along. The last they saw, it was passing between the piers of the Chester bridge.

LESTER CALCULATED IT WAS JUST AS WELL THEY DID NOT GO TO SOME PUBlic place to celebrate. He proposed they return to Ste. Genevieve and drive out to the point at the mouth of Gabouri creek where he would treat them all to some hooch from the bootleg barge. There on the bank among the willows—where he and Ethel shared their first embrace—they could over-imbibe to their hearts' content, whoop, holler, cut didoes, and commit whatever foolishness they must without strangers to note that these five were together on this night and carousing and carrying on in a peculiar frame of mind.

IT WAS AS HE FEARED WITH ETHEL. NEXT DAY WAS SUNDAY AND HE WAS TO meet her after church, which he did with a throbbing headache and uncertain stomach. Their habit then was to walk out the ferry-landing road to the Anvil and have their pleasure of one another in his room, and then to take their Sunday dinner downstairs at the common board. Frank and Emma Janis had come to regard them as an old couple and supposed they were as good as engaged, and Lester supposed as much himself.

As they crossed the north fork which had risen another six inches in the night Ethel remarked, "I have seen no sign of Holt Hardy."

He was silent.

"Have you?"

"Not this morning."

She caught him with sidelong glances as they walked along.

When they reached the Anvil and went up to his room and had disrobed she asked about a scratch along his arm, "What is that?"

He said it must have happened at work.

She noticed a swelling about his eye and asked, "Have you been fighting?"

"You might call it that."

"With Holt Hardy?"

"In a manner of speaking."

"Where is he?"

"I do not know."

"You had better tell me," she said.

He could not lie to her, though he softened it in the telling that they persuaded Hardy to leave town.

"You *persuaded* him?"

"He agreed that he would leave here and not come back."

"How did you persuade him?"

"We caused him some discomfort."

"You and your friends...How many?"

"Four."

"Five men against one."

"Quick as that he will draw his knife. He done it last evening."

"A pathetic hangdog man without family or a friend in the world."

"He tormented you night and day. He set that fire. He would have killed me with his knife."

"Five against one."

He resented her dwelling on that.

"He will return."

He imagined she was right. He had better have killed him. By himself. Without four other fellows to swear that mum's the word and any who peached was a dead man. Yet when it came to my neck or yours, he might very well conclude to save his own. As for Little John and Walter, he saw how they did in the matter of Clyde.

She had put her chemise back on. "Lester Dodge," she said, "I never want to see you again as long as I live."

15.

THEY HAD BEEN HEARING TALK OF WHAT THE LIME COMPANIES WOULD DO when their contract expired in June to where Lester put it out of his mind. Then one day it was June and at ten o'clock in the morning the word came that they were shutting down. It was the first Thursday in June.

Henry said, "All right, boys, separate out your own tools. Then we must police things up here before we go, so the sons of bitches can't hold nothing against us and charge we committed sabotage."

They gathered up the drill rods and pry bars and hammers and spikes and laid them in the crates and closed the lids. Walter checked the oil on the generator. They counted the dynamite and caps and Henry entered the numbers in his little book.

Little John said, "We may be searched."

Although Hardy had not been seen or heard of in some time Lester continued to tote the Bulldog Special. He sifted behind a pillar of rock and took it from his dinner pail and put it in his pocket and stuffed his handkerchief down over it. Sure enough there were two Pinkertons as they filed out the gate inspecting lunch pails. What they were concerned about was dynamite and caps.

Lester and other men drifted along the railroad tracks uncertain what to do. It was early to commence drinking but a number of them congregated at the Anvil. Janis told them what the bosses did was to play like they were negotiating with Dick Secour to his face while all the while behind his back they were fixing to lock them out.

Different fellows were of different casts of mind. For some it was like the schoolhouse burned down. It would be a holiday from toil. Others like Lester wondered how long it would continue and what the outcome would be, and if it was more than a week how they were going to eat.

He had a mug of beer with his work mates, then took a notion to catch some fish. He had seen two or three cane poles in the barn with line and bobbers wrapped around. He went and untangled them and it was three sound poles eight or nine feet long with screw eyes in the joints, and each with line tied to the fat end and run up through the eyes to the tip. What hung free was just long enough so you could hook the hook in the fat end. All three had sinkers and there were two cork bobbers.

He went in the tavern and in all the clamor when he was able to get Frank's attention, he asked if he might borrow a fishing pole. He said take all three. "Tomorrow is Friday, Lester. Go and catch us a whole mess."

He told him he would work on it, and went to the kitchen and got a wine cork for a bobber and two spares and some spoiled liver for bait. He found a coffee can in the trash and by turning over some rocks he got some worms, and taking all three rods he set out.

First he went to the point a quarter mile down from the ferry landing where the bank cut in and there was slack water with little whirlpools and sticks and trash and flecks of foam that you did not like to think just what it was.

He baited two lines with worms and one with liver and cast each with a swing of the pole and set the poles in forked sticks in the rip-rap. The sinkers were not heavy enough and the corks kept washing in too close. He ate his dinner from his dinner pail of a corn dodger and a chunk of sausage and watched the corks drift in, and when he surmised the hooks were dragging he went down and swung them out again.

After an hour and a half he lost patience and gathered up the rods. Instead of going back the way he came he went down the bank to a creek mouth with willows to either side and water had backed up and spread out on both sides to make an oblong pond of nearly an acre. The water was two and three feet deep along the sides where stout trees and brush grew and standing almost still so some of the mud had settled out, and he could see little waves and rings on the surface from fish.

He put fresh worms on all three hooks and cast out and almost at once one of the corks dove under and planed along. He pulled back and swung the rod so the fish was lifted out of the water, and it was a nice eating-size channel cat with a slender back and creamy flanks and the belly almost white. He left it on the hook and laying well up in the weeds, cut a sapling down to a fork for a stringer, and ran the pointed end up through the gill and out the mouth. In forty minutes he had a nice mess of a dozen and three bullheads.

When he showed up with them at the tavern kitchen, Hildegard the hired girl and the Missus made a fuss. "Bring us fish like that, Lester," she said, "and you can earn your keep."

He did not know if she was funning but it made him feel proud. As they hustled and bustled this way and that to serve the extra trade from the lime workers getting locked out of work, he found a corner out of the way and cleaned the fish himself taking care not to prick himself on the spines. And the girl opened the bottom compartment of the hotel-size icebox, and he laid them in a row along the ice.

When he went out front to have another beer, Little John told him Dick Secour was making the rounds of the taverns to say they must all come to the big union meeting that night at the Red Men's lodge.

THE RED MEN'S LODGE WAS ON THIRD STREET IN WHAT USED TO BE A BREW-
ery that was shut down with Prohibition. They sat on fold-up chairs among the brew vats
while Dick Secour talked to them from a fork-lift palette.

"Well, you know they acted like they was negotiating in good faith," he said, "while all
along they planned to lock us out before we had a chance to vote a strike. They jumped us
from behind thinking to catch us disorganized and split us up. Is their divide-and-conquer
tactics going to work?"

"No!" they shouted. It was loud and clear.

"You already know they are trying to take back our union shop. Are we going to let
them do that?"

"No!" they shouted.

"And they want us to take pay cuts of ten per cent...plus some niggling cuts in the dif-
ferential for firemen and dynamite-setters and for drillers. So it comes to more than ten per
cent."

He asked for a strike authorization vote. They discussed it back and forth. One man said
that maybe they had an advantage under the law to let it stand as a lockout. Others hooted
him down. Dick said either way, he had a stronger hand to play if he got their strike vote.

A fellow *from* Peerless called the question. There was a second, and they voted. It was
not unanimous. About two-thirds called, "Aye!" But one of the *noes* wanted a show of hands
and a count.

The secretary Ralph Grannaman counted and said, "Three hundred and sixty-three
aye, and seventy-eight *no.* The *ayes* have it!"

Oscar Kampf the business agent hollered, "All *right!*" and started to clap. Most of them
joined in clapping and standing up.

Dick Secour thanked them for their confidence, and their next order of business was
to organize what they had no better word for than to call it the strike. "The first thing is no
rough stuff. Don't get in fights. No vandalism. And that means watch your consumption of
alcohol. We get rowdy and they call in the law on a fight in the street or at the gates of one of
the plants, that is just what they want. They will provoke you. Give them the least excuse and
they will call in the National Guard.

"Watch your money. Don't spend half of it on alcohol....We don't know how long this is going to last...Now, we need pickets ...twenty-four hours a day seven days a week...and any back roads or trails into the quarries and kilns like at Bluff City, that old path in from White Sands road by Fallert's cave...the back way to Peerless by Lime Kiln road. They will try to sneak in scabs on us.

"What they are doing here locking us out is a lot like what old Jenkins done at Jenkins-Gillis--"

"And brung in niggers!" a man named Crowley said.

"What are we going to do about that?" another man asked. "The nigger quarry?"

"Not this evening, all right?"

Secour went on to appoint picket Captains for each company—Henry for Bluff City; for Peerless an older man, Clarence Theriot; and for Alton Lime and Western Lester did not catch their names.

THE GOVERNMENT TOLD THE LIME COMPANIES THE CLAIM THEY WENT out of business was a sham and threatened to sic a court order on them. So they made an offer that took back the closed shop and cut pay twelve and a half per cent across the board, and the men refused, and it was a strike.

Lester was in a strike once before and was not keen to be in one again. The first thing was you are bored. The job can be boring too, and hot and dangerous and wear you out and give you aches and pains. But you know you have to do it and it fills the time. In the strike even when you are busy doing something, you have in the back of your mind you are slacking. You blame yourself. He looked at his Grandpa's railroad watch at four o'clock and put it up. After he calculated an hour had passed he looked again, and it was twenty past. You eat, go on the picket line, come off, wait until you go on again or eat. Your bowel movement is a big event.

Then you worry about how you pay for what you eat. Frank and Emma Janis told him settle up when the strike was over, and his catching some fish from time to time helped out. But they were hurting too. More than half the paying jobs in town were from the lime works. The barbers ran a notice asking union men to support them and their union and not patronize unlicensed barbers during the strike, but a lot of the unlicensed barbers were wives and sweethearts or you cut your own hair. The movie theater was showing just on Saturday night and the Sunday matinee on account of the strike. The groceries let strikers' families run a bill, but still had to pay the jobbers who supplied them what they sold.

One day after Lester had brought in a mess of fish and was enjoying a draft of lager beer on the house, Hildegard was talking to the Missus about Charron's Market. They cut off credit to the men on strike but old Charron will make exception for a striker's family if they have a pretty daughter, or he fancies the wife and she gives him what he wants.

"What about the woman's husband?" Lester asked.

Hildegard said, "The woman is ashamed to tell."

IDLE HANDS ARE TOOLS OF THE DEVIL HIS GRANDMA USED TO SAY, AND IT was the truth for Clyde's married brother Leon. Off work on account of the strike the same as Lester and Little John and Walter and five hundred other fellows, he lost patience. He took it into his mind he could pull off a big-time bank heist. Little John said he bragged he maybe could get him in on it and asked who had Clyde's Bulldog Special.

Lester was out on a long ramble, taking his constitutional he called it, as he often did during the strike. He had gone along by Elder Shirtwaist and cut through the Old Cemetery to be sure Holt Hardy had not returned to lurk there and spy on Ethel, and he was walking down Merchant street when he saw a fellow with a bobtail shotgun come out of Rozier's bank and jump in this car that was already moving by the curb. And it roared up toward him and he scrunched over against the wall of the Catholic church, and it skidded on the gravel turning onto Fourth street and on past him so close he felt the wind, and went highballing on out of town.

Not a minute later here came the town marshal's own car that he had to drive himself on duty because the town was too cheap to buy a police car, and a fellow in a khaki shirt, Chief Deputy Ziegler, came running up with a rifle, and the marshal's car barely stopped and he jumped in, and they took out after the robbers.

SURE ENOUGH LEON GOT CAUGHT. FRANK JANIS SAID YOU COULD BLAME IT on his little wife who was one of the trash LaSource girls, only he already had done time in the penitentiary for stealing gold from dental offices. Lester had nothing better to do so he went along with Little John and Walter and Ralph to see him at the jail. But only Ralph was allowed in because he was family. They were waiting on the bench outside when Deputy Pappas came along and gave them a hard look.

Ralph was there perhaps three quarters of an hour and would not speak until they were a block away. He said they accused him of being in on the heist and tried to sweat him down. "They are transporting Clyde and Pyles up to City Jail at St. Louis with all the niggers because it is a Federal charge. He can get twenty years."

ONE THING LESTER DID TO PASS THE TIME WHEN HE WAS NOT ON THE picket line or fishing was to read in the books Ethel gave him to improve himself. They were Little Blue Books with paper covers but the ones she wanted him to read were two inches thick—*The Story of Mankind* by Hendrik van Loon which in parts was like *Ben Hur* at the picture show; and *The History of Philosophy* by Will Durant, and that was heavy going. One he could hardly put down was *The Jungle* by Mr. Upton Sinclair about a poor Finnish fellow in the Chicago stockyards, and he favored Mr. Jack London too, and a book on how religion was mostly hokum. Some she lent him and some she gave him as a gift and he was not sure which was which. She said they were put out by Mr. Haldeman-Julius and his wife in Girard, Kansas to educate the working man and woman, and some had sold half a million copies and they loaded them in freight cars at the printing plant. One of the big sellers was *Human Sexology* by Dr. Havelock Ellis, but she said he must read the others first and save that for dessert.

Lester's idea was that if he read all these books and improved himself, she would be sweet on him again and take him back.

One Sunday when her friend Mary Ann came to the Anvil seeking him out, his heart leapt up.

It was not as he hoped.

"A friend...." she said and stopped. She started over, "I am sent to tell you Holt Hardy is back."

They had sent her up to Lester's room and she was uneasy on account of that. She stood in the hall well back from his doorway as if she was afraid he would seize her and drag her in. When he came out to show her down the stairs, she said that is all and turned to hurry off. He followed her and asked after Ethel. She shook her head and skittered down the front way to the public room. Passing through, he felt people staring as if they thought he had made unwelcome advances. He caught up to her in the yard and blocked her way. "Look," he said, "I am only asking after Ethel's health."

"That is no concern of yours."

"Then why did she send you——?"

"She would do the same for anyone."

"I *am* concerned."

"She said you might be in danger."

"*She* is in danger. He will be tormenting her again."

"She does not need you to protect her anymore."

"What do *you* say, Mary Ann?"

She was startled that he recalled her name. She looked off down the hollow to the ferry landing as she spoke. "She said on no account to tell you this...but perhaps I am a better friend if I do."

Lester waited. He had an idea what it was.

"She is going to have your baby."

"Then we shall marry!"

"She says on no account. She has an aunt in Kansas City."

"No! I must see her...talk with her. *Please--*"

Mary Ann darted around him like a spooked horse. If he chased after her she would cry out.

ANOTHER WAY LESTER EARNED HIS KEEP IN THE STRIKE WAS TO ASSIST THE Missus and Hildegard with chores about the tavern and as they grew more used to him toting crates and clearing tables, they spoke more freely in his presence. The next afternoon when the Missus came in from the market, she said to Hildegard, "You will not believe what Edna just told me."

She took all her trade to Edna Okenfuss who was one of those who still carried her old customers while more and more of the merchants in town were cutting off credit to the families of men on strike. Hildegard stopped sloshing glasses in soapy water and was drying her hands.

"When I walked in," the Missus said, "she was talking to a woman--Louise...I will not tell her whole name--who lives out past Division Street. She would go to Charron's Market."

That was the only grocery north of the creek and it was mostly working people in that end of town, and a lot of the colored traded there too. It was a big store, half again as big as Okenfuss and Oberle's put together, or that new A & P in Festus. You heard Griswold put Bluff City money into it and was a silent partner, so it was a Company Store on the sly. They cut off credit to the families of men on strike after thirty days, just like the electric company.

She said the husband was out on strike and three little children at home. Louise' oldest daughter was married and lived with her husband on a farm out at Staabtown. "Her second oldest, Catherine is a very pretty girl but mentally slow. She lives at home."

He leaned his mop against the wall and rested his elbows on the bar.

"Sure enough Don Charron cut them off at the store after thirty days. Her husband Ed got temporary work with a contractor paving the Flat River highway. Catherine worked from time to time cleaning houses. Her oldest, Estelle, helped out all she could by bringing them tomatoes and squash and corn from her garden and meat when they butchered a hog ... But the day finally came when they had nothing to eat. The three little ones whimpered and fretted and went to bed hungry. Louise and Fred talked it over, and she decided she would go to Charron and beg.

"He asked after Catherine. She said she was about the same. Then he asked her what she wanted and when he seemed as if he would let her have it, she told him and he wrote it down and it was a long list. Then he said it would take him a while to get it all together, and she should send Catherine around to pick it up.

"So Catherine went to the market and came home with two big baskets of everything Louise asked for. She said Mr. Charron said next time they needed things, her mother should make a list and send Catherine over to pick the things up. Louise had a funny feeling but it passed. Why kill the goose that laid the golden egg?

"So it went on like that, Charron giving them credit, and Catherine taking the list of things they needed and going to pick them up ...Then one morning Catherine was sick at her stomach. She didn't have a cold or the grippe. She just threw up. And she acted sullen and sulky instead of her good-girl self. When it was time to go to the market again with the grocery list, she refused. She wouldn't tell why or make excuses. She just refused.

"Louise had an idea what the problem was but could not believe it. She called Estelle, and she came in from the farm to talk to Catherine....Well, I imagine you know by now what I am talking about."

They look askance at him as if to say shame on you too Lester Dodge for one of them who will use a woman so, as if they knew what Mary Ann had told him just the day before.

16.

THEY HAD BEEN OUT ELEVEN WEEKS WHEN THE TOWN WORTHIES AND LIME bosses started the meetings at the high school. The Mayor, a fellow named Paultier from the Chamber of Commerce, the old priest they called Father T., and the Colonel of the American Legion sat behind a long table up on the stage. Behind them was the Lions' Club band and spread out high on the wall above was an American flag big as a bed sheet, and to either side green dragons for the ball team. Lester and Little John and Walter were sitting in a row near the back. Henry said the meeting was to make them turn scab just you wait and see, and in the morning tell him about it.

After the band had played oompah music and some red-white-and-blue and World War tunes and the Ste. Genevieve Dragons fight song, the Mayor tinked on his water glass with a spoon and asked Father T. to lead them in prayer.

Then the President of the Chamber of Commerce Paultier got up and reported that at their regular meeting at the Knights of Columbus after an excellent supper served by the ladies how they talked about the strike at the lime plants and the hardships everybody was suffering, and they elected a committee to meet with the union men and then the lime company bosses and find out what is what and get this strike over with and the cash registers to ringing again. A number of people clapped and said *Amen*.

"So on Friday morning I went over to the Knights of Pythias Hall and met with Dick Secour here the President of Local 829 and the Business Agent Oscar Kampf, and a man from the District Office of the A. F. of L. international in St. Louis, a Mr. Femmer. And in the afternoon I met with Harry Spink the attorney for the lime companies. What it comes down to is the situation is about the same. The A. F. of L. international union wants their closed shop, and the lime companies ...they say they are whistling Dixie."

The ones who were clapping and saying Amen before grumbled and shook their heads and looked at each other.

Then it was Dick Secour's turn. He said, "I am going to remind you gentlemen of the history of our union here....We was granted our charter in April of last year. That May we called a general strike in the five lime plants for recognition and a closed shop. In two days four of the lime companies signed an agreement to recognize us and the closed shop. The fifth was Jenkins-Gillis. They shut down and claimed they were going out of business, and you all know the rest of that story and it will be the story at the other lime works if we lose this strike."

People in the crowd looked at each other in a different way. He did not need to spell it out. Lester imagined there were those who would say it in words to this effect *or we will go the way of the nigger quarry* and more and more of them will move up here from the cotton fields and this becomes a nigger town, like Hayti down in Pemiscot County or East St. Louis, Illinois. It was a strong thought.

"So we negotiated on pay and seniority at the other four companies," Secour said. "Bluff City Lime Company signed on June 1st. On June 8th Peerless White Lime Company signed the same contract. On June the 9th Alton Lime and Quarry Company signed. Western Lime Company signed the next day. The four contracts was identical.

"The average increase per man come to five cents an hour. The contracts put a limit on the hours a man can be required to work. The companies with one exception kept up their end of the contract, and so has Local 829. They also recognized our seniority rights, and until June of this year the relations between Bluff City, Western, and Alton with Local 829 has been the best.

"Last October Peerless Lime stopped paying the wage scale we agreed on. They took to paying boiler firemen as common labor at 50 cents per hour when scale is 60 cents. They classed drillers as common labor at 50 cents instead of 52-and-a-half cents. They started paying powder men 55 cents instead of the 60 cents we agreed on. When I went to talk about them welshing on the contract, they ordered me off their property.

"We called a strike. In one week they settled, and from last October until this last June, everything was hunky dory again. Then it come time to renew the contract, and they said *Oh, no, you can't have your closed shop no more.*

"They persuaded Alton and Bluff City and Western to go along with them. No closed shop. On June the 2nd we went on strike against Peerless, Alton Lime, Western, and Bluff City. Our organization is five hundred strong, and we will go back to work for Peerless, Alton and Western, and Bluff City when they agree to the closed shop...And nobody else is going to work one whit for the likes of them *until that day!"*

He looked around the auditorium and some of them commenced to clap and holler and then they were on their feet clapping and you can hear some *boos* from fellows that were sitting down. The auditorium was full and if you took the number of chairs in a row times the number of rows, that was 600 and more than half were standing up.

The Mayor tinked on his glass again and they settled down, and he recognized local trades-people one after another who stood up and said how they gave to the collections for the families of the men on strike and gave them credit at the store but they were losing money like water through a sieve and have growing debts themselves and are tapped out and it had to end, and whatever it takes they support the effort to end the strike one hundred per cent. Lester was thinking *now what does that mean?*

One man he recognized because he had purchased items at his store and he repeated his name *Don Charron*, the biggest store in town and the only one in the north end. He said his trade was almost entirely lime workers and poor people and colored, and he was next door to filing for bankruptcy. "A number of my customers work at Peerless Lime and some of them still had unpaid balances from their wildcat strike last fall." He said he carried them as long as he could but had to cut some of them off. "I am being sued by Monarch Brands for what I owe them. Vess Beverages will not deliver any more until I pay my balance with them. Since I expanded, my electric bill has doubled....Something has to give."

He would bring tears to your eyes except everybody knew he was the first to cut off credit in the strike. And if women talked among themselves as Lester imagined they did, some of them knew more than that.

Then a portly man from Rotary got up and he said a lot of businesses in this community were just days from going under. The President of the Savings and Loan said homes and farms were going to be foreclosed if the misguided fellows who signed on to this international outside union didn't wake up and get their lazy butts back to work. You can imagine what Lester and his friends thought of that, but there were others who hollered and clapped.

A few more trades-people got up and some of them who had gotten up before got up again, and they declared that fellows who came to their senses and signed the pledge cards might keep on running a tab and even in some cases they might forgive a family's debt. The hard-heads of course would remain shut off. The one who said it first was Charron. The pledge card started off, *"I herewith and hereby sever any connection whatsoever with Local 829..."* That is all that Lester read before he tore his in half.

Little John did the same, and Walter folded his into a glider and flew it out over two rows ahead until it hit a fellow who was talking scab in the back of the neck.

ONE EVENING WHEN HE CAME INTO THE PUBLIC ROOM THROUGH THE kitchen from cleaning a mess of fish out back, who should he see in the Anvil but Jack O'Hare—the man who passed him the CIO handbill that was the cause of his discharge from Crystal City Glass. He was at a table by the wall with Emma Janis and a pretty girl, their heads close together and talking low as if they were deciding where to plant a bomb and he was not about to interrupt. But just as he had settled at the bar and Hilde had drawn him a beer on account of the fish, O'Hare called out, "Lester Dodge! Just the man I am looking for."

He sidled over to them and O'Hare shook his hand and introduced the pretty girl with dark eyes as his sister Madeleine. At Crystal City Jack was a journeyman in the machine shop where Lester was the apprentice and acted like a big brother to him. He guessed he was thirty-five years old and was medium size with stick-out ears and wore wire-rim glasses. He told Lester once that his mother was Red Kate O'Hare who went to prison for making a speech against the World War, and she and his papa ran a workingmen's newspaper in St. Louis called the *Rip-Saw*. They insisted he must fetch his beer over and join them.

Jack told the story of how Lester was discharged for the handbill and he blamed himself, but he ought to have known the company kept a rat watching the toilet stall at all times. And Lester said how he owed the roof over his head to the mention of Jack's name, and the Missus said that was the truth.

Jack also had gotten the boot from Crystal City and now he was a paid organizer for the CIO. He asked Lester what he thought of the discharge of all the colored men. He said it was in the *Labor Tribune* and Emma was filling him in.

"I told him how you brought the man you worked with here… and you and your boys drank with him in the yard."

"Otis. Otis Bouchard. … He was let go for backing me against a crazy man."

"What do you think of that?"

"It was unjust."

"Who is to blame?"

"The lime companies."

"The A F of L does not allow colored."

"Local 829 never wrote 'colored' by their names … It was Otis backing me against Holt Hardy that spoiled it. He went and complained."

"You take that lying down?"

"I went to Bondurant. … We took up a collection."

"What good did that do?"

He thought on Otis the last he had seen him. "Not much."

"Did you know you *can* do something about it."

Now he knew where this was going. "You are paid by CIO."

"I told you that right off."

"Fellows here don't care for it."

"Why not?"

"'C. I. O. … Colored Included … heigh ho.' It's what they say."

"Who benefits from that?"

"The son-of-a-bitch lime companies … Beg pardon," he said to Jack's sister who followed with her eyes but did not say one word. She had a big school tablet on her lap and the paper did not have lines and she was drawing in it.

"Why are you on strike, Lester?"

"…Because…Mainly because they want to take back the union shop."

"And what makes them think they can get away with that?"

"It is hard times. More fellows out of work than jobs to go around."

"How does what you call 'the nigger quarry' figure into that?"

"It is Jenkins-Gillis to me."

"They hold it over your head. If you don't toe the line, they will do what Jenkins did."

"Over our dead bodies."

"When it comes to talk like that, the companies will call in the tin soldiers."

The Missus said, "You see what Jack is driving at?"

"…C. I. O."

"So long as the lime companies can hire colored men for half the pay, why should they pay union scale to you…? The *colored excluded* from your union is the companies' ace in the hole."

Lester said, "I thought Frank was paid-up Local 829."

Emma said, "He has an open mind."

"The answer is a union the colored men can join," Jack said. "Then you have got *solidarity.*"

Lester took his point.

"You know what happened in Flat River in the World War?"

"My uncle Douglas was one of them laid off because he was subject to the draft."

The American miners rounded up all the immigrants the lead companies brought in to bust the union and put them on the next train out of town with one-way tickets.

"And East St. Louis?"

"I have heard it spoken of." Lester's mother was visiting her cousins just across the river and she said you could see the red sky over East St. Louis from the fires the white people set in the tenements to smoke the colored out. Then they shot them.

Jack did not have to spell it out for him but he did—how many were killed, left homeless, how they were fleeing for their lives all night long over the Eads Bridge to the Missouri side. "And you know what caused it?" he asked.

Lester had a general ideal. It was a long strike in the stockyards and people saying it was unpatriotic.

"Mayrose brought in colored to break the strike."

All three of them looked at him—Jack, the Missus, and Madeleine, who was drawing something on her tablet.

"Lester, what you have got here is a time-bomb."

He bowed his head like it was his fault.

Jack's sister Madeleine tore the page out of her tablet and handed it to him. It was his picture, and a fair likeness. "Would you like to have that?" she asked.

He was tickled pink. He said if he was not on the outs with his jo, he would give it to her to make her think he was handsome.

"There is one thing you could do for us," Jack O'Hare said.

Lester cocked his head.

He gave him a card with blanks for your name and to sign it. "That is for the United Mine Workers," he said. "I just want you to think about it."

THEY HAD ANOTHER MEETING AT THE HIGH SCHOOL AND THEN ANOTHER and tried to make it a regular thing night after night like a revival to shame you and twist your arm to surrender your life to Jesus, only this was to make them all turn scab and sign the pledge cards. Lester and Little John went again one night they said as a lark but also to spy on who else came and see if any fellows they knew crumpled and signed the card. Most men do not want you on any account to know of course if they did sign, except the braggart anti-union men like Bucholz and Ralph.

The bunch up on the stage beneath the flag big as a bed sheet was pretty much the same as before—the Mayor and Leonard Paultier of the Chamber of Commerce, the old priest Father T, the American Legion Colonel Ed Kiefer—except that there was one fellow in a seersucker suit. Lester concluded he was the professor from the Jesuits' college at St. Louis that the posters around town said would give a talk about the new law for labor unions.

The band played their oompah music and World War songs and the Dragons fight song like before, but this time they mixed in some old wheezy old come-to-Jesus hymn tunes. After the music stopped and the old priest gave the invocation, the Mayor tinked his glass again. He wanted to thank Len Paultier for the tireless efforts of his Back-to-Work Committee on behalf of the whole community and for organizing these fine meetings with so many in attendance. He started to clap and people here and there joined in the round of applause, while Lester and his mates booed and heckled.

Then Paultier got up and said, "It is my great pleasure to introduce to you our special guest for tonight, The Reverend Doctor Alphonse Eberle who is Dean of the Business School of St. Louis University. He will talk to you about your rights under the so-called Wagner Act. He is a famous authority on this subject and will enlighten you on the facts, and dispel the misinformation and propaganda that has been coming to you from outside agents of the A. F. of L. and CIO unions ... Please welcome Dr. Alphonse Eberle...!"

The crowd that was against Lester and his friends hollered and clapped.

The professor was like a weasel with sharp little eyes and slicked-back hair. He got up in his seersucker suit and vest and nodded and grinned and raised his hands and grinned some more. "Thank you, Leonard," he said, "and Mayor Schwendt, and Father Van Tourenhaut, and all of you good people of Ste. Genevieve who have come out to this meeting tonight.

"I am simply going to give you some facts about the law passed recently by the United States Congress known as the Wagner Act. It is not in any sense to give professional labor unions an exclusive right to represent you. Let me repeat that...*The law does not say that only professional unions like the A F of L and CIO have the right to represent you.*

"It applies just the same to worker-managed independent unions. Any propaganda you hear that contradicts that is false ...You have the right and it is guaranteed by this law to form your own independent local union without any tie whatsoever to a national or international organization.

"The National Labor Relations Board or NLRB has been swamped with complain'ts based on misunderstandings and deliberate misinformation from the professional labor organizations such as the A. F. of L. and the Communist Industrial Organization or CIO. ... *It will take months ... years ... for every complain't to be acted upon....*"

He let that sink in, then reminded them, "Nothing prohibits you from forming your own independent union." He answered some questions from the anti-union crowd and people up on the stage, thanks them for inviting him, and sat down.

The snake oil he would sell them was company unions.

Paultier came to the edge of the stage and held up a fistful of the little cardboard pledge cards and peeled one out and started to read what it said:

> "I herewith and hereby sever any and all con-
> nections with the International Hod Carriers
> and Common Laborers Union of America Local

> Number 829, and in my own behalf propose to my
> employer that it open its plants and that my future
> employment be on the following terms...

Lester and his mates commenced to boo and holler and more and more of them stood up and they walked out.

THE CIO MINE WORKERS CARD WAS DIFFERENT FROM THE BACK-TO-WORK card, but the idea of signing it was shameful to Lester all the same. He would be ratting out on his friends when what they all must do was hang together in their solidarity in the union they had and win the strike.

He did allow himself to be persuaded to take Jack O'Hare and his sister to the joint in the old Creamery across the tracks where the colored men went to drink. He felt somewhat obliged for the picture of him that she drew, and she came along with her tablet.

Lester recognized an older man, solid, barrel-chested, with big shoulders and arms. He was Zeno, one of the Ribeau brothers where the boy Cletus stayed and he was Cletus' supervisor. He recalled Lester. He was courteous, even friendly, but cynical, the way a lot of colored people were in Lester's opinion and he did not blame them. They were still working at the non-union quarry, but they well knew at half the pay the white men were striking to keep.

Jack was respectful with him and round-about. After a while he had him talking about what he wanted him to talk about. "I been working seventeen years in the lime plants since I returned from the World War. Union come in, sign up mens, go on strike, company bust the union. In a while a new union come along or that same union try again. Mostly they A. F. of L. unions, no colored allowed."

Jack talked up the CIO, how they are for everyone, how they extend the brotherly hand of Solidarity not just to the white race but for one and all, to the *human* race. He told of the Guide Lamp sit-down strike that forced General Motors to recognize the United Auto Workers, how John L. Lewis defied the National Guard.

"Not here," Zeno said. "Go up to St. Louis...Chicago."

"What if you have a grievance?"

"Say you a 'malcontent.' You fired." He told how the other lime companies recognized Local 829 but Jenkins-Gillis shut down. "Old Man Jenkins say he going out of business before he allow a combination of working mens organized by outside agitators to dictate to him how much he pay, who he hire, when he fire, and diddly squat....Then he open up again with turned-off croppers from down South."

"You know that is a violation of the Wagner Act?"

"Tell that to old Jenkins. Now we the nigger quarry. He making money hand over fist."

"Is that right?"

"I telling you the truth."

"I mean is it *right?*"

"That how it be."

"What if you sign the card for C. I. O. United Mine Workers, get John L. Lewis to go to bat for you?"

"Old Man Jenkins call out the American Legions…or he shut down for real, take all that money, buy him a race horse."

"That's fatalism."

"Call it what you want. I has to buy groceries….No call for me to sign a card for the C. I. O. I be making union scale my own self. Don't be right but it the truth."

All this time Jack was occupied with talking to Zeno Ribeau, but Madeleine was sketching him. When Zeno saw what she had done, he was touched. He took it, and she gave him a UMW card.

THEY WENT TO YET ANOTHER MEETING TO WATCH OUT FOR FELLOWS WHO might lose their sand and sign, and to shame or if need be perhaps to intimidate them out of it. This time the special treat was the old priest giving them the benefit of the sermon he preached this last Sunday on the strike.

He came out from behind the table to the edge of the stage and talked like he really was your kind old papa and you are his boy that needs his guidance. "I hope I can announce from the pulpit next Sunday," he said, "that the strike has been settled and the lime kilns are operating again."

He told how he had met with Dick Secour and Ralph Granaman for the union and then with Mr. Spink who was the attorney for the lime companies, and Mr. Spink assured him they would not lower wages or retaliate against anyone. "The companies do not want to break the union," he said. "They invested millions of dollars here. They are losing money and customers. What a calamity it would be if our lime kilns shut down! All they want is the right to run their own business, and who can blame them for that?

"They are losing money and going into debt. You are losing money and going into debt.

You are running up a bill at the grocery store. You owe your landlord....How many months have you been unable to make the rent? Or if you are so fortunate as to be buying your own little home, you have missed mortgage payments. You are taking advantage of the patience of Mr. Rozier and his bank. But even that kindly and forgiving gentleman will be pressed in turn by *his* creditors, and he will have no choice but to foreclose. And all you have scrimped and saved for over many years will be lost. *Everyone* in our community is losing money, and many are sinking under the crushing load of debt.

"In the *Our Father* in English our Methodist brethren say not *Forgive us our trespasses* or *mea culpa* but *Forgive us our debts.* We falter and are dragged down by our debts, just as we are dragged down by our burden of sin and guilt. Sin and Debt. As only Our Savior can redeem us of the one in the hope of Everlasting Life, the other must be paid from the wages of honest work.

"You are not only hurting yourselves and the lime companies. You are hurting the honest storekeepers and professional men who have been so generous in extending you credit.... You are hurting your wives and little children.

"Our Holy Father teaches us to respect the dignity of work. You have our moral support. Our hearts go out to you. We understand and sympathize with your struggle for what you feel... *or have been led to believe...*is your right.

"But the time comes when you must pay attention to the cost of your strike for others. The time has come for you to take the hand we reach out to you in the spirit of Our Savior. *Do not insist on exaggerated small differences.* The time has come for you to submit.

"In the name of Our Holy Father and our dear Savior and Our Blessed Virgin, *Amen!*"

What stuck in Lester's craw was *exaggerated small differences* as if their union shop was a small difference. Take that away and they were all the same as at Jenkins-Gillis.

The Mayor thanked the old priest—the old union buster with a backwards collar—and said he hopes those who have ears to hear will ponder his words in our hearts. Then he called on Paultier for the report of the Back-to-Work committee.

Paultier got up and started reading off the names of the lime companies one by one and how many of the men he claimed had signed the pledge cards, and he took packets of cards out of his pockets and shoved them in the faces of the union men. "Peerless Lime, fifty-one cards. That is thirty-seven per cent...Western Lime, thirty-two cards. That is--"

"Scabs!" one fellow shouted. Others joined in and they shouted him down. *"Scabs! . . . Scabs! . . . Scabs! . . . Get the scabs! . . . Get the scabs ! . . ."*

Three or four men jumped up on the stage, and right in front of the Mayor and the Priest and the oompah band they grabbed Paultier and dragged him down and out on the floor.

A whole bunch of fellows slapped him a few times and took all the cards from his pockets. People were yelling and screaming for the Sheriff and the police and rushing out the doors.

Lester and the staunch union men bunched together up front more than a hundred of them and they were together and nobody trying to stop them. When they were satisfied they for sure broke up that meeting, they walked all together out the wide auditorium doors and up the street. They did not need anybody to holler hup-two-three-four. They were in a strong line like soldiers four abreast, the rank and file of Local 829 and without thinking mostly in step. They were marching. Lester glowed with pride. He was thinking: *Now this is Solidarity.*

They marched on up Fourth and across the North Fork—that was up out of its banks— to LaHaye Street and the Red Men's lodge in the old brewery that was their unofficial strike headquarters now because you could not cram them all into the regular union hall.

They heard rumors back and forth about how the bosses would get an injunction against them or call in the tin soldiers but nothing much happened and they did not have any more meetings for several days, and by then all anybody was thinking about was the flood.

17.

MOST YEARS THE RIVER ROSE IN THE SPRING, FLOODING THE LOW END OF the Big Field and some duck hunting clubs up at Establishment Creek. This year it did that but had scarcely gone back down at all by the end of July. Gabouri Creek stayed backed up to just under the bridges on the North Fork and South Fork. The old town lay between the forks, almost all of the stores and businesses and old French houses. The Ribeaus' house, Leola Amoreaux, and Green Tree Tavern were just south of the South Fork on the St. Mary road.

By the last week in August water was up over the bottoms from the ferry to the railroad embankment. Floods were not supposed to come in August, but you tell that to the river. Those who had electricity listened on the radio. The reports said a big flood was coming down from Davenport Iowa, Hannibal, St. Louis, down from Omaha, Nebraska, St. Joseph, Kansas City too, the biggest flood in twenty, fifty years, then they were saying a *100-year flood.*

Cap Ribeau was the mail man, going from here to there in town and out on his rural route. He drove and walked the streets carrying mail to people. Everywhere on poles and posts and tree trunks was green tape for how high the water would come if the levee broke.

Up in the north end of town people were ordered to evacuate. Main Street was closed off at the North Fork. He drove over the Third Street bridge, taking mail to houses on the high ground. He went to the V.F.W. hall where they were filling sandbags in the parking lot on the edge of the bluff that looked across the expanse of water that covered the bottoms to the bluffs on the Illinois side. Evacuated people were staying there. Cap called out like mail call in the Army when he was the mail clerk, "Johnson, Veronica."

A white woman who was trying to keep her two whiny little boys amused with filling sandbags said, "That's me."

He gave her the mail, two bills and a return-to-sender from her ex-husband who was dodging his child support.

"What you doing here, Mrs. Johnson?" Cap asked, funning to cheer her up. "I thought you stay up on North Main."

"Wrong side of the tracks," she said.

"Got you two good helpers."

"They get cranky."

The boys were supposed to hold the bag open so she could shovel in the lime screenings. They had plenty of that from the lime companies, instead of sand. When the bag was full the bigger boy was supposed to tie it shut but she had to tie it over again.

At night Cap and Lon and Zeno took turns on the patrol. With Leola and the Brooks and Leo Geisler and Hector St. Gemme from the Green Tree, they kept up the levee on the South Fork from Seraphin Street to the train track. Neighbors on the St. Mary Road patrolled there too. If they saw a sand boil or a leak, they plugged it.

Cap patrolled with Otis Bouchard. Their levee was forty-six feet high that night. He shined a flashlight down on the creek side. You could see the water creep up. He shined it out toward the river, just stinking water and the tops of cottonwood and pecan trees.

Irene Bouchard came with sandwiches and a thermos of coffee, insisted he eat. "I don't know if I be helping much," she said. "Can't think on nothing else. Can't sleep."

They watched a mattress float by low down in the water like a drowned person.

Cap walked the levee in the moonlight, with a fog ring around the moon. He walked on the railroad embankment that was what the levee there consisted of--sometimes walking on the ties, sometimes along one side, sometimes on the other. Where the ballast rocks came just to the tops of the ties was the best. Now and then he walked the rail to see how many steps he could take and keep his balance. He would get to a hundred, once to more than five hundred. But he quit, thinking somebody would come along and see him acting childish.

Down by the depot most of the cribs and shacks toward the river from the embankment were flooded to the eaves. At Mabel Detchmendy's joint they had built up their own wall in a u-shape to the levee with Mabel and some whores and bar flies filling sandbags, the sports piling them up.

People tried to protect their own houses, piled sandbags around them, stayed up all night watching. A LaHaye Street a young white boy in thick eyeglasses was walking round and round his house by the sandbags. Cap asked him, "How you doing, young soldier?"

He said, "I wish this never happened."

"I hear you."

"I'd rather be reading my book."

"What book?"

"*Twenty-Thousand Leagues Under the Sea.*"

"Jules Verne," Cap said.

"How do you know that?"

"*The World Book.*..I read in *The World Book.*"

"We take turns," the boy said. "Grandpa's asleep."

Cap came to a large woman named Sue at her little house by the levee and sandbags on the North Fork, with water up six feet above the yard. She was watching a row of electric pumps with hoses up from the basement over the wall sucking the water out. She said if the pumps went, the mud and horsehair bousilage in the walls would crumble and that old posts-in-the-ground house just fall apart.

Her young daughter came out with barbecue and coffee cake.

"We just eat to pass the time," Sue said.

They offered Cap some. He said thank you, he just ate a sandwich. She was heavy woman, and the girl was going to be.

"I don't know whether to play double solitaire with Rose, or catch some sleep."

"You and the girl go sleep," Cap said. "I watch."

They went in the house. He sat up on top of the sandbags watching the brown water inch up, turning a flashlight on it now and then. Clouds came sneaking and swelling and blotted out the moon. Raindrops fell, lightning flashed off a ways to the northwest, then came distant thunder over the hum of the pumps.

Sue came out again. "Too scared to sleep," she said. She was eating a piece of coffee cake.

NEXT MORNING CAP WENT OUT ON HIS ROUTE SOUTH ON THE ST. MARY road. Houses on the bluff side were still dry, but everything out on the river side of the road on the Grand Champ was flooded. A johnboat came across the field past the tops of the pecan trees along Aux Vasse creek and on past a barn roof and a silo. It came put-putting up beside the road, an old man in the middle with a suitcase by him and in front a pig. The younger fellow in back running the outboard motor called and waved his arm.

Cap leaned out the window of his mail truck.

"Say, can you help us out?"

His name was Adam and Mr. Biggs was his father-in-law. He wanted Cap to take old Biggs and the pig into town so he could go back and fetch the other pig and a cow and her calf.

"All in that tippy little boat?" Cap said.

"Just the pig and calf," he said. "Her mama will swim after."

Cap said he was not supposed to interrupt U.S. Mail delivery, but with people flooded out his route was not taking so long. Cap was thinking why not take that boat on as far as the Gabouri bridge? Adam said he would but it would take too long and he was worried about the other animals, with water up to the calf's chin and her mama bawling. Cap said he would take Mr. Biggs but not the pig.

The old man said, "Hoover is my friend. He will follow me like a dog."

"That pig shit on the U.S. Mail, I lose my job."

As Cap was driving Biggs into town, the old man hollered. Cap looked in the rear view mirror and saw the pig. He slowed down, and Hoover trotted along behind.

Cap left the pig at his own place with Lon, and drove on by the Fourth Street bridge over the South Fork into town thinking to take old Biggs up to the VFW where Veronica Johnson and the others evacuated from North Main street were staying. As they were passing by the Valle high school yard where a hundred people were toiling to fill sandbags, Biggs said *stop*. "What's all that State Police?"

Two State Police cars and a black Packard limousine were parked by the Catholic Church on Merchant street across from the Valle school yard that was called the Desert because it was it was covered with macadam and had no trees. Up on the schoolhouse back steps was Vern Schwendt the Mayor in a tin hat like the men had to wear in the quarries. Beside him was a man in a straw hat and a bow tie. Old Biggs wanted Cap to stop.

So they sat there and listened. Sister Josephine the principal of the high school introduced the man in a bow tie, their Congressman Banjo Curtis from Herculaneum. A microphone was set up between him and the Mayor, and what they said came out on the public address. The Congressman told everyone what a brave effort the people of Ste. Genevieve were making and all the volunteers and soldiers and yes the prisoners from the county jail and from the Potosi Correctional Facility, all of them, women and men, white and colored, young and old, and so on. He said it was just inspiring to all America and all the world how the people of Ste. Genevieve and all the towns up and down on the river in the Third Congressional District carried on their brave fight against the flood, and be sure to vote Democratic in the August primary. Vote for him because he loved them all and fought for them tooth and nail in the halls of the U.S. Congress.

Vern the Mayor said thank you Mr. Congressman and we sure could use some government money, and what about that promise of a U.S. Corps of Engineers forty-foot levee the Senators welshed on. "This town goes back two hundred years to the time of the Frenchmen. We are having our Bicentennial Pageant and President Roosevelt spoke to us on the radio. We are the oldest town in Missouri. We have got to save the old buildings..."

He had to stop. Tears ran down his face. He was not a Holy Roller or some kind of Praise-Jesus Baptist, as if he were crying for joy because of the holy spirit. He was just a grown man crying. People up by him looked at each other then away, embarrassed.

The Congressman said yes, well, he can't help the Senators. His friends in the House of Representatives passed it, and they all were doing a wonderful job and god bless you, and he raised up his arms like he expected everyone to holler and cheer for him.

A few here and there clapped their hands a time or two to be polite. Mainly they went on filling sandbags and ignored him.

NORTHERNMOST ON CAP'S ROUTE WAS SULPHUR SPRING TWO MILES BACK in off the highway, houses on the terrace in the gap where the river ran smack against the bluff. He came to where to turn in, then saw the sign:

ROAD

CLOSED

The regular road wound along the bottom by the creek. The creek was flooded from one side of the hollow to the other, wide as two ball fields.

He saw four john-boats pulled up and chained to stout trees, and on the other side of the highway in the church parking some old cars and trucks. But it was not Sunday or Bible study or choir practice. He saw them parked there and the boats.

He drove on a quarter-mile to where a steep gravel road climbed up to the top of the hollow and ran along the edge way above the creek. That was the back road. He turned in past a sign:

FLOWER

HILL

FARM

St. Louis people named Pflager had owned it, the man an inventor and philanthropist. In the Twenty-Seven flood, Sulphur Spring people were welcome to use the road. Cap wound on up in first gear. Then coming near the high ground that ran mostly flat, he shifted to second. Tall trees closed on both sides of the gravel road, oaks, hickories, gum and beech.

As Cap came around a turn he saw a gate, and a man in khaki pants and shirt with a gun on his belt. The gate consisted of a white pole, and counter-weight on the short end of the post with a pin through it. The man raised his hand commanding him to stop.

Any fool could see this was a mail truck. Cap leaned out the window and snapped, "U.S. Mail!"

The man came up beside him puffing up like a pigeon. "This here's a private road," he said. "You are trespassing."

"I am delivering the U.S. Mail."

"To Flower Hill Farm...Mrs. Wells Gladney?"

"Sulphur Spring."

The guard shook his head.

"Twenty-eight families here...on my route."

"Use a boat."

He turned off the motor. He stared straight ahead out the windshield. He would not curse this jackass. He would not pull the revolver from under the seat that he was not supposed to carry—because he would rather be fired than dead.

"What is wrong with you?" the stupid man asked.

"You interfering with delivery of United States Mail."

"If the mail ain't for Flower Hill Farm sanitorium or Mrs. Gladney, you're trespassing."

Cap looked at him, a red faced white man with his gut hanging over his belt and mean eyes. He asked, "To whom am I speaking?"

"The Law."

Cap looked out the windshield. He could say *What law?* He could say *You let me pass or you committed a Federal Offense, U.S. Attorney Dowd 8th District St. Louis get you indicted,*

Judge send you to Leavenworth Penitentiary, and just you see if I be lying.

"You simple-minded?" the stupid man asked. "You understand English?"

Cap stared out the windshield.

"Now turn this truck around and get your cotton-picking ass off Mrs. Gladney's property...That's an order."

Cap started the motor. He could whip the truck to the left, knock the guard down, run him over two, three times, and roll him off the edge to the hollow into the swollen creek. He would float on through the gap out into the river, and the flood would hustle him along past Memphis, New Orleans, to the Gulf of Mexico for the fish to pick his bones.

Or he could pull the pistol from under the seat, and pop a hole in his forehead while he was still grabbing at his belt.

He turned the truck not quick as he could but as if he misjudged, and the man had to jump to get out of the way.

"Hey!" he hollered.

While Cap was backing up to finish turning because the road was too narrow to make a U-turn, the man moved in front of the truck, his hand on his gun, then came around to the driver's side again. Cap pulled his revolver, tucked it tight under his leg in his right hand, and rested his left hand on the steering wheel.

"I could run you in for that."

Cap looked out the windshield, took a breath, and tried to say it matter-of-fact, "Tomorrow you be talking to a United States Marshal."

The window by Cap's arm was still open, the guard's

red hand with sores from some kind of skin disease holding on to the door by the window frame. Cap had an impulse to roll up the glass so he would have to snatch back or get some fingers smashed. But that would be childish. Cap waited. The man gaped at him with his mouth half-open at the astonishing idea that this Negro mail man might be telling the truth, and the scrofulous hand was removed.

Cap acted calm. If he hollered and got all righteous, the man would think he was bluffing. Maybe he was.

The guard stepped back. Cap let the clutch out. He drove on slow in second gear, taking his time. Going down the steep part he shifted to first and let the engine brake.

Down at the highway he pulled over. He was shaking, breathing funny. He was not scared of the stupid white man. He was scared of *what he almost did himself.*

A JOHN-BOAT CAME UP THE CREEK WITH ONE MAN IN IT, TOWING ANOTHER john-boat with two old women and an old man. The man in the first boat ran it up the bank, got out, and chained it to a sycamore tree. Then he pulled on the rope and the old man pushing on a pole helped get the other boat up the bank, and they chained it to another tree.

The first man—Cap knew him—was Gary Price. He stepped down in the water to help the old man he called Bo disembark. Then Gary and old Bo helped the first woman who was Bo's wife Helen Taubold get out. They pulled some more on the boat so almost all of it was out of the water, and helped the other woman—her mother Mae Sago, who was ninety years old. They all were colored, Gary Price white.

Old Mae had a bandage around her head.

They were going across the highway to Bo's truck in the church lot to drive her to the doctor so he could take the stitches out. Cap followed along, watching out for cars on the highway.

"Mama suppose to have her stitches out last Friday," Helen said. "I try to do it myself, but my sight is weak. The stitches just too small."

"We going to come in our boat," Bo said. "Then the motor don't start...Gary here very kindly offer to help us out."

"Ain't nothing, Mr. Taubold," Gary said. "I was on my way to work." He worked at Brickey's coal dock, but the swing shift didn't start until five o'clock.

They helped old Mae up to the cab in Bo's truck, and Helen got in beside her. Bo went around and climbed in the other side. Cap came around beside him. He said "You know about the road?"

"I know now."

"Mr. Pflager sell the place to that Catch Wells woman. She rich from Seven-Up, run a sanitarium up there for rich peoples from St. Louis to dry out. The sight of us raggedy-ass poor peoples might drive them to drinking again."

"Hoosier say he the Law, run me off."

"Oh, he the law. He a deputy. Sheriff in this county look out for the rich peoples."

Sulphur Creek was the county line.

Bo started the motor, and drove out on the highway going to the doctor in Festus.

Gary said he brought his car out the last day the road was passable, and drove on to work. When he came back after his shift at two o'clock in the morning, the regular road in to Sulphur Spring was flooded and the road closed off. He went walking up the high road and came to the gate. The Deputy told him he can't come that way. He walked back down to the highway and waded a mile and a half to get home in water to his belt and in some places up to his arm pits. He said old Bo had to do the same thing when he drove his truck the last time to take Mae to the doctor. He had to leave her and Helen in the truck, wade in by himself, and get his boat to fetch them.

Gary told Cap he could use his boat, and when he was done chain it to the tree with one of his padlocks for mailbags. It was like neighbors did all on the same road when they wanted to keep a common gate locked. Each one had his own lock hitched in the chain, his own key, any one of them could open and lock it up again. Two other locks were on the chain with Gary's. Not all of the people in Sulphur Spring had a good boat. They shared.

"If you want to kick in some gas," Gary said, "it's a quart of oil to a gallon of gas. Just pour the oil in the gas tank."

Cap said if his if his postmaster didn't authorize it, he would will bring his siphon hose. The Postmaster was fair-minded for a white man but scared of the rules and regulations.

WEDNESDAY THE *FAIR PLAY* HAD A STORY AND LETTERS ABOUT THE SUL-phur Spring people and *Madame* Catch Wells Gladney, how her sister Luciana owned the St. Gemme-Beauvais house everybody was pitching in to save, and Catch Wells herself was one of the Colonial Dames with Mrs. Griswold and they were begging everybody to save the Bolduc house by the South Fork. They were rich because their daddy invented Seven Up, and Mrs. Catch Wells Gladney was a benefactress of the St. Louis Symphony Orchestra. Some-times her husband gave them an extra big hunk of money to let her wave the baton for a night.

One letter was from *Anonymous*. It said when Mrs. Gladney wanted to save her Colo-nial Dames' old French house, she was happy to let working people hump sandbags. But if they came to use her back road, she didn't like how they smelled.

18.

MR. ROZIER WANTED LON TO DRIVE WHERE PEOPLE NEEDED HELP, DRIVE them to get groceries, the doctor. He said he wished he could fill sandbags. He gave money to the flood relief and donuts for the patrol. His bank would give people loans at one per cent for fixing their houses when the flood went down.

He liked talking to Lon when he drove him because he knew how to listen to a white man. "The flood is a calamity," he said, "but it brings us together."

"Yes, sir." Lon said *yes, sir* or *um-hmm* or *that's a fact* or *I hear you* to whatever Mr. Rozier said, just about. If he begged to differ or changed the subject, Mr. Rozier did not get mad, just confused. Lon studied to listen, show he was paying attention. As the old gentleman's chauffeur, he considered it part of his job.

"You see people from all walks of life down there in the school-yard filling sandbags, out on the levee passing them along. Father T. himself goes down there two hours every evening, and he must be seventy years old. Sister Josephine pitches in...You see the transient Colored from Smoketown...the lime workers on strike. You see high school boys and girls and little children...And wasn't it a shame that Valle high school girl who fell off a truck and died? Ken Oberle and Joe Schappenkotter and Odalie Papin, the shopkeepers, Ernie Kohl the barber, the National Guard boys---God bless them, from Festus, Flat River, DeSoto, even convicts from Potosi and inmates from the county jail, all together now, to save us from the flood. There is a famous German poem that Ludwig van Beethoven set to music in the last movement of his Ninth Symphony. You know who Beethoven was, Lon?"

"Yes, sir. A musical composer." His brother Cap read in his *World Book Encyclopedia* and he read on all manner of things, and told Lon and Zeno more than they wanted to know.

"Have you ever heard Beethoven?"

"I don't believe so, sir. We don't have electric but Zeno got us a wind-up Victrola, plays his records...Blind Lemon Jefferson, Howling Wolf...music of that nature."

"Beethoven is sublime. It goes like this..." Mr. Rozier whistled a tune, then he sang in his old-man's voice,

All men become brothers
Where thy gentle wings . . .

"'Where thy gentle wings...' 'Gentle wings' something..." He whistled the tune again.

"Brings tears to my eyes, like the World War...of course that was against the Germans."

Lon hazarded a thought of his own. "Mr. Rozier," he said, "suppose it be in the war time, you suppose the Germans and us fight the flood together?"

"Why, I don't know, Lon. That's an interesting question."

"With all that poison gas...and the U-boats."

"I imagine some of Kaiser Bill's Germans would, and some wouldn't."

"Yes, sir."

"...And the volunteers," he said. He did not like you to change the subject. "The volunteers from St. Louis, and Rolla, those school teachers from Atlanta who heard about us on the radio, the firemen from Ohio because they had a bad flood on the river through their town, the Scioto River. Rich and poor, male and female...Wets and Drys...I cannot think of one group of people that has not pitched in. I just wish we could pull together like this all the time..."

"Umm-hmmn."

"What's that?"

"Yes, sir!"

He wanted Lon to drive to St. Mary road, stop at Ribeaus, and see the cow and calf and Hoover the pig. He had to get out, walk with his cane to the muddy yard, reach through the fence, and scratch the kinky brown hair on Hoover's back. The pig rubbed himself on the post and like a cat purring but a pig sound back down his throat *gldh-glgh-glgh*.

"You certainly have a way with animals, Lon," Rozier said.

"Till they taste the medicine...or the needle go in."

"I couldn't get along without you, of course," he said, "but you could make a living at this."

"Not without no license."

"Who ever asked you for a license?"

"...Be a sideline."

Hoover flopped down for Mr. Rozier to scratch him on his stomach. He just purred and purred in his pig language.

"Did you hear about the island on the Illinois side where they found all the different animals?" Mr. Rozier asked.

"I hear something about that."

"It was a big island and as the water rose little by little they kept moving to the higher ground. The high ground is always the upstream end of a bottom or an island, you know. They gradually moved up closer and closer together in the trees on the high end until the river cut through the chute and I suppose by then they were scared to swim. A deer will swim, you know. Thinks nothing of it."

"Umn-hmn."

"So by the time these two farmers went out there in a boat, the animals were crowded together in just a half-acre or so of woods. Deer, opossum, rabbits—you expect that. Raccoons, some chickens, the three heifers the farmers were looking for—and get this: a fox, a hawk with a broken wing, and a *bobcat*. You don't see bobcats much anymore."

"No, sir. That is a fact."

"...All crowded up together there. The lion lies down with the lamb."

"Yes, sir..."

ALL WEEK CAP DELIVERED TO SULPHUR SPRING IN GARY PRICE'S BOAT. Twice he siphoned gas from the truck to a coal-oil can, mixed in oil, and put it in the motor.

Late one afternoon when he was just out of sight of the highway in the shadow of the tall trees putt-putting along easy with his mail sacks in the front of the boat, he saw a man sitting against a sycamore tree with a gun across his lap. He waved for Cap to come up by him. Maybe he was fixing to rob him, and his pistol was back under the seat in the truck. But if he did not stop the man might shoot him.

It looked like a two-barrel combination .410 shotgun over a .22 rifle, a meat-for-the-pot gun. Then Cap recognized the man. It was that Holt Hardy fellow who caused Otis Boyer and all the colored men in the union quarries to lose their jobs.

His tangled hair was down past his ears with bits of twigs and green leaves in it and he had not shaved or changed his shirt since who knows when, and Cap wondered if he had a cloven hoof? His eyes would fix on you like a cougar trying to hypnotize you before he jumps.

"You want some fresh squirrel?" he asked.

Cap saw he had a number of squirrels laid out in a row on a bloody piece of newspaper. They were skinned and gutted, and appeared to be fresh. "Well, I might."

"I would say take them, only I am hard up from the strike."

From what Cap heard Otis Boyer say, he was not hard up just on account of the strike. Vigilantes took him out in the woods, advised him to go away from around there and not come back. They would do that, mostly with Colored. "How much?" he asked.

"How many you need?"

"Me and my brothers, the boy Cletus...make four."

"Fifty cents."

"I should give you more than that."

"It's enough."

Cap fished out his pocket change while Hardy wrapped the squirrels in a piece of newspaper. He handed them to him, and Cap slipped an extra dime in with his money. Fifteen cents a piece was not a bad price for fresh squirrel.

Hardy said, "I sell to the people going in and out on their boats."

"They having a hard time."

He cursed that rich old woman in her mansion on the hill sounding like a Bible verse, but he twisted it around.

Cap said, "Uh-huh."

"You deliver to Ethel Fahnstock?"

"She on my route." Holt Hardy was too, on the next farm and it was all overgrown and rundown. Before they ran him off he was staying in the old schoolhouse the other side of Fahnstocks on the highway. Now and then there was mail for him, and Cap left it in the schoolhouse mailbox. It would be gone from the box next time.

Hardy looked as if he might say something more, but he just stared at him again like an animal fixing to pounce. As Cap turned to start the motor up again, he said, "She is a kind and lovely person."

"Um-hmm."

"She *helps* people in the flood. Works all day in the shirtwaist factory, then goes to the school yard and ties sandbags every night."

Cap recalled he saw her from time to time with that white boy Lester who worked at Bluff City with Otis Bouchard, and came to their place looking for him. This Holt Hardy had her on his mind. Cap surely hoped he never have *him* on his mind.

CAP WAS COMING UP FROM THE WHITE-TRASH NORTH END OF TOWN WHEN he saw a young white woman walking along Sugar Bottom road. She turned at the sound of the motor, and waved him down. In a mail truck the steering wheel was on the right side so you could lean out stick the letters in the roadside mailbox. He stopped by her.

She was crying, her face swollen up. She was wearing cut-off bib overalls and her blouse was mussed and not buttoned right. "Yes, ma'am?" he asked.

She said, "I'm lost."

"Where from you lost?"

"St. Louis. I came to help. ... The creek was flooded so you couldn't cross, and a motorboat was tied up and an old truck parked by the bridge. I asked the men how I could get into town where people were filling sandbags."

Cap supposed she drove a car from St. Louis, and he asked if it broke down or she had a flat tire.

She said, "That's where the men are."

He imagined they had gone somewhere else but she did not study to fetch her car. She bit on her lip to stop crying. He asked her, "You want to go to the Sheriff's?"

"I don't know."

"...Or a doctor?"

"I just don't know."

"I can take you to Dr. Deichman...or direct you."

"Is he nice?"

"...Or Beaulah. Beaulah Misplaits. She a midwife."

"The Midwife."

He drove her around to Beaulah's on South Gabouri street. "Beaulah colored," he said.

"That's fine."

The young woman's name was Jessie. She said say she was going to college in Massachusetts. He asked her, "The mens colored?"

Her face got hard. "They were white."

"What kind of truck?"

"An old white truck. It must have been a milk truck."

"Any kind of name or sign on it?"

"It was painted over, faded....P-something."

"It's a town Pevely up past Festus."

"It might have been Pevely."

"Be a Pevely Dairy."

"There were racks with bottles....and jugs. It wasn't milk."

"Sound like bootleggers to me." He did not tell her they were protected. They could be from Illinois, anywhere. Lots of influential white men were their customers.

He went up on the gallery. Beaulah came to the screen. He told her about the young white woman. She said she would do for her what she could.

19.

AT LEAST THE FLOOD WAS SOMETHING TO DO WHEN YOU WERE NOT ON THE picket line. Dick Secour and the Union to a man were humping sandbags to raise the levees, to make them thickest at the bottom, and stop the sand boils and leaks. Dick said he knew they would pitch in anyhow, but it was no harm done if they were well-represented among the able-bodied men fighting the flood. They were used to hard labor with calluses on their hands and strong backs. Lester doubted many would dispute him if he said Ste. Genevieve would have washed away long since without the heavy lifting of the lime workers hour after hour, day and night.

He never once did see any of the bosses or Tertius Griswold or his friends. His mother made a clamor to save the old French houses above all, and working people whose homes were ruined be damned.

Lester and Little John and Walter generally worked together as a crew with Henry. They tended the levee on the north fork of Gabouri creek, which was the upstream end of town. It bore the brunt as levee after levee upstream burst and fresh surges of the foul brown water roiled down upon them.

One afternoon Ralph and Bucholz were working with them and Bucholz must clown with a bundle of iron fence posts that they were driving into the soggy ground to hold a line of stout planks to anchor the bottom row of sandbags. Standing on the tailgate of their truck he had raised them up over his head like the strongman at the circus but lost hold and dropped them so one sharp corner scraped down Lester's thigh and cut a nasty gash.

They wrapped a shirt-sleeve tight to stop the blood and Lester would go on with their business, but Henry would not permit it. He drove Lester himself in the truck to the office of an old doctor on Third Street across from the jail named Hertig, who stitched and bandaged him up and said, "Keep it dry. Understand? Or you will get lock-jaw."

Also he must not exert himself or the stitches would tear loose. "You bled a good deal already. You can lose blood pretty damn quick if that opens up."

Henry wanted to drive him around to the Anvil, but Lester persuaded him to let him off at the school-yard. He said, "I can set on my butt all day and hold sandbags open for others to fill, and not strain them stitches one whit."

Henry said, "I wish you would not do that, Lester," but he stopped and left him off.

Lester granted his leg had gone stiff but he tried not to limp as he moved along the walk by the side of the gymnasium above the crews that were filling the bags and stacking them just so onto skids.

He was four to five feet above the yard with five concrete steps down that people sat on for bleachers to watch games. Every twenty feet or so was a pile of screenings from the lime plants, and around each pile a team of three people. It was down to a system. One sat on an overturned five-gallon bucket holding the bag open, another filled it with a shovel, and another bent over or squatted down to tie it shut when it was full, then slung it into place on the skid---three side-by-side and another three side-by-side end-ways to the first three. The next row was the same except it was two bags end-to-end across the three sideways below it, then just three bags across the second row, two across them and one on top in a lumpy pyramid shape, 18 bags on each skid.

A man with a fork-lift moved the skid out in the yard and left it in a row. Later he or another fork lift loaded the skid into a truck to take out to the levee. People out there passed the bags up the line like a bucket-brigade to where fellows with strong backs, mainly lime workers, slung them where they belonged and pushed and kicked them in just so. Besides lime workers were National Guard and convicts at the business end.

Here and there in the school-yard you saw just two people or two and a child trying to do all three jobs that on a team of three that had the hang of it just slung them out like clockwork. Near the end furthest from the gate, he believed he saw someone he knew.

It was Ethel Fahnstock and her friend Mary Ann.

HE GIMPED ALONG BY THE WALL OF THE GYM TO JUST ABOVE THEM. ETHEL sat on an overturned bucket holding the bag open, then tied it herself while Mary Ann dragged the last tied bag over to the skid, then came back and took up the shovel to fill the next. He believed they knew he was there but they did not look up.

He hobbled down to them and said, "…Ethel?"

She looked up and gave him a sad smile. "Why, Lester! What have you been doing with yourself?"

"Humping sandbags when I am not on the picket line…reading in all them books you lent me."

She looked down at that.

"You suppose I could work along with you and Mary Ann?"

The women looked at each other. Mary Ann shrugged, and Ethel said, "I don't see why not."

He was embarrassed that he must favor his leg but they divided it up like the others with him sitting on the bucket to hold the bags open, and they switched off with Ethel to shovel and Mary Ann to tie them shut and sling them on the skid.

At first he was happy, even joyful to be so near his dear girl once more, but now and again her skirt hung against her belly and she had begun to show. Surely Mary Ann had told her she told him what she told her not to tell, but he supposed he had better not let on he knew. Yet he wondered if she ought to be shoveling like that.

After a while she stopped and looked at her hand and said, *"Damn!"*

She had got a blister already from the shovel. He insisted she let him see. The blister was the least of it. Her fingers were all bloody from what she was doing before, tying the hard twine on the bags by the hour. He called to a soldier who was laying out more empty skids in the place of the full ones the fork-left just bore off, and when he came over to them Lester asked him if they had First Aid.

He was glad to help the pretty girls and said oh yes and right away fetched over the Corpsman. He had little ready-made bandages wrapped in paper and would put them on her himself, but a fellow in charge called him over to tend a man who had collapsed in the heat. He gave Lester the bandages and he wrapped them on her fingers, and two in an X-shape over the palm of each hand.

"I look like a mummy," she said.

"You will be one soon enough," said her friend.

"Mary Ann...!"

"Lester knows and you know that he knows, and--"

"If he says one word about it, I shall tell him he may no longer fill sandbags with us!"

"Yes, ma'am."

Mary Ann shook her head.

He took his horsehide work gloves that were still rolled together and stuck under his belt. "Here," he said. "They are grimy and worn, but perhaps they will help."

She took them and held her hand against one. Naturally it was smaller but not a child's hand, and she put them on. She caught his eye. "Thank you," she said.

A while after that Lester needed like crazy to take a leak. There was no holding it back much longer.

Along the south fence of the schoolyard were some outhouses on wheels from an outfit in Festus called Johnny-on-the-Spot that you see at construction jobs in a town where you can't go out behind a bush. With four in a row if you had to pay every time they got pissed in, that company would make a mint. A woman came out of the one Lester was waiting on and it seemed it was all-for-one/one-for-all women's or men's and he went in and breathed through his mouth against the stench and it was a great relief.

When he came back there was a fellow standing over the women and he had an idea who that might be. As he drew near he saw he had been correct. Even from behind he knew it was Holt Hardy.

He had been packing the Bulldog Special again since Ethel sent word Hardy had returned, but in his lunch pail. He did always have it nearby when he worked on the levee or was on the picket line, but when he insisted Henry let him out at the school-yard he left it in the truck. He edged toward a nearby pile of lime screenings with a shovel sticking up in it.

He was thinking better that Ethel shoo him off herself than if he joined in the scene and Hardy would feel he must show his manhood. She was giving him a piece of her mind.

His clothes were tattered and filthy, his hair long and tangled with bits of twig and green leaf in it and he had plaited some kind of headband with vines that looked like greenbrier. Perhaps he had become one of those half-horse/half-man creatures in the mythology book Ethel passed on at the same time as the sex book. Or did he suppose he was Our Lord Himself, or John the Baptist fasting in the wilderness?

He hung his head. Ethel was motioning him to move along now and out the school-yard gate.

Mary Ann saw Lester. Hardy could tell that she was looking at something behind him, and he turned.

"It is *you!*" he said.

Lester was frozen in his baleful stare.

"Go on, Holt Hardy!" Ethel said to him loud and clear. *"Pretty damn quick!* ...Or I shall call the soldiers on you!"

Already people nearby had turned to look, more than one of them soldiers.

Hardy took a step toward Lester.

He snatched up the shovel.

Two of the soldiers drew near and he saw a third out the corner of his eye.

Hardy edged off slant-ways up the stair, and out of sight around the corner of the gymnasium. Lester caught a glimpse of him slinking up Fourth Street.

He stuck the shovel back in the pile of screenings and when he came up to her, Ethel told him, "He wanted to take your place working with me and Mary Ann."

"He said you were doing the girl's job sitting on the bucket," said Mary Ann.

"That is true enough," Lester said.

"Holding the bag open between your legs…"

"He talked coarse to you?"

"He is changed….He does not stay at his farm," said Ethel.

Lester said, "He looks like he lives in the woods in a cave."

"He had been watching us…"

"He does that…I seen him."

"Just now?"

"Other times."

"…So you spy on me too?"

"I spy on *him* spying on you…"

She looked at Mary Ann.

"It ain't the same…"

She looked again at him. "Holt Hardy says he killed a man…"

He had heard he was suspected of killing an old farmer named Williams on a squirrel hunt when they found two of Williams' hogs on Hardy's farm.

"*…For my sake.*"

"How is that?"

"Last week…as if to win my heart."

Again Lester had the chill of dread. This fit the idea he had of him, like setting the fire.

"Perhaps he was only boasting."

"I believe it," said Mary Ann.

"There was that deputy at Sulphur Spring," Lester said. He read of it in the *Fair Play* newspaper. The Deputy was enforcing the wishes of that rich old woman to keep the riffraff off her road.

"Shot from the woods," said Mary Ann.

"*He* done it."

"We don't know that," Ethel said.

NOW JUST AS HE MIGHT WISH TO HAVE WALTER AND LITTLE JOHN NEARBY with Holt Hardy returned, they were arrested and booked into jail as accomplices to Clyde in killing Falkner. Henry bailed them out, and Walter said it was Clyde's lawyer getting to him to lie and spread the blame. Not long after that was the trial and they were obliged to testify, and Lester received a notice from the court that he must be available to be called.

He heard no more of that, and the second day the verdict came in. The Prosecutors Huck and Petrequin had charged Clyde with murder in the first degree and asked for his death as punishment. What the jury came in with was second degree murder and a sentence of 35 years in the evil old state penitentiary in Jefferson City. From all that was said of what went on in there, Lester was not sure but that he might prefer to be hanged.

After Clyde was sent away, Little John told Lester that he and Walter both had their way with his sister more than once. But she told him the baby was Clyde's.

CLETUS WAS IN DREAMLAND WHEN *WHUMP..!* AND THAT LITTLE BARN where he stayed out back jenked altogether from the rock wall it sat on to the roof-tree as if a giant gave it a love tap or a one-jolt earthquake up from New Madrid, just a taste of what it *can* do and the sound right after treading on its heels *WHAM...!* What it was was dynamite that burst the Valle Spring levee.

He pulled his pants on, ran out in the yard barefoot, and heard water rushing. He found Cap and Zeno on the gallery in front. By the star light, you could hardly see it. Just hear the water spread out in the *grand champ* and lap up to the road. You felt it in the air that you were closer to water now and it seeped up across the road and behind them and rose, just rose up toward them. It rose nearly to the gallery floor.

They went around to the back. It had stopped just three feet before his crib where the ground sloped up.

"That be on purpose?" Cletus asked. There was talk when all the levees upstream burst to dynamite the north outer levee to let water out and take the pressure off the inner levee.

"Dynamite don't go off by itself," said Zeno.

"Just you wait," said Cap. "Them peckerwoods blame it on the nigger mail man."

"They don't always be thinking about you."

"Some say I set that fire."

People mostly laid it on that strange white man the vigilantes ran off but said he snuck back, living in the woods. *Hoke, Hank...* some *H* name. Hoke Hardy that said Otis Boyer crossed his path.

The water out back was up to his knees, but got shallower going to below the little barn. They came and went by walking up to where it was still dry and across the Brookses and Amoreaux back lots to Seraphin Street, then into town over Fourth Street.

CAP HEARD THE CREST WAS GOING TO BE 39 FEET ON TUESDAY, THEN THEY were saying 43 feet on Thursday, then 47 feet the next Monday. Finally they said 49 feet, and after that the water actually was going down some. He read in the newspaper 49 feet seven inches at the ferry landing. Little by little the water came down and everywhere was a mess.

Old Biggs came to fetch his pig Hoover in a truck. Next morning Hoover was lying in the mud under the gallery. His brother Lonzo and that boy Cletus had spoiled and treated him like a pet. He wriggled himself loose and came back. Biggs came and fetched the pig again, acting like it was their fault.

The next morning, Hoover was lying there under the gallery steps. His brother shook his head and moaned how Biggs was a mean old son-of-a-bitch, and said they were trying to steal his pig. He carried on like an old woman and begged and pleaded with Cap to take that pig in the U.S. Mail truck back to where he belonged.

Cap said old Mr. Rozier had Lon drive him around helping people. He could return the pig.

"In Mr. Rozier's Lincoln Zephyr automobile?" Lon said it like Cap asked him to take down his pants.

"I suppose to take him in my U.S. Mail truck?"

"You done it before."

"That pig just *covered* in mud. You bake him, suck the pig out, you got a pig statue...a pig-size piggy bank. How you like it I hand you a letter all filthy with mud and pig shit?"

"Now there you go, exaggerating. Be how you get youself in trouble, run you mouth and exaggerate."

Cletus was squatted down by Hoover scritching behind his ear. He said, "I take him back."

"Not in my U.S. Mail truck!"

"Not in Mr. Rozier's automobile!"

"He follow me....Give me a carrot."

Cap and his fussy old woman of a brother looked at each other. Lon shook his head, went in, and came out with a carrot.

Cletus broke off a piece, fed it to him, scritched him behind his ear. "Come on, pig," he said. "Sou-ee...sou-ee...!"

Hoover got himself up on his feet.

Cletus backed out from under the gallery, and the pig followed. He held the carrot down by his leg, made a noise just like a pig some way in the back of his mouth. He walked around to the front and down the road, and that pig followed after.

IN THE FLOOD CLETUS AND ZENO WERE LAID OFF WORK WITH ALL THE REST at Jenkins-Gillis except watchmen. Water didn't come up to the crusher and kiln but it covered the bottoms road and railroad tracks. You would suppose the flood had crested when the water came down a little, but then it would go up higher than before. Finally with what seemed like it *was* the crest, water came down a little and a little more.

Cletus helped out the flooded people and some gave him pocket change, not like paying him but more a tip. Water still surrounded the Creamery joint on three sides but you could get to it walking the track. Cletus would go in, and socialize mainly with CJ or Taylor. He believed they were living off Vera Fox, one of the immoral women Lon was always going on about.

When the old white farmer's pig was lying there pig-happy in the mud under the gallery steps a second time and Lon and Cap went to quarreling, Cletus led him home with a carrot. Old Biggs lived out in the Bois Brule bottom in a rundown mansion. Passing the biggest Indian mound Cletus saw a row of posts cheek by jowl just barely above the water that was still covering the fields to each side.

Biggs said he was about ready to get in the truck and fetch that pig back again. He said, "You niggers put voodoo on him."

Cletus was not sure if he was disrespecting him on purpose or supposed he was making a joke. Reverend Whitfield said you can't help white people calling you nigger among themselves or thinking of you as nigger in their minds, but you can speak up and ask them not to call you nigger to your face. Cletus said, "Sir, I asking you not to call me nigger."

"Now, boy. No offense."

"My name be Cletus."

"I mean the Ribeau boys."

"Cletus Johnson."

"Everybody knows old Lon sells charms."

"First I hear of it."

"To Colored."

"He doctor animals with scientific medicines from Mr. Vital Amoreaux. He a pharmacist."

"Lon is a damn fine animal doctor. We agree on that."

"Yes, sir."

"And I know he was not trying to steal my pig."

"Yes, sir."

"I spoke in fun, boy."

Everybody knew the law on a stray pig. If your pig strays in my garden, I can impound it, and make you pay a fine at the court house before you get that pig back.

"You done me a favor bringing him back."

"That pig, he take a shine to us. I feed him carrots and talk to him in pig talk."

"He is a smart pig and contrives to get loose."

"Be a shame you has to cut his throat for pork chops."

"That is the nature of things for pigs."

"Yes, sir." And Cletus was thinking to the mind of a white man, the nature of things for Colored is you do the same work for half the pay. And when you ask him politely not to call you nigger, he calls you boy. He gave Hoover his last piece of carrot. Hoover said thank you in pig talk and rubbed some dried mud off his shoulder against the side of Cletus' leg.

"Unless you want to purchase him at the market price…or Lon, he might."

"No, sir. No, thank you." Cletus had 15 cents in his pocket. "Then one day I set down at table to eat his chops myself."

"You are a clever boy."

"Yes, sir. Thank you." If he were in reach of his arm, Biggs would be patting him on the head.

Biggs was an old man by himself who wanted to talk to pass the time of day, even to a nigger. His son cropped the fields with a new Ford tractor, and lived in town. Now in the flood you could see that the old house and farmyard buildings were on a low flat Indian mound that Indians built up to live on in a flood.

Cletus took pity on this old white man. He said his son and little wife did not pay him any mind. He was truly perplexed how to keep Hoover from wriggling loose again. He showed Cletus where the pig dug under the fence and the next time broke through a rotten board in the last stall in his hay barn. With nothing better to do, Cletus stayed and helped him out mending fence. When they were done he gave him a dollar.

Considerable time had passed and more water had drained off into the ditches. Back a ways from old Biggs' place Cletus saw another low mound and more close-together posts in a line. Mostly the fields were mud now and here the flood had scoured down, while other places it dumped new dirt and some fields further down were spoiled with a foot of pure white sand. He saw more posts in the corners around a square and dents in the ground and he wondered if it could be Indian houses and there were Indians living in houses instead of Indian tents.

When he came to where the road was near the biggest mound, he walked out toward it by the row of posts that stuck up now nearly a foot and were big around as telegraph poles. He was counting his steps. In the mud he saw a piece of bone and picked it up. It was long as his little finger and shiny smooth where it came to a point. He knew from Buddy when he ran together with him and JT that it was an awl. He put it in his pocket.

He found a piece of smoky flint you could see light through, and pieces of Indian pots with little grooves across the lip and lines on the side like you draw with a sharp stick when it is soft clay, and he put all that in his pocket.

Two steps were a pace. He took 85 paces to where the mound started. A pace was five feet, so that made it 425 feet from the road. He walked up on the mound to where it was highest. It was fifteen to twenty feet higher than that bottoms mud all around. From there he saw another mound lower down, and out to the mound old Biggs's house and yard set on, and two more low mounds. If you drew a line around them and the one he was standing on and Biggs', it made a oblong bigger than the courthouse square and the blocks on each side and more on the ends. It was a whole Indian town bigger than Ste. Genevieve rising up in the Big Field bottom. But they were not wild Indians on horseback like Custer's last stand. They made pots and houses and mounds and put big posts in the ground so all the town was like a fort.

The top half of the mound stayed dry in the flood and had some woodchuck and chipmunk holes. He squatted down by one and in the dirt the woodchuck threw up were more broken pieces of pot and a little piece of the flint you see light through, and it was a flat three-cornered piece big as his thumb nail and had notches by two corners. Buddy called that kind a bird point. He put it in his pocket.

He thought again on how he used to be friends with Buddy and J.T. He learned his lesson. A white friend will deny you.

He commenced to go from one hole to another looking in the dirt around it. Almost every one had pieces of broken pot and bones. One had a little black corncob no bigger that his thumb and you would think that woodchuck would have eaten it but the corn grains were still on it all burnt shiny black.

Down on the bottom walking back to the road he was looking at the row of posts, then places with dents in the ground, posts in the corner. Here and there were what he thought were pumpkins or cantaloupe. He went out and looked at one. It was the top half a pot like a face, sticking up half a foot. The next one had designs on it, rows of sharp dots like from sticking a sharp stick in the clay and lines side by side. Buddy said a old pot that never was broken was worth good money. You need a shovel and patience to dig one out whole. He said to himself he would come back.

The sun down low, near supper time. He humped along back to Ribeaus.

CAP LOOKED UP MOUND BUILDERS IN THE *WORLD BOOK*.

> Mound Builders, a highly civilized race that
> flourished before the Indians came. Who were the
> Mound Builders? Survivors of sunken Atlantis?
> Egyptians and Phoenicians wandering far from
> home?

RAIN FELL IN THE NIGHT.

Rain and wind whipped up a storm they said as far north as St. Louis, lightning and thunder and rain like what fell on Noah. Lightning struck the big old mocker-nut hickory behind his crib. His ears were ringing from the thunder-stroke.

Water covered the fields again, but not just from the rain falling on them. It was from rain falling on the hills all around that ran down through little creeks and branches flowing into the South Fork and the North Fork of Gabouri Creek that came together where that crazy man dynamited the levee. For the first time since the flood, since way before the flood, water flowed in the creek higher than the river. Before, the river backed up into the creek.

The next day, the water was down again. Cletus went out to look. The town of the Mound People was gone.

Where water scoured off before, now it had laid mud and silt down. He thought maybe because it came from behind. The biggest mound was still there, and the low mounds. All the posts and pots like the heads of people were gone.

Zeno came walking out the road into the field. He was curious. Cap and Lon were curious too but they had to go to work. Cletus was standing on top of the biggest mound when Zeno came up to him. "Be all covered up again," Cletus said.

Zeno stood looking around.

"You think I lying?"

20.

LESTER AND LITTLE JOHN AND WALTER AND AS MANY OF THE LIME WORK-ers as were not flooded themselves were big on helping out. People appreciated you and that made you feel good. But the strike did not just go away.

At first they were saying oh wasn't it wonderful how they all pulled together in the flood. Now all they had to do was join hands in the same spirit and end the strike. This idea came particularly from the Chamber of Commerce and the lime bosses and the old Priest.

The Back-to-Work revival meetings started up again. Now they were tolling the women in to get the strikers by the short hairs. The notice in the *Fair Play* said the Chamber of Commerce labor committee ...and the newly formed Independent Lime Workers Union extend this invitation to the women of Ste. Genevieve so that they too may become informed as to the aims and purpose of the movement to return the men to work.

Wives and sweethearts of those who had signed *or who have not signed* cards should all come and were welcome to participate in the meeting. It was in the public school auditorium and they were expecting a crowd of 1,000, and refreshments would be prepared for that number. A guest speaker would be on hand and the Lions Club Band would entertain one and all with a lively concert.

What set a chill down Lester's back was the item after that:

At last Friday night's meeting the Committee informed the 600 men present that over 51% of the workmen of the Bluff City plant had signed for an independent union and that the other two plants were rapidly nearing a majority.

It was a bare-face lie but when they said it like that in the newspaper, some of the fellows who had been wavering would say *What's the use?* And cave.

WHAT THEY DID WAS TO RALLY THE TROOPS. THE NIGHT OF THAT MEETING they gathered in the Red Men's hall in the old brewery on Third at LaHaye street. The places of those who had fallen by the way and signed the pledge cards were more than made up by retired men and kith and kin and stout school boys, although Lester imagined a few that did sign the cards were among them wavering back, or to spy.

The word went out to honest working men round about, and a hundred CIO fellows from Crystal City Glass were in their number, more than fifty from the Flat River lead mines, marble and building-stone quarrymen from Bloomsdale and Ozora and Weingarten, men from the broom factory at St. Mary and the Perryville brick works, fellows from the railroad shops at DeSoto that Lester's papa used to work with. To cap it all they had more than two dozen coal miners from Sparta, Illinois, John L. Lewis boys with Mother Jones in their hearts.

They were crammed in the old brewery and gathered in bunches outside the windows and doors.

Oscar Kampf went up on the little stage on the grain bin between two of the beer vats and said a few words to welcome their brothers from far and wide and he called out each group, "The Crystal City Glass boys...! Flat River Lead...!" *The Coal Mine fellows from Sparta!"* and they all hollered and clapped.

Then Dick Secour got up there. "Numbers talk, boys," he said. "We don't need to knock heads or smash things up. That is just what the lime bosses want, so they can call the tin soldiers on us....*Don't give them no excuse!"*

They lined up four abreast and set out. In close order they were three blocks long as they crossed the North Fork, and swung a column-right on Washington Street. They just rolled along, an old soldier here and there counting cadence to himself and they were mostly in step without thinking about it, smooth and rising up like the river. By the weight of their numbers they rolled along.

Then the front stopped.

Some of the rest of them jammed up together before they could stop. It was the Sheriff and one of his three deputies and two town police, which was half the force. Lester was in the 4th rank back and was not able to hear all they said. It seemed like everybody was acting civil to each other, and Dick Secour and Oscar Kampf and Ralph Granaman followed the Sheriff around to the side door to the auditorium and went in.

Frank Janis was up in front as the man in charge now. Lester called out just loud enough for him to hear, "What if they cuff Dick and Oscar and Ralph and haul them to jail?"

Frank answered just matter-of-fact, "We will mob the sons of bitches and set our boys loose, and go home and get our guns."

The ones in earshot liked the sound of that and passed it along the line. Lester imagined he was not the only one who would not put it past the bosses to attempt any and all kinds of dirty tricks. Whether mobbing the law would work out as they might wish, what Frank said made them feel better. They had the weight of their numbers and the bosses must be mindful of them, if only on that account.

LON'S NEIGHBOR GERALDINE BROOKS HAD HER OWN CATERING BUSINESS
on the side, and sometimes he helped her out. When the flood went down she had a job to cater
at the high school for the big Back-to-Work meeting when women were invited, to provide refreshments. Geraldine had made little three-corner cucumber sandwiches and cut the crusts
off. Mrs. Griswold allowed her to use her kitchen when all her regular work was done and
store the hors d'oeuvres in the old ice box. Lon would carry a tray around serving them, and
mix up the cherry phosphate punch and keep the bowl filled.

They still were setting up on the trestle table by the back wall behind the rows of folding
chairs when the word came down there was going to be trouble. The whole quarry and lime
workers union Local 829 except for the pitiful scab fellows in the hall that signed the pledge
cards were on the way marching there. Besides them were the CIO men from Crystal City
Glass, lead mine men, coal miners from Illinois all marching up to the auditorium going to
barge right in and take over.

The men in the chairs--they all were white--got up and most of them went outside to
see or protect the women. Just women and children and a few men were hanging back. Then
behind Lon somebody was coming in the side door.

He went to the entrance hall. Toilets were on one side, on the other a room with a big
table and a blackboard. It was the Sheriff and Secour the Union boss and his sidekick named
Kampf and Mr. Granaman—who was a older man. Lon went back and put glass cups of the
phosphate punch on a tray and took it to the door of the meetings room. Around that big table
sat the Back-to-Work chairman Mr. Paultier and two more Chamber-of-Commerce men, and
the three Union men, and the Sheriff. They saw Lon and he asked, "Any of you gentlemens
care for some refreshments?"

Nobody wanted refreshments, especially not that punch.

He took the tray back and left it on the table. "You messing up my business, Lonzo?"
Geraldine asked.

"Just ease-dropping."

She said something he did not quite hear, and he went out in the hall again, and leaned in
the corner by the open door. They were talking loud back and forth, Paultier saying the gang
outside was mostly from out of town, and had no right to come to the Ste. Genevieve meeting.

"They are in the public street," the Sheriff said.

"These men here are responsible," said one named Chadwell. "Arrest them!" He was the one whose wife fired Tillie Beauvais because the jackleg doctor, Deichman, said she had the syphilis.

"On what charge?"

"Conspiracy. Inciting to riot!"

"There's no riot."

"Do something!"

"I have got four men."

"Call in the State Police! The National Guard!"

"If it come to calling in the Guard and you convince the Governor, you wait two hours before any of them get here ... more like four."

They hollered back and forth a while, but finally Paultier said like a little boy when you just won all his marbles, *"All RIGHT the meeting is canceled."*

"But we will have our regular meeting next week," said Chadwell. "They can't expect their goons to come all the way here every night."

Lon listened so he could tell Zeno and Cap and Cletus. Zeno wanted to be Union and if the white men's would not allow Colored, he wanted that union that made them welcome. He could lose his job agitating to get CIO in since that Jack fellow from Crystal City came to town trying to organize Jenkins-Gillis without Old Man Jenkins knowing about it until too late.

So the Back-to-Work men went up on the stage and Paultier said, "Jack Chadwell and Kurt Ketting and I refuse to knuckle under to the Union's ultimatum that their whole crowd be allowed in here to just take things over. We will not permit that. Most of the crowd out there are in no way connected with our local strike situation. They are not citizens of Ste. Genevieve or this county and were hauled in here for the sole purpose of trying to intimidate us.

"So on the advice of Sheriff Picou...this meeting is adjourned, and we are asking you to return peaceably to your homes...and avoid confrontations with the Union men."

Nobody questioned him or made a fuss. The Back-to-Work men came in and gathered up their women and sniffle-nosed children and slunk off. They were all quiet and subdued. Here and there a child piped up, and some of them were grabbing the little three-corner sandwiches on the way out.

DICK SECOUR AND OSCAR KAMPF AND RALPH GRANAMAN CAME OUT
and told them the meeting was canceled, and they must go back to their hall and decide what
to do next. They did not holler or carry on. They just gave the lime bosses a set-back but the
war was a long way from over and they were not of a mind to celebrate. Not yet. They about-
faced and marched rout-step back the way they had come. People on their galleries and front
stoops watched them pass in the twilight and Lester imagined a number of them by now
were Back-to-Works and anti-union but nobody messed with them in word or deed, and that
included the Law.

When they were back at the old brewery Dick Secour got up there and told them, "Boys,
you done good. *That* was discipline. We did not in no way give them the least excuse."

Here and there men spoke up saying that's right, we done good, but nobody cheered or
hollered. This was sober business.

"So what is next?" Dick asked. "Do I hear a motion?"

Three or four fellows said almost at the same time and treading on the heels of one
another and not all just the same words but pretty nearly, "Shut down the nigger quarry!"

"Do we have to call it that?" Frank Janis asked, and Lester supposed he had his missus
on his mind. When he told her later just what they did—and she would want to know—he
could tell her he said that.

Some of them made a joke of it saying things like *Call a spade a spade* and such like,
but Frank had a point.

"The *scab* quarry!" a fellow called out and there was back-and-forth about that.

Frank asked, "What do we want them to call it in the newspaper?"

Lester was impressed. In his book Frank Janis had his head on right. He studied things
out with his little woman and she was plenty sharp. They had two newspapers in town, the
Fair Play and the *Herald,* and you knew they would have their stories of what came down
that night. What with their old French houses in the flood and their long and bitter strike,
they sometimes made the St. Louis papers too.

Henry Maheu got Dick to recognize him and he said, "Jenkins-Gillis…"

"That's better," said the Secretary old Ralph Grannaman.

"*The non-union quarry,*" Frank said.

"Now can we word it as a motion?" Dick Secour asked.

That went back and forth until they agreed and called the question and Ralph Grannaman read it out:

Resolved: Local 829 will set up picket lines and

> prevent any and all operation of the Jenkins-Gillis
> quarries and lime works until such time as Man-
> agement recognizes A.F. of L. Local 829 Labor-
> ers, Hod Carriers, and Quarry Workers Union
> International as the sole bargaining agent for its
> employees, and agrees to limit employees to dues-
> paying members only.

Nobody objected or had a question but one of the older fellows who was hard of hearing said he missed part, and Ralph who kind of liked the sound of his own voice was happy to read it again.

"We ready to vote now?" Dick Secour asked.

A number said yes and all right and others nodded their heads.

"All those in favor say *Aye*."

It sounded to Lester like just about everybody in the room and in ear-shot at the open windows too said, *"Aye!"* That included the fellows who came from far and wide to back them, and nobody objected to that. Nobody hollered. Sometimes when just a few want something they will yell it out as loud as they can so you think they are more numerous than they actually are, or that they are such stout fellows you had better not cross them. The *Ayes* were like the weight of water breaking through the levee not loud but scarcely any sound at all save a rushing at first and when a barn or large tree is in its path simply rising and moving across the land.

"All opposed?" Secour asked.

Out of the 12 hundred and more men within the sound of his voice, nobody said *No*, not even a cut-up or one old crank. It was a moment of silence, like in memory of the dead.

THEY PROCEEDED ON AS THEY DID BEFORE, MARCHING FOUR-ABREAST and for the most part silent. They went down LaHaye street by the North Fork and swung a column-left onto North Main which about there started to be called Modoc road or the road to the ferry landing.

Dick Secour had told them again that they must be orderly and give those who wished them ill no excuse. The night men running the kilns would be frightened. "We must be calm and respectful and treat them decent," he said, "while we are firm that work there must cease. They are not our enemies. Colored are men the same as us. Old man Jenkins tolled them in with advertisements in the Southern papers. They sweat and strain hour after hour as we do in constant danger of accidents that kill or maim and cripple you for life. The difference is they are doing it for half the pay and while that injured us, they themselves are not to blame."

And this will cease.

No one thought to mention that once Jenkins-Gillis had shut down, the by-laws of the union forbade the enrolling of colored men. Perhaps they would assist them in joining another union, say the CIO mine workers. And then what? Would the John L. Lewis boys stand by and let A.F. of L. Local 829 represent the other lime plants? Lester thought *We often fight each other as mean as the bosses fight us.*

With all the foresight in the world you could not plan all things out ahead of time. Nor were they philanthropists. They were fighting for their jobs in hard times, the few that remained.

A HALF MILE FURTHER UP THE TRACKS FROM BLUFF CITY, THEY CAME TO the gate shack at Jenkins-Gillis. You could hear the slap and whir of conveyor belts and the low grinding of the pulverizers as they reduced the cooked rock from the kilns to powdered lime, but little else save the sounds by the river of the country night—the katydids, the peepers and here and there a bullfrog in the slough, a coal train passing on the Illinois side, and a whippoorwill along the bank.

Ther orders were to form a line across the mouth of the hollow and wait.

It was on toward midnight when they saw a colored boy with a dinner pail coming up the tracks and after him a darker heavy-set man. The boy saw them us first and stopped as the man came up beside him, said something, and they both continued on. Lester would not blame them being scared. For all they knew they were there to lynch them.

A few feet away they stopped and the man said, "Good evening, gentlemens."

He was the man who recognized him at the joint across the tracks, and Jack O'Hare and his sister proceeded to vamp on him for the CIO. The boy Cletus stayed by him and his brothers.

Several of the white men answered back civil enough *Good evening...How do you do?* Frank Janis did the talking. "We mean you no harm," he said. "We are Local 829 and we are shutting down this outfit until Mr. Jenkins recognizes us as the sole bargaining agent for his employees and signs a closed-shop contract."

"I understand you," said the older man.

"So until then, this here is a picket line. There will be no trouble so long as you respect it."

"I don't study to mess with your picket line."

Frank Janis nodded and asked him, "Aren't you one of the Ribeaus?"

"Yes, sir....I be Zeno."

Frank told him his name and acted like he was about to shake his hand but thought better of it.

"I do have a request, sir."

Frank nodded for him to say what it was.

"I be the night foreman on the kilns. We was coming in for the graveyard shift...If the swing-shift boys just walk off, be all that melted rock. Leave it to go cold, it stick to the furnace walls. Have to go in with a hammer and chisel to get it off before the kiln fire up again."

One fellow said that's Jenkins' problem, another how that happened in the short strike at Peerless last November and the company lawyers made a big to-do over it. Henry said it would give old Jenkins his excuse to hold out until Kingdom Come and law us in the bargain.

Frank decided to let them empty the kilns before they shut down, and sent Henry and some other men with Ribeau to help, and, make sure all the Jenkins-Gillis men in there came out when they were done. This required a certain amount of time.

Frank said to the boy Cletus, "You are free to go."

"I be waiting for Zeno," Cletus said.

"Nobody's going to mess with you."

"I prefer to wait, if you don't mind."

"Suit yourself."

After a while Lester sifted over to where he was, leaning back on a big railroad tool-box with a padlock on it by the tracks. "How you doing?" he asked.

"I remember you," he said. "Come to give that money to Otis' wife."

"Lester. Lester Dodge."

"Cletus Johnson." He offered and Lester hesitated, but he did shake his hand.

He imagined they could speak of any number of things—of where he came from in the Boot Heel, of chopping cotton, of his kinfolks, if he had a jo and how he took to school. On his part Lester might tell him of digging tiff, of Uncle Roy getting him on at Crystal City Glass, and of Ethel who allowed him once more to walk by her side.

This boy Cletus and Lester had much in common. They both set out on the road of life in the worst hard times in memory. They both were screwed over by the lime bosses and not the sort to take it lying down. Yet he was colored and Lester was white.

While he would have been wrong to pretend he did not know him, yet it might be just as well not to make too much of a show of their acquain'tance. They met like soldiers in the night between the lines when a truce is called to bury the dead. Lester said if they set them one against the other, "I will not bust your head unless you are fixing to bust mine first."

Cletus shrugged, "I be agreeable to that...only--"

"Only what?"

"White mens come to whip my head, I scoot."

As Lester returned and would lose himself among his fellows, he felt some of them take notice that he was fraternizing with Colored.

"Who is *that?*" Walter asked.

21.

ZENO RIBEAU SAID THAT IT HAPPENED SOON AFTER THE WHITE MEN SHUT them down at Jenkins-Gillis because Negroes were not allowed to belong to the union, and that made them scabs. Two white men who were on strike from Peerless Lime, Chomeau and Rauscher, went out Saturday drinking. Rauscher drove a truck. He did not know just what Chomeau did except that he had a jack-leg insurance business on the side, the kind where you pay in twenty-five cents a week, and he had been out collecting from his customers. Both white men were married, with children. They had an idea to go down to the end of Merchant Street past the depot to a Negro place, and watch the Negroes dance.

Vera Rogers—who they say stabbed a man in Crystal City—hustled them to buy her drinks. After a while she mentioned a craps game up at Modoc landing. The white men were interested in a Negro craps game, and they agreed to give her and her two friends a ride out to Modoc landing for a dollar and fifty cents. Her two friends were Lee Guy Taylor and Columbus Jennings who worked under Zeno Ribeau's direct supervision at Jenkins-Gillis Lime Company.

The way Zeno heard it, when they came to the Frisco trestle just before you go down to the river Taylor said, *Now stop and turn around.*

Rauscher the man driving reached in back see if Taylor was armed and he was, and the other white man said, *Is this a hold-up?*

Rauscher jumped out of the car and went around in front as if he was going to crank it. The colored men hauled Chomeau out, backed the white men under the trestle, took ten dollars and a fountain pen and a watch from Rauscher and thirty-five dollars from Chomeau.

Taylor said, *You have got more money than that.*

No, honest. I haven't, Chomeau said. He started to say something else but Taylor shot him, and he crumpled to the ground saying, *Oh...!*

The other white fellow Rauscher was a big man and he grabbed Taylor from behind and they were fighting shoulder to shoulder.

The woman sid, *Shoot that man behind and do it damn sure and not let him get up on you.*

C.J. ran up and tried to shoot but he did not understand how to work the automatic gun, and smacked him upside the head. Taylor whipped around, shot the big white man with his .38 revolver right up next to his belly and he fell.

He lay there playing dead. The woman and C.J. took and hauled him by the legs over the rip-rap to the river bank, and shoved him in. Taylor had grabbed the dead man, Chomeau, dragged him over the rocks, and heaved him in the water too.

Rauscher was paralyzed from the bullet stuck in his spine, but he could paddle with his hands. When they saw he was still alive, the colored men and the woman threw rocks at him. After a big rock from the rip-rap hit him in the head, he did not holler any more.

A freight train spooked the woman, and she ran past the Anvil tavern, and hid in the shed. The two men couldn't get the car to start, so they walked the Frisco tracks back to town. The woman caught up to them. Taylor said, *Girl, you sure can run fast.*

She said, *Be a time to run.*

He said he had to get rid of his pistol.

JUST DOWN FROM THE LANDING WAS THE MOONSHINE BARGE. THAT SAME Saturday in the afternoon Revenue men seized the barge and a fast boat with two 80-horsepower gasoline motors tied up to it. They found 1,500 sacks of corn sugar on the barge, 140 five-gallon cans of moonshine on the boat, a .32 caliber rifle, a .22 caliber rifle, some revolvers, two 12-gauge shotguns, and field glasses. They arrested eleven men, five white and six colored. When they took the moonshiners to the lock-up, they left watchmen on the boat and barge.

One of the watchmen heard the shots and went down the gangplank to walk along the river bank and saw Chomeau's hand sticking up above the water. He pulled the dead man up on the bank then saw Rauscher lying half on the rip-rap with his legs in the water and pulled him up too. An ambulance from the Basler Funeral Parlor took him up to the St. Anthony Hospital at St. Louis. He recovered consciousness, and talked to police.

WHITE PEOPLE WERE ALL STIRRED UP, FEARFUL AND ANGRY. THEY TALKED to their neighbors and gathered in the street. Men waited by the jail for news to come down.

The Sheriff's men brought in transient Negroes from the shacks by the depot, and sweated them down. One told Sheriff Ben Picou he saw Legrand Taylor and C.J. Jennings and a woman name Vera from Crystal City get in a car with two white men about one o'clock in the morning. They arrested the woman, and she denied it. They questioned her some more, and she admitted she got in the car with two white men but ran off as soon as she saw the colored men had guns. C. J. knew she copped on him, and he said he was in the car and had a gun but no bullets in it. Taylor had blood on his clothes. They searched his crib, and found a bloody handkerchief. He said he had a nosebleed. They read him what the woman and C. J. told them and signed their names, and Taylor said he shot the white man because he hit him in the mouth.

Before the men in the street knew the Negroes confessed, the Sheriff snuck them out the back to a fast Packard automobile confiscated from the bootleggers and ran them up to Festus.

LON RECALLED HOW FATHER VAN PREACHED A HOMILY THAT SUNDAY JUST like always from a Bible verse. He preached from *Galatians 3:28*. He lined it out: *Be neither Jew or Greek, slave or free, male or female…We are all one in Jesus!'*

He said the Frenchmen who came there two hundred years ago and prayed Bishop Dubourg to send them a priest were not so afflicted with racial prejudice as the mostly Protestant Americans who came in after them. The faithful Catholics married the Indian women and African women who warmed their beds at night and gave them children. "Some of their descendants live among us today and are members in good standing of our parish family."

Lon scrunched down and ducked his head so if people turned to look at him he would not know it.

"We must not let our feeling over the deaths of Harry Chomeau and Paul Rauscher attach itself to them...or to any other good colored people here. Race prejudice has no place among us. It is a sin.

"Thou shalt love thy neighbor as thyself!

"In the long and bitter strike at our lime kilns ...in the depths of a national depression when millions of men...and women... seek work and cannot find it...fear gnaws at our hearts. Many have lost their life's savings in the failures of the banks. Our houses and farms have been seized for debt. ...Our children go to bed hungry. We are susceptible to primitive emotions.

"We have a grim reminder of that in Germany where the National Socialists and Herr Hitler stir up hatred of the Jews. Scarcely a week passes without an item in the *Herald* or the *Fair Play* about a lynching somewhere in the South. Just last week in *Caruthersville, Missouri* a man was dragged behind a car, bound to a tree with baling wire, and burned to death.

"I was awakened in the small hours of the night. I opened my window and looked out. A large number of men...and some women...were gathered in the square between the courthouse and our church. I believe they contemplated mobbing the jail... Some of you were among them.

"I have no wish to embarrass you. When others come forward to the altar rail, I must ask you to remain seated and reflect... After you have come to Confession...to beg forgiveness for the race prejudice in your heart...*then* you may hope to partake again of his holy body and most precious blood...and the promise of everlasting life. ...*Amen.*"

White people down in the pews were looking behind and this way and that, whispering and muttering out the side of the mouth. The Old Father was saying they were *excommunicated*. They would complain on him to the Archbishop at St. Louis. And that Archbishop, Glennon, like a lot of the Irish did not study Negroes. Not one bit.

Lon sat up in the colored gallery by the stair. He preferred to be down to the vestibule and out before Father came to greet people as they left. Sometimes he was quick and caught Lon, held on when he shook his hand, made sure to visit and make his white people wait. This time Lon had beat him.

On the church steps was Doctor Deichman with a paper. What it said was: *All colored have to leave town by five o'clock tomorrow.* People came up, signed the paper. Trash white men loitered in Market Street and between the church and the court-house. Lon sifted on across to between the Knights of Pythias and the hardware.

Father Van came out like always to shake hands and visit his people after the mass. He stood in the red doorway looking down. He waited. All around people stopped their talking, looked up. It was so quiet you could hear a towboat on the river a mile away.

Deichman turned and cocked his head saying, "Why, good morning, sir."

Father Van said, "You are not one of my flock."

"Your *flock*…?" Dr. Deichman was not even Catholic, just some kind of Lutheran by his family. But he told anybody who would listen that he was a Free Man, a Free Thinker. He said priests and preachers take your manhood. He was not a Mason either. Or a real doctor. He was an osteopath.

"You are trespassing!"

"Trespassing?" Deichman said, looking around like he was being mistreated. "Why, this is a public place…"

"What is that?"

Dr. Deichman said a *petition*.

"Let me see it!" Father held out his hand.

"I have the right—anybody has the right to circulate a petition."

"Not on the steps of my church!" Father came after him.

Deichman backed down the steps, stumbling. He scuttled off sideways like a crawfish.

EMIL DEICHMAN WAS KNOWN AS THE NIGGERS' DOCTOR, WHICH WAS NOT what his papa had in mind. He was so proud when he came home from Kirksville. He had fitted up the parlor as his office and made the furniture and fixtures himself to look like pieces he found in a catalog. Emil's kid sister Edith acted as his receptionist.

Ste. Genevieve already had two well-established physicians and he believed it was the wife of one of them who started the whispering around town that he was not a real doctor. He was licensed to practice osteopathic medicine, including surgery and writing prescriptions. He owed that to the advocacy of his beloved Old Doctor Still and the international fame of the college he established, and to the thousands of patients successfully restored to health by his students. The American Medical Association might not recognize osteopathy but the state of Missouri did, and he was proud to display his diploma on the office wall.

Deichman granted that to some extent he might have started off with a chip on his shoulder. In the beginning family members came to him out of curiosity, then extended family and their friends who imposed on him one after another without a thought in the world of offering any compensation for his professional services. His first real patients were Colored who paid what they could, or could only promise to pay. He had to take out a loan from Papa to pay Sis.

That was how it went for the first three years. Oh, he got to where he was making a living at it, but his patients were almost entirely colored people.

Then a whole wagon load of dynamite exploded at Jenkins-Gillis Lime. About nine o'clock in the evening there was a flash, and two seconds later a sensation like an open hand smacking your chest. He went out at once, and all up and down LaHaye Street the neighbors were coming out to see. They knew it must have been an explosion at one of the quarries, and from the direction it had to be either Jenkins-Gillis or Bluff City Lime. People heard it for miles around.

Deichman did not have long to gossip with the neighbors. One of the ten-ton Mack trucks from Jenkins-Gillis came rumbling up the street and stopped right by him. It was Tyrone Misplaits, who was hired in spite of his prison record as a favor to the old priest. He said, "Be a explosion, a whole wagon load of dynamite! Say to fetch you damn quick!"

He rode with him in the cab of the truck trying to maintain his dignity. Tyrone was the *type* of the *bad nigger*, thought he could intimidate you and cut you down to his level with physical menace. He drove too fast. The truck jolted and careened over the ruts and pot-holes between the tracks and the towering limestone bluff. He asked, "You bring you doctor bag?"

The almost-new bag was in his lap, a gift from his father.

"Be real bad in there. Lots of mens hurt."

He asked if any were dead and he said, "Dead mens too."

They came to the gap in the bluff where the drainage of a nameless creek had cut down through the clay and limestone, and he swerved the truck to the left with a spray of gravel and Deichman was thrown against the door. When he stomped on the brake, he jerked forward over his black leather bag and his forehead came within an inch of smacking the windshield.

A bow-legged little fellow with tight curly white hair almost like a Negro—who he knew only by sight as Jenkins—scuttled over from the old Frisco caboose that served as his office. Just as Deichman was opening the door, Jenkins arrested it and insisted on talking through the open window. "Hertig is on a call out in the country," he says. "Report to Dr. Claiborne."

The Negro jerked at the gear handle and popped the clutch so they jolted forward. The truck ground along in a low gear.

They passed three old stone chimney-kilns that were still in use, and on the lime screenings that covered the ground was fresh debris of loose rocks and twisted pieces of metal and here and there a piece of cloth, a shoe, a blackened helmet. They wound up the hollow past gaping tunnel mouths you could drive three of those trucks into side by side. Strings of overhead lights disappeared into the darkness hazy with lime dust. They passed one with the lights out, then around a slight bend, a tunnel with the roof caved in down the middle and fresh blackening around the sides.

The truck stopped. At the walls were openings back into the tunnel and at the larger one to the right was a cluster of men standing and moving around, and laid out on the ground to the side along the bluff face three rows of men. Some looked dead, others nearly so. One cried out, another moaned, another writhed this way and that. Others bent over them, one in a soiled white coat.

Deichman went to him. It was Claiborne the epitome of Southern gentility whose manner toward him was mildly reproving, coming as he did from a family of low Germans fresh off the boat. He looked up from splinting a humerus, and said, "Yes, a... Doctor...Dreckman—"

He corrected him, "*Deichman*, sir."

"Thank you for coming."

He mumbled and shook his head. It was not a favor to *him*. Deichman was not even sure Claiborne had deigned to ask for him. More likely it was Jenkins.

"If you will, start on the third row...at the far end."

"How many are there?"

"We don't know yet. So far, seventy-five or eighty have been accounted for. Those men there, and nineteen who were able to walk out. More than fifty are not accounted for. I believe most of them are still in there."

He abruptly turned back to the man he was attending to.

The hulking young Negro still hung at his side. He turned on him, "*That will be all, Tyrone.*"

He stood there with his chin at an attitude and a smirk on his face as if to say *I have something on you, white man.* For a moment he wondered if he expected a tip, or wanted him to offer one so he could act insulted.

Deichman went to the last man on the back row. He looked like a statue knocked supine. As he wiped the lime dust off his face he knew he was dead. Still he opened his shirt and put his ear to his chest. He remembered his stethoscope, took it out and hung it around his neck, then put the knobs in his ears and pressed the shiny disk to the sternum. To a man nearby who was watching he said *He's gone*, and moved on to the next.

His face was a bloody pulp, his chest concave as if it had been pressed in by a giant thumb. From his maw came a regular burbling whistle. He filled a hypodermic with a dose of morphine and injected it into his arm.

He worked on through the night. Someone told him Doctor Hertig had come. He wanted to say *Bully for Dr. Hertig.* The work went on.

Well after sunrise when they had done all that could be done at the scene—although men were still loading ambulances and hearses from as far away as Sikeston and Rolla, he slipped away down the hollow. He was relieved to see no sign of Tyrone Misplaits and his infernal truck, and no one else took notice to offer him a ride. A sense of grievance added to his satisfaction as he trudged along bone-tired yet strangely elated down the railroad tracks at the base of the bluff.

He went straight to bed.

When he awoke late in the afternoon, his sister gave him a list she said was from Dr. Claiborne. "It's the ones you're supposed to see."

Once they were able, most of these men came to visit him in his office. Their families came. In time as a result of the Jenkins-Gillis explosion, he had a respectable white practice. As he began to charge them the same as the white, his colored patients dwindled to an appropriate minority. He was no longer *the niggers' doctor.*

22.

MATT ZIEGLER SHOULD HAVE KNOWN BETTER THAN TO GO TO THE LEGION Hall that night. He made a precarious living from his Tobacco & Art Supplies shop and what was left of the income from his family farm after paying the hired man. He was no longer able to work it himself because his right leg was shorter than the left and he had to wear a platform shoe. The accident at Peerless quarry he could thank for that was seven years after he mustered out of the Army. He had served in the 793rd Field Artillery in the Argonne Forest and came home without much interest in trading war stories at the Legion hall. It was when he was on the mend from the accident that he started dropping in there from time to time to lose his change in a few hands of penny ante poker or a game of cribbage.

It was not a regular meeting but most of the fellows there were members of Kiefer-Bucholz American Legion Post 150. And they ran it like a meeting by the Rules of Order. A motion was made and seconded, something like: *Resolved: that all Negroes in and around Ste. Genevieve be notified to leave town by five o'clock tomorrow.* It might have said *permanently* but he believed that was understood.

Then there was discussion. At first you would think the question was whether to have the honor guard at the front or the rear of the Armistice Day parade to the cemetery. It was ten-thirty, eleven o'clock at night and fellows had been drinking but their discussion was businesslike and serious like when a man really is loaded but he walks dignified. Matt called it pompous drunk.

The motion was made by the osteopath Deichman, and he could not tell you who-all seconded. Several.

A farmer known as Big Jim Shackleford who at one time had been a Justice of the Peace stood up. He felt compelled to argue the matter with himself as a legal precedent. "The St. Louis newspapers may call it mob law," said he. "Well, it was mob law when the Patriots of Boston dressed up as Indians and threw the tea into Boston harbor. It was mob law when the people of France pulled the Bourbon kings down from the throne and set themselves free from the power of the aristocrats and the priests."

The dig at the Catholic church did not go over well in this crowd and some fellows grumbled and told Big Jim to sit down.

"I am not finished," he said. "Just hanging those three particular niggers for the murder of Rauscher and Chomeau does not solve our problem. The problem is *all* the niggers... Now, there is no law on the books that says we can force them to leave town. We have to...*motivate* them. If that is *mob law*, it is time we had some right here in Ste. Genevieve, Missouri!"

"Who cares what they call it, Jim," said Johnny Pape.

Deichman arose to argue for his own motion. "As a medical doctor," he said, "I have a scientific point of view. Negroes are anthropologically inferior to the Aryan race from Northern and Western Europe that has made this country great. It is a matter of civic bacteriology. Coming up here from the cotton fields they carry diseases—syphilis, cholera, and tuberculosis. They are the sewage of the body social. It is time to flush them out."

In the front row Reuben Biggs—whose son had taken over farming his place—said, "I object!"

"Doc has the floor," said Tony Parent.

"I have given my opinion," Deichman said..

"They are not all the same," said Biggs.

He was another of the old soldiers from the Spanish-American War and the Philippine Insurrection Matt's father used to throw cards with and he asked, "How is that, Reuben?"

"Niggers are like dogs," he said, "all different varieties. You have dogs that hunt, dogs that herd sheep. Some are friendly and wag their tails, lick your hand. Some are mean and will bite you and you have to put them down. Some are lazy and good for nothing. Just lay around under the porch scratching, eating, shitting, climb on each other's backs and try to fuck your leg. Some will bark all night so you can't sleep."

"What's your point, Reuben?" Tony Parent asked.

"Well, some of the niggers here are useful, do nigger work like janitors, cooks and maids, you know, that are beneath a white person."

"Is this in favor of the motion, or against it?"

"Now you take Lon Ribeau. He is a *good nigger...*"

"Maybe he wants to amend it."

"Chauffeurs old Mr. Rozier around...tends his garden...goes to mass...does his animal doctoring."

If Big Jim Shackleford was pompous drunk, old Reuben could scarcely follow own his own train of thought. Someone hollered, "Sit down, old man."

"He pissed his pants!" said Johnny Pape, and the fellows by him hooted and snickered.

"Let him finish," said Tony Parent

"If anybody tries to run Lon Ribeau out of town, I personally will kick his butt. Understand...? You all understand me?"

"You want to make an amendment, Reuben?"

"...Different kinds, you know."

"He means the bad and useless niggers have to go, and the useful well-behaved ones can stay."

"How do we tell?"

"Make a list, the Good Nigger List and the Bad Nigger List."

"Is that what you want, Reuben...as an amendment?"

He sat down, and slumped over with his head on his knees, his arms slack and his knuckles on the floor.

Matt considered trying to say what Reuben Biggs meant as an amendment or make it himself. Something like '*The motion applies to the transient Negroes brought in here by the lime companies,* not to the decent, hard-working Old Colored who go back generations to before the families of most of us.' But that would be condoning it. He should be standing up to these fellows. His aunt was a nun and she would rap their knuckles. He imagined—if he had it with him—pulling his service forty-five and saying *The first one of you sons of bitches that moves I will put a hole in your head.* He was not about to attempt any such thing, not with his orthopedic shoe. Or could he get away with it because of that? To tell you the truth he did not much care for Colored except for certain individuals such as Zeno Ribeau who he worked with at Peerless quarry before the accident, or his brother Lon, or Geraldine Brooks who catered for his aunts when they entertained the Ladies' Auxilliary.

Someone did propose what seemed to be the drift of Biggs' rambling as an amendment, but people were getting restless and impatient. The meeting was falling apart into different conversations, and it was never voted on. Tony called for a vote on the original motion, and just about everyone shouted, *Aye!*

From behind him Matt heard Deichman saying to Herman Steiger in a just-between-us voice, "Someday of course there will have to be a Final Solution...but the Bad Niggers List is a start." He did not like the sound of that—as if for now just telling them to go away was enough, but finally they would have to put them in concentration camps.

The crowd was breaking up into gangs, *task forces* they called them, to go five and six to a car all around town where colored people lived and give them the ultimatum. Matt eased on out before someone tried to bully him into joining them.

LESTER DODGE WAS ON THE PICKET LINE AT THE BACK ENTRANCE TO BLUFF City with Walter and some fellows from Peerless he did not know. A number of Colored had moved up there since the flood, and the pickets were supposed to keep an eye on them. Some were staying in the rundown house and farm buildings and the sheds from when the quarry was working out of there. Others made do in shacks and shanties they put up from boards and tin roofs and such from their old cribs in the bottoms.

A Chevrolet coupe rolled up with a drunken fellow riding shotgun in the rumble seat. He climbed down and two other fellows got out the front, and one of them had a lever-action rifle and the other a big old automatic pistol in his belt and he was wearing an American Legion cap. The other two backed him as he walked up to them and said, "How you boys doing?"

Lester did not like the looks of this one bit. His first idea was that they were company thugs to bust their picket line and intimidate them for Griswold to sneak the colored in and scab them out. If that was their game, Henry had returned the Bulldog Special with a few choice remarks. But it was in his dinner pail over by the walnut tree.

"You all know about the nigger murders?" asked the one with a shotgun that was in the rumble seat and Lester recognized him as a driver for Peerless named Crowley like the ridge and one of the ones known to have signed a pledge card.

"Don't nobody not know about that," said Walter.

Lester was edging off to the side by the walnut tree.

"They confessed," said the one with a lever-action.

"By the time we heard about it," said the American Legion, "that damn Sheriff snuck them off in a fast car to Festus."

That sounded like a good idea to Lester.

"So?" Walter said. He and the other fellows acted as if they saw the matter as Lester did and supposed that these three gun-happy sons-of-bitches came to mess up their picket line.

"They are low-class transient negroes from down south," said the American Legion. He went on to tell how they had a meeting and came to a *ruling* that all the colored have to leave town. Lester took him for some kind of salesman.

"We are going around everywhere they are staying," said the one with a rifle, "and telling them they have to be gone by five o'clock tomorrow."

"The ones that Jenkins brought in to work the nigger quarry," Crowley said.

So that is what this is about said Lester to himself and he would have nothing to do with it. But Walter nodded, and to him and the others on the picket line it was just a fine idea and should have been thought of before. Those evil nigger murderers of honest white men just gave them the excuse.

"We already shut down Jenkins-Gillis," Lester said, "and they are not going to open up again and none of the other lime companies either until they sign for a union shop!"

"Well Sol-i-dar-i-ty, dog my cats!" Crowley said.

Walter seemed to think that was to joke about. If they were trying to make it so Colored can't take their jobs, the closed shop did that already. Unless they switched to the CIO, and the colored issue was why they rejected them in the first place.

"Who are *you?*" American Legion asked.

"Lester Dodge," he said. "Who wants to know?"

"People you better keep a civil tongue in your head when you answer," Crowley said.

"We are going around to where Colored stay to give them the word," said the one with a rifle.

"I am Herm Steiger, Vice-Commander Kiefer-Bucholz Post 150 American Legion," said the one in the cap. "You boys come along."

"We are on a picket line," Lester said.

"It accomplishes the same thing, don't it?" said Herm Steiger. "And gets rid of the undesirable element at the same time."

"No, thank you...*sir*," Lester said. He eased down to squat by the tree and his dinner pail.

"You best come along," said the one with a rifle, who had a shanty Irish way of talking.

He thought what was the difference if he came when Walter and the others made six more of them? Then he thought how what they were doing was against the law and maybe they supposed a man was less apt to snitch if he was tarred with blame same as them.

"You with us or against us?" Steiger asked.

"Or is he one of them that his heart bleeds for the niggers?" Crowley asked.

"The *ruling* can apply to you too...Lester."

He had got his hand down inside his dinner pail. He told them, "You go to the penitentiary your way....I will go mine."

The three with guns looked at him and the fellows supposed to be on the picket line shifted their feet and edged away.

Knowing what Lester had in his dinner pail, Walter said *Don't mind him, he's just contrary* and joined with the vigilantes as they all went off to terrify the Colored.

Lester did not stand about gawking after. He cut down the path by Fallert's cave and on out through the quarries, dodging the regular picket line out front.

At the Anvil he had a tall one in a clean and lighted room where nobody that he knew of it wished him harm.

AFTER DARK CLETUS WENT ON DOWN TO THE JUKE JOINT. MABEL HAD cleaned it from the flood that finally broke through her private levee, but on the wall where the water came to was a stain up higher than you could reach and everything smelled of mildew. She was dry in her sandbag fort by the railroad embankment until the crazy man dynamited the levee. Her place was concrete-block and stayed put. But the wood shacks and cribs floated off.

Cletus took a shot of white whiskey with Vess Cola, and minded his business. He nursed it, listening to Blind Lemon Jefferson on the Victrola. Just a few people were in there besides him—Otis Bouchard, two old men playing dominoes, a wino woman, a couple having a domestic dispute, and two whores together making eyes at some young gentlemen in the corner who looked like they were planning a crime.

Then these white men came in, five, six of them. Two had shotguns. He saw pistols in their belts, billy clubs. One he knew named Stokeley from down St. Mary road, some kind of jack-leg preacher. Another was a driver for one of the white quarries named Crowley. The little one Paddy Ryan was a bartender and had a rifle.

The man acting like he was in charge wore a Legion cap and was named Steiger. "Mabel?" he asked, "That your name?"

She asked, "What for you white mens come in here?"

"There's been a *ruling.*"

Mabel had a shotgun herself back there. Acting like she was not in the least intimidated she said, "I know you ain't Klan cause you show you faces."

Most week nights there would be three times as many people in there. Friday and Saturday there would be a hundred inside, and in good weather as many out in the yard. Black people were staying close to home because of the killings. Lonzo said the white men had some big meeting to decide what they were going to do.

"All Colored must leave town by five o'clock tomorrow."

Cletus was not sure he heard that right. The other customers here and there in the place looked at each other.

"Who say that?" Mabel asked.

"I am Herman Steiger, Kiefer-Bucholz Post 150, American Legion."

"American Legion?"

"The meeting at the Legion hall. It was so moved, discussed, and the ayes had it. Then we made it unanimous."

"Who 'we'?"

"The meeting of the town."

"All the peoples of Ste. Genevieve stuffed in that Legion hall?"

"'*Cursed be the race of Ham,*' said Stokley. "'*They shall be the hewers of wood and drawers of water.*'"

"Who empty you piss pot when we gone?"

The peckerwood Crowley reached across and slapped her.

Cletus was holding his lock-blade knife in his pocket.

Ryan the one with a Winchester rifle drew down on Mabel.

"...By five o'clock tomorrow afternoon," Steiger said.

They stood there, waiting to see if anybody else back-talked.

HERM STEIGER COMPLAINED THAT ALL AROUND THAT END OF TOWN THEY congregated at the corners and in vacant lots. You passed young Negroes who would just as soon cut your throat as look at you. Besides the forty-five in his belt he had a nickel-plated .32 in his pocket. His advice was if they jump you, be deliberate and get one with each shot.

You saw their children everywhere—all sizes of pickaninnies, the big girls taking care of the little ones, hanging out the wash. They were turned off from the cotton fields and came up the railroad tracks from down south. You constantly heard that suggestive nigger music. They had nothing else to think about. "They breed," he would say. "Before long there'll be more of them than white people and they will take over like in Memphis."

Down at St. Mary last summer one of them had grabbed a little girl picking blackberries and dragged her off into the woods and exposed himself. Another one watched from the cane until a young farm wife Heidi Jokerst was alone and pushed in the door and threw her down on her kitchen floor and tried to force himself upon her. When her screams brought her husband in from the fields, the Negro cut him from elbow to wrist with a linoleum knife so that he no longer had the use of that arm.

Steiger would grant you a few of the Old Colored were upstanding citizens. He sold George and Geraldine Brooks a Chevrolet Tudor sedan with 70,000 miles for a hundred and sixty-five dollars, and they paid in cash. They had just one child. She gave piano lessons. He heard one of her pupils was white and he did not know what he thought about that, but they were letting them alone.

You had to steel yourself. The last place they found anyone before they called it a night was a rundown old house on the South Fork. A woman with one eye swollen shut and a cut lip said she had to get to her job at the shirt factory because her husband was laid off and he drank. Stokley said she was lying. "They don't hire niggers at Elder Shirtwaist."

She mumbled something.

"Well, you be gone by five o'clock tomorrow. That's the ruling."

By the time they got back to the Legion Hall where the other fellows had parked their cars and trucks, the sky was light over the bluffs on the Illinois side.

IN THE FOG HOLT HARDY COULD SEE ABOUT AS FAR AS HE COULD SPIT, AND he would stop to listen. It was hoofs like a plow horse taking his sweet time. He sifted on back into the cane and lay down behind a wash tub amongst the trash thrown off the bluff.

A horse and a mule hitched to a log-chain came along pulling a beat-up Model-A truck loaded with household plunder and Colored. They were perched on top and hanging off the sides and packed together like clowns in a flivver. More of them followed after, one pushing a two-wheel cart, another leading a mule with rolled-up featherbeds and a rocking chair on its back, but most with what they could carry on their own back or in their hands. They just walked along. Women and girls kept children in line and toted babies on their hips, old aunties told them hush. Altogether it was more than a hundred.

Holt Hardy continued on his way.

He came to an old woman lying back on the rocks and dirt from off the bluff, by her a grip tied with clothes line. He asked, "Why are you people walking up the road in the middle of the night?"

"My chirren left me here to die among the rocks."

He walked on.

23.

IN HIS DEPOSITION ZENO RIBEAU STATED THAT GANGS OF WHITE MEN drove all around that evening to where Colored lived saying *a word to the wise, you leave out of here by tomorrow five p.m.* It was supposed to be that just the transient Negroes had to leave, and let the old French Colored alone. But the gangs were mostly ignorant American Legionaires who didn't know the difference.

All day Monday Colored left in old cars, on the train, or they walked. By five o'clock p.m., the people the lime companies had brought in from down South were gone, and just about all of the local Colored too.

The Sheriff called the Governor, and he sent in the National Guard. Eighty men of Companies M and H from De Soto and Flat River came in with Captain Christy, and they guarded what Negroes remained. In the afternoon people were saying that when the doctors at St. Anthony Hospital operated to take out the bullet by his spine, Rauscher died. That made two white men the victims of brutal murder by Negroes. American Legion and the riffraff were going up to Festus, and take those Negro murderers from the jail and hang them high as Haman. The Sheriff heard about it, and sent them on to City Jail at St. Louis. Captain Christy told the Governor all was quiet in Ste. Genevieve, and the Governor said the National Guard could go home.

Once the soldiers had gone, white men gathered in the street again.

LON RIBEAU HAD JUST COME BACK FROM THE DAIRY SHOW AND CAP WAS lying on the gallery floor stone inebriated. Zeno said some trash niggers that worked for him killed two white men and they best lay low, when Cap stirred himself. Their voices woke him up and he supposed it was his business to go into town and find out what was going on.

Then he had to start making speeches.

Lon and his older and wiser brother were used to him, how he would run on from his *World Book* and his *Fair Play* newspaper at the dinner table with his home-made wine. Lon scarcely listened, just went *Umn-hmm….Is that a fact?* A preacher who preached in an empty church, that was their least brother. Cap imbibed the red wine and he preached on and on. But that night he was doing it in the street, and not just Colored heard him.

It would have been better if he had done like Zeno and Lon, kept quiet and minded his business. But, well, he was intoxicated, Lon said, and he had strong feelings and he said a lot of things he should not have said. His words came home to roost. That is what caused them trouble. Their own trouble.

AT TEN-THIRTY TUESDAY NIGHT CAP RIBEAU WAS READING HIS *WORLD Book*, and Lon and Zeno playing cribbage when light shone in the windows. They went to look out, and it was headlights. Five, six, a number of automobiles had stopped along both sides of the road, and were shining the lights on their house from three sides. Then they were getting out, four, five men from each car. Cap saw a shotgun, a lantern, pistols, American Legion caps.

Cap supposed they came for Cletus who stayed out back because he was wanted down in the Bootheel, and he said so himself he cut on a white boy.

Herman Steiger the car salesman and Paddy Ryan who ran a tavern on Merchant Street came up on the gallery. "Ribeau?" Steiger asked.

All three of them were Ribeaus. Zeno stood looking at them out the screen-door, his hand on *Grandpère's* 10-gauge double barrel goose gun that leaned by the jamb. He asked, "What you-all want?"

"The mail man..." Ryan said.

"Louis....*Cap!*"

"He having his bowel movement."

"How long does that take?"

"He a reader," Zeno said.

"What's he read?"

"The *World Book Encyclopedia*."

"He will not be harmed," Steiger said.

Cap was off to the side where they couldn't see him, and he had their papa's big old revolver out from under the mattress. Lon had his .410 rabbit gun. Leola next door let them use her phone sometimes. They did not have electricity. The coal oil lamp was on the floor between the windows, the windows open.

Zeno asked the men, "What you all want with my brother?"

"He has to leave town," said Paddy Ryan.

"He commit a crime..? You here to arrest him?"

"For his own protection."

"You deputized?"

Steiger said, "We represent Bucholz-Kiefer American Legion Post." He was on Cap's rural route.

Cap asked himself *Why the Legions come around for me? Cause I be high yellow, say I could pass? Or because I have a white man's job in the U.S. Postal Service?* You live amongst white people all your life, never for sure know their mind. Or was it because he stole the *Wanted* poster for that boy off the post office wall? If he was out there, he had better lay low. Cap would get down in the root cellar if he was him.

The men at the door asked if Cap was finished.

"He take a long time when he go to crap." Zeno said. "Take longer when you make him nervous—"

At the back door a woman called, "You hoo...!"

"...Have a shy bowel."

It was their good neighbor Leola Amoreaux and she was white, walked right in. She said, "*I called the Sheriff!*"

Steiger and Ryan looked at each other, shifted their feet.

"Gentlemens, I ask you politely..." Zeno said. "Get off our front porch." He did not show the shotgun. It was in his voice.

The white men backed off. Down in the road they looked this way and that, disputed among themselves. There were six carloads of the vigilantes. The tin soldiers were gone, and Sheriff Picou had two hired deputies.

Zeno was a war veteran too and by the window he was messing over his dynamite. He had ported it out one stick at a time in his lunch pail over seventeen years laboring for Jenkins-Gillis and a year before that at Peerless Lime.

"Let's cut out the back," Lon said.

"They got car headlights shined on the back."

"Charley Garesche' hiding in the church basement."

If that boy Cletus was out there in the old crib, he was sitting tight.

Cap saw a man named A. J. Crowley who drove a truck for Peerless Lime. He was another one on his route and he would sic his dog on him. He hollered, "That nigger's taking long enough to crap a baby!"

Alonzo sifted to the back door.

You could spit from their gallery steps to the road.

Zeno had two sticks of the dynamite taped together with a cap with a short fuse down by the lamp flame. He said, "I will make some white mens *hop!*"

Cap said, "Then what?"

"What you mean, 'Then what?'"

"A Negro...kill some more white mens?"

"They trespassing. Herm Steiger have a big old .45 model 1911 in his belt. Fixing to string you up from the pecan tree."

They were men they knew the name of. They had done nothing wrong. Cap set their papa's revolver on the window sill and started out the screen door.

Zeno caught him by the belt in back. "You crazy?"

"I be going on down there before my brother commence to throw dynamite."

"Hold your horses!"

Cap jinked loose and went out on the gallery and said, "Gentlemens, what you want with me?"

"We aren't going to hurt you," said Ryan.

"You will be escorted out of town," Steiger said.

"What crime I do?"

"The ruling was--"

"The *'ruling'*?"

"From the nigger list," Crowley said. He was inebriated, and not the only one.

"We made a list of all the decent property-owning colored people," Steiger said. "They are allowed to remain...Any of *them* that left yesterday are welcome to return to their homes."

Ryan said, "We're just cleaning out the transient Negroes from down South."

"...Who harbor the criminal element."

"The cotton-picker scabs," said Johnny Pape who worked at Western Lime.

"My family own this house a hundred years...What for you call me out?"

"We went down the list," Steiger said. "You will not be harmed."

Cap hung on to the gallery post, studied to control his bowel.

They went and fetched their white neighbor on the other side Gary Schramm, and Steiger said he would come along to guarantee his safety. Gary was mad as a hornet cursing them to get their damn hands off. He hollered, "Cap! Don't trust these drunk sons-of-bitches!"

They shut him up.

ONE REACHED OUT AND GRABBED CAP BY THE ANKLE, AND THEY DRAGGED him back in the dark, hit and kicked at him, pulled him this way and that. They were not of one mind. Cap messed his pants.

Headlights came down the road. *It had to be the Sheriff.*

Light shined on them crowded in the road. A car slowed down and almost stopped, then started up again and peeled on out of there. It was a young girl and her boyfriend driving home from the picture show, thinking the men were going to rape and rob them. He stepped on the gas. The girl's white face scared to death whipped on by, men knocked every which way.

Cap slipped off in the dark.

The road followed the edge of *Grandchamps* bottom, with the houses on the uphill side. He cut the other way down to Gabouri Creek, and ran hunched over by the stone wall past Green Tree Tavern and under the bridge. Someone hollered, *"Where's the nigger at?"*

He heard a commotion back on the road. Motors gunned, tires peeled off in a hurry.

He kept on up the creek under the bridge for 4th Street, climbed up the bank and walked along to the priest's house, and hid in the basement with old Charley Garesche'. He was out of his mind. He cried, laughed, and carried on all night. Next day Father T. put him on the train to Arsenal Street sanitarium at St. Louis.

CLETUS THOUGHT THE VIGILANTES CAME FOR HIM BECAUSE HE CUT ON J.T. He ducked down in the root cellar under just part of his crib. Then he scrunched up in the space between the floor and the ground where it was not dug out and crawled to where you could see light from the headlights they left shining up into the back yard. It was coming in from between two of the up-and-down wall posts and he got out his knife and scraped away more of the chink between so he could see out some. He could see men at the side of the house and there had to be more around in front. He imagined they were talking to Zeno and them up on the gallery saying call him out. If he ran, they would see him for sure. But maybe they did not know he cribbed out back. He was thinking did he blow out the lamp?

They were taking a long time so maybe the Ribeaus were trying to shuck and jive or Cap, he would bogart them. Lon was the one most likely to tell where he was. Cletus told himself act like the buck rabbit when you come to hunt him, sit tight.

Some kind of commotion was going on, the men he could see shifting around. A car motor gunned and peeled off and they yelled and cried out he believed saying here come the Sheriff, then more car doors closing, motors gunned, gravel was flying, tires peeled off. It sounded like the vigilantes decided mostly to scoot.

This might his only chance. He scrunched backwards to the cellar and scrambled up through the trap door and grabbed his work shirt and cut out the back, and slunk along by the line of bushes and trees up the hill a ways. Then he jinked back down the dirt alley to the creek where the track ran beside it and he went along under the bridge and squatted down.

Short trains from Peerless and Alton Lime came off and on all night taking bags of cement and chemicals and hopper cars of crushed stone to the landing where they loaded off onto barges. He waited maybe three-quarters of an hour sitting tight under the bridge before he heard one coming, a little yard engine puffing along slow for the curve and street crossings through town. It had just four cars. Cletus jumped the third one. He grabbed the ladder and hunkered down under the pitch-roof bottom of the hopper only they could see you there. He swung around the ladder and climbed up and lay down on the load of crushed rock.

He felt in his pockets. He had his knife and handkerchief and some change and small bills but he would count it later. He believed it came to eleven dollars and some.

MANY OF THE VIGILANTES WHO EVADED THE SHERIFF AT RIBEAUS' ON THE south side of town went to the north side to the hastily abandoned houses in the creek bottom below Ziegler Street, doused them with coal oil, and set them on fire. The first was the home of Beaulah Misplaits and also where she conducted her practice. The second in the row was the home of Jim Cobb and his wife and their five children. The third was that of Jim's cousin Will Cobb and his three children and Will's sister Maria Moss and her little girl Fancy. The last was Uncle Ben Kelly's. They also burned his chicken coops and more than forty chickens, which were how he made his living.

No one was charged, but people suspected Deichman the osteopath was behind it. Then one of the workingmen from the lime kilns was heard boasting that he and his two buddies actually set the fires, while Deichman watched from his car up on Ziegler Street. He paid them five dollars each. The boastful fellow, named Bucholz, laughed and said they would have done it for nothing—even "would have paid for the fun of it, burning the niggers' houses."

24.

MATT ZIEGLER IN HIS DEPOSITION STATED THAT AFTER THE VIGILANTES went around Sunday night to every colored person they could find and told them all to leave town by five o'clock Monday afternoon, they did. Some took the train. Others left in old cars and trucks, and many set out on foot with what they could carry. They were gone by sundown.

Even Geraldine Brooks who worked for the Griswold family and her husband George the high school custodian fled to Jefferson City where their daughter was a student at the state college for Negroes. Sarah and Charley Garesche' were cowering in Father Van Tourenhaut's basement. Mabel Detchmendy and a bootlegger and his whore hid out on the Illinois side until they felt safe enough to show their faces for business as usual at the Creamery. Only the Ribeau brothers stayed in their house.

Some National Guard straggled into town late Monday night, but that was locking the barn after the horse was stolen. Ziegler saw Ed Kiefer and Leonard Paultier and some other civic booster types drinking beer and playing pool with them at the Legion Hall, and by the next afternoon they were persuaded that everything was hunky dory and they left. They had not been gone three hours before another vigilante gang had gathered at Ribeaus.'

WHEN THE NATIONAL GUARD CAME TO TOWN AGAIN MAJOR ADAMS OF the State Adjutant General's staff came with them, and he took a different tone. They arrived not long after midnight in a convoy of olive drab trucks and a Department of Corrections bus, 80 men from Company M in Festus and Company H in DeSoto.

The next morning when Matt Ziegler walked up Market street from getting a putty knife at the hardware, he looked up to see the muzzle of a .50 caliber machine gun at the corner of the Catholic church at Dubourg square sited to command two sides of the courthouse and the entrance to the jail. It was chest high on a stanchion mount with three legs, with a long belt of vicious-looking cartridges. Two old soldiers manned it, and a rank of uniformed men with fixed bayonets stood to either side.

They called a meeting at the courthouse Wednesday afternoon, and Matt was in attendance. The hall was packed, mostly with local business men. The *Fair Play* put the crowd at 250. He scarcely had elbow room in his perch on the stairs.

Mayor Schwendt presided and said the meeting was called to enlist the citizens of the town against mob violence and to curb the unfavorable publicity they were getting over their reaction to the killing of Harry Chomeau and Paul Rauscher by Negroes. He introduced Father Van Tourenhault.

The old Priest said they should welcome Major Adams who was there as a personal representative of the Governor and Captain Christy of Company H from DeSoto and Lieutenant Fogelsang of Company M from Festus. They must co-operate with them in every way to combat disorder and mob violence. "Until recently Ste. Genevieve has been known for the harmony we have enjoyed with our Negro people whose families have lived among us for many generations...as opposed to the strife that has afflicted other communities such as Flat River and East St. Louis. It is our duty to curb in every way the spirit of racial animosity that has been expressing itself over the last three days."

Prosecuting Attorney Petrequin, Dr. G.M. Claiborne and others were allowed to have their say. Finally the Mayor called on Major Adams who was on the staff of the State Adjutant General. He said his instructions from the Governor were to restore peace and harmony to this town. "I ask each and every one of you to cooperate with us, and with Mayor Schwendt, and Presiding Judge Siebert, and with Sheriff Picou....The Governor also instructed me to inform you that if we are called here again, we will remain for six months and you will be put under martial law."

This did not sit well.

JUDGE SIEBERT CALLED A SPECIAL SESSION OF THE COURT IN THE MATTER of the six men arrested in the incident at Ribeaus—Russell Stokley, James Hurst, Johnny Pape, J.A. Crowley, Herman Steiger, and Louis Paddy Ryan. It was in the big courtroom that took up most of the second floor, and like a number of others from the meeting Matt went in to watch the proceedings.

With a nod from the Judge, the Clerk Leo Karl read the charges. "...Attempted kidnapping, threatening to do great bodily harm, inciting to riot, and interfering with a Federal employee in performance of his duties."

"How do they plead?" Siebert asked.

Their lawyer Hans Wulff got up and said, "I thought we agreed to a lesser charge."

Siebert looked to the Prosecutor Harry Petrequin, who said, "They offered to plead guilty to disturbing the peace and...making threats."

"No, sir. That's a felony."

"The Clerk will enter a plea of innocent to the charges...We have examined the defendants and heard testimony. They will please rise."

The six of them stood up with different expressions on their faces—Herm Steiger dignified and respectful, Crowley and Pape looking around and shaking their heads as if to say *this is bullshit*, Ryan sheepish, Hurst ready to take his medicine, and Stokley with a *Jesus-loves-me* smirk on his face that Matt would dearly have loved to see Frank Siebert wipe off.

"We find you guilty of disturbing the peace, trespassing, and making threats. You are sentenced each to six months in the county jail and a four-hundred dollar fine."

People around Ziegler gasped, shook their heads, and some said out loud *No! That's not right!*

Siebert smacked his gavel and adjourned.

AS THEY EMERGED FROM THE COURTROOM, WORD SPREAD OF AN URGENT meeting at the Legion Hall two hours hence. Matt set out fully intending to drive on home in his trusty Model-A to the farm, but saw no harm in stopping off for a beer at the Flash Café across the highway from Peerless Lime. Some fellows who were at the courthouse were there and Mike McBride bought him a beer so he must buy him one and then another fellow he knew bought for both of them, and they were going to the Legion Hall and Matt ended up tagging along.

This was an official meeting in the hall, not the bar. Over their heads along the balcony rail to either side were ranks of flags and unit guidons with names of places where they served---1st Infantry, 138th Field Artillery, Chateau Thiery, the Marne, the Meuse Argonne. They came to order and recited the Pledge of Allegiance, and Chaplain Andy Laird who was an ordained minister of the Episcopal Church gave the invocation.

The Post Commander Ed Kiefer welcomed the special guests, Major Adams and the officers of the Guard companies Captain Christy and Lieutenant Fogelsang. They were sitting behind him on the platform with Mayor Schwendt and Sheriff Picou. From the lectern off to one side Ed said, "We called this meeting at the request of Dolph Schwendt and Ben Picou. They are asking us for assistance in main'taining order ... and to protect all our law-abiding citizens and their property. ... Do I hear a motion?"

The President of the Chamber of Commerce Leonard Paultier so moved, "...That Kiefer-Bucholz American Legion Post 150 pledges to uphold law and order, and to serve as sheriff's deputies in any emergency." There was not much discussion and the question was called. It passed with some grumbling but no distinct Nay votes, and they made it unanimous.

Major Adams congratulated them.

Then Big Jim Shackleford got up to complain about what was being said about the town in the press. He railed at the Kansas City Star, the Des Moines Register, and the St. Louis Star-Times. The account that particularly roused his ire was in a St. Louis Negro newspaper called The Argus as reported extensively in their own Herald. "Listen to this...," he said. "Old Citizens Driven From Ste. Genevieve, Mo....Pioneer Mississippi River Town Becomes Bloodthirsty After Underworld Killing and Vents Feeling on Respected Negroes....Families Banished from Their Historical Homes....Members of Knights of Columbus Participate in Move Against Their Own Catholic Church Communicants....Protesting Priest Ordered to Keep Mouth Shut.' ...That is a pack of lies!"

Matt watched Adams' face with sagging jowls and quick little eyes. So far as he could tell he did not take offense.

"There has been no violence nor any bloodshed other than the murder of Paul Rauscher and Harry Chomeau that set us off, and rightly so! Except for the misunderstanding last night between some fellows who had too much to drink and went to have a few words with the Ribeau brothers, there has been no rioting or disorder. No shots have been fired ... by or at anyone ... citizens of this town, the men at Ribeaus, or military or police in the four days since the trouble began. ... Ben Picou called for the state troops as a precautionary measure, and although some of us might question the necessity for that, Ben and his men should be commended for keeping the lid on and preventing violence."

A man in back moved a vote of thanks to Sheriff Ben Picou and his deputies. It was seconded and passed with general approbation and a round of applause.

Another man offered a resolution that Post 150 "guarantee protection to certain native property-owning Negroes whenever they might wish to return to their homes." Big Jim Shackleford wanted to a add a proviso, "However, *no other Negroes* will be permitted to return to the community." This drew cheers and an outburst of applause. Someone else said they needed to round up the suspicious tramp characters who had drifted in on the chance of taking the jobs vacated in the general exodus of the colored people. This was added as an amendment, and it all passed on a voice vote.

Matt looked to see how this was going down with Major Adams. He was beaming and nodding his head.

Nobody said a word about the burning of the houses on LaHaye Street.

The next day, Thursday, Matt learned that Judge Siebert had ruled that the fines and jail sentences he imposed on the six men guilty of offenses against the Ribeau brothers were suspended, so long as they behaved themselves. They were free to go home, although they faced arraignment on the Federal charges in St. Louis.

That afternoon Major Adams returned to Jefferson City, and the National Guard was pulling out. By Friday morning they had all gone home, and the whole town was on good behavior.

CLETUS KNEW HE HAD BETTER NOT BE IN THAT CRUSHED ROCK WHEN THE train stopped and it fell down the chute into the barge. But if he raised up to look, the dock men might catch him.

He sat tight.

A clanking and clinking in the couplings jinked from car to car and they moved back the other way to the side track by the barges in the flood lights. He eased over the edge and down the ladder and as the train was going faster he jumped, and ran two steps but his body was going as fast as the train and too fast for his feet and he fell out by the track on the ballast rock. He scrambled up, and got into the sumac at the bottom of the bluff. His wrists and knee were skinned but it would scab over.

After a while when nobody came looking for him, he went walking up the track. He passed a sign the size of a car license but up endways on a fence post, 64. In a while he passed one just like it, 63. These were mile posts. To St. Louis.

He walked all night sometimes between the tracks, sometimes on the ties outside, most of the time on the dirt beside the ballast chat. The best walking was when the chat was level with the top of the ties. When it was not and you tried to land your foot on a tie every step, it was either too long or too short. Now and again he cut up, walked on the rail, seeing how many steps before he lost his balance, and had to put his foot on the ties. Sometimes he counted his steps, two steps was a pace, and each time your left heel came down was five feet and some. Mrs. Nolan taught them in geometry a mile was a thousand paces from the old-time word for a thousand. Most miles had posts. 59...58...57, but some had been stolen and others had holes shot through them or indentations from bird-shot.

He walked all night, then went up a hollow, and lay down on the little soft brown needles in a cedar thicket to catch some sleep.

It must have been around noon time when he woke up, and walked on. His new work shoes were broken in but he felt a rubbing on his heel where he had a hole in his sock. Next time he stopped, he took the shoes and socks off, and switched each sock to the other foot.

Mostly the high bluff ran by the tracks. Sometimes there were bottoms off to the other side, other times you were on just a shelf by the river. Towboats went by, up and down. He walked almost as fast as boats going up. He counted barges, fifteen, twelve, empty or full. Now and then a little hollow opened up on the left, with a quarry or a farm. He watched for dogs.

He recalled his papa talking to Mr. Snow when he came to Cropperville to see how they were making out, something about Reverend Whitfield. Where he was staying in St. Louis was Meacham Park. Cletus was going to Meacham Park.

WHEN HER MAMA CALLED, ALL CLEMMIE BROOKS COULD UNDERSTAND for sure was that her parents were jumping in the car right now and driving to Jefferson City. Her mama said something about white men being killed and a lynch mob and the American Legion going around to all the colored people in Ste. Genevieve saying they had to leave town by five o'clock Monday. It made no sense, except that whatever happened this was not play-acting. Her mama was scared.

They arrived after midnight and you would not believe what all Mama brought with her in the back seat of the old car—the family pictures and bric-a-brac from the living room, a picture of trees in the wind that Clemmie painted in grade school, her white teddy bear. She was wearing her three best church dresses one over another all rumpled from the long drive and her little cloche funeral hat with a veil. Papa was numb.

The housemother Mrs. Ludington said they could stay there that night in the emergency, and she would help to find a room for them tomorrow at one of the boarding houses for colored near campus. One of Clemmie's suite mates was home for the weekend and the other two stayed that night with other girls. Papa would sleep in one of their not-much-more-than-a-closet sleeping rooms and Mama in another. Clemmie and her mama stood guard on the hall landing while Papa was in the bathroom.

He went on to bed, but naturally Mama had to come in Clemmie's little room and talk.

"I am devastated," she said. "I will never look at a white person the same way again."

"Did they come to our house and threaten you with guns?"

"They don't have to, child. They come to Ribeaus *right next door*....and the scariest part was, they did not wear bedsheets or pillow cases over their heads or black their faces. *They do not care who knows who they are.*"

That *was* scary. Growing up Negro in Ste. Genevieve, you hear different things different times about Klan. They are the boogey man when you are little and scared of the dark. You try to guess who they are. At least they always had enough shame—or at least enough sense, depending on who won the last election—to hide their faces. If the men were bare-faced, what did that mean? All the white people now were Klan?

She knew better than that.

She asked about her mother's friends.

"Father T. hid Charley Garesche' in the church basement," she said, "and Sarah is staying there too. Of course *they* know they be there now, but you would think...the church...

"Irene Bouchard went to her aunt's in Crystal City. Otis, you know, took to drinking after he got laid off because he protected that white boy. She would throw him out and he sweet-talked his way back, then they fight again. I imagine he went on up there with her. Zeno Ribeau, of course, he will not be moved. Lon stays on there with him...Cap is in the sanitarium up at St. Louis. Irene says they heard from him and he is more like himself, but he swears he will never set foot in Ste. Genevieve again."

Clemmie asked her, "What about that sharecropper boy, Cletus?"

"They don't know....He disappeared."

"I hope nothing bad happened to him."

"Kind of pert, if you ask me."

"He is a highly intelligent young man."

"He could learn some respect for his elders."

"What kind of respect all this teach him, Mama?"

"Any of us, child. Like I say....All my life I try to get along with white people."

IN THE MORNING MRS. LUDINGTON HAD HOT-CAKES AND SIDE MEAT FOR breakfast in honor of Mama and Papa, and the girls wanted to know their experiences. Adele James and Cynthia Bolt were in Professor Langston's American Civilization class with Clemmie, and they actually did drive down with him to the Boot Heel to help the sharecroppers. Mama was not shy, she would tell her tale if you had patience to hear it.

"These two white men go trolling for skunk in the Negro part of town. Some way they contrived to get a woman named Vera who had more to drink than she ought riding in their car out to the ferry landing, but her two friends Taylor and C.J. ride along to look out for her. Well, the white men get crude and vulgar and her friends take up for her, and they fight, and when it was all over the two white men be dead. Cry goes up *Colored murdered two white men!*"

Mama told how the deputies sweated them for false confessions and white people mobbed the court house to lynch them. When the Sheriff got them out of town to the jail at Festus, the mob took it out on all the Negro people they could find and said they had to leave. Cynthia and Adele and the other girls hung on Mama's words.

Papa was flustered and bashful being the one man at the sorority-house table, afraid to dribble syrup on his shirt in front of all the attractive young ladies. Of course they did not have a Southern mansion with white columns type of sorority house with a hundred blue-eyed coeds like the Pi Phi's and Alpha Phi's at the white university up at Columbia. Their house was an old frame bungalow with a wing added on and they had eleven members.

When Papa went to get gas and oil, Clemmie had a chance to talk to Mama now that she was not so agitated. They sat on the front porch swing and she asked her, "Mama, what you and Daddy going to do?"

"I don't know, Clementine. I simply do not know."

"I just can't believe that all the white people want every single black person to get out of town....Who's going to do their menial work?"

"You think I *menial?*"

"Mama!"

"And you papa?"

"I am not being disrespectful, Mama. You wash and iron clothes and scrub toilets for Mrs. Griswold....Daddy the janitor at the white high school, bring in the mop and bucket when a white child puke on the floor....It's what you do."

"We *menial.* Embarrass you with your friends."

"Mama, my friends' parents just the same. Adele's papa a mail man in Kansas City, her mama has a little beauty shop. Cynthia's mama is the cleaning woman for some dentist and doctor's offices. All the girls, Mrs. Ludington, we the same people. Nobody looking down at you."

"I want better for you, Clemmie."

"I know that, Mama."

Papa drove up to the curb.

"Mama," Clemmie said, "you call Mrs. Griswold on the long-distance telephone. She will beg you to come back."

THE *ARGUS* AND THE *POST-DISPATCH* TOLD OF REFUGEES ARRIVING IN ST. Louis. "All night long the flight of the fugitives went on. Some of the children were almost naked and the women but scantily clothed. They waded the creek and climbed the hillside beyond. Once over the ridge they were out of danger for the time being.

"Women who had babies bore their infants close to their breasts. Some of the smaller children were carried by the men. Other terrified little ones, not comprehending the nature of the incident but knowing that something terrible was happening, stumbled along striving to keep close to their mothers.

"Some of the Negroes returned to town and were told that all must leave before nightfall. A few came back and packed up some of their household goods. Many remained in the woods hungry and almost naked until their friends took them scant supplies or they walked across the fields and along the country roads to other towns. At intervals they met armed men patrolling the roads and were told to move on. Each Negro was warned never to return on peril of his life.

"Two Negro preachers, Rev. S.S. Pitcher of Kinloch and Rev. L.M. Smith of Meacham Park were in Ste. Genevieve during the excitement. They were driven out with the rest. Mr.

Pitcher, pastor of the Missionary Baptist Church of Meacham Park, tells this story of his flight:

"Rev. Mr. Smith and I had made arrangements to open a colored camp meeting at Ste. Genevieve. We went down Monday intending to put up our tent and start the meeting that night. But the murder of the two white men so excited the town that I was warned by some of the citizens not to start the meeting.

"Monday night we were stopping at the house of James Cobb, later one of the houses that were burned down.

"We walked eight miles to Bloomsdale, then two miles and a half to Valles Mines, then fifteen miles to DeSoto—more than twenty-five miles in all. There we took a train for St. Louis, arriving Tuesday night.

"On the road toward Valles Mines we saw a man plowing in a field. He ran to his house, got his shotgun, and came into the road in front of us. We explained that we had to leave Ste. Genevieve and asked him the way to DeSoto. But he seemed so savage that we passed on.

"I am utterly worn out with a night and a day of walking amid hostile white people. The whole country between DeSoto and Ste. Genevieve seemed to be aroused. My church tent is still up at Ste. Genevieve and I don't know when I can get it."

About 75 of the fugitives went to St. Louis. A reporter named Robertus Love interviewed a number of them. James Abernathy a railroad porter who lived at 1838 Lyon Street in the Mill Creek neighborhood was harboring 21 of the Ste. Genevieve refugees, mostly women and children, in his two-room flat. Most of them had fled only partially clothed. Some had been permitted to pack their trunks and put them aboard the train Monday afternoon.

At Abernathy's were Mrs. W. S. Cobb and three children, Mrs. J. W. Cobb and five children, Mrs. Maria Moss and her little niece, James Cobb, and William S. Moss, the two latter being railroad firemen. They had gone out on their runs.

"Miss Pinky Cobb, a well-educated girl, almost white, was also at Abernathy's. Miss Cobb was one of the belles of Ste. Genevieve's colored population. Her sister Mrs. Moss is also nearly white, and the husband of this woman shows only the fain'test trace of Negro blood. The children of the Moss family are whiter than their parents.

"Miss Pinky Cobb told me a thrilling story of her escape. She was in the two-story house at Ste. Genevieve occupied and owned by the Cobbs and the Mosses, who are related by marriage. This is the house in which the two Negro preachers were staying.

"'When the white men with guns came to tell us we must leave,' said Pinky Cobb, "my sister and her children got under a bed. I ran to the cellar but feared that they were going to burn our house, so I went up the back stairs and started to run away toward the creek. I jumped into the water and bent down low. Finally I got far enough along without being seen and escaped up the hill.

'After the white men went somewhere else I crept back. I was so afraid up there among the trees that I just couldn't stay. Some of the folks had returned to the house and barred the door. I had to break in the door to enter.

"Miss Pinky is a bicyclist. She left her wheel at Ste. Genevieve. She wears a handsome silver watch and shows much taste in dress. She apologized for her appearance. 'My good clothes are all at Ste. Genevieve,' she said.

"Mrs. Cobb, mother of one of the locomotive firemen, said that she came from Fulton, Kentucky. 'That's the South too,' she said, 'but give me the South in preference to Ste. Genevieve. They are supposed to hate colored people down south but I never was treated like this. Kentucky is good enough for me.

"'I want no more of Ste. Genevieve, though I want to save my property there if I can. We have all worked hard to buy our little home from old Mr. Rozier at his bank, and if there is any law and justice in Missouri I do not see how they can beat us out of it. I had to sell my cow for ten dollars. She was worth three times that. Our furniture is all smashed and burnt now.

"'Every one of us believes that if a Negro committed that murder no punishment is too severe for him. But we don't believe that the innocent should be made to suffer for one man's crime. Especially the women and children.'

"When the trunk of Mrs. Maria Moss was thrown off at Union Station, three bullet holes were observed in the side of it.

"The two men of these families were absent on their railroad runs when the raid took place. The women and children when they went to the depot at Ste. Genevieve to take the train for St. Louis were not permitted to board from the platform. They had to walk nearly two miles up to the Modoc ferry landing.

"Old Uncle Ben Kelly whom everybody liked is nearly 80 years of age. He lived alone in a small house just in the rear of the home of French Godley, which was burned. Uncle Ben was a chicken farmer. His chickens netted him a living. 'Them chickens was all I had for my livelihood," said Uncle Ben. I don't know why the white folks wants to run poor old Uncle Ben out of town. I was there here thirty years and I never done nobody no harm, sir. Nobody at all, sir. I'm going down to my gal at Crystal City cause that place ain't no home no more for Uncle Ben.'

Uncle Ben's gal at Wagoner is his married daughter.

25.

MATT ZIEGLER WAS PLAYING CARDS AT THE LEGION HALL. WHEN HIS FRIEND Tom Wilder the Postmaster pulled up a chair to join their game of penny ante, Luther Mott refused to make room for him and none of the others would budge either. Tom asked, "What's wrong, boys? Afraid I'll win your pay check?"

"This is a closed game," said Luther.

"...Do I smell bad?"

"I lost enough," Matt said and started to get up.

Al Moeller puts his hand on his arm.

"Take my place, Tom."

"He is not welcome," said Dolph Schwendt.

"Well, anyhow, I'm folding." Matt threw in his cards.

He went to the bar and asked for a Four Roses and a chaser and the same for Tom, and they settled at the small table in the corner between the last bar stool and the picture window. Nobody came within a ten-foot pole of them. You would think they had a highly contagious disease.

They both knew what all this was about.

Tom said, "Those six men were in violation of the Federal law, Matt...and a lot of other fellows too."

Matt had seen the piece about it in the *Fair Play*. The penalty for conspiring to intimidate or prevent by force any person from performing his duties for the government such as delivering mail was up to ten years in the penitentiary and a 5,000 dollar fine.

"Frank Siebert may give them a slap on the wrist and send them home. After all, he serves at the pleasure of the voter—"

"If the soldiers weren't here," Mat said, "and he threw the book at them, the fellows in the courtroom and out in the street would have mobbed him and set the whole bunch loose."

"But I answer to a different crowd."

Matt said it appeared to him that Henry Wallace and Mrs. Roosevelt and their friends were trying to bring in their anti-lynching law by the back door, after the Southern filibuster killed it again in the Senate.

"You think *Boys will be boys?*"

"I'm not saying that. Just, to people in this town ten years in the penitentiary seems harsh for what amounted to a shivaree at Ribeaus'."

"Cap was a nervous wreck. For all he knew they were going to hang him, burn him alive. He jumped the next train to St. Louis and signed himself in to the Arsenal Street sanitarium."

"That's regrettable."

"*Regrettable?*...Can you imagine what it's like to have people turn on you, talk about you behind your back and—?"

"*Tom*. People are staring."

"I don't give a god-damn. You serve your country in the World War...."

A lot of them did, including Matt Ziegler and the men who were shunning Tom.

"I was in the Lost Battalion. You know about that?"

"Only in a general way."

He went on to tell him, "It was in the Argonne Forest with our trenches across here.... and the German trenches across there."

He moved two swizzle sticks on the table to show where the lateral trenches were. "Then we had connecting trenches," he said. The so-called Lost Battalion was most of the 2nd Battalion of the 308th Infantry Regiment and some of the 3rd Battalion. "They told us to attack up the connecting trench," he said, showing him with his hands. "Only the Germans were ready for us. They really were ready. They pulled back to the ends of the trench like this...and let us go right through. Then they closed in behind us...It was a little closed-in valley like one of the hollows here where the quarries are, and Germans up all around the rim with machine guns, and in the middle, one spring.

"The Germans had their machine guns ranged on the spring, and whenever one of our boys went out with some canteens for water, they shot him up like Swiss cheese....We were cut off for four days. Out of seven hundred men, a hundred and fifty survived."

He took out his wallet and thumbed through the cards, some of them quite worn. It took him a moment to find the one he wanted, and he showed it to Matt. It was light blue with black printing, from the Veterans Administration. "Number Four," he said. On the back was a list of stipulations and directives in very fine print. Number Four read: *Members of the Lost Battalion will receive blood whenever needed without charge from any facility.* Tom put away the card. The Lost Battalion had given its share of blood. Matt bowed his head.

He was over there too but in the rear with Corps Artillery. What happened to his foot was after he got back, you could say in the war between Labor and Management. Only Peerless Lime did not give you a purple heart.

"You come home...." Tom said. "Your wife that you loved as your own life has died of the influenza. Your nerves are shot. You wake up in night sweats. Your hand shakes....You try to get hold of yourself, and cast around for what you will do."

He was telling Matt this not simply as the crowning injustice of how the Legion fellows were treating him, but to recall the most trying time of his life. If he could get through that, he could say of what was happening to him now in Ste. Genevieve, *This too shall pass.*

"My dad's harness and saddle business has dwindled to a hobby in his old age, and the livery stable where I worked is a gas station. In the Army I was a mail clerk until the Argonne offensive when they gave that to a replacement and threw me into the line. So when the postmaster job comes open, you think what's to lose? And you apply, and with your veterans' preference you get it, and other fellows that wanted it resent you. You hire a well-qualified colored man as a letter carrier because it is department policy not to discriminate, and people in this town look funny at you for that...And then these murders...which have nothing to do with anything...Could happen anywhere...red men, Chinamen ...but the Dixie yahoos here jump on it as their excuse---only a large part of the Dixie element are Germans who need to show how American they are, that their hearts don't go pitty-pat for the *Vaterland* and Kaiser Bill--and they go to lynch Cap Ribeau, who had absolutely nothing to do with any of it."

"They *said* they just meant to make him leave town—"

"You believe—?"

"For his own protection."

"You believe that?"

"Well, maybe it's what some of them thought they were doing...or believed afterward that was all they were doing."

"They were a gang of drunken vigilante fools. They—"

"*Tom!* We better go someplace else."

They walked down Rozier Street and across the Gabouri bridge. He told Matt there had been vandalism to mail trucks. He got threatening phone calls, a brick thrown through the window of his house out the St. Mary road, a note stuck under the windshield wiper of his car. "When I go around town, people I knew for years don't speak to me. It's childish. If I go in a place and people are talking, they clam up. The rough element tries to intimidate me. The nice people give me the cold shoulder....I'm being ostracized."

Matt said it was not right.

"That's what the Greeks did, you know? Cast you out .... Now, if I just clear out of here, where am I going to get another job? Not in the Postal Service.

"I grew up here. My dad lived here all his life. I can't believe this. I went to school with these people. I thought I knew them better than anyone else in the world. Now it seems like I never knew them at all…how spiteful they can be.

"You know, I couldn't stop the Federal prosecutors from going after those six fellow if I wanted to. The Sheriff arrested them, and he and Petrequin knew Federal Law was involved here, and they notified the Postal Inspector at St. Louis. He is the one that investigated and turned it over to the Prosecutor. Maybe I could have lied to get them off but all that would do is make them think I'm yellow, and prosecute just the same. But people seem to think it was some kind of personal vendetta of mine to testify against those men. I wasn't there. All I can testify to is that Cap Ribeau did not report for work the next day.

"I wake up in a sweat. I can't get back to sleep. My hand shakes. It is like when I came home from the World War and my wife dead all over again. I have this nervous tic in my left eyelid. I can't control it…I can feel sorry for myself, you know?

"Then I start to think how it must be for the colored people…

"A gang comes to your door and not just trash…respected citizens…and says be out of town by five o'clock…Can you imagine that?"

Matt could, and he was ashamed to admit when he saw them doing pretty nearly the same thing to Tom, a white man, it came home to him. When it was just colored, well, this had happened, and worse, to them in other places, and to other kinds of people. He believed it was more likely to happen in hard times.

He did walk out on that poker game.

THE POSTMASTER SENT THE FOLLOWING TO THE *FAIR* PLAY, WHICH WAS printed as a letter to the editor:

> TO SET at rest the many false and unfounded
> rumors about the reason for my resignation of the
> Post Mastership of Ste. Genevieve, I wish to state
> that the whole reason is because my war-shattered
> nerves demand that I give up this exacting and
> confining work if I am to regain and retain my
> health.
>
> L. Tom Wilder

LESTER ACKNOWLEDGED THAT DRIVING THE COLORED FROM THEIR MIDST was a mark on the book page of the town. The good people who stood by ought to be ashamed, and he might have done more himself to stop Walter and Little John from tagging after those fellows with guns. One thing they accomplished though was to take the starch out of the lime companies.

You may read in the papers how it was a lynch mob deprived of the three negro murderers by Sheriff Picou doing his job, how trash was the perpetrators and among them a number of the Ku Klux Klan, and in anger and frustration they turned on all the Colored they could find. They will tell you American Legion and Knights of Columbus were foremost among them.

That is true as far as the Boston Tea Party was real Indians. Just like in the whole town, half the Legion and K of C were lime workers. And most of them who rode in gangs packing guns to give the ultimatum to the Colored to leave town by five o'clock on Monday were Union fellows.

It served their cause.

Now the Colored were no longer there for the other lime companies to go the way of Jenkins-Gillis with an open shop and half the pay. The workingmen of Ste. Genevieve not only showed their resolve in keeping up the strike week after week and a militancy to reckon with in trashing the Back-to-Work meeting. When they calculated it was in their interest, they did not scruple to set the law at defiance and impose their will.

The bosses and their lawyers had food for thought.

Then the Federal charge against them of unfair labor practices came down. The hearing would be Monday in the Ste. Genevieve courthouse at 10 a.m. Commissioner Dorothy D. Schweinitz of the National Labor Relations Board said they committed industrial espionage, interference with union activities, threats, attempts to discredit the union, and coercion of employees. She had filed a separate charge against Bluff City Lime for not bargaining in good faith and locking their men out.

The *Fair Play* had to remind everybody what the Professor from the Jesuit College at St. Louis said, how this was a lengthy procedure and the Board in Washington DC had hundreds of cases waiting, and the lime companies will appeal any ruling against them. The courts can take months before they get around to a decision on their little complaints. The idea is they might as well sign the pledge cards for the company union because any justice they might hope for would come too late. They all would have starved to death. Of course the lime companies would not have done a whole lot of business in that time either.

So Monday morning came, and Commissioner Schweinitz called the hearing to order in the courthouse basement. Right off the bosses' lawyer Henry Spink announced Bluff City had settled and signed a closed-shop contract with Local 829. He said a copy of this agreement was forwarded to the Board at Washington with a request for permission to dismiss charges against the company.

On Wednesday Peerless, Western, and Alton Lime settled, and that night the lime workers had a big parade from up at their hall in the old brewery down La Haye street and up Main and around by Market to the courthouse. It was Local 829 five-hundred-strong and their women and children too and it looked like half the town. Dick Secour and Ralph Grannaman talked to them over the public address.

Dick told them they did themselves proud. "The strike is settled. We are called back to work with a deal we can live with, if the lime companies keep their word. Let us give them the benefit of the doubt until they show they don't deserve it. Whatever differences of opinion, whatever animosities we felt, or harsh words that has been spoke, so far as we are able let us forgive and forget."

The Guiannee singers sang and Little Beau Herron and Charley Paschia fiddled for them, and right out there by the jail they danced in the street.

Maybe some were dancing because they drove the colored out.

You don't like to think about that.

ETHEL HAD RELENTED AND WAS KEEPING COMPANY AGAIN WITH LESTER, and she would stay the night from to time but would not bide with him. She must help her mother with farm chores. When he said then he should stay there himself, she would not hear of it. "What of Holt Hardy?" he asked.

She said, "I have not seen him since the flood."

He said she knew as well as he did that he lurked about.

"The town accuses him of any evil or misfortune that occurs."

"With good cause."

"He is blamed for dynamiting the levee."

"Because he done it."

"Some people say it was the colored mail man."

"You know better."

"They say he reads in Marcus Garvey and plots revenge on the white race."

"You fault a man because he *reads?*"

"I mean it as an instance of the lies people will spread."

She had told him there was talk of her among the spiteful girls at Elder Shirtwaist.

He blurted it out, "Then *marry* me!"

"If I do, I will be discharged."

He had heard of this in the schools and elsewhere that women worked. In the hard times that seemed never to end an already-married woman might keep her job. But any single woman who married must give up her place for a man.

26.

IT WAS ALMOST DARK OUT WHEN REVEREND WHITFIELD HIMSELF CAME TO the screen door. He said, "Cletus Johnson! What you doing here?"

Cletus told him, "I be on the run."

"It's that bad?"

He nodded.

"We heard about it, of course, reading all kinds of things in the newspapers."

Cletus realized Whitfield thought his being *on the run* meant just like all the other Colored who had to leave town. He sweated it as he was walking the last miles how to explain himself when he got there, but maybe he could just let him think what he thought.

"I heard from people down in Cropperville that you were in Ste. Genevieve....that you found employment there."

"Yes, sir....in the lime works."

His wife Zella appeared, and behind her the two little girls Barbara and Shirley. When they got together they used to climb all over Josephine, beg her play to games with them.

"Zell, you remember Cletus," he said. "Walter Johnson's boy."

"He Josephine's brother," said the older girl Barbara. They called her Bar-bar because that was how Shirley said her name when she first was talking.

"I certainly do," Zell said. "Owen, what's wrong with you? Let Cletus in the door. We feed him up. He look like he didn't eat for a week....one of those starving Armenians."

Whitfield opened the door wide and grinned and asked, "How you find us...? How you get here?"

"I mostly walked."

"That's sixty miles! ....Hold up you foot."

He looked at the bottom of Cletus' work shoe, just a plain clodhopper shoe but at least it didn't have a hole in it. He said, "On the railroad track."

"With all them bums and jailbirds?" Zell asked.

"I be scared mostly of the brakemens. And dogs. Say I be trespassing. I only rode the cars a little ways at first."

"How you know just where to come?" the Reverend asked, as if he was worried everybody knew just where to find him.

"I remember from my papa Meacham Park....When the mile posts down to seven I ask a porter at a depot. He say it the colored section of Kirkwood...out Big Bend Road, cross from the white cemetery."

Cletus had asked at the flower shack across from the cemetery gate. An old white woman scared he would rob her said it was right behind her back lot but you couldn't see it through the trees. The way in was the next cross street where it said Filmore on the right hand in Kirkwood, and Milwaukee Street to the left was Meacham Park.

He turned up Milwaukee Street, and sure enough past the woods was a regular little town by itself. New York Street, Chicago Street, cities up North that Colored moved to, and more cities, where they moved from--Memphis, New Orleans, Nashville. He crossed Attucks Street, Douglass, Garvey. He knew he was in the right place. People were all Negro, most were friendly, directed him to where the Whitfields were staying, a little house like a cropper cabin on Memphis Street.

Mrs. Whitfield fed him up on gumbo and cornbread, and the little girls Shirley and Bar-bar watched him eat. The house had a inside toilet, a bathroom. She said he had to take a bath, and put him to bed in the back room, drew the shade and curtain. In no time he was asleep.

THE NEXT DAY HE WOKE UP AT FOUR O'CLOCK IN THE AFTERNOON. ELEVEN hours he slept. He lay there on the cot that must be in Reverend Whitfield's study with book cases, a desk. Just slivers of yellow light came in the crack around the shade. He lay there, thinking he had to tell them the truth.

He got up, had some corn bread and chicory coffee. Mrs. Whitfield was light skinned, big but a young pretty face. Cletus would bide his time, tell her husband later. She had to know too, but he would wait. As he sat at the kitchen table, she offered him some rhubarb pie. He saw the little girls playing a game on a board with dice in their room.

Mrs. Whitfield asked what possessed the mean white people to drive all the colored people out. She knew about the murders.

He told about the lime workers afraid colored would take their jobs at half the pay.

"*Argus* blame the Knights of Columbus."

"We the non-union quarry, nigger scabs."

"You think that *justify* how they done you, Cletus."

"No, ma'am. Only...*explain* it."

"White peoples the spawn of the Devil...Don't tell my husband I say that."

"No, ma'am."

"My husband preach *Don't hate the white man. We tractored off. Be dollars and cents, not white against colored.*...He think Mr. Snow his best friend."

"A white friend will deny you."

"*Amen.*"

He felt restless, stood up, tried to walk but his knees were stiff. He could only swing his legs from the hip joint.

Bar-bar looked up, saw him, and said, "Cletus be Uncle Sambo." Shirley came to look and he did it again like on purpose to cut up, and they laughed.

Zella saw what was going on, said, "You girls hush!"

He sat down again, asked her who Uncle Sambo was. She said he was a white man on stilts with shoe polish on his face and a sign that said front and back: *Get You Feet on the Street! Sam's Bail Bonds.* She put her hand behind his knee, rubbed up and down, asked does that hurt?

He said what hurt was if he tried to bend it.

She rubbed up inside his leg.

He was getting a hard on. To be away from her he went to sit out on the back stoop. He watched the birds catching bugs in the light sky after the sun went down. Leaves had turned orange on the gum trees. The air was still, shirt-sleeve weather. He heard children playing, a screen door slam.

Zella called to him that she was feeding the girls and there was some for him when he was hungry. He said he would wait, but when he smelled it he changed his mind and went in to dinner and ate, hog jaw and greens and sweet potatoes. When they were done she set a plate in the oven for her husband. She said he was out seeing rich men and white preachers, all the time trying to get help for the sharecroppers, and now the Ste. Genevieve people too. He saw the Scarlet Bishop, and a white woman that wrote a book, pestered his friends at the newspapers.

HE DID NOT COME HOME UNTIL PITCH DARK AS SHE WAS PUTTING THE girls to bed, reading them their story. He poured himself a glass of port wine and offered some to Cletus which he took. Some old church Negoes laid that against him, wanted a thou-shalt-not type of preacher. He called and asked, "Zell, you want some wine?"

She said leave it on the table for her.

Cletus said he had something he had to tell him.

Whitfield looked different at him and just sat there after his long day and he already had taken off his preacher's collar. He sighed and stood up and said *Come on then*, and he went out on the back stoop and Cletus followed.

He said he was not be on the run like all the other colored in Ste. Genevieve. He was on the run from the law.

"What for?" Whitfield asked.

Cletus told him the truth about it.

Reverend Whitfield looked at him. After what seemed a good while he asked, "You tell Zella?"

"No, sir."

He supposed he would tell Mrs. Whitfield then and they would talk it over and decide about him like the Ribeau brothers, but instead he just said he must not speak one word to her about it.

Cletus was thinking he has secrets from his wife. And when he was gone so late, was it only trying to get help for the poor croppers?

"Be a reason..." He was looking back over Cletus' shoulder, speaking low, "I explain later."

Cletus turned, and she was standing there with her glass of port wine just inside the screen door.

REVEREND WHITFIELD RODE WITH HIM ON THE STREETCARS TO DOWN-
town where the lawyer's office was. On the corner by the white high school they took the
Kirkwood-Ferguson 01 car, then at Clayton courthouse changed to the University 11. The
Reverend said nobody would tell you colored had to sit in back but mostly they did.

Cletus tried to read all the street signs on the corners because he was staying in St.
Louis now. But the streetcar jinked this way and that so he lost track. Then they were on
Olive Street going east toward the river. He looked up at the whitest tallest building he ever
saw, sun shining off the high-up windows. He asked *What that be?*

Reverend had no idea what he was talking about. He pointed up through sooty window
glass. He said, "Oh the Continental Building," that some fool from Arkansas built just before
the stock market crash and it was half empty now, winos on the stairs.

The biggest city Cletus ever went to was Paducah, Kentucky to visit his auntie Arline.
She worked at the Jackson Purchase Hotel. At seven stories, it was the tallest edifice in Paducah. She was a chambermaid, said she could get him on to bellhop.

Down on the sidewalk they were in the midst of tall buildings like river bluffs with windows. People passing this way and that would not say one word to you. Fog and coal smoke
hung in the air, so if you stay you will cough up black bloody phlegm like a coal miner just
because you live in St. Louis. Maybe Cletus would go to his Auntie Arline in Paducah. Automobiles and trucks moved slow and impatient, streetcar bells went ding-ding, and people
hollered and cursed. He saw some old horse-drawn drays too.

They were at 705 Chestnut Street, with windows broken and boarded up. When you
went in by a row of mail boxes and up the stairs, you left footprints in the soot. Mr. Redmond
was on the 6th floor. He had black and gold in frosted glass in the door:

> Sidney R. Redmond
> Attorney at Law

Reverend Whitfield knocked. A voice said come in. An older colored woman was typ-
ing with a black snuff box over one ear, clipped to her head and a wire coming out of it. She
listened, then typed; listened some more, typed some more. Four chairs stood around the
walls, open doors to two offices. One was empty. The man in the other looked up from his
desk, waved for them to come in. Reverend Whitfield had already talked to him about Cletus
on the telephone.

MR. REDMOND WAS MOCHA BROWN, WEARING AN OLD GRAY SWEATER THE
kind with buttons down the front only you wear it mostly unbuttoned, and a red bow tie, and
a white shirt. He got up, shook hands with Reverend Whitfield, and with Cletus. "So you've
been staying in Ste. Genevieve?" he said.

"Yes, sir."

"I just got back from there. It was not a pleasant experience."

"Sidney is representing the people accused of killing the two white men," Reverend
Whitfield said.

Cletus said, "Lee Guy and C.J."

Mr. Redmond seemed surprised. He told him he worked with them on the lime kiln.

Reverend already told Cletus he had to go on to a meeting, and he gave him car fare to
get back to Meacham Park by himself. He said, "So I leave my friend Cletus here for your
good counsel."

"Gentlemens," Cletus said, "I cannot adequately express my gratitude for—"

"Now, Cletus, just doing my preacher job."

"Don't thank me yet, boy," said Redmond, looking at him over the top of his eyeglasses.

Reverend Whitfield left, and Mr. Redmond nodded for Cleuts to sit down in the chair
facing his desk. Behind him Cletus saw out the window across to the high building on the
other side of the street. The smoky fog was so thick that even things that close looked fuzzy.
"Well, now, Cletus," he said, "...Jackson?"

"Johnson."

He wrote on a yellow paper tablet on his desk. Not much, maybe just his name. "Owen
Whitfield tells me you have a problem with the law."

"Yes, sir."

"That you have been charged with a serious offense...?"

He nodded.

"Can you just tell me about it....what they say you did....what you say you did....how
whatever it was happened....or didn't happen?"

Cletus told about their last camp at Sweet Home church and what J.T. did to his sister,
and how he did him in turn. He told it as close as he could to just how he told Reverend Whitfield, and maybe the Reverend already did tell him that.

"And they call it 'assault with intent to kill?'"

"Yes, sir. That be the part I remember."

"Did you intend to kill him?"

Cletus thought on that. "Maybe I don't care if I do....Say, I want to *hurt* him....bad as he hurt Josephine."

"How bad is she hurt?"

"Have a trick baby."

He talked some more, asked him questions. Cletus allowed if he studied to sure enough kill JT, he would clip him up first. He was hurt too bad to fight back. Didn't holler. Nobody to witness. He could easily have killed him dead.

Mr. Redmond said, "All right, young man. I can suppose you did not have *intent* to kill. It was assault. With a deadly weapon. An honest judge could find that."

"....I has to turn myself in?"

He thought on this before he said, "A compassionate judge....without prejudice....might give you probation....under the circumstances."

"I be telling it to a judge like that?"

"Not in Stoddard or Dunklin or Pemiscot or any other Bootheel county in Missouri... not in that whole judicial district, or the 27th either."

"So I going to the penitentiary?"

He looked at him a while. "An attorney is an officer of the court," he said.

Cletus was thinking they tricked him.

"Who else knows about this?"

He said Reverend Whitfield, Ribeaus in Ste. Genevieve, besides his family and Law down home.

Mr. Redmond advised him the same as Ribeaus. Stay out of trouble. Keep his mouth shut.

He said his practice was mostly in St. Louis and he saw prejudice and indifference and outright injustice every day of the week. But after he went down to Ste. Genevieve on this Rauscher-Chomeau murder, he saw the judges of St. Louis as veritable Solomons of enlightenment. A colored man knew prejudice in his bones and all his life, and he might think he knew all about it out in the country and small towns and down south. He had been disrespected, insulted by white people. But he never before felt what he felt in Ste. Genevieve. Almost the whole town. Almost. They hated colored people. They wished them not to live amongst them. They had caused them to leave under threat of death.

"I am taking a chance on you, Cletus," said Redmond. "Don't you go down to Cropperville to visit your mama any time soon."

Cletus was not planning to.

"That is my professional advice."

Cletus waited, not sure whether he should stand up to take his leave or if something else was expected of him. "I am extremely grateful, sir," he said. "I will certainly pay you when I get some money together."

"Don't even think of it."

"If there is any way—"

"But it would be helpful...You said you were acquain'ted with my clients, that you worked with them on the lime kiln."

"Yes, sir. They bad Negroes."

That was when Redmond got him to talk about the labor situation in Ste. Genevieve at the time the white men were killed. He was particularly interested in how the local union officers protected the jobs of their Negro members but turned on them as the bitter strike wore on. He called Mrs. Simmons in to take notes.

27.

HE LEARNED OF IT FROM HILDEGARD THE BARMAID. AT THE END OF THE work week Saturday noon Lester went in the public room of the Anvil for a pint. As she drew it she stared at him. "Lester?" she asked.

"That's my name."

"You hear about Ethel?"

"Ethel Fahnstock?"

"Your jo."

"*What?*"

"She is....she was shot."

"*Shot?*"

"With a shotgun."

"When?"

"She died."

"*When?*"

"Early this morning," Hildegard said. "She was shot when she went to milk the cow."

He said, "It was Holt Hardy."

She said, "They are seeking him."

He took a long draught of his beer, wiped the back of his hand across his mouth, and stood up.

"Now don't you--"

"I am going to see her mother."

He climbed the stairs to his room first, left off his lunch pail, and stuck the Bulldog Special into his pocket.

WHEN HE CAME OVER THE RISE HE SAW A NUMBER OF TRUCKS AND CARS at the Fahnstock place, among them Basler's van that if she were alive would be an ambulance. As he came down the lane and turned in at the mail box, two men came out onto the porch with what could only be Ethel on a stretcher with little wheels.

Her mother and another woman came out after her and stood watching. Perhaps he should pay his respects to them first but he went to the open doors at the back of the van. He stood just out of the way as they slid her in and one of them tightened a strap to secure the stretcher cart.

When the man who was doing that climbed out, Lester stepped up against the rear bumper so they were unable to close the doors. "Hey, what do you think you are doing?" said the other man, who was older and wore spectacles and might be Basler himself.

"I am her fiancé....Lester Dodge."

The man turned and looked up at Ethel's mother on the porch, and she nodded.

In the back of the van his sweetheart lay the height of his chest as he stood on the ground. When he went to fold back the blanket nobody stopped him. Her face was the color of your fingers when you are frost-bit, her lovely cheeks drained of her natural blush. Two shotgun pellets had lodged in her forehead and scalp, another in the side of her chin, and around each her flesh was bruised and puffed out like a boil. It was not buckshot but the next thing to it that you use on turkeys and geese. He touched the back of his fingers to her cheek and it was not quite stone cold. One eye was half open, the other more nearly closed. He put two fingers to her pale cold lips, then bowed his head and kissed her farewell.

He stepped back and nodded to the older man. "....Thank you."

They closed the doors, got into the front, and he stood and watched as they drove slowly out of the yard, turned into the lane, and passed on between the fence rows down the long hill to the Flat River road.

He said to himself *So that is what dead is.*

ETHEL'S MOTHER WAS IN HER BIG OLD FARM KITCHEN WITH FRIENDS AND neighbors and near relations that included her grown daughter Laverne and two of her grown sons Douglas and Harold and their wives, and the woman who was on the porch was her sister Mrs. Sprot.

On the long table where you could feed a threshing crew at one sit-down were covered dishes and plates and platters of little sandwiches, cold meats and bread, cakes, pies, cookies, pickles and deviled eggs. A big pot of coffee was on the stove and another pot of bean soup, and on two sideboards were bottles of hooch and seltzer and glasses and pitchers of lemonade and ice tea. He had seen such spreads before but only now did it strike him that the food was not only to spare Ethel's mother labor and for those who gathered there to eat. It was how Ethel's kith and kin shared their grief.

He went to Mrs. Fahnstock and offered his condolences. She put her hand on his arm, then embraced him and for a moment held him close against her bosom. "She cared for you, Mr. Dodge," she said at his ear. "For the longest time she would not tell me you wished to marry and take her away from…this."

"Yes, ma'am."

"She said she could not leave me and little Delbert here alone on the farm….I told her….I *begged* her to go….If only she had."

He hesitated, then asked, "You knew she was going to—?"

"Oh, yes….That poor disturbed man took two lives this morning." She sobbed once and was very still.

He said he would try to learn from her charity, but to himself he could not help recalling and now it was fervent that *He wished he had killed him when he could.*

As he stepped back he noticed all talk among the dozen or more people in the kitchen had ceased and they were frankly looking at them. Although he did not know all of them by name, it seemed to be generally known the relation that he stood in to Ethel as her accepted sweetheart—as opposed to the deranged man who took her life. He felt some of their particular sympathy extended to him, and he was moved to turn away and wipe the back of his hand across his eyes.

NEXT HE SOUGHT OUT YOUNG DELBERT, AND FOUND HIM BACK OF THE barn with some of his friends. One of them had a .22 rifle and they were taking turns shooting at brown bottles in a row along the side of the woodpile, and he recalled Ethel saying her father brewed his own beer.

When one of them saw him he hollered, "Cheese it!" and all of them ran off every which way except Delbert and the biggest boy, whose gun it seemed to be.

Lester stopped by the back of the barn several feet away and Delbert asked, "Are you going to *tell?*"

He looked at him and his friend and he shook his head. Somehow it pleased him to see this, Delbert acting like a natural boy while the grown-ups inside pulled long faces and said the pious things you were supposed to say. "Why, no, Delbert," he told him. "I belive if your sister saw what you and your friends are doing out here instead of play-acting like good boys inside, she would smile."

Delbert looked close at him for a moment as if to see if he was being sarcastic, then turned to his friend and said, "This is Ethel's real fellow, Mr. Dodge."

"*Lester* Dodge." he said.

"Gus Offenburg," the biggest boy said, and they shook hands.

"My sympathy, friend," Lester said to Delbert and he shook his hand too. "You were one of her favorite people in the world."

"Well," he said, "if you have to have a big sister, it could have been worse."

Lester was thinking that from a 13-year-old brother that was high praise indeed.

"You want to take a shot?" Gus asked and offered him the gun.

"Why, thank you," Lester said. He believed this should fully convince them he was not going to tell. He sat with one hip against the back of the barn at an angle to the line of fire so he had a firm rest with his elbows on his knees. It was a Sears Roebuck imitation of a Remington bolt-action youth model with a spring-clip magazine. He popped off at one of the bottles and was surprised at the splatter of amber liquid. "Why, that looks like good beer," he said.

Delbert tried to suppress a giggle and Gus looked away, and it occurred to him they might have tried some of it out.

"Shoot some more if you want," said Gus.

"One more," Lester said, thinking it would not be right to shoot up the boys' ammunition.

"It is Mr. Hardy," said Delbert. "We killed him seventeen times."

"Yours makes eighteen," says Gus.

Lester squeezed off another shot, and another brown bottle burst with a satisfying splat. "Nineteen," he said.

Delbert said Ethel told him, "He tried to kill you."

"I believe he would have."

"Why didn't you kill him?"

"With all my heart I wish I did....I had the chance."

"He spied on us and lurked about. They ought to kept him in the loony bin."

"They are seeking him," Lester said.

He started to hand back the .22 to Gus and he nodded at Delbert and he gave it to him instead.

Standing up flat-footed he fired off four or five shots as fast as he could work the bolt, missing some, but two bottles splattered.

"Careful," Gus said. "They will hear us inside."

Lester looked at the back of the barn and up at the hay mow. "Is this where it happened?" he asked.

"I seen it out the window," said Delbert.

"Her getting shot?"

"She went to the barn to milk the cow like she always done. He was hiding up in the hay mow."

"Here?"

"Around in front." Delbert went around to the front of the barn where it faced the house, and Gus and Lester followed. Delbert pointed up, "That's where he was at. I heard a shot and looked out. She was close to the barn, and where he was standing he had to shoot near straight down and only nicked her. If she had ran in the barn it might have been long enough for Mama to come after him. She has her shotgun too and she keeps it by the back door. But my sister screamed and run toward the house, and the second shot you could see her jerk. The last shot it all went in her back. It turned her lungs to sausage meat."

Delbert said he saw Hardy come out of the barn and walk off across the fields to the old schoolhouse where he lived before he went away. Ethel was unconscious but still alive, and he helped a neighbor and his mother carry her in and lay her on a pallet in the front room. Dr. Hertig came in just a few minutes, but said that little could be done. She died about nine-thirty.

Lester walked toward the house. He thought of how Delbert and Mrs. Fahnstock had spoken of Holt Hardy. He did not fear and loathe him as before. What Hardy did was the worst stroke of fortune Lester had borne in his short life, taking from him his beloved and their child. Yet he felt toward him as if he were a great bear who mauled her to death, or a lightning bolt. His madness was a force of nature and he himself might have had some role in whatever strange fancy moved him to this, yet he did not feel it so much as a personal affront.

Perhaps he should. Perhaps a number of those gathered there would have him tracking him down over hill and dale with blood in his eye. He felt no great urge to do that. Before this he so keenly felt his menace and alone in comprehending it that he did presume to make him business he must tend to on his own. He enlisted Walter and Little John and Bucholz and Ralph to act in concert against him, but he was not ruthless enough. Now by *doing* what he most dreaded that he might, Hardy had made himself the business of the posse comitatus and the hue and cry.

Lester went inside and sought out Ethel's older brothers. They were with Deputy Pappas, in the front room by the telephone. The brothers knew who he was but not by name, which he told them, and they told him theirs, Douglas and Harold. Pappas was the one who sweated Lester and Walter and Little John over Clyde shooting Falkner.

"Well, they have caught him," Harold said.

"May he hang and burn in hell to the end of time," said Douglas.

"And then some."

Stout young farmers with families and spreads of their own, they exchanged a hard look. He heard later that both of them were expressly forbidden to join in the posse seeking Hardy.

Pappas was glowing with satisfaction. He told it Lester imagined not for the first time how Sheriff Picou ordered men to every crossroads for miles around and notified the farmers by telephone. "We told them to be on the look-out," he said, "and sure enough old August Mussig from out near Miller's Switch he called in to say Hardy appeared at his farm and said he was ready to turn himself in. He kept saying, 'I will surrender peacefully. I am right with Jesus. I surrender.' And sure enough....when Ben showed up with Pete Drury and George Rozier at the farm, Hardy come out of the house with his hands in the air."

Others had gathered around to hear Pappas tell his tale again. "He kept saying he surrendered. He surrendered peaceful because Jesus told him. He did. They put cuffs on him and brought him in the car to the county jail."

There was no rejoicing. People nodded, looked at one another, said a word or two. It was a relief but was expected. It would not bring Ethel back.

28.

THE FOLLOWING WEDNESDAY REDMOND AND ESPY WERE IN STE. GENE-
vieve again, in a small court room before Magistrate Judge Francis X. Siebert. County Attorney Petrequin was also present, and a number of white men who did not wish them well
occupied the back row. The clerk read from their plea for a change of venue that they "cannot
have a fair trial in said cause in the 27th Judicial Circuit---consisting of the counties of Bol-
linger, Ste. Genevieve, Madison, Perry, and St. Francois---because the inhabitants are so
prejudiced against the defendants. This petition is supported by the affidavits of....five cred-
ible disinterested citizens of this county..." He stopped reading.

Siebert said, "Please continue, Mr. Kerl."

"That's all. It doesn't have any signatures."

"None at all?"

Kerl shook his head.

"Not one single—?"

Redmond interrupted. "Your honor! ... I ask the clerk to read the last line of the form."

"'The last line of the form'?" Siebert asked, as if this were a strange and suspicious
request.

"Yes, your honor."

The Judge threw up his hands as if he never heard of such foolishness, but he would
humor him. "Mr. Kerl..."

The clerk read "'*unless the facts be within the knowledge of the court and no further
proof is required.*'"

The Judge did not like it one bit how Redmond had stood his ground. He called him to
stand before the bar. He remarked that he and Mr. Espy had been appointed to defend the
three Negroes because they were indigent, and it was the responsibility of the Court to be
sure that they were competently represented. "Mr. Redmond," he asked, "did you make any
effort at all to find witnesses in support of your motion?"

Redmond took a deep breath to control his fury at this attitude and the assumption
behind it—that he might present himself as an attorney but was still a lazy Negro you have
to keep your eye on, or he will take your money and not do the work. Redmond told him in a
patient voice that he and Mr. Espy spent an entire day calling on residents of Ste. Genevieve,

most of them local business people and their employees. "A number of them—I would say six or seven—stated that feeling ran high against our clients and they could not possibly get a fair trial here. However, they were reluctant to go on public record saying so because they would be ostracized. They would lose most of their customers. They feared vandalism. They feared for their safety ....I have a list of local residents that Mr. Espy and I called upon in person. We visited more than that. There are thirty-three names on that list."

"And all of them said there was prejudice against your clients?"

"No, your honor. Six or seven. Several people were hostile and rude to Mr. Espy and myself. They exhibited obvious prejudice against us as People of Color."

"Who are the six or seven residents you say told you there was prejudice, but would not go on public record to say so?"

"To tell the Court their names would expose them to the same hostility and prejudice we are trying to establish...It would be disrespecting their wishes."

"Well, Mr. Redmond, who am I to question your high-mindedness! But your substance seems to be....that most of the people of this town are ignorant bigots....and to tar me personally and the entire judiciary of this five-county circuit with the same brush....and to tell the court that the six or seven people who said we're prejudiced are too cowardly to stand up and be counted....and we must take your word for their existence."

One of the loungers in the back row laughed out loud.

Redmond did not attempt to conceal the resentment in his voice as he related with some heat what was written with soap across the windshield of his car and that all four of his tires were slashed.

"You may request reimbursement for the cost of the tires."

"I shall, your honor."

Then he elaborated on the incident of the men who were following him and Espy. "I asked one of them, 'What is your name?' And he said, 'Crowley. Mister Crowley to you, nigger.' "

Redmond was aware of discomfort in the courtroom.

"I said the name sounds familiar. One of the others said to the first man 'You had better go home, A. J.' Well, in less time than it takes to get to the outhouse when you have got the flux and your bowels are about to explode, those men jumped in their cars and *vamoosed*. They were gone....Now what was all that about...?

"I have since discovered that A. J. Crowley was one of the six men Sheriff Picou arrested after the incident at the Ribeaus....and that you yourself, Judge Siebert, found all of them guilty of various offenses, fined each of them 400 dollars, and sentenced them all to six months in jail..."

Siebert stared like a statue in a marbled hall.

"I surmise, your honor, that *you thought* they had been doing something wrong..."

Siebert's shoulders heaved with a deep intake of breath, then letting it out. "All right, Mr. Redmond," he said, "we take your point."

"Thank you...I come back to the last line of our petition after the blanks for witnesses, '*unless the facts...be within the knowledge of the judge of the court and no further proof is required.*'"

"Are you done, Mr. Redmond?"

"Yes, your honor."

He smacked three times with his gavel. "Court is adjourned for twenty minutes....We will reconvene at eleven o'clock." He smacked the gavel down three more times, hitched up his robe, and ducked out the little door behind his throne—Redmond imagined to take a leak.

He had in mind the same business for himself. As he headed out and around to the crooked little stairway down to the toilet and urinal in a broom closet for Colored, Espy chided him, "What got into you?"

Over his shoulder Redmond said just doing his job.

"All that lawyering and not even the trial yet?"

"Half the time, that's where you already lost. The venue ....and jury selection."

"You wore that judge out."

"*Thank you.*"

"You ever gigged for contempt of court?"

He shrugged. "They suppose to warn you first."

WHEN THEY RECONVENED JUDGE SIEBERT ANNOUNCED THAT THEIR MO-tion for a change of venue outside the 27th circuit was denied. However, he would permit a change within the circuit to St. Francois County. They would be on the docket in Flat River for trial early in December.

Walking out to the car Espy tried to congratulate him. He shook his head, "Whiddle-dycut."

"What you mean *whiddledycut?*"

"People in this town cast us out. Those hillbilly lead miners at Flat River never allowed colored among them in the first place."

"Sidney, you take a pessimistic view of human nature."

On the drive back to St. Louis he told him about what happened at Flat River in the World War. Management at the lead mines had replaced native-born white men with Italians and Bohemians fresh off the boat on the excuse that the immigrants were not subject to the draft. The native miners responded by rounding up all the immigrants, forcing the company clerks at gun point to pay them off, marching them to the railroad depot to buy one-way tickets, and herding them onto the train for St. Louis.

WHEN ESPY AND REDMOND PRESENTED THEMSELVES AT THE ST. FRANCOIS County jail in Flat River to meet with their clients early on the morning they were scheduled to begin trial, the turn-key told them they were not there. He said he was told to have two cells ready for them but they did not show up. Sheriff Buncombe was out with Federal agents raiding a still and hooch warehouse in a old lead mine at Shibboleth.

They went upstairs in the courthouse and sought out the County Clerk. He said their case was dismissed because of a "technicality" in the papers granting the change of venue. When he asked if he might call the Ste. Genevieve Court on his telephone, the Clerk said that was long distance. Redmond said he would pay for it.

The Clerk made the call himself and handed the receiver over the high counter. Redmond finally got through to the clerk Leo Karl who said they were scheduled for a special hearing there on Saturday morning, and the prisoners were transferred back to the Ste. Genevieve jail last night. When Redmond told Espy he rolled his eyes and just shook his head.

SO THEY APPEARED SATURDAY MORNING IN STE. GENEVIEVE, AND A DEPuty and a turn-key brought in their clients in old-fashioned jailhouse stripes, hand-cuffed and in leg irons. Redmond objected to the restraints, and the cuffs but not the irons were removed. Magistrate Judge Siebert presided.

He tapped his gavel and said this was a special session of an adjourned term. "Mr. Redmond and Mr. Espy, I am advised that we must go through the motions of an arraignment."

Redmond stood and addressed the Court, "Your honor, I have here substantially identical forms waiving the right to a preliminary examination for all three of my clients, each signed and witnessed."

"How do they plead?"

"Innocent to all charges."

"The Clerk will record a plea of innocent for the three defendants."

When this had been done the Judge says, "We will now entertain a re-submission of the Defense motion for a change of venue."

For practice Redmond let Espy summarize their arguments in favor.

Judge Siebert gave his ruling on the spot, almost word for word the same as before. "The motion is overruled….for the reason that the petition is insufficient both as to form and substance. However---"

Redmond interrupted. "Your honor! I respectfully---"

"*However*…without affirming or denying the supposition… but wishing to avoid the least appearance …we order and adjudge that the venue be changed to the Circuit Court of St. Francois County….and that this case be set for trial December 16th."

So they were back where they were the week before. The hold-up was the State admitting *prejudice within the knowledge of the Court* that Siebert neglected to include in the papers he sent over. Petrequin smiled and acted nice.

Redmond asked about the disposition of the prisoners.

"They will be transferred to the St. Francois County Jail in Flat River."

This was better than Ste. Genevieve, but not much.

On the 16th they appeared at Flat River and asked for a continuance to allow time to prepare their case and notify their witnesses. This was granted. They would be continued to February 10th.

REVEREND WHITFIELD TOOK IT UPON HIMSELF TO MINISTER UNTO THE Colored run off from Ste. Genevieve besides the croppers put off the cotton farms. He went to visit Cap Ribeau in the Arsenal Street sanitarium, came back and said he was sane as you or me but now the white doctors were keeping him there to teach him a lesson and he was depressed. Blues had him by the ankles like a ball and chain. He said if Cletus went to visit it would cheer him up.

Cletus did not study going in with all the crazy people. If you go in, maybe they won't let you out. Only Cap was his friend.

Reverend Whitfield talked to Mr. Redmond. *He* was going to see Cap. Cletus felt shamed. He took the Manchester 55 car from the same stop a block from the high school, changed in Maplewood to the Arsenal Street.

Mr. Redmond was not there yet, so he sat on one of the waiting chairs.

One of the guards had just come off shift and was waiting for his wife, and Cletus got to talking with him. He had a fresh cut over one eye. He asked him, "Excuse me if I getting in you business, but did one of the crazy peoples do that on you head?"

"Don't be nothing," the Guard said. "Probably one of the other fellows on the response team."

He told him there were supposed to be four of them but today was just three, and they had to subdue a little old woman who thought the Devil was crawling up her vagina. Cletus asked if it was true that crazy peoples had superhuman strength. The Guard said no, nothing like that. It was not hard to subdue an individual if you didn't care if you hurt him. People were fragile. It was when you were trying to do it and not hurt them, that they got in their licks.

The Guard's wife emerged from the end of her shift, and they hurried out to catch their bus.

Mr. Redmond came, and told the man and woman at the counter who he was and who he had come to see, and he sat by Cletus on the waiting chairs.

After a while a phone rang, and a white doctor bald on top with white hair around the sides and a white mustache came out and asked, "Mr. Redmond...? I am Dr. Ludwig," and he shook hands with him, then with Cletus, and Cletus told his name but the white doctor did not pay attention. He took them down to the end of the row and they all sat on waiting chairs.

He said Cap was improved. At first he was scared of his shadow and said everybody was talking behind his back to do him harm. He no longer had the nervous tic in the eye and two fingers or the panic attacks. Now he mainly was depressed, still had trouble sleeping, didn't want to eat.

Mr. Redmond said Cap told Reverend Whitfield they were keeping him there to teach him a lesson.

The Doctor shook his head and said that was a symptom. "Our concern was he might harm himself. At the meeting this afternoon I plan to say he should be discharged....We know about the situation that precipitated this. He's in a quandary what to do next." He turn to Cletus, asked, "What's your name again?"

He told him. He asked what his connection was to Mr. Ribeau. He told him Cap's brother Zeno was his boss at the lime works and he was staying in the old cabin out back from their place.

Dr. Ludwig said, "Oh. You're *Cletus*. He was worried. Didn't know what had become of you."

He took them to the door he had come out of, and showed them through. A guard locked the door after. Dr. Ludwig shook their hands again, said an orderly would conduct them, and he went about his doctoring business.

The Orderly was an old colored man with one eye all white as if it had turned sideways in his head. He said follow me please. They went down a hallway, turned a corner, down another hallway, and turned another corner, and by this time Cletus had no idea which way was which or how to get out of that damn place.

Cap was in the Colored Men's Day Room. He sat in a chair with a book by the row of windows that looked out on a brown grass yard with windows to other parts of the building on the sides and across, with benches in a hollow square, and a dead catalpa tree. One end of the day room was a counter where guards, nurses, whatever you called them watched and did paper work and talked on the telephone. Crazy men were sitting in most of the chairs around a long table.

Men walked back and forth, around in circles, talking to themselves, humming a tune, saying things out loud. A dispute flared up over a chair. A little man with a smashed in face had an old-time football helmet that came down over his ears and was strapped tight because he banged his head on the wall. One man opened his trousers, took out his penis, and began to play with it. A guard come over to him. A fat man commenced to sing a revival song, *Jesus on the Telephone,* clapped his hands. Cletus did not want to see all the crazy people doing their craziness but you couldn't help it.

They went to the counter, and signed in. The orderly said they would call him or another man when they were ready to leave.

Cletus was keeping his eye on Cap. He hardly moved except to turn a page. He believed he knew they were there but was acting like he didn't notice.

They went up beside him. He scarcely moved, did not look at them. Cletus said, "Cap…. how you doing?"

He let the air out in kind of a grunt, "Hunnh…" He sat just looking out over the brown grass yard.

"This here Mr. Redmond. He a lawyer."

Redmond said, "Reverend Whitfield….Owen Whitfield spoke to me about you, Mr. Ri-beau."

"I know Whitfield," Cap said.

They talked some about how he was being treated. He grumbled about the food, the crazy people running around loose. Supposedly the dangerous ones were in the east wing. He loosened up some, explained for them as if he were their guide to this place. He said there really was such a thing as the padded cell. When a patient got obstreperous, they put him in there where the walls were padded so he couldn't hurt himself. There was such a thing as a strait-jacket too, with arms twice as long as you natural arms, that they wrapped around and tied the ends so you couldn't move. Attendants would put you in a cold shower in the strait jacket to cool you off, then the padded cell.

Cletus wanted to ask Cap if they did him like that but it would not be polite. He turned and looked up at him, halfway grinned and said, "No, Cletus, I never was in the padded cell or the strait-jacket. Not yet."

Redmond said Owen Whitfield told him they were holding Cap against his will to teach him a lesson, and that was illegal because he came to them and committed himself.

"No, well, that be how I was talking last week."

"You know you still got your job if you want it," Redmond said.

Cap said he did not know that. He said the last he heard the six men out of the carloads of ignorant white vigilantes the Sheriff actually did arrest were let off on good behavior.

"They are not out of the woods yet." Redmond told him about the Federal prosecution on charges of interfering with a government employee. "They can get seven years in prison a piece and each a ten-thousand-dollar fine on that."

Cap could not help himself. He looked up at both of them and actually smiled, a big old watermelon grin across his high-yellow face.

29.

WHEN HOLT HARDY WAS DELIVERED AT THE JAIL, THEY TOOK OFF THE handcuffs and put him in a cell with a flush toilet and a wash basin and a wide shelf of a bed and a straw mattress. They said take time to relieve himself and when he was ready he could make a telephone call, and then they wished to talk with him.

After a few minutes Deputy Rozier came back to his cell, and he told him he could not think of anyone to telephone. He supposed that was when to call a lawyer or your kin to get one for you, but he could see no need for a lawyer and could not pay for one if he did. His only kin were his Aunt Isabella and her husband Raymond Surdyke at Flat River, and they would have nothing to do with him anymore.

Rozier went off and returned with Sheriff Picou, and they took him into a little room with just a table and three chairs, and no window. He sat on one side of the table, the two of them on the other. He was not handcuffed again or put under any other restrain'ts. Rozier asked if he would like a cigarette.

He said, "No, thank you. I never acquired the habit."

Then Sheriff Picou said, "Mr. Hardy, you are entitled to a preliminary hearing before a magistrate. That would be Monday before Judge Huck."

He told them he just wanted to get on with it.

"You need not decide until Monday morning."

He said, "Yes, sir."

"Now, would you like to tell us what happened this morning?"

"That is what our Lord says I must do."

Picou and Rozier looked at each other.

"Ethel is my darling. We shall be joined in Paradise."

The Sheriff nodded for him to go on.

"Her father wished us to be married. He hired me on at Bluff City Lime, and I often took dinner at their place....Near every Sunday after he died."

"Did Miss Fahnstock return your affection?"

"She was contrary....just a young girl, you see....She consented to go with me to a dance at Weingartens.' You know it?"

"Oh, yes."

"Old Weingarten's house, the entire third floor is the ballroom. All are welcome, ten cents for the music. And you may purchase food and beverages, and if you care to stay the night, it is ten cents for the gentlemen on the ballroom floor, the same for ladies on beds and pallets on the second floor....and in the morning you could purchase breakfast for a reasonable price."

"I have been there myself....with the Missus," said Rozier.

"So Miss Fahnstock accompanied you to the dancing at Weingartens?'"

"Yes, sir. On a Saturday night."

"When was that?"

"Oh, more than a year ago. It were in July, July the 18th."

"You remember it well?"

"Oh, yes. I bring it to mind over and again."

"Did you and Miss Fahnstock have a pleasant time?"

"I surely thought so....I did not object to her dancing with other fellows....so long as it was known I was the one that brung her."

"So she....you both were having a pleasant time?"

"I was, although it pained me the other fellows cutting in....I was big about it. And I surely thought she was enjoying a pleasant time....But we had a disagreement."

"How was that?"

"She objected to my consuming alcohol."

"That is against the law, you know."

"Yes, sir."

"Although we are hard-pressed to enforce it everywhere at once."

"Weingarten don't sell hooch, however. You must bring your own or obtain it off others with some to spare. Weingarten, he just provides you set-ups."

"....Did Miss Fahnstock object because your consuming alcohol was against the law?"

"No, sir. She declared I was consuming it to excess."

"Were you?"

"No, sir. I sincerely believe I was not....but she is a young girl, you know....skittish like a half-grown horse."

"How much had you consumed?" Rozier asked.

"I brung a pint. It weren't all gone."

"Half a pint would be too much for me."

"Different fellows have different capacities, of course. But I sincerely believe I did not have too much according to my capacity....The trouble was, she had it in her mind I took too much. She *seen* it thus....and she held it up to me tales she had been told that I acted wild and crazy when I was drunk."

"Is that so?"

"Tales grow in the telling. People around here are given to gossip and bearing tales...."

"The tales are not so?"

"When I was her age....and younger....perhaps now and then I got out of hand....years ago...."

"....You were sentenced to five years in the penitentiary for assault with a deadly weapon."

"Who told you that?"

"And before that you were committed to State Hospital Number One at Fulton....and remained there eighteen months."

"Who went and told you all that?"

"It is public record....We have it from the Attorney General's office and the state police."

"That was....long ago."

"Did Miss Fahnstock know of your prison time and your confinement to a state mental hospital?"

"....She might not have understood."

"Did her father know?"

"He knew my people. I would not be surprised if he did in a general way. He never held it up to me."

The Sheriff and Rozier looked at each other and shifted about in their chairs. The Sheriff said, "So you and Miss Fahnstock had a disagreement?"

He pondered how he should reply. The Lord had bid him speak the truth. "She never again would go with me after that."

"Never?"

"No, sir....Oh, she would be civil, inquire after my health.... But never again would she consent to go with me to a party or a dance....Still I would take Sunday dinner with her and her mother and young Delbert, and sometimes I would come to call of an evening....She was ever civil....but she made excuses, would say she was out of sorts and remain in her room.... or after work would go to her friend Mary Ann in town....She joined the Guionee chorus for the Bicentennial just to spite me so she would have rehearsals as her excuse to remain in town....She commenced to walk hand-in-hand with her curly-haired boy....that imp of the Devil Lester Dodge....to bide all night in his room....and yet I was steadfast in my love.... She was always with me in my heart....ever in my mind and fancies the livelong day....and in my dreams at night....I could not help myself. I am forever bound to her....You might say I delude myself....I say to you....I was keeping a holy trust....like my love and faith in our dear Lord Jesus...."

Here he could not help himself. He shuddered and shook and broke down and wept, as he did when the Holy Spirit came upon him. Sheriff Picou and Deputy Rozier kindly waited him out.

When he resumed he felt a hardening against her in his heart. "What it come to is....she persistently refused to have anything to do with me....would keep up only the barest civility in the presence of her mother....I became angry....*enraged*....At times I would walk the byways with ideals of a terrible deed I might commit....I stayed, you know, in the old Zell schoolhouse by the Flat River Road....and across the fallow field I could see her house and barn....*I would see her*....my dear cold-hearted Ethel, my darling, in the yard going to-and-fro at a her chores....or tossing a ball with Delbert....or chasing him to snatch him in her arms and give him a Dutch rub for some boyish mischief he had committed against her....Oh, that give me such a pang, to see her hold his head close against her bosom as she rubbed his scalp with her fist round and round to make him squirm....At night when I lay in bed I would see her dear face in my mind. During the day I would sit by the window to watch for her to come out in the yard....and when I had caught a glimpse of her I would go back to my bed and lie down and cry....A grown man, I freely confess to you....I would take to my bed and cry....I resolved to ask her one more time to go with me....to attend a motion picture show I knew she would fancy, Norma Talmadge in *The Woman Disputed*, and if she refuses me this time I will conclude I may never have her in this life....And if I may not have her, no one else will.

"Once more she refused me, and sealed her fate.

"*If I may not have her, no one else will.* I thought that many times and the more I thought it, the more sure I became that I would kill her....Last Thursday I went to the Fahnstock home with my shotgun and waited for her to come out, but she remained indoors all day. The next day I tried again but she came out with her brother and I did not want to kill the boy. Friday night I went home and thought the whole matter over. I decided that I would kill her the next day no matter what....In the morning I went and hid in the hayloft of their barn while it was yet dark and waited for her to come out to milk the cow. It was then I fired the shots."

ANOTHER DAY THEY TOOK HIM AGAIN TO THE LITTLE ROOM WITH NO WIN-dow and Sheriff Picou asked him, "Why did you dynamite the levee?"

He was truthful in his reply, "Because my darling would not permit me to assist her filling sandbags."

"What kind of a reason is that?" Deputy Pappas asked. Sheriff Picou and Deputy Rozier made the inquiries when he first was brought in and both were courteous in their manner toward him. This time Sheriff Picou was called away, and he was left with Pappas and a deputy from Festus he had not seen before.

"Why did you fire the picture show?" Pappas asked.

He believed he had done as his Savior would have him do when he freely confessed to Sheriff Picou and Deputy Rozier. He felt no such call to oblige this rude fellow.

"Are you going to answer me, or do I have to knock some sense into your head?"

He held his peace.

Pappas struck him with the flat of his hand. He tasted blood where a tooth had cut the inside of his cheek.

They asked him why he killed the deputy at Sulphur Spring. This he had freely confessed to his blessed girl. He told her yes, my dear, I shot the law man. *I bring him to you in my teeth like Cinnamon when he leaves a fresh mouse on your pillow.*

Pappas and the other fellow continued to strike and abuse him until the one from Festus said, "We do not want to leave marks on him that will show in court."

30.

REDMOND AND ESPY DULY APPEARED ON THE MORNING OF FEBRUARY 15th. Taylor was tried first. Tuesday and Wednesday were given over to selecting a panel of thirty possible jurors. The State rejected six, and the defense rejected twelve for various reasons. This left twelve to serve on the jury, without any alternates.

The main show was to begin at nine o'clock Thursday morning. Women with children in their arms and sacks of lunch arrived early to secure seats, and the benches filled to capacity. People sat and stood in the aisles and in the back and scrunched into corners. The large courtroom and the hallways and stairs were packed. People unable to get in crowded around the courthouse waiting for news. Among them were many denizens of Ste. Genevieve who had motored the thirty miles over to Flat River and some from the countryside in wagons and on horseback.

At the prosecutors' table sat an old Kansas City cop with a night school law degree sent by the Governor to back up the locals, Assistant Attorney General Don Purteet. Beside him Henry Petrequin shuffled papers, and the attorney for St. Francois County cleaned his fingernails with a pen knife.

Judge Eustace Threlkeld entered the courtroom at precisely nine a.m. by the jump-hand clock above his dais. The clerk intoned *Please rise.* They did. The Judge said *Be seated,* and as they complied there was a mumble and buzz. He smacked down his gavel three times and said, "Court will now come to order....in the matter of Brownie 'Le Guy' Taylor....charged with murder in the first degree in the death of Paul Rauscher....on October 12th this last year."

Purteet then rose to state the charge against Redmond's client, based on two counts in the death of Rauscher, the first for shooting him and the second for dumping him in the river and throwing rocks at him when he saw that he was still alive. They were right if they thought the second count was more heinous, showing premeditation and no question of self-defense unless you could plead self-defense against the chances of getting caught. Trying his man on just one of the deaths was also smart. It kept things simple with less for the defense to gig them with on appeal. If they lost, they could try him again for Chomeau.

They were not going to lose. Redmond's one slim chance was to argue that Rauscher finally died from the surgeon trying to dig the bullet out of his spine, not from the gunshot or from hitting him on the head with rocks. He would need the Doctor to testify to that, and it would leave him open to a malpractice suit. Realistically the best the defense could hope for was that their two bad boys and one bad girl did not hang.

So Purteet laid out the story one more time, or, the Prosecution version of the story. First he read it from the Information For a Felony in righteous and redundant legal talk. "'... This Brownie Taylor alias Lee Guy--'" They persisted in writing that wrong in the court papers. His name was *Ronnie*, not Brownie. "'...On the 12th day of October last in the County of Ste. Genevieve....upon one Paul Rauscher....then and there....feloniously, willfully, with premeditation, deliberately, on purpose and of malice aforethought....did make an assault with a dangerous and deadly weapon, to wit, a revolving pistol then and there loaded with gunpowder and leaden balls....and did shoot, strike and wound the said Paul Rauscher about a vital part of the body....the abdomen .... giving him....one mortal wound....'"

Then Purteet lined out the Second Count, "'....And the said Paul Rauscher by reason of said mortal wound ...became unconscious and was insensible and in a stupor of body and mind and was then and there helpless and wholly in the power and control of the said Brownie Taylor alias Lee Guy....and his accomplices....and well knowing the helpless, unconscious and insensible condition of the said Paul Rauscher, and wickedly contriving and intending to kill and murder him....the said Brownie Taylor, Columbus Jennings and Vera Fox nee Rogers did then and there feloniously, deliberately, willfully and of their malice aforethought take the said Paul Rauscher by the body into their hands and drag, carry, cast, throw and push the said Paul Rauscher into the Mississippi River nearby situated ... wherein was a great quantity of water, and the said Brownie Taylor and his accomplices did then throw, cast, and hurl large stones from the bank of the Mississippi River upon, at, and against the said Paul

Rauscher while he was struggling in the water....and did hit, strike, and wound him....upon the head and body....and by this means Rauscher was choked, strangled, shocked, exposed, and suffocated....by reason of which he did languish, and languishing did live ... until on the 14th day of October, he died.'

"That is the official charge that you will have before you as you deliberate. What it comes down to ... in plain English ... They shot him ... and dumped him in the river and threw rocks at him."

At this point the Judge asked for all the witnesses to rise and come before him, and he told them they would have to be excluded from the courtroom except when they were called to testify. "I trust you understand the necessity for that," he said.

When the witnesses were gone, Purteet continued with his opening statement of how the State was going to prove its case. He listed the witnesses he would call and gave the jury teasers of what they would say—the St. Louis police captain who took Rauscher's statement, the doctor who tried to remove the bullet, the Revenue Agent who pulled him out of the water, Stanton the Undertaker, and Sheriff Picou. He stressed the evidence purporting to show how the defendant Brownie Taylor with his accomplices Columbus Jennings and Vera the Fox Rogers threw the body of Rauscher into the river and stoned him, inflicting wounds to the head and body from which he later died. He told them the State had a signed confession from Taylor, from Jennings, and from Vera the Fox Rogers. "If ever there was such a thing," he said, "what we have here is an open-and-shut case."

Redmond stood and objected to his referring to Mrs. Fox as he did and the court papers calling her Vera Rogers *alias* Vera Fox or the other way around, rather than Vera Fox *nee* Rogers the way they would if she were a white woman. This was greeted with snickers and hoots.

The Judge brought down his gavel twice. "Objection sustained," he said. "The clerk will take note of Mr. Redmond's objection, and see that court papers are corrected so that she is referred to by her correct name. Mr. Purteet, you will cease referring to her as *Vera the Fox*."

A number of people laughed out loud. Redmond had seen a Judge clear a courtroom because one spectator laughed, and rightly so. It was contempt of court. He imagined Threlkeld was capable of this but did not choose to take offense. It was a bad sign that he was *playing to* this crowd. On the other hand, he might be calculating to be as fair as he could under the circumstances. He would sustain their objection, but he would not come down on the hillbillies laughing. Perhaps they were not laughing so much at the Judge as at Redmond, the uppity Negro complaining how a Negro woman is referred to or addressed. He banged the gavel once and said pro forma, "Order in the court."

Purteet finished at ten o'clock. The Judge granted a short recess and when they convened again, he asked the jury to leave for the purpose of qualifying Captain John J. Carroll of the St. Louis Police Department as a State's witness. Petrequin called Carroll before the Judge to describe an interview with Rauscher at St. Anthony's hospital not long before he died.

The jury came back in and Carroll was sworn and sat down in the witness chair, and Petrequin led him through his testimony about what Rauscher said. Carroll related the gist of his conversation with Rauscher at St. Anthony's hospital and gave pretty much the same story that was brought out at the coroner's inquest and reported in the *Fair Play*. He said Rauscher declared he did not believe he could live, that the doctor told him he was in a serious condition and that he "wanted to tell the truth."

He described the details of the alleged holdup, how a gun was stuck under his chin, that he was ordered out of the car, that the other Negro man shot Chomeau and then turned the gun on him and shot him in the abdomen. Carroll told of how Rauscher's eyes filled with tears as he described their dragging him down to the bank of the river, how they took him by the wrists and ankles and swung him back and forth between them and heaved him out as far as they could into the water, and when he cried for help they threw large stones at him until they thought he was dead. When they had gone, he said, although he had no feeling from the waist down and could not move his legs, he finally managed to paddle to shore with his hands and pull himself part way out of the water. He recalled nothing after that until some men who had heard him cry for help were loading him in the hearse that also served as an ambulance. He remembered Mr. Stanton telling him they were going to St. Anthony's hospital in St. Louis, and nothing after that until he was coming out from under the ether and the doctor was telling him about trying to remove the bullet.

When Petrequin finished the direct of Carroll, Redmond had no further questions.

Petrequin called Dr. J. J. Pullian of St. Anthony's hospital to the stand. The Doctor had four x-ray pictures. The State secured admission of all four of the pictures and gives them exhibit numbers and showed them to the jury. Petrequin asked Dr. Pullian the cause of death. "The cause of death was the result of a wound to the head, a bullet wound in the abdomen with the bullet lodging in the spinal column, and shock as a result of these injuries."

When the defense was given the opportunity for cross-examination, Redmond asked, "Dr. Pullian, is it true that you operated on Mr. Rauscher in an attempt to remove the bullet lodged in his spine?"

"Yes."

"Is that always indicated in cases of this nature?"

"....No."

"Could you explain for us lay people why sometimes it might not be indicated?"

"There is a danger of course of more damage to the spinal cord....of more nerve damage....or the fluid leaking out."

"Sometimes the medical judgment is to leave the bullet where it lodged....to do no harm?"

"....That is correct."

"Is it possible that if you had not attempted to remove the bullet from Mr. Rauscher's spine, he would be alive today?"

Petrequin stood up so fast his chair fell over, "Objection!"

Judge Threlkeld asked, "What is your objection?"

"Well....the line of questioning is irrelevant and--"

"Mr. Redmond?"

"Your honor....If Mr. Rauscher might otherwise be alive today, then the cause of death could just as well be the attempt to remove the bullet from his spine, and--"

"You can argue he wouldn't have died if he stayed in bed that morning," said Petrequin.

"Objection overruled."

"....If he died from the attempt to remove the bullet, then the charge against my client should be *assault*, not first-degree murder."

Doctor Pullian was excused, and the Judge called a recess for lunch. Knowing they would not be welcome in any of the local eating establishments, Redmond stopped at a grocery and bought bread and cold cuts and soda pop, and Espy wanted a bag of Saratoga chips. They ate in the car.

Like in Ste. Genevieve the accommodations for Colored were in the basement of the Flat River courthouse. The nasty stench from the overflowed toilet and cigarette smoke suffused the air. You had a choice of the urinal or the commode-without-a-seat but with both of them in there at once, Espy's ass was up against his hip. If he moved his feet carefully, the half-inch of diluted piss on the floor did not quite reach to where the upper of his shoes was stitched to the sole and he could keep his socks dry.

31.

AFTER THEY RECONVENED, THE STATE CALLED DR. PULLIAM ON RE-DIRECT
to try to discredit Redmond's suggestion that Rauscher died from the attempt to remove the
bullet.

The next witness for the State was Roy J. Dugan of the St. Louis Custom House who
was guarding a confiscated bootleg boat captured the day before by James A. Dillon and his
deputies, and was tied up near the scene of the crime. He testified that he heard Rauscher's
cries for help, and when he went to his assistance found him lying partly in the water and
partly on the bank. He pulled him out of the water, and Rauscher told him he had been held
up and shot.

Dugan said he saw another man lying on the bank and asked Rauscher who it was.
Rauscher replied, "It's my buddy. He is dead." Dugan said the bank was an incline of about
sixty degrees and that it would have been possible to pull or carry a man down it. After getting Rauscher out on the bank, Dugan said he notified the Sheriff.

Next they called Warren J. Stanton of Ste. Genevieve who was an undertaker by profes-
sion. Petrequin got him to tell the exact position of Rauscher's body when he was picked up
on the river bank near the Modoc ferry landing.

Then the prosecution called Ste. Genevieve County Sheriff Ben Picou, who testified that
he found Rauscher in a critical condition on the river bank and his car nearby. He arrested
Taylor about nine o'clock that morning, six hours after the shooting. "He implicated a man
whose name was 'Lee Guy.' I released him, but later when I arrested Jennings, he told me
'Guy' was a name Taylor went by ....So I arrested Taylor again....After his second arrest,"
Picou says, "Taylor told me he shot both Rauscher and Chomeau and carried Rauscher and
dumped him in the river, and that Jennings carried Chomeau and all three of them threw
rocks at Rauscher."

"The Rogers woman too?" Petrequin asked.

"Yes, sir."

"At both of them?"

"That's what he said."

REDMOND USUALLY ADVISED A CLIENT NOT TO APPEAR AS A WITNESS IN his own defense. However, in this case the verdict was pretty nearly foregone. His hope was for prejudice that he could document for an appellate court. Taylor's claim of self-defense would not cut much ice. His complaint about how he was treated in custody and how his confession was obtained might not either with this courtroom crowd or the jury, but was grist for the mill on appeal.

So the defense called Taylor as their first witness, and Redmond conducted his direct examination. "Mr. Taylor," he said, "first I would like to ask you about the circumstances of your so-called 'confession.'"

Petrequin was on his feet, "Your honor, it was a *confession*, witnessed and signed. 'So-called' is a misnomer. I object."

"Overruled."

"Mr. Taylor?" Redmond asked.

"It was a mob outside. They be wanting to *lynch* me.... Lynch all of us. They holler and shout. I can hear through the jailhouse window. They making *threats*."

"Do you recall any of these threats?"

"'Nigger, say your prayers!' .... 'We going to *cut* you!' .... 'Burn, nigger .... Burn!'"

"And how were you treated by the officers of the law?"

"Sheriff Pappas *struck* me so I bleeding from the head."

"Are there any marks on you from that beating?"

"This scar....here." He leaned forward pressing two fingers to a spot over his left eye."

"Objection!"

"Mr. Petrequin?" the Judge asked.

"If any scar at all is there, it's *old* .... We would need a doctor to examine it."

"Mr. Petrequin, I am going to rule against you because the proper place for you to raise that objection would be in your cross-examination."

Petrequin sat down. He was still is in a salty sore-head sulk.

"What did Deputy Pappas *say* to you?" Redmond asked. They had gone over this.

"He say the Ku Kluxers outside bust in there any minutes, wire me to a tree, soak me down with coal oil, and *burn* me to death if I don't confess up."

"He said, 'Ku Kluxers?'"

"Yes, sir."

"You believe that?"

"I don't actually know, sir. Down home at West Memphis, I believe it....I *believe* it!"

Petrequin interrupted to ask for a sidebar, which the Judge granted and then called a recess.

WHEN THEY RESUMED, REDMOND CONTINUED WITH DIRECT OF TAYLOR in his own behalf. He asked him if he discharged a firearm. "Yes, sir," he said, "in self-defense."

"Can you tell us your best recollection of what happened?"

"Yes, sir....One of the white mens, he start a fight."

"How was that?"

"He insult Vera....*Mrs. Rogers.*"

"In what way?"

"Talk dirty to her. Reach around, try to feel her up."

"Then what happened?"

"I *told* him stop acting that way. I say, *You would get sore your own self, a Negro talk that way to a white woman.*"

A stir went through the crowd that was part ridicule and part outrage at the very idea of a black man so much as entertaining such a possibility, and to have the impertinence to speak of it out loud in a court room in the hearing of white people. What they were saying in effect with hard stares at Taylor and at Redmond and Espy and out the side of the mouth to each other is *And you can be damn sure we would not just get a sore head about it.*

Redmond nodded, and Taylor continued. "He stop the machine, reach back and hit me in the stomach. He say, *So you are sore, are you?* Then he hit me again. He turn around in the front seat hitting at me and I trying to clinch him up and my elbow hit the door handle some way and I fall out to the ground, and he jump on me, we wrestling....C. J., Vera, the other white man all scramble out the car. Vera, she yell, *That white man have a gun!*"

He stopped, his eyes looking here and there in the court room. Redmond nodded as if to say it's all right, go on and tell your story.

"So....I pull out my revolver and fire to one side. Bullet hit that other white man and he fall....I keep on firing, empty my gun cause I be afraid the man I fighting with, he get hold of it and shoot me....He fall down too....He a *big* man."

"That was Rauscher."

"All I know he a fat man, drag you down, roll over on you like a big old hog. He the one still alive."

"That *was* Rauscher."

"Yes, sir."

"You *believed* one of the white men was armed?"

"For a fact."

"Which one?"

"The other white man."

"From the one you were fighting with?"

"Yes, sir. Vera, she holler, *That other white man have a gun!*"

Redmond turned to the judge and said, "Your honor, I submit, a sincere belief the other party has a gun is grounds for a verdict of self-defense."

"Address the jury," Threlkeld said.

"....Whether he actually did have a gun, or not."

"Counselor, you will address the jury."

"Yes, your honor."

He ended his direct examination of Taylor there because he knew what he would say about subsequent events, against his advice. Sure enough on cross, Petrequin got him to deny he had any part whatsoever in throwing Chomeau and Rauscher in the river and in stoning Rauscher when he tried to swim to the bootleggers' barge. Then over Redmond's objections that this was hearsay and inadmissible unless he called them to the stand, Petrequin read the statements of Jennings and Mrs. Rogers that contradicted Taylor.

That threw cold water on any disposition a juror might have to believe the story he drew out of him on direct. He himself could believe that story. He also could believe the story Rauscher told of Taylor ordering him to stop the car and turn around.

When Petrequin was through, Redmond said no more questions.

The Judge slammed his gavel three times and called a recess. Then after a sidebar he excused the jury and told them to report at 9:00 o'clock the next day.

ON FRIDAY MORNING THE STATE CALLED SHERIFF PICOU ON RE-DIRECT TO refute the defense claim that he used the mob clamoring to lynch Taylor to terrify him into saying whatever he wanted him to say. With flagrant leading of the witness, the prosecution would have it believed that the National Guard was called in purely to protect the decent law-abiding Colored in town. It was true that Taylor and Jennings and Vera Fox were long gone to Festus by the time the Guard finally arrived.

Redmond saw little to be gained in another cross. What he needed was witnesses. He said, "No more questions."

The Judge called a recess for lunch before they had closing statements.

THE CROWD IN THE SQUARE AROUND THE COURTHOUSE HAD GROWN, and now some of them recognized Redmond and Espy. Walking to their car across the street they were subjected to hard stares and catcalls and muttered threats and insults from people close by who barely gave them room to pass.

As he was unlocking the car door Redmond looked up and saw three black-face effigies made of clothing stuffed with straw. They were dangling by ropes around their necks from third floor windows of the Knights of Pythias hall above a hardware store. He felt people watching him see them, and he cut his eyes down before he could make out the hand-lettered signs pinned on them. He supposed they included names, either Taylor, Jennings, and Mrs. Rogers; or, Taylor, Espy, and himself.

They got in the car and slowly backed out of the angled parking place, people moving out of the way in their own sweet time. In first gear they had to creep along slower than walking. The crowd seemed to want them to know they could stop them if they pleased at any time and serve them like the straw men. And if Redmond and Espy gave them the least excuse, they would.

They passed the stalls and carts of hucksters selling donuts and coffee, hot dogs, little Confederate flags, American flags, and Black Sambo rag dolls. After they turned the corner the side street for two blocks down the hill was as crowded as the square. Redmond estimated more than five thousand people had congregated for the trial, half the population of Flat River, Bonne Terre and the nearby lead mining villages of Desloge, Elvins, Rivermines, Esther, Mineral Point, Federal, and Cheatham combined.

They went to the same grocery and bought cold cuts and cheese and bread and soda and a large bag of Saratoga chips. They ate where they were parked two doors down from the grocery. When he turned on the motor and idled it to run the heater, the windows steamed up and they had a semblance of privacy.

JUDGE THRELKELD CALLED THE COURT TO ORDER AND ASSISTANT ATTORney General Purteet straightened his papers, rose with dignity to his feet, and came strutting up to the jury like a dandy at a barn dance. He told the Prosecution version of the story one more time, relying mainly on Rauscher's statement to the St. Louis police captain, but also the confessions of Jennings and Mrs. Rogers shrugging as much of the blame as they could off themselves and onto Taylor.

"Brownie Taylor himself admits," Purteet sayid, "that he fired the shots....And according to the other two Negroes and to the victim himself, he threw rocks at Rauscher when he saw him trying to swim to the barge....The question is not whether he killed Rauscher or whether there was calculation in throwing rocks at him....That he is guilty of murder in the first degree is foregone....The only question that remains....is how he shall be punished."

Redmond was thinking Purteet had not overstated his case or slathered it with words like *heinous, vile, unconscionable.* He took notes furiously trying to get down everything he said.

Then he went into his peroration asking for the death penalty. It was as if a microphone descended from the ceiling and began to broadcast their proceedings to the mob that pressed up the courthouse steps and jammed the yard and streets all around the square. You could distinctly hear different voices holler out, "Hang him high as Haman!....Hang him high!" And, "Burn, nigger....Burn!" Some settled into a chant, *"HANG the nigger!...HANG the nigger!"*

Many inside the courtroom were looking at each other, nodding their heads. Here and there one joined in, mouthing the words. Judge Threlkeld scowled at them, took hold of his gavel.

Purteet could not help warming to the crowd inside and outside the courtroom, but still he glanced out the corner of his eye from time to time at Redmond taking notes, and over at the official court recorder supposedly taking it all down in shorthand.

"Gentlemen of the jury," he said---they did not often have women on juries then, certainly not in murder trials. "The People are watching. You can hear their voices...."

And indeed you could from all sides around the square, the closed windows vibrating from the chant like rolling thunder, *"Hang the nigger!....Hang him high!"*

"They are waiting," said Purteet. "They are waiting for you....They are waiting to learn whether you decided to do what must be done....*or they will do it for you...!"*

The fountain pen still in his hand Redmond rose and called out, "Objection!"

"Yes, Counselor," said Judge Threlkeld as if he was wondering when the defense attorney would get around to this.

"The Prosecution threat of mob violence is highly prejudicial."

"Objection *sustained!*" said the Judge. He turns and said to the jury, "I strongly admonish you to disregard any threat of popular violence!"

He said to Purteet, "If you again make reference in any way to mob rule, you will be found in contempt of court!"

There was an ugly stir among the spectators.

The Judge banged his gavel twice. "Any further demonstration like that, and the courtroom will be cleared!"

Purteet waited with his head bowed and his chin in his hand against his chest until the Judge nodded and said, "You may resume."

With a quick glance at Redmond as if he was thinking he must have written all that down too and as if he was afraid of making matters worse, he quickly concluded, trying to catch the eye of the foreman of the jury, "Bring in the death penalty....and you will receive the commendation of the *law-abiding* people of Missouri."

The Judge was displeased. As Purteet returned to the Prosecution table and sat down, Threlkeld seemed about to admonish him again. But the stir among the spectators had resumed and they were in an ugly and rebellious mood, and the chanting outside had not abated, *"Hang* that nigger!....Hang him *high!"*

Threlkeld thought better of whatever he was about to say, and turned to Redmond.

In his closing statement he went through the motions, recalling Taylor's claim that his confession was coerced, his account of the white man insulting Mrs. Rogers. The defense had no hope of a favorable verdict, and Redmond's safety and that of Espy and of Taylor himself was a matter of legitimate concern.

The spectators in the courtroom had become part of the mob outside. They were like rabid fans at a sporting event, a herd of buffalo milling around before they stampede. All he studied was not to set them off.

He finished what he had to say, shut up, and sat down. His chance to serve the client was in the appeal.

The Judge read his instructions to the jury and sent them out.

Scarcely any of the spectators left the courtroom, afraid that as soon as they did someone else would take their places. They seemed to think they would not have long to wait. In this they were correct.

The jury was out for less than an hour.

The Judge smacked his gavel three times for order. The jury filed in and at a nod they sat down. Threlkeld asked, "Have you reached a verdict?"

The foreman, a little man in glasses and a bow tie, rose and said, "We have, your honor."

"What is your verdict?"

"We find the defendant guilty as charged...and recommend a penalty of death."

The courtroom exploded in raucous cheers and whoops like the home team kicking field goal in the last seconds to win the big game. As the news spread, a roar of approval and cheering resounded from all around the square. There were celebratory gunshots, the honking of car horns.

Taylor did not accept his sentence with Christian humility. When Redmond turned to him to offer his condolences and assure him they were immediately filing an appeal, he shouted and cursed. "Thanks for nothing, you jackleg sack of bullshit!....Hire a nigger for free and you get what you pay for! You didn't do diddley-squat!....You *fired!*"

After he had been shackled and led out by three bailiffs, the Judge summoned Redmond to the side of the bench and said, "The defendant spoke in the heat of the moment, Counselor....Until and unless you are notified otherwise by this court, you will consider yourself as his attorney of record."

The halls of the courthouse were jammed with rowdy celebrating people who were not especially friendly to the Negro attorneys for the defense. Espy and Redmond attached themselves to a passing bailiff and pretending not to know the way, they asked him to show them to the County Clerk's office. He complied. When they had finished the routine paperwork and officially filed for the appeal, the bailiff was still waiting outside the door. Redmond asked him if someone might escort them to their car.

32.

LESTER DID NOT ATTEND HARDY'S TRIAL. THE NEWS OF IT WAS THAT THE jury required less than two hours to return a verdict of guilty of murder in the first degree and to recommend his hanging. His lawyers called on a doctor from the state mental hospital to testify that he labored under hallucinations and was insane or that he suffered from a social disease that affected his mind, but to no avail. A week later the judge passed formal sentence that he would be hanged on December 17th. But his lawyers filed a "writ of error" so his case might be appealed to the State Supreme Court.

The Anvil took the Ste. Genevieve *Fair Play* and left it out for guests to peruse. Lester usually would page through it, and now and then he found an item pertaining to Hardy and read it with some interest. The paper the week after his sentencing had an item about an attempted jail break and how Hardy did not take part. Another man condemned to death was the instigator. He and an accomplice used a stove grate to dig through the soft brick wall into the Fire House next door and would have made their getaway if the Fire Chief had not come in to check to see if the machine was in running order and heard strange sounds. When he was caught the condemned man Williamson said, "Why, Sheriff, if you was in my fix you would do the same thing." Hardy was reported as saying he was not in on the plot. But if the boys had gained entrance to the Fire House and secured a bar to break the lock on his cell, he would have walked out with the rest of the gang. Lester was alarmed to think the man came that close to escaping, but also did not like the way the matter was treated as an instance of boys will be boys.

The next news was that the higher court had agreed to review his case. Their decision did not come down until the third week in November. It was nevertheless what was to be hoped for. His death sentence was affirmed and he would be executed on December 18th at the Ste. Genevieve Poor Farm. This was a new wrinkle. Previously the hanging was to be at the jail or in the courthouse yard at Flat River.

The next news was that the new Governor had given Hardy a reprieve until January 22nd so that he could study his sanity report. The same item declared that the Sheriff had stopped all preparation for the hanging. The scaffold with its enclosure in a stockade 16 feet high had already been erected and was ready for use, if the execution finally did come to pass.

Lester was not alone in his exasperation. The closer they seemed to come to the event, the more keen he was to have it over with. This was not so much out of the fear and loathing he felt for the deluded man when he was running loose, but like when you need so bad to take a leak that you are doing a little dance. Or when you have been suffering for several days of constipation and drunk a quart of castor oil and are bursting to empty your bowels, but are unable to get to where you may do that. The whole town seemed out of sorts. They needed to get Holt Hardy out of their system.

Finally the item of February 27th declared HARDY TO BE HANGED FRIDAY AFTERNOON. Beside the main story was a smaller item "Sheriff Busy Issuing Passes for Hardy Hanging" that said he believed about 300 would be in the stockade to witness the event. Lester presented himself at the courthouse and when he told the clerk his relation to Hardy's victim, he issued him a pass. It was a printed slip of paper that said *The bearer,*

_____ with his name inked in on the blank line, *is appointed a special deputy for the occasion of the execution of:* _____ and Hardy's name inked in there, and the time and date and place. The time was one o'clock in the afternoon.

Also from the item in the paper he was informed that a number of women from various towns in Missouri including some from Ste. Genevieve would be in attendance, and that a majority of the requests for passes were from doctors, lawyers, newspapermen, and law enforcement officers. One request was from the editor of the Sedalia *Bazoo* in the western part of the state for a number of subscribers who had booked a special railroad car for an excursion to attend the hanging. It stuck in Lester's craw, and when he spoke of it in the public room of the Anvil, he found others had also taken note. Expressing their scorn of the morbid curiosity of the *Bazoo* Hanging Excursion from Sedalia was like scratching a serious itch from chiggers or poison ivy. All of them of course were superior to such shameless behavior, except that he heard a good deal of grumbling from those who applied for passes and were denied.

Ethel's mother had been issued a pass, but a request for one for her younger brother Delbert was denied on the grounds that he was under age.

THE FIRST WEEK IN MARCH REDMOND AND HIS CLIENT APPEARED IN Threlkeld's court in Flat River for sentencing. The jury had recommended death and the outcome was foregone. Still as he waited beside him in his shackles at the table for the defense, Taylor had a childish hope that his life would be spared.

The courtroom was not packed as it was for the trial but the first few rows were filled with more than thirty people, including Mr. Le Clerq Janis of the Ste. Genevieve *Fair Play* and a man whose name he forgot but believed was with one of the St. Louis papers. Threlkeld called them to order with his gavel. He addressed his first remarks to the lawyers for the defense. "Mr. Redmond and Mr. Espy, your motion for a new trial is denied."

This too was foregone. Redmond did not protest.

"We proceed to the sentencing of Brownie V. Taylor, alias Lee Guy....The defendant will please rise."

As Taylor stood you could hear the shifting of the chain that connected his leg irons. He was dressed in his Sunday suit and white shirt but without a necktie.

The Judge rapped his gavel again and read from a paper in his hand, "It is therefore considered ordered and adjudged by the Court that the defendant, Brownie Taylor, having been found guilty as aforesaid be taken to the jail of St. Francois County from whence he came and there securely kept until Thursday the 16th day of April and on that day within the walls of the jail at Flat River at the County Seat of said County of St. Francois, if the jail is so-constructed that the execution can conveniently take place therein, but if said jail is not so constructed, then in an enclosure surrounded by a wall palisade or fence higher than the gallows and sufficiently closed as to exclude the view of persons on the outside of said enclosure to be adjoining to or as near the jail as possible between the hours of eight o'clock in the forenoon and six o'clock in the afternoon of that day, he, said Brownie Taylor, be hanged by the neck until he is dead; and the Sheriff of St. Francois County do the execution of this sentence."

This time instead of cursing his lawyer he fell to his knees and wept as if the dam that pent up all his grief since he was in knee pants had burst, and he yearned with all his heart to be consoled. "Mama…Oh, Mama…*Mama!*" he said. He was wracked with long shuddering sobs, involuntary, without self-consciousness or shame. He had to be pulled erect and escorted from the courtroom by two stout bailiffs who bore his weight on his elbows and forearms. His legs were limp as a ventriloquist's dummy and his cardboard feet fluttered along. He had wet his pants.

THE DISTRICT COURT RULED AGAINST HIM. THE FOLLOWING THURSDAY, Espy and Redmond filed an appeal on Taylor's behalf to the Missouri State Supreme Court. Until their decision, Taylor's execution was postponed and almost certainly would not take place on April 16th.

ON JUNE 1ST THEY APPEARED AGAIN IN THE COURT OF JUDGE EUSTACE Threlkeld in Flat River, this time for the trial of Taylor's codefendants Columbus Jennings and Vera Rogers. On advice of Counsel Jennings entered a plea of guilty. Redmond called him as a witness and asked him to outline to the court how the crime was committed. In the main his account agreed with what emerged in Taylor's trial, except that he greatly minimized the part played by Mrs. Rogers.

In cross-examination Assistant Attorney General Purteet asked only about Vera Rogers. "You say she did not join in throwing stones at Rauscher in the water?"

"No, sir," said Jennings. "She make herself scarce....Catch up to her later down the railroad tracks."

"The statement of Rauscher said she did join in."

"He down in the water, sir, in and out of conscience. He was mistaken, just a honest mistake....sir."

"You did join in yourself?"

"Yes, sir."

"No further questions."

When the Judge gave Redmond a chance to ask more questions on re-direct, he passed. The Judge banged his gavel and declared a recess until eleven-thirty.

After calling them together again, Threlkeld gave Jennings life in prison for killing Chomeau and life in prison for killing Rauscher, "the sentences to run concurrently." He put down one piece of paper and took up another. "In the matter of Mrs. Vera Rogers, we find that the testimony of Columbus Jennings casts reasonable doubt on the recollections of the victim Rauscher while he was half-paralyzed and semi-conscious in the river. The State chooses to dismiss the case against her, and after completing some paper work with the Clerk of the Court, she is free to go."

At this Mrs. Rogers clapped her hands together and cried out, "Thank you, Jesus!" Suffused with the Holy Spirit she looked ready to dance and speak in tongues. Then she looked to Jennings as if expecting him to share her joy. He stared straight ahead. Redmond heard him say under his breath, "You welcome."

THE WHEELS OF JUSTICE COULD GRIND SLOWLY INDEED WHEN YOU WERE awaiting an uncertain outcome. Their appeal on behalf of Ronnie Taylor was filed in the first week of March. By the anniversary of this appeal to the Missouri Supreme Court, they had learned nothing.

Taylor languished in the St. Francois County jail in Flat River. When Redmond visited him from time to time he would be fretful and morose at best, and sometimes hostile and abusive. To his credit, when there was a spectacular jail break, he made no attempt to escape.

Someone threw a bottle of nitroglycerin against the steel bars of one of the windows of the bull-ring of the jail where prisoners were permitted to mingle and amuse themselves outside their cells during the day. The explosion that followed blew out the window. Twenty-four of the prisoners, Taylor among them, made no attempt to escape. Of the seven who fled, one was fatally shot, a second seriously wounded, and five gained their freedom at least for a time.

Finally in June a year and three months after filing, they received the decision of the Supreme Court. Espy and Redmond were notified by registered mail. And the same day they received the written decision, they read of it in the *Post-Dispatch* under the headline:

Brownie Taylor Given New Trial By Court.

Signed by Commissioner for Division 2 of the Missouri Supreme Court Henry J. Westhues, it was based on closing remarks by Assistant Attorney General Don Purteet to the effect that the people were watching them to determine if it would be necessary to resort to mob rule, or whether the Law was sufficient to punish such crimes as those committed by Taylor. Westhues found the remarks highly prejudicial and that they tended improperly to influence the jury. "The argument of the Special Prosecutor can only be interpreted to mean that if the jury in the case refused to convict the defendant and assess the death penalty, a mob would do so."

Westhues granted that Threlkeld sustained Redmond's objection to the argument and admonished the jury to disregard any reference to mob rule. "There are, however," he wrote, "some cases where the trial court is powerless to extract the poison that has been injected into the case."

In December at a new trial in Flat River, also before Judge Eustace Threlkeld, Taylor was sentenced to a life term in the penitentiary on each count, the terms to run concurrently.

Although his client showed little appreciation, Redmond was pleased. He had no hope of acquittal in the first trial. This was the one outcome he could work toward. The nol pross of Mrs. Rogers was lagniappe. To celebrate, he and Espy treated themselves and their wives to a steak dinner at the Victorian Club in the Ville, where they were entertained by the incomparable blues-man Henry Townsend.

33.

FRIDAY WAS MILD AND CLEAR, ONLY A FEW DAYS AFTER THE THAW AND break-up of an ice-jam at the ferry landing that stretched to the Illinois side of the river and back along the Missouri shore for half a mile. The Poor Farm looked like a big old red brick factory with a belfry and a gallery across the front and along the wings that stretched back on either side. It sat at the foot of the bluff line across a yard that used to be a pasture of perhaps ten acres along the Bottom road, before it crooked around a limestone outcrop and you come to the Landing and the Anvil.

After they lay down their tools at the quarry and the other fellows went to settle down with their lunch pails, with Henry's leave Lester had the afternoon off. When he came in sight of the Poor Farm already there was a crowd, and sure enough on the railroad siding was a car with a banner along the side:

> BAZOO SPECIAL Holt Hardy Execution Ste.
> Genevieve, Mo.

Around on the grass outside the stockade were all ages and sorts of people and two refreshment stands with weiners and beverages, and a fellow with a cart and two or three others with boxes and chests on straps around their shoulders with things to eat and drink and souvenirs.

He saw a printed card with a picture and picked it up. The picture was Holt Hardy, cleaned up some but he needed a shave. It read:

> HOLT HARDY EXECUTION For the Murder of
> Ethel Fahnstock.

Under that was a time-table and the cost, and on the back was printed a Special Deputy Pass, and in fine print at the bottom: *J. West Goodwin, Editor, Sedalia Bazoo.* Lester stuck it in his pocket. That would be his souvenir.

A fellow was playing a sad tune on a mouth organ and Holy Rollers were beating a drum and shaking tambourines. There was an organ-grinder with a little monkey and a man in a top hat on stilts with signs on him front and back for the Southern Hotel. A buxom girl was selling sheet music of a sad song about Holt Hardy and his doomed love for fair Ethel.

The stockade was like a fort from *The Last of the Mohicans* but up close you saw it was not whole logs but just sawmill trash slabs bark-side-out in up-and-down rows. It was high though. He calculated that standing on the shoulders of a man his height and reaching his arms straight up, he could still not touch the top of it.

He drifted along and came to the people bunched up at the entrance and for a while he waited his turn. But the state policeman called out, "Step back, please, if you do not have a pass....You must have a pass to enter....Step back, please." Lester concluded to push his way through. He showed the trooper his pass, and he allowed him in.

Inside was less elbow room, and he would say it was more than 300 people, and among them scarcely any women. The scaffold was at the west side toward the bluff, the floor of it higher then his head so you could see anyone upon it from wherever you were at. The gallows itself loomed up more than twice as tall, the rope with a noose hanging down. Here and there he saw someone he was acquain'ted with and nodded, and then up close to the side he spotted Ethel's grown brothers Douglas and Arthur.

Arthur saw him and motioned with his head for him to come there, and he said something to a deputy. It was Pappas and he saw Lester too and made his way toward him. When he got close enough he said Ethel's brothers said he should have a place close by them, and he followed. Arthur made room for him, and they were in the front row at the left where you could reach out and touch the scaffold posts and see a ways underneath. Lester said, "Thanks."

Arthur nodded.

They had no need of speech as they waited there side-by-side.

YOU COULD HEAR A COMMOTION ALONG THE BACK WALL, AND A DOOR HE had not seen right by the platform opened and a preacher came through and after him Holt Hardy, two state police, Sheriff Picou, and a little fellow in a black hood. They nearly brushed against him as they passed by, then around to the front, and Hardy went up the steps two at a time. On his face was a smile that stayed the same as they bound his legs with straps and his wrists behind his back.

All talk had ceased. Word must have been spreading among the throng outside the fence, as they too fell silent.

At a nod from Picou, Hardy spoke. "Friends, I am proud to admit my trust in Jesus. He has been a great comfort to me through the long months waiting for this day....I feel no malice, not even toward those who have been so bitter against me." Here his eyes turned in Lester's direction, and in spite of himself he shuddered and his bowels clutched tight. "I am prepared to meet my Master and...my golden-haired darling in Paradise."

His lips trembled, and after a pause he said just above a whisper to the Sheriff, "That is all."

The hooded man set the noose just right around his neck with the knot behind his left ear, and offered him a blindfold which Hardy shook off. The man stepped back and put his hand on a lever that stuck up from the floor. Lester counted to himself *A thousand and one... .a thousand and two....a thousand and three...to seventy,* when the trap was sprung.

Underneath he could see him from the waist down writhing and twitching. It went on for some time, like a grasshopper suffocating in a jar. His knee had scraped as he fell and the cloth tore and blood had soaked through. Like Lester nearly did himself he had messed his pants. You could smell him like a baby that shit its diaper and under that an unwashed body smell. More than five minutes and he still gave a twitch now and then, one foot knocking against a post.

People whispered and talked low among themselves but no one moved to leave. They were waiting him out. They had waited a year and a day and then some through endless appeals and stays. To think he still might suffer made it sweet. Finally at two-fifteen three doctors went under there to check and Dr. Hertig that attended to Ethel was one of them. They pronounced Holt Hardy dead.

People began to talk and a few to joke. If beforehand they were like jaspers at the fair crowding the hootchy-kooch, now they were polite and moved slowly like after church.

Lester invited Douglas and Arthur to join him in a glass of lager beer and a shot of schnapps but they were going to their mother and young Delbert, who had remained at home. They insisted however in driving him the short distance to the Anvil in Arthur's new Ford truck.

"He is like the bull that gores the heifer turned out for him to tread," said Douglas, "or the sow that eats her farrow....You must put them down."

"He will trouble us no more," said Arthur.

Lester was numb. Hardy had done his worst. Perhaps there was a lake of fire where he would twist and writhe in eternal torment, perhaps not. As for his dear girl Ethel whose name he took in vain, he thought of lines she fancied in the *Treasury of Immortal Verse* that was one of the Workingmen's Library Blue Books that she passed on to him. One lay-about Sunday morning they were turning over the pages together when she stopped and said *Oh, this is one Miss Marple liked....from an old play,* and she read it to him. The end of each verse was almost the same, and that is what he remembered.

> *Golden lads and girls all must*
> *Like chimney sweepers come to dust.*

He heard the words in his head as if on Dictaphone wax to the sound of her voice.

34.

CLETUS ASKED THE COLORED MAN AT THE SHOESHINE STAND IN THE LOBBY of the big hotel across from the Governor's house, and he directed him to Lincoln Institute. He recalled that Clemmie was a member of the same sorority as Miss Anita James and that it was Delta Stigma. Something like that.

He found it after a while, an ordinary clapboard bungalow house with a new part out back that had white shingles on the sides, and a sign in front: *Delta Sigma Theta*, over a triangle, a sideways *W* and a zero with a line cross the middle.

Clemmie was not sure what to do about him. They sat in the little front room with a worn-out couch and old chairs where the young ladies of the sorority entertained their young gentlemen. A big mirror hung beside the wide door for them to check their appearance before they stepped out. They sat in two chairs in the corner between the mirror and the window that looked out on the wide gallery across the front and the scraggly lawn to big run-down houses across the street with signs for rooms to let.

"I am glad to see you safe, Cletus," she said. "We were concerned." She knew about the vigilantes going to Ribeaus.'

He told her how he saw Cap in the sanitarium, and he was going back to his postal service job. And now Cletus knew the men came for Cap, not for him.

"Why would they come for you?" she asked.

He just shook his head. Mr. Redmond advised him to keep that business to himself, and on the streetcar Reverend Whitfield explained how it's to protect Zella that he did not want her to know either. "After I be getting death threats and flee up to St. Louis," he had said,

"Zella stayed on at LaForgue with Shirley and Barbar. Three white men with guns come to the door looking for me, asked where I am and when I come home." He said it was better she did not have to lie, she honestly did not know. It would the same if the Law come to her asking for the cropper boy that stayed by Ribeaus.

"Why you come to Jefferson City, Cletus?" Clemmie asked. "What you going to do?"

What he had in mind was how she taught him on Sunday afternoons for the high school test. Maybe he could pass it, matriculate as a student at Lincoln Institute. She gave him to understand how he might possess the ability to succeed in that. Only she did not seem glad to see him.

Before he could think what to say, she anticipated. "If you expect me to be tutoring you again for the high school equivalency, I just don't know where I could find the time."

"....That's all right."

She said how her mama and daddy come to her when the white people of Ste. Genevieve ran all the Colored out. "Like I am the Underground Railroad."

She told him how she made her mama call Mrs. Griswold long distance. And sure enough the rich white B-I-T-C-H begged her to come back to polish her silver and wipe her toilet, and her daddy went back to his custodian job in the high school. She said the letters to spell the word, just did not pronounce it, *bitch*.

Reverend Whitfield said he would do better staying in St. Louis where there were a whole lot more colored people and mostly Negroes in certain parts of town. Not everybody knew everybody's business, and his chances of employment were better. Jeff City he said was bigger than Ste. Genevieve and had a certain number of Colored, but the white people there year round were not much different. He said *They look you over, wonder if you escaped from the Penitentiary. Or paroled.* All this came to Cletus' mind. He turned and pretended he was looking at something interesting out the window so she did not see tears in his eyes.

"Oh, now, Cletus," she said and patted his hand. "We'll see..." She went on to say how it was her summer vacation when she did lessons with him before and now she had her school-work and practice teaching, and her fiancé was jealous of her time.

Then she asked how he was going to support himself.

He looked out the window again.

She sat there thinking, shook her head. "We have to find someplace for you to stay."

He was her guest for dinner in the sorority house dining room, and Miss Adele James and Miss Cynthia Bolt were there. They asked about the people in Cropperville. The House-mother Mrs. Ludington was nice, said she had an idea of a situation for a young colored man with turn and references of three of her senior girls.

She said her sister worked as a domestic for an old white widow Velma Sellars who was almost blind and lived alone in a big old house on Dunklin Avenue. Mrs. Ludington took Cletus to meet her sister, and it worked out. He had his own room out behind the kitchen. In return for his room and board he did chores around the place, went with Mrs. Sellars to the store. In a while she trusted him to pay her bills from her check book.

He did odd jobs with neighbors for some pocket money, and Clemmie found time to *tutor* him, and sent off for information on the high school test.

LESTER HAD AN IDEA TO STAY ON AT STE. GENEVIEVE JUST FOR A WHILE AND help out Ethel's mother from time to time with chores she needed done. He would see what kind of dutch Delbert was into and stay to Sunday dinner but not as a regular thing. Ethel's friend Mary Ann would be there sometimes, and after a while he concluded he might ask her to the picture show.

One evening as he was having a draught in the public room at the Anvil, Frank Janis told him they needed a man in the machine shop at Jenkins-Gillis if he did not mind working with Colored. Lester allowed he might be interested. Frank pointed out a man named Burke as who he heard it of. Lester contrived to have a word with Dick Burke and he told him who to talk to, and one thing led to another and he was hired.

Henry Maheu told him he was sorry to lose a good man. But with any job at all hard to come by, when he had a chance at something better he was right to move on.

ZENO WAS GLAD WHEN HIS BROTHER CAP CAME HOME FROM THE SANITAR- ium to working for the Postal Service, only at first they had him stay and sort letters. A clerk made his deliveries. Both kept their old jobs on paper, but for a while that new postmaster had them trade off. He was afraid for Cap out alone on the rural route.

Lonzo continued in service to Mr. Rozier, with his animal doctoring on the side. It seemed like that picked up some. Lon told Redmond that old white farmer Biggs said he was ashamed for how white people of the town did them. He said *I don't care if you are a nigger or a Jew, you are the best damn doctor of veterinary medicine between here and Perryville.*

As for Zeno and the other colored men who grew up in Ste. Genevieve and worked in the kilns and quarries, a number of them returned. Old Jenkins wanted to open up his quarry and kilns, and he hired them on. Starting out he gave them the same as the sorry-ass down-and-out sharecroppers, only they were gone and not coming back. They went on a while, got some paydays under their belts, stocked up on rice and beans.

What Jenkins did not know was that they had been organizing CIO. They had a union vote. It was almost unanimous, 78 to 3.

Old man Jenkins would not recognize it.

They went in the next Monday morning for the day shift, but the graveyard shift men stayed on. They had all their tools out, dynamite chests unlocked, all the kilns cooking full of melted rock, and they sat down. They would stay right where they were until they got the same pay as the AF of L men in the white quarries. Send tin soldiers in, they would blow up the whole concern.

They said *We will not be moved.*

SIDNEY REDMOND WAS THE FIRST AFRICAN AMERICAN IN MISSOURI TO BE appointed a circuit court judge.

Books from Gival Press - Fiction and Nonfiction

Boys, Lost & Found: Stories by Charles Casillo
ISBN: 978-1-928589-33-4, $20.00

Finalist for the 2007 *ForeWord Magazine*'s Book Award for
Gay / Lesbian Fiction / Runner up for the 2006 DIY Book Festival
Award for Compilations / Anthologies.
"...fascinating, often funny...a safari through the perils and joys of
gay life."
—Edward Field

The Cannibal of Guadalajara by David Winner
ISBN: 978-1-928389-50-1, $20.00

Winner of the 2009 Gival Press Novel Award / Honorable Mention
2011 Beach Book Festival Award for Fiction / Finalist National Best
Books 2010 Award for Fiction & Literature.
"...a devilishly delicious and disorienting novel. Food, sex, ghastly
travel experiences, tantrums, Cannibal has it all, along with one of
the most peculiar versions of the family triad in literary years."
—Joy Williams, a Pulitzer finalist, received the Strauss Living Award
from the American Academy of Arts and Letters

A Change of Heart by David Garrett Izzo
ISBN: 978-1-928589-18-1, $20.00

A historical novel about Aldous Huxley and his circle
"astonishingly alive and accurate."
—Roger Lathbury, George Mason University

Dead Time / Tiempo muerto by Carlos Rubio
ISBN: 979-1-928589-17-4, $21.00

Winner of the 2003 Silver Award for Translation, *ForeWord
Magazine*'s Book of the Year.
A bilingual (English / Spanish) novel that captures a tale of love and
hate, passion and revenge.

Dreams and Other Ailments / Sueños y otros achaques by Teresa Bevin
  ISBN: 978-1-92-8589-13-6, $21.00

  Winner of the 2001 Bronze Award for Translation, *ForeWord Magazine*'s Book of the Year.
  A bilingual (English / Spanish) account of the Latino experience in the USA, filled with humor and hope.

The Gay Herman Melville Reader edited by Ken Schellenberg
  ISBN: 978-1-928589-19-8, $16.00

  A superb selection of Melville's homoerotic work, with short commentary.

Gone by Sundown by Peter Leach
  ISBN: 978-1-928589-61-7, $20.00

  Winner of the 2010 Gival Press Novel Award.
  "Almost no other novel treats the creation of sundown towns. *Gone by Sundown* thus amounts to a one-volume antidote to American amnesia. On top of that, it's a good read."
  —James W. Loewen, author of *Lies My Teacher Told Me* and *Sundown Towns*

An Interdisciplinary Introduction to Women's Studies edited by Brianne Friel & Robert L. Giron
  ISBN: 978-1-928589-29-7, $25.00

  Winner of the 2005 DIY Book Festival Award for Compilations / Anthologies.
  A succinct collection of articles for the college student on a variety of topics.

The Last Day of Paradise by Kiki Denis
  ISBN: 978-1-928589-32-7, $20.00

  Winner of the 2005 Gival Press Novel Award / Honorable Mention 2007 Hollywood Book Festival.
  This debut novel "...is a slippery in-your-face accelerated rush of sex, hokum, and Greek family life."
  —Richard Peabody, editor of *Mondo Barbie*

Literatures of the African Diaspora by Yemi D. Ogunyemi
ISBN: 978-1-928589-22-8, $20.00

An important study of the influences in literatures of the world.

Lockjaw: Collected Appalachian Stories by Holly Farris
ISBN: 978-1-928589-38-9, $20.00

Winner of the 2008 Appalachian Writers Association Book of the Year Award for Fiction / Finalist for the 2008 Golden Crown Literary Society Lesbian Short Story / Essay Collections Category / Finalist for the 2008 Eric Hoffler Award for Culture / Finalist for the 2007 Lambda Literary Award for Lesbian Debut Fiction.
"*Lockjaw* sings with all the power of Appalachian storytelling—inventive language, unforgettable voices, narratives that take surprise hairpin turns—without ever romanticizing the region or leaning on stereotypes. Refreshing and passionate, these are stories of unexpected gestures, some brutal, some full of grace, and almost all acts of secret love. A strong and moving collection!"
—Ann Pancake, author of *Given Ground*

Maximus in Catland by David Garrett Izzo
ISBN: 978-1-92-8589-34-1, $20.00

"...*Maximus in Catland* has all the necessary ingredients for a successful fairy tale: good and evil, unrequited love and loving loyalty, heroism and ancient wisdom...."
—Jenny Ivor, author of *Rambles*

Middlebrow Annoyances: American Drama in the 21st Century by Myles Weber
ISBN: 978-1-928589-20-4, $20.00

Current essays on the American theatre scene.

The Pleasuring of Men by Clifford H. Browder
ISBN: 978-1-928589-59-4, $20.00

"...deftly drawn with rich descriptions, a rhythmic balance of action, dialogue, and exposition, and a nicely understated plot. *The Pleasuring of Men* is both engaging and provocative." —Sean Moran

Second Acts by Tim W. Brown
ISBN: 978-1-928589-51-8, $20.00

2011 Runner Up for the New York Book Festival Award for Science Fiction /
2011 Winner of the London Book Festival Award for General Fiction. "Really clicking, *Second Acts* is a picaresque, sci-fi / western, such as Verne or Welles might have penned it, but with tongue planted firmly in cheek. Tim W. Brown's tale of a husband's search for his fugitive wife takes readers on a whirlwind tour of America, circa 1830. In subverting history Brown's tale celebrates it, with a scholar's eye for authentic details and at a pacing so swift the pages give off a nice breeze."
—Peter Selgin, author of *Life Goes to the Movies*

Secret Memories / Recuerdos secretos by Carlos Rubio
ISBN: 978-1-928589-27-3, $21.00

Finalist for the 2005 *ForeWord Magazine*'s Book of the Year Award for Translations. This bilingual (English / Spanish) novel adeptly pulls the reader into the world of the narrator who is vulnerable.

Show Up, Look Good by Mark Wisniewski
ISBN: 978-1-928589-60-0, $20.00

Finalist for the 2009 Gival Press Novel Award.
"..a rollicking, laugh-out-loud romp of a novel, a picaresque spin through fin-de-siècle New York as seen through the eyes of its intrepid, Midwestern-born heroine...."—Ben Fountain, author of *Brief Encounters with Che Guevara*
"Wisniewski: a riotously original voice."—Jonathan Lethem

The Smoke Week: Sept. 11-21, 2001 by Ellis Avery
ISBN: 978-1-928589-24-2, $15.00

2004 *Writer's Notes Magazine* Book Award—Notable for Culture / Winner of the Ohionana Library Walter Rumsey Marvin Award. "Here is Witness. Here is Testimony."
—Maxine Hong Kingston, author of *The Fifth Book of Peace*

The Spanish Teacher by Barbara de la Cuesta

ISBN: 978-1-928589-37-2, $20.00

Winner of the 2006 Gival Press Novel Award / Finalist for the 2007 *ForeWord Magazine*'s Book of the Year / Award for Fiction-General / Honorable Mention for the 2007 London Book Festival. "...De la Cuesta's novel maintains an accumulating power which holds onto a reader's attention not only through the forceful figure of Ordóñez, but by demonstrating acutely how ordinary lives are impacted by the underlying social and political landscape. Compelling reading."—Tom Tolnay, author of *Selling America* and *This is the Forest Primeval*

That Demon Life by Lowell Mick White

ISBN: 978-1-928589-47-1, $21.00

Winner of the 2008 Gival Press Novel Award / Finalist for the 2010 Texas Book Award for Fiction / Finalist for the 2009 National / Best Book Award for Fiction.
"*That Demon Life* is a hoot, a virtuoso tale by a master story teller." —Larry Heinermann, author of *Paco's Story*, winner of the National Book Award

Tina Springs into Summer / Tina se lanza al verano by Teresa Bevin

ISBN: 978-1-928589-28-0, $21.00

2006 *Writer's Notes Magazine* Book Award—Notable for Young Adult Literature. A bilingual (English / Spanish) compelling story of a youngster from a multi-cultural urban setting and her urgency to fit in.

A Tomb on the Periphery by John Domini

ISBN: 978-1-928589-40-2, $20.00

Honorable Mention for the 2009 London Book Festival Award for Fiction / Finalist for the 2005 Gival Press Novel Award.
"Stolen antiquities, small-time thugs, a sultry femme fatale.... a book that takes the trappings of noir then transcends the genre...." *Bookslut*

Twelve Rivers of the Body by Elizabeth Oness
ISBN: 978-1-928589-44-0, $20.00

Winner of the 2007 Gival Press Novel Award
"*Twelve Rivers of the Body* lyrically evokes downtown Washington, DC in the 1980s, before the real estate boom, before gentrification, as the city limped from one crisis to another—crack addiction, AIDS, a crumbling infrastructure. This beautifully evoked novel traces Elena's imperfect struggle, like her adopted city's, to find wholeness and healing."
—Kim Roberts, author of *The Kimnama*

For a complete list of titles, visit: *www.givalpress.com.*
Books available via Ingram, the Internet, and other outlets.

Or Write:

Gival Press, LLC
PO Box 3812
Arlington, VA 22203
703.351.0079

www.ingramcontent.com/pod-product-compliance
Lightning Source LLC
Chambersburg PA
CBHW030409020726
47493CB00003B/996